LADIES' OWN BAKERY SEASON ONE

The Collected Episodes

JUDITH LYNNE

Books by Judith Lynne

<u>Lords and Undefeated Ladies</u>

Not Like a Lady

The Countess Invention

What a Duchess Does

Crown of Hearts

He Stole the Lady

No Titled Lady

<u>Maids Done Waiting</u>

The Lord Trap

The Lady Escape (Forthcoming)

<u>Cloaks and Countesses</u>

The Caped Countess

The Clandestine Countess

The Castaway Countess (Forthcoming)

<u>Ladies' Own Bakery</u>

The Regency romance comedy serial

This is a work of fiction and as such its characters, events, words, and places are the product of the author's imagination informed by history.

Readers of my books will know that this book takes place in the world of 1813. This work is deeply researched, but fictional.

This is for the Ladies' Own Bakery readers, and all women building lives of their own.

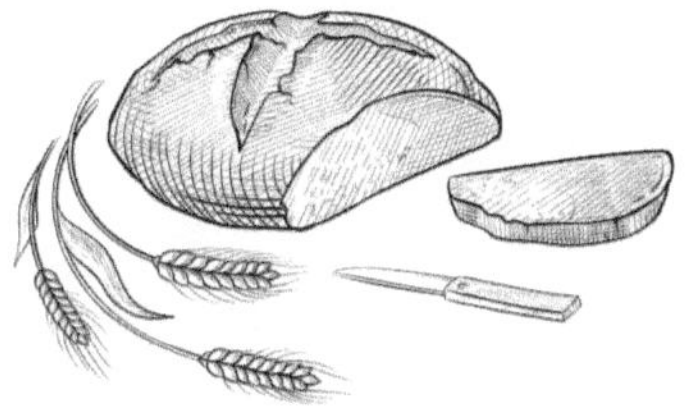

Preface

Welcome! The Ladies' Own Bakery is something a little different: a Regency romance comedy serial. It's a comedy sandwich stuffed with tasty Regency romance filling. My faithful readers got the episodes right to their inboxes. Now that the season is over, I'm delighted to bring you the collected season.

Like your favorite show, the season isn't over at the end of season 1. The loves and lives of our Bickering sisters will go on, planned now for three more seasons. **So you've been warned—this story doesn't end at the end!**

Rose, Emery, Jane, and Anna, and their whole world, will return in Season Two!

Learn more about Judith Lynne books, or sign up to find out when more Ladies' Own Bakery is released, at judithlynne.com!

Episode 1: The problem of men

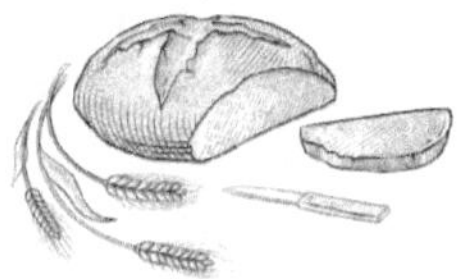

Inside was everything they'd ever known, and outside, some man was knocking.

Anna smoothed back her hair, a column of ruffles and uncertainty in the middle of the floor. The knocking was loud; this was it. Her last moment in the rooms that had been her home since she was born. She was the oldest, and their mother was gone. She had to go to the door.

She could do this, she had to do it. With grace.

She opened the door to the rough batch of men who were there to take everything she still owned to her new hope, their new home.

"Yes," she said with great solemnity. "Thank you, sir, I—"

"I cannot find my hairbrush!"

"I already packed all the ribbons. We only have one each. I put it with them."

"There are five ribbons and four of us. That's a ribbon and a quarter for each of us."

"Some of us didn't get to go to elegant school, you know."

"Or any school at all."

"Why don't you have your bundles with you?"

"Oh, bundle this. Why can't we take our *furniture?*"

Only three sisters, but it sounded like a thousand. It always had and it always would.

Anna, the oldest, wished she had any memories of the two years before Jane had arrived. They must have been quieter.

"Ladies." Anna called over her shoulder while trying to look as if that wasn't what she was doing. If she turned around she'd see all the hubbub behind her. "The new tenants have paid us for the furnishings, as you well know."

"Then what are *we* here for?" the man at the door wanted to know.

"We are so glad for your help," Anna told the four squat, muscled young men outside, who smelled of dust and horse. She tried to focus on the closest. "You're Mr. Pierce, you've come to take our things to Leicester Square?"

"That I am, and I've got half my brothers with me." The bow-legged fellow jerked a thumb back over his shoulder. "And we've a cart, so just point us at what you want carried."

"Well, it's everything, really..." She took in the bare walls with a wave of her hand. It all looked so much colder now.

"But not the table and chairs, Anna," murmured tall, dark-haired Jane from where she'd retreated to the corner.

"No, and we've got our bundles here." The youngest, Rose, half-bent her knees and pointed at the wad of clothing at her feet. Her scarred eyes made clear why she didn't look down; she couldn't see.

"The beds must go, and the mattresses, and such." Emery had scraped her lighter hair back from her face and tied it tightly with string rather than ribbon. She was tall enough to see over everyone's heads. "The things in the other two rooms, if you please, and that crate of pots, and the one of dishes."

"How about that pot, miss?" One man waved to a covered ale tankard at her feet.

Emery swept it up in one long hand. "I'm carrying that myself."

"Does it matter?" Anna patted her golden-brown curls as if heading to the drawing-room of someone important, but then clearly didn't know what to do next. "We are all going to the same place."

"Are ye?" Mr. Pierce turned back. His brothers trooped into the bedrooms and began to dismantle the beds with some banging. "Room in the cart for your things, but not all of you."

"Oh." Anna looked at her sisters. Her mother wasn't here. Anna should know how to do this. But she *didn't* know how to do this. "Do we... do we draw straws? Should I just decide? None of us should go alone."

"We haven't any straws," Rose pointed out.

"She means, who's going in the cart." Emery clutched the ale tankard as the noises of breaking apart the beds continued.

"You and Rose should ride in the cart, obviously." Jane deferred to Anna as her older sister. "Emery and I will walk."

"Because I'm fragile? No." Rose picked her clothing bundle up and gripped it with both hands.

"We can do this, you know." Anna wanted to brace them all up.

"Of course we can do it, we are doing it, who else is doing it?" Rose had been blind since she was eight, but she'd always been that blunt. Her curls, so like Anna's, were a lie, Anna thought. "We've all agreed I'm not fragile, and there's no need to put me in the cart."

"I don't know if it's best for you to walk, Rose." Anna was leaning toward the bedroom, trying to glimpse whatever was causing the unholy racket in there. She winced at a particularly loud *crunch*. "It's not a matter of being fragile."

"Then I'm walking. I'm blind, I'm not broken."

"I thought you were lazy," muttered Emery.

"Maybe not if I get a chance to do things," Rose shot back.

"Rose is neither broken nor lazy, but clearly she should ride. And so should you, Anna." Jane, her back ramrod straight in her best dotted linen, usually ignored Anna's dithering; but accepting Anna's plan was a sign of being gentler with her since their mother's funeral.

"I'm riding. I need both hands to hold on to this tankard all the way there." Emery kept one hand wrapped through the handle, even as she swung her bundle over her shoulder. The bundle clanked; she had quite a few kitchen implements inside it.

"Yeah?" Mr. Pierce had come out of the bedroom, along with men carrying pieces of one bed. Pieces that might or might not go back together. "That tankard that important? What's in it, jewelry?"

"Our chance at freedom," Emery told him, and followed him out.

Rose seemed to be waiting for her older sisters to say something final as she rocked back and forth on her feet.

Anna tapped her shoulder. "You walk with Jane, you'll be fine. We're all grown now, and we've decided to go out into the world, haven't we?" Anna jumped again as there was another crunch from a bedroom.

Jane just looked at her. "Will you be all right?"

Anna's laugh trilled lightly, harpsichord notes in search of a harpsichord. "Why ever should I not be, Jane?"

"Because you've sat in these rooms for a quarter of a century hoping one day we'd be rich again, and we won't. We aren't. None of us are married, and that includes you. And Papa and... and Mama are gone."

Anna leveled her eyes at her sister. Where Jane's brown eyes looked inky, Anna's were warm velvet. But there was some stony determination in their depths. "It isn't as if I were alone, Jane. We are doing this together."

And with that, she shoved Jane toward the door. "So you and Rose had best get started, otherwise we'll have to wait for you. I hate waiting for you."

"CAN'T WE GO INSIDE AND SIT?" ROSE WAS TIRED, EVEN though all they'd done was walk from one London neighborhood to another. It was tiring, leaving one's home.

Jane peered at every passing wagon and carriage. "The cart will be here before long; we must wait. And there are no chairs, you know!"

"I wish we hadn't sold the table and chairs."

"The new people wanted them, and we could use the extra coins. They're practically all we have to live on till we do business."

Rose pondered this. When she was thoughtful, she bent her head, and now her face was hidden by the girlish linen bonnet with three ribbon roses on it—her nicest.

Jane couldn't quite see through all the carriages barely moving through the square. "Someone has caused a commotion ahead. I must go look, will you be well here for a moment?"

"Jane, no!" They had agreed that they ought not to go abroad except in two's. They had walked here together for just that reason.

"I'll be right back!"

Of course Jane would be the one to break the rule they'd all agreed to, thought Rose with annoyance.

The roadway just in front of her seemed full to bursting with the *neighs* and *clops* of horses. There was the rattling of all sorts of leather straps and buckles, and wooden wheels.

There was even the squeaking of thick iron springs. Men called to each other, on the far side of the carriages, in what must be the square; and Rose could hear the narrow heels of ladies and the thick heels of boots in all the steps streaming around her.

Would she let all this noise and hubbub overwhelm her, or might there be the tiniest pleasure in the freedom to simply stand outside and be one of the crowd?

"See, I was only gone for a moment. There is such a snarl ahead, I don't know when Mr. Pierce will get the cart through."

"Jane, what's going to happen?"

"We'll have them take the beds upstairs and they'll go right back together, never you—"

"I mean to us. All of us. What's going to happen?"

"No one knows, muffin." The unexpected childhood name was quiet as Jane drew closer. "No one ever knows, but we'll be all right."

"How do you know?"

"I don't," Jane said, pressing her shoulder into Rose's, "but we must keep on, just the same."

Dust motes danced in the air of the bakery as if nothing had happened there for a long, long time.

Then that all changed.

Crash! Went the chipped old door against the wall, and all four young ladies, who had all been pushing on it, nearly fell inside in a tumble of skirts and bonnets.

Anna untied her bonnet to cover that she was catching her breath. "We had better get Mr. Scrope to fix that door."

Emery carefully set her tankard on the counter before she

peered at the warp at the top of the door. "I believe I can fix that."

Jane shook her head. "Don't you dare. The landlord will only charge us more if your repair doesn't suit him."

"Look at the door, Jane." Emery stood in the open door, pointing at its humped top with an accusing and steadfast finger.

Rose had kept her balance by keeping a hand on the door. She trailed in, following her fingers. "If the door doesn't open, it can't suit *us*," she agreed.

"Enh," Emery said for Rose's benefit, and shrugged. Two-handed, she scraped and shoved the door mostly closed again.

"It may only be because it hasn't been used." Anna shook her hands. "Please, all of you. I thought this would be a new day for all of us. Can we not leave our bad habits at the door and start fresh with one another?"

"That's not how bad habits work," but Jane only muttered it quietly, and everyone pretended not to notice.

So Jane pretended not to notice them not noticing. "Where is the till box?" Shaking out the skirts of her best dress, the primary sign that she felt the day was just as important as Anna did, she put her bonnet on the deep counter and began searching the shelves behind it.

Emery's head was adorned with only a linen cap; she took it off and shoved it in her pocket, and rolled her eyes. "There won't be any money in it."

"Mr. Scrope said he would give us the use of it as part of our lease. We ought to use it."

Anna reminded herself, too, to leave her bad habits at the door. Perhaps this was the day she learned how not to be impatient with Jane. "Certainly we shall use it, when we have customers, which we do not."

Which idea seemed to prompt Emery to stalk through the shop area, past all the tilted wooden trays on shelves, to the door in the back that led to the bakery proper. "Nothing to sell till we start baking, so I'll have a look."

And Rose continued having a look her own way, letting her fingers touch the windowsill and the tables and working her way around to the counter, which was deep, and along its used, pitted top.

Anna regarded that pitted top with some dismay. She wasn't sure customers would wish to buy their bread from such an obviously aged and used surface.

But as the oldest sister, she had worries beyond just the start of their little business.

"Emery. Please. Wait one moment. Jane, Rose. Please."

Jane, who had finally discovered the till box on a lower shelf, was poking around its empty interior as if coins would appear if she only searched for them.

Emery, though, stopped. With her hand on the door handle. Ready to fly at any moment.

And Rose, still in her girlish bonnet, turned.

"Can we not—I think Mother would want us to put aside bickering and be... different, here."

Jane was still examining the box. "Hard to put it aside when it is our name."

Anna closed her eyes. She had to set a good example. She was the oldest sister. It was her *responsibility*.

"Jane, stop poking at that thrice-bedamned box and listen to me for a moment."

Jane finally looked up.

That was not a good example. That was not the right example, *at all*. Mother would be so disappointed.

Well, Mother wasn't here. And she was Anna, not Mother.

"This is a business." Anna folded her hands in front of her. She had never been as tall as Emery or Jane, and she never would be; she had learned how to make herself as visible as they were, from childhood. She used that now, standing tall, speaking up, and looking at each one of them in turn. "This is *our* business. We must make this work, ladies. Mother did the best she could with what Father left her. Now we must make the leap into a new life and find our own way. All of us, together."

Jane didn't frown till she heard the *together*. "How long will it be before one of us marries? We won't be together all that long. Rose is the youngest, and she is nineteen. Sorry, twenty."

Emery, arms folded again across her chest, leaned her shoulder against the wall. She looked rangy and boyish that way. "Jane, you're so blasted in love with marriage, why aren't you married yet?"

Which was a low blow; they all knew Jane's spinsterhood at the ripe old age of twenty-four was not for lack of trying.

Jane was openly scowling now. "It won't be long now." She waved toward windows fogged with wheat chaff, at the bustling street outside. "We are on display, here. Someone will be bound to snap us up."

Rose's nose wrinkled. "I thought we were selling bread, not ourselves."

Anna tightened the clasp of her hands so she didn't make fists. "No one is selling themselves. And if we wish to marry, it won't be for money. Am I right?"

"You absolutely are right." Rose had never pursued any unlucky suitors, unlike Jane, but neither did she despise the whole idea, as Emery did. "We well might marry; people do. But that cannot be the purpose of our lives day in and day out, can it? What a dreary life that would be."

"Thank you." Anna put all her very real gratitude in her voice. "And we are sisters. No matter what, we will always be sisters. That is how we came into this world and what we will have for all our time in it. So we had best get along, and nicely, as customers won't want to walk into a bickering bakery."

"Not going to put Bickering Bakery on the sign, then?" Jane put one hand on her hip, apparently impatient to get back to poking at the till.

Why did she always harp upon their name? "We haven't discussed that yet. Do we want Bickering Bakery? I thought…" Would this sound too silly? "I thought perhaps Ladies' Own Bakery."

"Oh, that's lovely, Anna, I like it!" Rose clapped her hands and smiled her sunny smile.

Emery, still leaning against the wall like a bored society youth, frowned this time. "Will people buy bread from ladies?"

"If not, then signing papers to lease this bakery was a very poor plan." Jane had finally ceased poking at the till, but was now down on her knees behind the lower shelves, presumably to see if any loose coins had fallen down back there. But they could all still hear her muttering.

"We *have* signed the lease, though, and a bakery this will be." Anna must have a conversation with Jane about how customers would also want to do business with a shop assistant who wasn't surly.

"But… putting it on the sign?"

Rose, as she often did, offered a compromise. "Why not put it on the sign and see how business does, and then change it if we feel we need it? I think it an excellent name, Anna, I do."

"Emery? Jane?"

Emery shrugged. "Let's try it."

Jane stood, brushing dust from her skirt. "I did not think it wise to use our only funds to lease a bakery. I was voted down. I did not think it wise to come to Leicester Square. There too I was outvoted. I don't wish to be outvoted again, but I don't think it wise to begin our business under a name that won't stay. And I have no confidence either that people will buy bread from ladies."

That was the shadow hanging over all of them, of course. It wasn't at all proper, or popular, for ladies to conduct business.

But they were all excellent bakers, thanks to their departed Mother, and it seemed a trade they could make pay.

It had seemed like a door to a better tomorrow, that one advertisement in their one paper, a gift from a wealthier neighbor. "Bakery to let, all the fittings," the advertisement had said.

So here they were.

And if they couldn't make it pay...

The door to the shop started to open, stuck, and then someone crashed their own shoulder into it, rather less forcefully than the sisters had done.

A woman in a flat cap and knotted shawl leaned in. "Any buns today?"

It was an odd question, as there clearly were no buns; there were no loaves, nothing at all.

There was a brief silence of confusion before Anna gathered her wits enough to say, "We have not opened to do business yet, ma'am, but we hope you will return when we do."

"Oh aye," said the woman without much interest, and disappeared again.

Anna turned back to Jane, fixing her with her best *big sister* look. "It appears that we are in a neighborhood interested in buying bread from ladies."

Jane threw up her hands. "Fine! I agree! I said I didn't wish to be outvoted again."

Feeling a bit formal, Anna even smiled a little as she rapped her knuckles on top of the worn counter. "Ladies' Own Bakery it is then."

And for a moment, before Emery disappeared into the back, all four sisters were in perfect agreement.

"SPIDERS?"

The bakery proper filled the back three-quarters of the first story, with wide smoke-stained beams above and round arches of brick supporting them. The oven was built against the innermost wall, cold and shadowed now, but waiting for life.

Anna had looked into the half-barrels stacked against the back wall, then drawn back, and back, until she'd pulled back so hard that it seemed that she might fly off the earth and sail up to the ceiling. "Oh, *spiders*."

"Looks like," said Emery as she tipped the barrels over with relish.

The room was full of broad, heavy slab tables, good for kneading. There were slatted squares made of wood atop many of the tables, upon which the bread would cool, and many vast bowls.

One of which was indeed, like the half-barrels, full of spiders.

"We have to wash all these anyway, we might as well start now." Emery pushed the wooden lever to start water running through the pipe that came through the wall high up, and tilted down and down to the vast washtub that took up nearly the entire back wall.

With a clank, the water trickled, spit, then ran through the pipe.

It was brown as shoe leather.

"Well," and Emery made a sort of *hmm* noise deep in her throat, "maybe once the pipes clear out a little."

Anna still looked as though she were going to faint. She

never had fainted, not even when she was eight and Emery had broken her wax doll.

"Anna," said Emery a little more gently, "I can't do this all by myself, you know. I'll need your help."

Anna shook herself and patted the smooth waves of her hair, which no spider had moved. "I'm going to help, you know I am."

"Are you? Because if you're just planning to get married and get this place behind you, Anna, let me remind you that I *won't*. I'm not getting married, and you know it."

"Oh, if you only..." But Anna's voice trailed away. It had been years since even their mother had tried to say *if you only met the right man* to Emery. Tall as Jane but rangy, strong, and with bright moss-green eyes the rest of them did not have, Emery wasn't just different from the rest of the Bickering girls. Anna truly couldn't imagine her standing next to a man and saying *yes, I take him to be my lawfully wedded husband.*

And Emery had never imagined it, either.

She came closer now, those eyes pushing down on Anna like a hand. "I'm not getting married. I'm staying right here. This is going to be my *life,* baking bread and earning my living till I die. So don't send this wrong for me, big sister."

"Well, but if I married well, or Jane—"

"You've been saying that all your life. If you marry well, or Jane. Never Rose or me, who never got to go to school, or Aunt Eden's parlor parties, or ever even had *talk* of a season."

"Emery. Really. Did you *want* a season?"

The idea of Emery dressing in virginal dresses to be peered at by men who wanted brides lay between them like a dead, wet frog.

"No," Emery finally said, "but I never had the chance to turn it down, did I? And what about Rose?"

"Aunt Eden is so nasty about Rose's marriage chances, as you know very well." Clearly trying to forestall more of this conversation, Anna laid her clothes bundle on a table and ducked under the shelf to poke the end of a long wooden paddle into one of the wooden vats. Presumably this was to send spiders packing.

"Aunt Eden is a nightmare," said Emery, "but I'm talking about you. And Jane. The fancy ones. Us not-fancy sisters need to live, too. And this bakery is going to keep us from ending up in the streets."

"But if Jane marries, or I do—"

Emery stuck her head under the shelf right next to Anna's, making her jump. "My life can't depend on your marriage. So stop saying it."

"I know. I know." Anna bumped her head on the shelf, trying to back up gracefully. She stood there rubbing the bump as Emery straightened, too. "We ought not to have to marry to live. You *know* I agree. That's why we're *here*."

"Just stick to it, Anna, and we'll all stick with you. You're the oldest, you know."

WHEN THE DOOR TO THE SHOP OPENED AGAIN, IT WAS Rose, followed into the bakery proper by a woman of perfectly ordered middle years. "It's Mrs. Scrope, An—Miss Bickering."

"Mrs. Scrope! Thank you for coming." Anna sailed over to greet their landlord's wife. "As you see, the key let us into the building perfectly well."

"Oh, I knew it would." The lady held her shawl tight in both fists in front of her and looked all around the bare shelves and tables. Anna wondered what she thought they'd already stolen. "I told my husband he needn't come. The arrangements are already made. I've told the man who sells me wood you want to keep buying from him, too."

"Thank you, Mrs. Scrope. Your help is much appreciated."

Rose folded her hands. They'd met Mrs. Scrope three times, and each time Rose seemed to make her uncomfortable. She preferred to pretend Rose did not exist.

Emery was far more interested in the fittings of their new establishment, few though they were besides the enormous wood-fired oven. "We're keeping the peels. The big paddles for placing the bread in the oven?"

"Yes, yes. All the ones under here."

"Would you mind if we fixed that front door a bit?" Anna smiled and tried not to wring her hands, just keep them clasped. It would look more ladylike, surely. "The way it sticks at the top?"

"Oh, fine, fine." Clearly, despite Jane's worries, Mrs. Scrope didn't much care.

They would just have to take her word that she represented Mr. Scrope, too.

"And... would you mind if we had that countertop finished again? To make it smooth."

"No, not at all, Mr. Scrope should have arranged that. In fact, I can send a man over, a friend of the family who has helped us before. Unless you've a man to do work for you already." Mrs. Scrope's eyes darted around Anna's hemlines and waist as though she expected Anna to have a man attached to her dress somehow.

"No," Emery said brusquely from her spot underneath the table, loudly re-stacking the baking paddles.

Anna held on to her shaky smile. "I don't believe we can pay a carpenter right now, ma'am, but perhaps if he would lend us his tools, or perhaps for a small fee?"

"Well, now." Mrs. Scrope, who was sturdy herself, took in Anna's not-very-large frame and small clasped hands. "Don't you ladies need a little help with some of that heavier work?"

"No," Emery put in again, still under the table.

"We really will be fine," Anna reassured her. "There are four of us, you see. And we were raised not to shy away from hard work."

"Mm hmm. But your father was a gentleman, you said."

Mrs. Scrope was as British as she was, Anna thought a little testily. Surely Anna ought not to have to explain the pitfalls of being a gentleman, but poor.

"A gentleman, but very much opposed to our starving to death." Anna seemed to have tapped a little of Emery's brusqueness on that one.

"And quite right, quite right. Well." Mrs. Scrope looked around the place again. The tables, shelves, basins and bowls were heavy, and good. But the place had been used, of that there was no question. "Let us say this. As a bonus for contracting to lease the place. You pay me, *mm*, three shillings and Mr. Scrope will match them, and we'll have the fellow plane the countertops."

"And the door." Emery emerged from rummaging under the table, brushing off her skirt as she stood.

"And the door," Mrs. Scrope immediately agreed.

"And the shelves," Anna added quickly.

She immediately regretted it. The woman had made a generous offer. Anna ought to have accepted it. Why must she always push? She didn't want to be like Jane, chasing down every penny, she did not.

But Mrs. Scrope just shrugged. "If you'll make it three and sixpence, fine. I believe he will do it for that. If not, I may put in an extra penny or two. After all, you have the entire rest of the year's lease to pay. It is an investment on my part in your success."

Inwardly, Anna sighed. "Thank you, Mrs. Scrope, we accept."

"It is Mr. Scrope's arrangement, not mine," said his wife who had just made the arrangement.

Emery had stuck her head into the depths of the cold oven. "I suppose you pay a chimneysweep, too."

For the first time Mrs. Scrope radiated a little tension, narrowing her eyes at Emery as she emerged with some soot in her hair.

"You won't want the chimney swept often," she pointed out. "Ashes would fall into the bread." Which they would be making at all hours of the day and night.

"Often enough we don't catch fire," Emery replied immediately. "We live upstairs, after all."

"If you burn soft wood, the chimney will get dirty," warned Mrs. Scrope.

"We intend to buy the wood from the vendor you've recommended, ma'am," Anna swiftly added.

"All right, all right. I'm leaving before you girls steal me blind."

But Anna couldn't tell whether or not she was really upset.

"I'll see you out, Mrs. Scrope." Surely she should leave while they were ahead, Anna thought.

Just at the front door, the graying woman paused.

"You girls know this isn't a game, don't you?" She clearly meant to sound pleasant, but her words had an edge. "You have signed that lease. You have a legal obligation to pay the lease. I've let you do it in payments—I mean, Mr. Scrope is letting you do it in payments, but you must meet those payments. You all understand that, don't you? As you've all signed it?"

Well, Rose had made her mark, not strictly signed, but Anna wasn't going to argue about it with a woman who used phrases like *steal me blind*.

"We do understand it, Mrs. Scrope." Anna opened the door and hung on to her smile even more tightly than she hung on to the door.

"It's just that, four young ladies… It's nothing to Mr. Scrope if you all get married and leave off this baking business, but you do still have to pay the money."

"We have no plans to marry, any of us," Anna said, pleasantly enough, though her grip on the door handle was white-knuckled. "We do not even know any suitable young gentlemen. As you may imagine, Mrs. Scrope, which is why we have entered into this business."

"Lucky to have four of you, I suppose, as there'll be plenty of work." Mrs. Scrope retrieved her shopping basket from the windowsill, reminding Anna of how the windows needed washed. "Bakeries come and go so quickly here, I never do understand why. Good day, Miss Bickering, and my best to your sisters."

"I don't see of what use I will be. But I must be of some use. I *did* sign too." Rose was darning socks in the sitting room of the apartment, upstairs from the bakery, that had come along with the bakery proper.

Fortunately, she didn't need light to do it, as Anna had no idea where to find the lamp. Well, she had until nightfall, she supposed.

The rooms were spacious, but with only their few belongings, the space was merely emptiness.

It's got to be here somewhere, thought Anna as she stared around at the pile of bundles they had brought with them earlier today. But if she found it, could she also find the lamp oil?

"I thought you could help at the counter as well as anyone. You can read a scale."

Reading the scale, Anna knew, wasn't the problem. Rose had little confidence for new things, and she also preferred sitting down and being quiet.

For the thousandth time Anna reminded herself that her sister wasn't lazy, she was blind.

Though she *still* suspected that one did not preclude the other.

"What if the customers talk to me?"

"They'll have to, if they want bread." Wiping her hands on her apron first, Anna untied one bundle to find it contained their flatware.

Brilliant, had they had any food.

Since, hilariously enough, they had no bread, Emery and Jane had gone to find any shops that were still open, and something to eat for a cold supper.

"I don't like talking to new people."

Suppressing a sigh, Anna reflected that Rose certainly had her own way of being just as stubborn as all the other Bickering sisters.

"I thought you might help with the bread-making too."

"Emery shouts at me."

"I think she wants your help, though."

"She wants to shout at me."

"No, dear, I don't think that's so. Emery likes to shout." That was true enough. Emery had always liked to shout, and climb walls, and poke about in the kitchen since she was small. She had a feeling for the way bread behaved and they all knew without ever discussing it that Emery would be in charge of the baking itself, just as they had all known that Jane would look for, find, and cling to that money box.

"Perhaps I shall marry?"

That made Anna take closer notice.

She came and knelt on the floor near where Rose was sitting with her legs crossed before her like a child.

"Would you *like* to marry?"

Rose bit her lip, her slightly scarred eyes looking straight ahead. "Why haven't *you* married yet, Anna?"

That made Anna settle more onto the floor.

She didn't want to lie to her youngest sister, but she didn't want to set a poor example, either. And she might well be setting a poor example by not marrying.

But no. She couldn't think that.

"It's when I think of Father, you know." Her voice softened a little as she told her sister this, in the emptiness of their new world. "Seeing him and Mother together, and how much they adored each other. They never passed by one another without a smile or a kiss. They held hands when they sat by the fire, unless one of them was working on something, or Father was filling his pipe." The memory was warm, and brighter than any lamp could be; Anna could see them now. "They were always beautiful. I loved looking at them. And I think... I think I want what they had, if I can find it."

Rose ran her finger across the eye of her needle, feeling the groove there. "None of the girls I knew ever thought that marriage was about love. They talked about what kind of house they could have, how proud they might be of their husband, how many children they wanted."

"Some of that might have been dreams about love that they didn't wish to say."

Rose nodded a little. "But... but when we run out of money, how will we eat?"

"We won't run out, little muffin. We are going to have a thriving bakery and live together as long as we like."

Rose's voice was wry as she said, "Yes, that sounds splendid, spending my entire life living with Jane."

Anna laughed. "Well, Jane might well get married. She's the one most determined to do it."

"You make it sound as if it's just like Emery planning to file down that door."

"I think Jane intends to put at least as much muscular effort into it."

Both of them laughed together.

Anna patted Rose's shoulder.

"None of us will ever be alone in the store, you know. We needn't be. There are four of us. And we will look out for you; don't we always? We won't let people *accost* you, you know. They might wish to buy bread, that's all."

The door opened; the noise made Anna and Rose both jump.

"We have apples and cheese and tea and *bread*," called Emery at the top of a voice that could only be described as gloating.

"For pity's sake, be quiet." Jane shut the door after them both.

"Why? There is no one in the building but us."

There were no chairs and no hooks as yet. Both sisters simply plumped down on the floor next to Anna and Rose.

And Emery uncovered a shopping basket.

Flipping out a folding knife, she pared cheese off the block in her basket, and tore off hunks of bread to go with it. Jane passed them around.

"I had to walk ten minutes even to find another bakery," Emery reported gleefully, her eyes dancing. "And Leicester Square is bursting with people. We talked to a fellow on the corner who runs a tailor's shop. He told us he clothes half a dozen earls living right off the square, as well as people from every country, musicians, people from the theaters, all sorts of people. People who do not bake, my little titmice."

"You really must not call us that where anyone can hear." Anna tried to sound disapproving and ladylike around a mouthful of bread and cheese.

Rose nodded and made a *hmm hmm* sound of agreement. Her mouth was full, too.

Emery considered that. "Would you rather I just say tits?"

Jane helped herself last. "I hear the Yankees in America call them chickadees."

"Chickadees? What an absurd word. I like it." Emery chewed it over thoughtfully, along with the bread. "Chickadees. Yes."

"We're not chickadees. We're serious ladies of business."

"Oh yes, so serious." Jane swallowed before putting out a theatrically shaking hand. "Ladies, it is of the direst urgency that I have half a pound of your lightest bread. Quickly."

They all laughed. Together, which made Anna the gladdest of all the things that had happened that day.

Emery had left the door to their new rooms open; after all, there was no one else in the building. They heard someone open the door at the bottom of the stair and yell up. "No buns today?"

Anna looked around at her sisters' faces. All four of them looked equally surprised.

She stood up and walked to the door, still ruffled, slightly less uncertain than this morning.

When she looked down the staircase, she saw the outline of a stocky woman in a knotted shawl. Surely that was the same woman from earlier who had shoved her way into the bakery shop.

"We have no buns yet, ma'am, we have nothing to sell yet. Please do come back when we are open for business."

"Well," the woman called back up, "how do I know when that is?"

Anna looked back into their new sitting room. "When is that?"

"Five days at least," said Emery, "maybe seven. I must feed the starter slowly enough that I don't kill it, and I've never baked a loaf as big as a half-peck loaf before!"

All the sisters were good at baking bread, but only Emery

felt she could tackle the massive loaves, more than eight and a half pounds each, that city bakeries made to sell by the piece.

"Check back in five days, ma'am," Anna called down, as appropriately as she could, given that she was shouting down a staircase.

"I'll check back tomorrow," said the woman.

"You don't want to walk back here if we have no buns, though, surely?" Anna hoped the rest of her customers wouldn't be this confusing.

"Of course not! I have bunions!" called the woman and slammed the door.

Turning back to her sisters, Anna just fluttered her fingers toward their door. "She'll be back. She has bunions," she told them, as if it made sense. She was the oldest. This was her role now.

Episode 2: Men don't buy bread

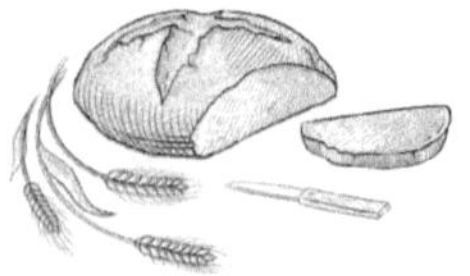

Emery wanted to whistle as she let herself out the door of their little flat. She didn't, because she *had* been raised to be proper, and she didn't want to wake her sisters. But she had the urge to whistle. Her own bakery to play with, and it was time to commune with the flour!

Rising dough was magical to Emery.

She was surprised to trip over a heap of clothes on the floor of their hallway. She had to catch herself against the wall to keep from tumbling over.

Even more surprised when the heap of clothes turned out to have a man in it.

"What are you doing in here?"

"I live here." He rolled over...slowly. He had hair turned dark through lack of washing, and sunken eyes over a wild mop of a beard.

Emery had never seen anyone like him, and didn't like seeing him now.

"You do not! We never heard a thing from you or about you!" It felt stupid, lecturing a heap of clothes with a man in them. Emery backed away, as far from him as possible.

He didn't seem to feel stupid, just flattened a hand against the nearest wall as though the hall were rocking. "How long have you been here?"

"Didn't you feel it when I tripped over you?"

"I mean," he said, slowly enunciating his words, "in this building."

"A day! Well, and a night." Emery's first impulse had been to scream, then to kick him. Now she wondered if his only defense was arguing.

"I need hardly explain that I was not in residence last evening."

"Oh! *Oh!* Are you drunk?" As brash as she was, Emery's mother had never given up hope that one of her daughters might marry well; that meant Emery had to behave properly, just in case someone with a title offered for Jane or Anna. She'd been as constrained as they were, to no purpose, since, as she'd been insisting to her mother since she was seven, she wasn't getting married. She'd never seen a drunken man.

The experience was underwhelming.

Emery glanced back at the door to the rooms where her sisters still slept. It was before dawn, in the small hours when fashionable people were just coming home from their never-ending round of parties. It was past time to get bread baking, if one intended to have bread in the morning.

She didn't have bread baking yet, but she needed to tend to the rising. And today was their first flour delivery.

"Look, get...inside your room or whatever you have."

"It's a room." The drunken man rolled over again, on his chest, then stretched a hand up and out toward a door she hadn't noticed, in the far corner of the hallway. "Why wouldn't it be a room?"

"I just thought it was a closet or something. Anyway, get

in it. If one of my sisters trips over you..." If *Anna* tripped over him, Emery thought to herself, there would be hell to pay. Though Rose might really fall. Jane would simply step over him and keep walking. "I have a blind sister and I don't want her to trip over you."

"Right. Right. No problem. Don't stop in the hall so people don't trip. I've got it."

But he still didn't move. In fact, he collapsed now on his chest, so that Emery was addressing the back of his shaggy head.

"Why don't you move?"

"Can't." He waved an airy hand, from his spot face-down on the floor. "No fear, no fear, I will, soon enough. Soooooon enough."

"For pity's sake." Emery took a step towards him, then back, clasping and unclasping her hands at her waist. Then decision hit her. Bending over, Emery grabbed the collar of his coat and the waistband of his trousers, and with one strong *heave* moved him four feet down the hall, in front of his own door.

"Good lord!" He rolled over to face her. "Are you a dockworker?"

"It's just like hauling flour. You've got to get inside before the sun comes up, will you?"

"Yes, yes." His assurances were no more reassuring from the front; he wore no waistcoat, and Emery's heaving had popped a button from the front of his trousers.

But that was the best Emery could do. She left him there. Flour was calling her.

"Come along when you are dressed, Rose!" Anna hummed to herself as she buttoned on her gloves.

"Why are you putting on gloves to go downstairs and work?" wondered Jane.

"Oh, I'm..." Anna shook herself a little, looked round the bare empty room where they'd sat on the floor to eat dinner last night. She didn't look like she had an answer.

"You're going down to evict spiders. I must go out and do the shopping. We must all work in the bakery but we still need to live and eat, and I must get soap and any number of other little things." And Jane put out her hand.

She wanted the gloves.

There was no one more trustworthy than Jane when it came to their few coins. Anna trusted her entirely to shop. But she didn't really trust her with the clean pair of gloves.

Anna thought to herself that if Jane brought the gloves home undamaged, she'd hide them, and wished she'd thought of it sooner.

"Yes, of course." She laid them in Jane's palm with a fake little smile, hoping Jane would take the offering in the spirit in which it was meant: unwilling.

She did. "Truly, I will do my best to return them in good order."

"Rose, are you coming? Jane must go out."

Jane tugged on the gloves. "She needn't come with me."

"Don't you recall, we agreed never to go anywhere except in pairs?"

"And how will that work when Rose and Emery are making the bread and you are waiting on customers?" Jane shook off the idea of propriety like a horse shaking off a fly, her body shivering with disgust all over. "It won't work and we must do the best we can. And we must have more soap. We will likely use all we have on hand, today."

"Yes, of course," Anna agreed faintly, just as falsely enthused about Jane going about alone as she had been about handing over her gloves.

SHE WAS STILL MULLING ON IT A QUARTER OF AN HOUR later as she attempted to sit on the floor without wrinkling her skirts. Why wrinkled skirts mattered today, she couldn't fathom. It was a habit not to wrinkle them, as what would people think?

A good habit, Anna decided as she knelt. Customers wouldn't want bread from a wrinkled person. Surely some of the same rules of behavior that governed a drawing-room could apply to a shop?

"Rose, why am I still waiting?"

"I'm brushing my hair!" Rose called through the door of the room she shared with Emery.

"Not *now*!" Anna had kept her hair short enough for the fashions required of social contact, but Rose's hair, so similar in golden-brown color and curl, was nearly to her waist, and brushing was a serious activity.

"Yes, now!"

"Why on earth now?"

"Because I want ten minutes of peace and quiet all to myself!"

It wouldn't do to develop the habit of muttering, Anna thought to herself, trying to keep all the muttering internal. "Then I am taking down the night bucket, and I'll see you in the shop."

They hadn't anything as elegant as a close-stool with a lid; they had the bare minimum, and the bare minimum was the large porcelain jar with its lid that they had used to relieve themselves since they were children.

There was a drain behind the building, there always was; she'd simply slip down and deal with it, then she could wash her hands at the pump there and be ready to start...scrubbing the bakery.

Which roughened and reddened the hands. She'd *need* those gloves if she ever met anyone from the upper echelons of society again.

She closed the door behind her. What did it matter if it locked? They had nothing to steal.

But when she reached the top of the stairs, chamber pot securely held in both hands lest she drop it, she realized there was a man at the bottom.

A man in what looked like a finely cut wool coat, though she couldn't see the color of it with the daylight behind him.

What does the *color* matter? Anna wondered wildly, concerned primarily that she might be about to be murdered with a chamberpot in her hands.

"Hello," he said, standing there.

Ugh, said something in the back of Anna's brain. *Someone ought to introduce us, and it ought to be him to me. I am the lady.*

But there was no one there, and as with everything now in life, if Anna wished it done she must do it herself.

"How do you do?" she said down the stairs. "I am Miss Anna Bickering, so delighted to make your acquaintance. And why are you in our bakery?"

"Lord Zachary Vane," said the interloper, "and clearly, I am not." She could just see his hand wave toward the door beside him, which led to the shop itself.

There must be a way to lock that door to the outside at the bottom of these stairs.

"My apologies, Lord Zachary, but this is our bakery and you must leave."

He didn't leave. He put a foot on the stair.

Anna gripped the chamberpot.

"It may be your bakery, miss, but it is my home, and I am only returning to it."

"This isn't your home."

"It is."

"It isn't."

He stepped up again. "We can do more rounds of this, but they will surely all end in the same way?"

"You go away, or..." Even Anna couldn't bring herself to threaten him with a chamberpot. A *used* chamberpot.

"Miss Bickering, I live here. You cannot simply send me out because you don't like the look of me."

"I can't even *see* you. I'm sending you out because we live here."

"You live in those rooms there, am I correct?" She could just see him incline his head toward the door behind her. He was holding his hat. *I can win with a chamberpot against a hat*, Anna thought. "I live above you."

Of course he was above her, if he was a *Lord* Zachary, Anna thought first, but then she realized he meant the top floor of the building.

"There are rooms up there?" Looking behind her, Anna realized that there was another staircase. So tiny she had not even seen it, across from a short, narrow door that must lead to a closet.

"Indeed, to the third floor, and I live above even that. I am just going there. Unless it will offend you in some way."

It could hardly offend her for the man to go to his own flat, but it didn't *help* her any. She didn't want him to get too close, and she *certainly* didn't want him to brush past her while she was carrying a chamberpot.

She made a decision. "Go out, and I will go into the bakery, and then come back in."

He stopped on the third stair. "I beg your pardon?"

"Just step out, if you will, and count to...count to twenty, and then you may proceed unimpeded up the stairs."

Lord Zachary paused for a moment. "Do you think I will need to do this every time I wish to come home?"

"No no. Just for now. If you please."

"Well, I can't refuse a mannerly request."

He paused on the last stair as if wondering if there were a way to refuse a mannerly request. But he must have some gallantry to him, as instead of demanding an explanation, he went out.

Anna let her breath go in a long, slow breath.

Then made her descent safely, but quickly. She only had a count of twenty.

Just as she was about to reach the bottom of the stairs, the door swung open. Another two seconds and it would have swung right into her face.

She tightened her already white-knuckled grip on the porcelain.

"Any buns today?" said the shawl-covered woman, sticking her head inside.

Anna could just see the back of Lord Zachary, politely turned. He stood a pace or two away. She'd thought the coat fine because it fit him well, though perhaps those shoulders were just the result of a clever tailor's padding.

"Ma'am, please come back when we are open. We would be glad to sell you bread as soon as the bakery is open."

"I can't be traipsing back and forth all day looking to see if there's buns," the woman said, her slightly popping eyes regarding Anna with deep disapproval. Not the chamberpot, Anna. "I have bunions, you know."

"I do know, ma'am, and I am so sorry." What was there to do but apologize?

"Hmmph," said the woman, and closed the door.

THE STREETS WERE EXCITING, JANE DECIDED. SHE LIKED the hustle and bustle. Whatever Anna saw in a quiet parlor, she couldn't imagine. It was so much more exciting just to see all these people, every kind of person, all dashing here and there, living a life she knew nothing about.

She had already walked round the square before, when they had all visited the bakery before signing the lease. She had some idea of the shop where she could readily obtain soft soap for cleaning, but suspected prices would be cheaper if she went farther from the square.

It did not escape her that there were no other nicely dressed young women of her age on the pavement along the packed-earth roadway. She glimpsed a young lady in an open-topped brougham, being driven somewhere with her mother; she had a bonnet not unlike the one Jane was wearing, decorated with some lovely turkey feathers. Jane had not been able to afford the turkey feathers.

But otherwise the women around her were dressed much more heavily, in coarser fabrics with worn edges. The young ones wore maid's caps, or had children hanging on to their skirts; the older ones had shopping baskets and the wrinkles that came from care.

Jane would need some heavier dresses, she realized, once they had money for such things. If they ever had money for such things.

Two fine young swells wearing Mr. Brummel's prescribed dark coat rode by, polished till even the hooves of their horses shone. One turned her way, but he didn't doff his stovepipe hat. Instead, he gave a long, low whistle.

It took all the pleasure out of the trip. Now, instead of being able to look around her, Jane could only be conscious of herself. And a man she did not know making a loud, rude gesture because of how she looked.

Jane had always been conscious of how she looked. She had dark hair and flashing eyes that set her apart from her sisters, and much of what had once been her father's social set. Her looks had done nothing for her. Her mother had hoped, quietly, almost silently, that they would catch Jane a husband before she was twenty.

When they hadn't, Jane had set about solving the problem for herself. She had thought it reasonable to suggest to that young man with two thousand pounds a year that she would be happy to help him run his estate. It had not been. Before that conversation, the young man had followed her through every musicale with big, soft eyes; after that conversation, she'd never seen him face to face again.

She didn't think he'd spread any rumors about her—he wasn't that type—but the next fellow wasn't so kind. He didn't need to be so choosy, Jane thought even now. He had a gut at thirty, and was losing his hair, and was not so charming he need think more women would fall at his feet. Jane was beautiful, she was smart; he ought to be glad of her suggestion that they make an arrangement.

He was not. Instead, he told his friends she was grasping, and after that, most of the mothers in London made sure their younger sons did not come into her circle.

Jane wasn't a saint. She was beginning to suspect that men were awful. Despite that, she'd approached their neighbor who owned a coaching line with what she thought was a fair idea. He was more attractive than the last fellow, and likely richer. She could help him become more rich. She'd always had a head for arithmetic, and she liked watching stores of money grow. He ought to take her up on the idea.

He hadn't. She could still remember his bellowing laugh as Jane, standing on his front step in her pelisse and bonnet, most properly not entering alone, made her point clear.

"You look good enough, that's for sure, but I am not interested in marrying. Now, if you'd like to spend a few hours—" And then he'd made some suggestion that Jane didn't understand, she didn't know *any* of the words, but she knew it wasn't honorable.

She'd turned and walked away.

She'd made her good faith efforts. She understood how she ought to behave, and she would push those boundaries to find a man she could help, and who could help her. What was wrong with that? Why were men obsessed with mating like horses? Why couldn't they treat her as the businesslike person she was?

No, her looks had done nothing for her.

But Jane was too clear a thinker to blame herself for the man's whistle. That was entirely on him, the rude thing. He'd taken away her pleasure in her little outing, but she'd be damned if she bent her head.

"ROSE, WHERE ARE YOU GOING?"

Anna had been at her from the moment she'd awoken. Emery had been long gone, of course; Emery was always an early riser, and from now on she'd be rising in the wee hours to give the bread a start.

Rose ought to get up with her.

The very thought made her tired.

Rose dropped the rag she'd been using to scrub the kneading tables in the bakery and dried her hands on her apron. Why were her sisters so full of energy and she so *tired*? She couldn't stop thinking of her last days with her mother, and how *much* she missed her. Why didn't the other three miss her as much?

They'd spent so much time in the rooms together all their lives, the rooms that were gone; these rooms were the wrong shape, and it took her ages to find anything even though they had little left, and no one but her seemed to miss her mother.

"Out," she said shortly, and let the door to the bakery proper close behind her.

The bakery shop was blessedly quiet.

But did she want quiet?

She was too young, *too young* to have nothing in her mind but her sweet, lost mother.

Everything will work out, Rose, her mother had always said, but it hadn't, had it? Because here she was, with no father and no mother and only her sisters. And Anna asking her to do more work, more work, more work, when all she wanted to do was sleep.

She had to get a breath of fresh air.

This was as much her shop as any of theirs. She could do as she liked with it, including leave it. She could judge where she was by the deep, wide cutting counter to her left, and knew the door of the shop was just in front of her.

She had to pull on that door; then really *pull*. She was afraid the handle would come out, and they'd all be trapped. But she could go out as well as any of them. She'd go *out*.

Before anyone could come and stop her, she *was* out.

Hands in front of her, she kept on walking, till she could feel the edge of the walkway with her feet. It was a little lighter outside; she could see that. The scars meant she could make nothing out, but she could see that it was sunnier outside than in.

It was a soft, sweet day outside. Rose pulled up short with a gasp, as if she'd been dunked in cold water. She hadn't expected anything specific, she'd have walked out into boiling oil. But the air tasted like cooled, honeyed tea, albeit with a tang of dust from the roadway, and there was so much happening, everywhere.

People talked and laughed as they streamed along the street in both directions. There was the thunderous noise of hard heels upon the flagstone walkways, and of hooves in the street—and dogs barking, it sounded like, and—*mooing?*

"You aren't planning to cross the street, miss? Those cattle are dangerous."

Rose turned at the voice next to her. Her bad mood had blown away. "Are there truly cows in the street?"

Her would-be protector sounded dubious. "Cows or bulls, I'm not familiar with them, miss, but they're large and the horns are long and I'd stay away from them if I were you."

"I wasn't going across. I only came out to get a fresh breath of air, and plan revolt."

"If it's revolt you want, you've met the right man," he said.

At that, Rose stepped backward. And bumped into someone. "Pardon me." She realized she had come out without a shawl, hat, or gloves, and must look quite flyaway. "I wasn't looking for a gentleman for revolt."

"Funny, as I am always looking for a lady willing to revolt."

Shocked, Rose stretched an arm back toward the door of the shop. Could her sisters see her through the windows? How far had she come? Why hadn't she told them she was going?

"My apologies, miss, I've been too startling. Here." The man did something, and then there were no more people.

"What did you do?"

"Just spread my arms to make a bit of a block. Walk right back, if you like."

"Oh, please don't—" *Please don't make a spectacle of yourself for me*, Rose thought.

But why not? What good was respectability now? Her mother and father were gone. There was no money left.

If there were to be no wealthy husbands for Anna and Jane, there *definitely* wouldn't be for Emery and Rose.

"Thank you," said Rose a bit more gaily as she shuffled back toward the door. If he didn't care, why should she?

"You're quite welcome, miss. Call upon me at any time."

Was he *flirting* with her? "A gallant offer, unlikely to be made good, as I won't know when you are passing."

"Well."

He paused so long that Rose wondered if she ought to have been more formal. She simply never met men, and her sisters had her so rattled—

He said, "I'll just have to make sure you know that I'm here."

Rose's face felt hot. "Thank you, I'll call upon you if I need the walkway blocked or if there are dangerous cows."

"You do that, miss. You do that. I'll answer to Mr. Russell."

Rose just nodded, and felt her door at her back. It must be her door. Should she say something? Good-bye? Something flirtatious? She'd never been to any of the social outings Rose and Jane had attended, she'd been too young to make calls to anyone but family; and she *had* no family, except their atrocious Aunt Eden who lived in the country. Had she ever talked to a man before?

"Good-bye." She settled on the simplest solution, and then realized he was going to see her shoving that door open with her shoulder. Because she had to get in.

It was looser than it had been the first day, but really it *must* be repaired.

After the third heaving shove, it came free.

Rose could feel her face flush with heat. Mr. Russell had surely stood there and watched the whole thing.

"Good-bye," she said again, and slipped inside.

EMERY WAS STILL CLEANING THE BAKERY PROPER, BUT ANNA had moved on to the shelves in the shop. As Jane had predicted, they were about to run out of the brown, soft soap used for cleaning.

Their first delivery of flour had been made, by a nearly wordless fellow who tossed massive sacks across his shoulder with a flick of the wrists. Anna had not been able to ask his name; Mrs. Scropes would have it. She'd kept her word about having the man serve them, that was clear. Hopefully the carpenter would come just as punctually.

Behind Anna sat one of their big serving trays, almost as wide as her arms would stretch, with three tiny home-sized loaves in it. Emery had coaxed the oven to life, and made a few small loaves just to get the feel of it. Also, so that they would have something to eat.

She focused her attention on attempting to rub pits out of the counter with her washcloth.

"Madame, I need a loaf of bread immediately. Quickly, please."

Anna whirled.

The man who had suddenly appeared in the shop—why hadn't she heard him struggling with the door? They must hang a bell—was large, tall and wide-shouldered, with a heavy wool cape still swirling with the motion of his leap into the shop.

And she was alone.

"We don't sell loaves, sir." Not that they were even open. No one, apparently, bothered to read the card she had placed in the window that clearly read *Closed*. She hadn't thought it necessary to lock a door that would barely open.

When they had loaves to sell, they would be the four-pound quartern loaves that families bought, but more often the massive half-peck loaves, or even peck loaves, that weighed over 17 pounds.

The little one-pound loaves that Emery had made were

tucked on the shelf behind Anna in their *closed* shop because they had to *eat*.

Had the fellow seen those through the *window*? Because he said, "Are you mad? I see the bread behind you. Quickly, quickly." Fortunately he didn't come any closer, but peered out the window at something.

Was someone pursuing him? Was he planning to stop them with bread?

Anna began edging out from behind the counter and along the wall to the bakery door. She *ought* not be alone. Why had she let Jane go out? With Emery in the back? Where was Rose? She'd been cleaning with them a while ago, but had disappeared.

"We don't have any bread for sale yet, but when we do, we sell it by the piece."

"By the piece?"

The man leaped toward the counter; Anna shrank back. Closer, he looked even more alarming, with tossed black hair and heavy scowling brows and skin that looked browned by sun. Why didn't the man have a hat?

Perhaps he had escaped from someone who ought to look out for him?

"Yes, of course by the piece." Still edging toward the door, Anna pointed a shaking finger at the pitted cutting counter. "We...we might have one in the back."

Had Emery finished one of her experiments in larger loaf baking? Anna ought to know what Emery was baking, she supposed. The whole shop was filled with the scent of baking bread, and likely would be, thought Anna, every day of the rest of their lives. She wondered if it would eventually take away her appetite for bread.

Right now she had *every* appetite for bread, and she wasn't giving their dinner—and breakfast and lunch and dinner tomorrow, too—to this man for a few pence.

The man looked as if he did not know what a loaf of bread in a shop ought to look like. "Well, if you have one in back, give me the whole thing then! I'm in a hurry."

He couldn't be serious. He really was not in his right mind. Even without weighing it, Anna estimated the weight of the loaf that Emery was trying to bake, and quoted the price.

That brought the man away from the window. "Are you serious? What ails you, charging prices like that?"

She shrugged. He wanted a loaf of bread, but not to pay for it. She couldn't support *that*.

The door to the bakery proper was at her back. She knocked on it, loudly.

But no one came.

"Those are the prices everywhere, sir." Anna was desperate to find another way of attracting Emery's attention —she must be back there!—without leaving this man alone in their brand-new bakery. And their dinner.

"Well, *that's* not true. Dammit, dammit, dammit, dammit, dammit!" The man tore back to the window and began to swear as he looked out again.

And the door to the shop swung open.

Jane walked straight into the flood of cursing.

"What do you *mean*, sir?" she snapped. "This is a bakery, not a theater!"

And the black-haired man spun around in surprise to look at her. "What sort of things do *you* do in a theater?"

"Don't go close, Jane; he may be mad," Anna shouted, her nerves giving way.

Jane took one look at her sister, shaking, with imploring outstretched hands, and pulled a sausage out of her shopping basket, which she immediately put to use beating the stranger about the head and shoulders.

"How *dare* you frighten my sister! An honest woman

doing an honest day's work, and you think you can come in here and—what? Are you threatening her? Making demands?"

"Yes, I demanded some bread!" he roared. He put up both his hands to ward off her sausagey blows, clearly torn whether to pay attention to whatever it was outside the window that so transfixed him, or the beating he was getting.

"Well, we don't cater to your sort here! This is a decent bakery, and you are not the sort of customer we want!" The door, still warped, had only partially shut; Jane opened it with one hand as she herded the unwanted man toward it by continuing to beat him with the sausage. "You can take your business in frightening people *elsewhere!*"

And when the man had been sufficiently backed out the door, still protesting about something, Jane slammed the door shut. Warp and all.

Upon which Jane rushed to Anna's side.

"Are you well? He must have frightened you so! Where are Emery and Rose? Don't worry, he's gone, he's gone."

And Anna, still shaking, though this time more with laughter, threw her arms around her sister. "Oh Jane. You *are* wonderful."

"Are you *laughing?*" In half a second Jane went from hugging Anna tight to shoving her away. "Oh my stars, I thought you were truly terrified!" She ripped her bonnet off as if she might start beating Anna with *that*.

"Oh I was, I was! And I am so grateful, so very grateful, that you came in just as you did! I was alarmed, truly. But it was so funny, you beating the stuffing out of him with that... with a *sausage...*"

Overwrought nerves gave way and Anna sank to her knees, alternately laughing and crying.

And after a second's thought, Jane smiled, then started to laugh herself.

"That must have been quite—"

"Oh Jane! I don't think that man has ever been beaten to within an inch of his life with a *sausage* before!"

And then both sisters were kneeling, laughing till they cried on each other's shoulders, when Emery finally appeared in the door to the back.

And stopped, surprised to see them so.

"What on earth?"

She stepped around them to swing a tray holding two massive, heavy loaves, appropriate to carve up for sale, on to the counter.

"Oh Emery, you should have *seen* it! I was all alone and the frightening man was waving his arms and demanding bread and getting more and more odd and Jane was like an angel, just like an angel armed with sausage!" Anna rocked back and forth, holding Jane tight.

"Odd? Why didn't you call me if there was someone behaving in a way you didn't like?"

"I knocked on the bakery door! Why didn't you come?"

"Oh, was that what that was?" Not looking particularly concerned, Emery began shifting one loaf to the wide tilted shelf behind the counter.

"Never you mind." Jane squeezed Anna right back. "We ought to rig a bell that you can ring, that any of us can ring, that will sound in the back."

"I ought to have some sort of weapon, too," said Emery with practicality. "I don't even have a sausage."

And on the floor, Jane and Anna just held each other, shouting with laughter, and rocking one another.

Frowning, Emery just took up one of the massive knives they'd washed, along with the counter.

Slicing through the center of one loaf, she held her breath.

Even Jane and Anna, on their knees on the floor, stretched to look.

The huge loaf was wet and doughy in the center. Clearly not baked through, though the crust was golden and perfect.

"Hmm." Emery didn't look discouraged, though. "I know how to fix that."

"The fire's too high?" They all let Emery take the lead, as bread truly excited her. But Anna was as good a baker as any of them, and they all understood what the problem must *be*; just not, at first blush, how to fix it.

"A bit. I can arrange the wood differently. I can fix this." Emery wasn't bothered. Slicing off a piece that looked perfect, she put it in her mouth. "Mmmm. Doesn't even need butter, like this."

"Every bread needs butter."

But Jane had come up from the floor and brushed her hands off on her skirt. She took the knife from Emery and began slicing around the uncooked center.

"What are you doing?" asked Emery, as Jane shoved her aside.

"Cutting off what we can sell."

She filled a tray with the pieces, then marched over to the door. Jerked her head to indicate Anna should open it.

"Fresh bread, going quick!" shouted Jane.

"Oh no, the laws say you have to sell it for a certain price, and you haven't weighed those!" gasped Anna, trying to pull on the back of Jane's dress.

"Let them arrest me. This isn't bread. This is a bread *trial*. And I'll be damned if I'll let it go to waste. Emery, do you think you'll have some to sell in the morning?"

"Two more days," mumbled Emery, poking her fingertips into the raw bit and wondering if she could put it back in the oven.

LATE THAT NIGHT, THE OLDER THREE SAT AMONG THE bundles in their sitting room, now open and with belongings scattered here and there.

Rose had already gone to sleep in one of their two wide beds. She was asleep in her underclothes, under one of the quilts.

She could not stop apologizing for not hearing Anna on the floor above, as she had been sweeping the basement.

Anna decided to wait until later to point out that Rose needed to be in the shop, not downstairs. Today wasn't the day to press that point.

"We had better make the best go of it we can." Jane spoke in that way she had that meant she had been thinking. "It's clear none of us will be getting married. Not from working in a bakery."

Anna nodded slowly. "Men don't buy their own bread."

It was wives and cooks and housekeepers who did the shopping. Even when Jane held a tray on the pavement, not one man purchased a bit. Not even that alarming person they'd sent packing through a great deal of determined sausage-whacking. Anna hoped *he'd* gone far away.

"We may not have many men as customers," Anna finally said, "but Leicester Square does have men *in* it."

Jane slumped back against the wall, staring at the little piles of coins in the light of their single lamp.

And said, staring at the coins, "You all aren't going to marry and leave me alone with this shop, are you?"

"Why on—whatever do you mean?" Anna was aghast.

"I *won't* be marrying." Emery, nearly asleep, still sounded quite firm.

"Jane, honestly. What made you say that?"

Jane's jaw locked firmly in its set, tense position, but she still did not look at her sisters. "I know you can all marry before I ever will. I am the practical one, and it is practical to notice that despite my...tenderness for some of the young men I knew in our old neighborhood, I do not appeal to their marrying instincts."

Then she finally looked up, and her eyes met Anna's.

"You will likely marry first, and when you do, please do not leave me to my own devices. Not with a bakery."

"I will not leave you to your own devices with *anything*. None of us are that likely to marry, Jane. Marriage isn't even offered to many women, and here we are, and I am not in my first youth. We are running a *shop*. We're in little danger of marrying. And I am in *none*."

"But you're pretty and kind and people like you, and—"

Squirming closer, Anna pressed her shoulder into Jane's. "It is our business. All of us, *together*."

Eyes closed, Emery nodded, head thumping softly against the wall.

There was an answering thump against the far wall, towards the back of the building.

"What was that?" Anna was too tired to jump, but her head whipped round.

"Likely nothing." Emery nodded sagely, with her eyes closed, sliding down to lie full length on the floor.

Jane and Anna looked back at the coins shining in the lamplight. Coins for hope, and independence. The chance to live their lives as they chose, looking for the love their parents had had, or proudly living without it, but never selling their lives for money.

More than cleaning the shop, more than baking their first loaves, this felt like the moment when their business was real. They all felt it. Somehow, Anna knew, they were all on the same page for one moment.

"*All* of us," Anna said again, squeezing Jane's hand.

"At least we can have peace and quiet from men in here," said Jane, scowling, for some reason.

And something far above them creaked.

"See? Old beams. Must be warming up from the oven fire downstairs," Emery added.

"Yes, it must be." Anna's voice was faint.

When her eyes lit on the coins, her expression turned into one of resolve, her jaw set rather like her sister's. "Ladies' Own Bakery is off to a start," she said softly.

Episode 3: The nature of customers

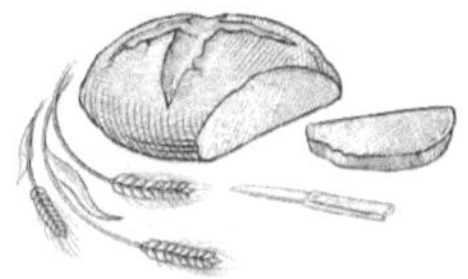

"Smells good, lady!" a wagoner called to Anna as she pushed open the shop door.

"Yes, it does!" Anna's smile was like sunshine, and she never saw his wink.

She had opened the door for exactly that reason. The bread smelled *good*, and they had bread for sale. Both the darker, rougher, cheaper maslin bread, and some very good loaves out of finer, sifted flour.

Anna didn't have a way of letting the Square know that the ladies' own bakery was open for business. No one had paid the least attention to her small card in the glazed window that said *Closed;* she expected they wouldn't read its other side, which now faced out, and said *Open*.

But no one could ignore the smell of good bread.

She paused. There ought to be something she could do to draw attention that wouldn't be too improper. Wave a hand-kerchief, perhaps? Drop one? Then it would be dirty; this wasn't a carpeted drawing room.

Anna stood there for a moment, blinking, hoping that was enough motion to draw the eye in the early morning light.

There were people about, milling in the chill dawn air. They ought to see her flapping eyelashes.

When she sailed back in, Jane was hovering near the loaves behind the counter, either to protect them or sniff them.

Jane nodded at the door. "We'll put that gap to work for us today."

"Won't we just!" It was downright hot in the bakery proper, but the shop was only warm; it didn't hurt to have some cool air coming in from outside, and the smell would be their best way of attracting customers.

Indeed, their very first customer appeared to be following the smell inside.

She was a slight young girl, in a linen cap; a maid, likely, but one entrusted with the shopping. Jane wondered if she worked for some nearby earl, as the tailor across the street had told her the square was home to several. Or perhaps she worked for another shopkeeper, perhaps one who could afford only a maid for help.

Whoever she was, she had a great sense of her own importance.

She and Jane regarded each other across the floor. Anna thought perhaps one of them might suggest a duel.

The maid marched herself up to the counter, head poised atop a long neck, and peered down her tiny nose at Jane. "You have bread for sale?"

Behind Jane, all there was on the shelves was bread.

"We do, yes," said Jane, fairly affably for her, Anna thought.

"It is fresh today?"

"It is fresh in the last hour. Just cool enough to cut."

"Would you say," said the girl, looking down her nose still, "that it is still so warm that it is likely to dry out once it is cut?"

Jane's eyes flicked toward Anna, who gave her a little shake of the head. Jane wasn't good with foolishness, but they must all learn to wait on all sorts of customers.

Jane looked back at the girl. "I would say that it would not. I would say that it is a very good temperature for being sold."

"So then if I take it home and serve it to my master and mistress, I won't be scolded for bringing them dry bread?"

"How long do you intend to wait before you serve it to them?" Jane asked practically.

"Miss Jane." Anna shook her head again.

"I assume," said the girl, "that if the bread is not to their satisfaction, I may come back here and you will return my money to me?"

Anna made a little noise, moving as if to start forward, but Jane just put up a hand towards her. "I believe I know the answer to this question, Miss Bickering." She looked at the girl. "You can safely assume that no money you spend in here will ever be returned to you. However, *I* assume that if the bread isn't to the satisfaction of the house, you won't return here to spend any *more*."

"I see."

The girl stared at Jane. Jane stared back.

Anna wanted to explain to their customer that Jane would win this game.

But she held her peace, letting Jane handle their first customer, and in a few more seconds that felt like years, the haughty young woman relented.

"Then I'll have two pounds. If you please."

"Very good, miss."

The shape Jane cut was square-edged, not a wedge, and the girl just nodded, took it and wrapped it in a piece of linen in her shopping basket. Then she started for the door.

Anna didn't need to interfere in *that*, either. Before the girl had gone two steps, Jane said, "Do excuse me, miss, but I believe you've accidentally overlooked the matter of payment." She said it in a *loud* voice, one rather at odds with the words.

"Oh. Quite." With no apologies, the girl circled right back to the counter and laid coins on it. Jane pocketed them. She clearly wasn't taking her eyes off this girl to secure the few coins in the till.

"Good day, miss," said Jane, and the girl nodded and went out.

"Oh." Anna let out the breath she hadn't realized she was holding. "You did so beautifully."

Jane just looked at her. "I didn't dance on stage, you know. It is not that sort of performance."

"But you did, you did so well!"

"What exactly did you think I would do to our first customer?"

"Oh. Our *first* customer." Anna clasped her hands and swept herself in circles all around the empty shop. "Our only customer. Our *last* customer."

"Surely not," but Jane didn't sound so sure.

There was so much bread. *So much bread.* What if no one else came to buy any?

"Someone else will come." Anna felt certain.

They stared at the door for a moment.

"Not that we must stare at the door."

"No," Jane agreed to that readily enough. "Surely not."

They stared some more. The stuck gap at the top kept it open almost a foot. The smell of bread escaped through the gap, along with their excitement.

"It didn't look hard," Anna finally said, looking back at her sister.

"No." Jane just looked puzzled. "It felt odd. Odder than I expected."

"Odd?"

"Yes. Odd. Wait till you try it."

That was when the creaking, half-gapped door opened again, and a troupe of rough, dirty men of middle years, shoving and shouting at each other, tumbled in like kittens.

Only to stop stock still when they saw Anna and Jane.

Both sisters were clearly torn between wanting more customers, and wanting customers like these.

"It's ladies," said one of them.

"It's women," said another.

"We can't come in here," said a third, even though they already had.

"Gentlemen, we are happy to wait upon you. Did you wish to buy some bread? The maslin, perhaps?" Anna folded her hands at her waist like she was singing at a *musicale*.

The men blinked.

"It's a shop," put in one in the back.

"They're going to *sell* us *bread*," leered the second one, but the first fellow elbowed him in the ribs.

"Shut up, you. I need to take the missus some bread or I can't go home. A pound, please," he said, very politely, to Anna, and then suddenly decided to take off his hat.

"You needn't, sir." She wished he hadn't; he was balding and much in need of a bath.

Jane cut the portion, and Anna took his coins. Then two others followed, and all of them went out in a subdued cluster, far quieter than they had tumbled in.

Both Jane and Anna could hear their muttering as they went. "It's *girls*!" "Shut your face hole, you lump." "I can't go home and face my missus without something to eat, she'll throw me out again." "We should have left the inn before sun-up."

They had just gone when the door creaked open again and

a squarish young man with friendly eyes stuck in his head and looked around.

Anna floated closer to the counter, her eyes flicking back and forth between Jane and the young man.

"I like the rate of improvement in customer quality," whispered Jane.

Once the young man had looked thoroughly around, he swept off his stovepipe hat. *His* hair was reddish-brown and clean, though cut bristle-brush short. "Isn't there another young lady, too?" was his singular greeting.

He still hadn't stepped inside.

Anna didn't think it wise to reveal how many sisters there were. "Can we help you with something?"

His bushy eyebrows tilted up. Was he surprised they hadn't answered his question? "My apologies, just looking for the young lady I met the other day. I haven't seen her outside since. I hope she's well?"

Jane glanced toward Anna. "A tall one with lighter hair, or—"

"Miss Jane!" hissed Anna.

Jane just gave her a shushing look that said, *This is too important for your silly proprieties.* The gentleman—or whatever he was—told Anna, "Not at all, one who looked rather like you, miss, but I believe she was blind." He nodded. Perhaps he meant the nod to be reassuring.

When had *Rose* met a *man?*

"She's not here at present," Anna managed to choke out, and the man just nodded.

"My apologies for interrupting you, I'm sure I'll be back." And he started to close the door!

"But—" Anna's voice stopped him. "Don't you wish to purchase any bread?"

The man just smiled. It was almost a grin, and almost inappropriate. He was several years younger than she was,

Anna realized, despite his bushy eyebrows; he had a square jaw and the near-grin made him look like a little boy, and far *more* attractive. "I won't be buying bread anywhere but here in future, I promise you, miss," and he was gone.

Anna just drifted closer to the counter. Jane's jaw had dropped open, too. She hadn't imagined that.

"Where did—"

"We'll have to ask her—"

"Should I have—"

But there was no more time, as the smell, or the sight of people leaving, seemed to alert Leicester Square that there was bread to be had, and then there were, all in a rush, more customers than either sister could remember.

WHEN THEY FINALLY HAD A QUIET MOMENT AGAIN, ANNA just waved to Jane. "Go get her, go."

Jane shook her head and suppressed a smile, but half-opened the door to the bakery proper to call, "Rose, Anna needs you, I think."

"I need her? We all need her! That young man doesn't need her! What *happened?*"

Jane just shrugged as Rose, floured from collar to knees, came through the door.

"What did you *do* outside? That is... No, what did you *do* outside?" Anna couldn't think of another way to put it.

"What? I've been in the bakery all morning!" Rose's face flushed with the heat, and her curls were escaping. She looked dewy and sweet and pretty, and Anna and Jane exchanged a look. Their baby sister looked a bit too alluring.

"A gentleman asked after you this morning! He didn't even come all the way in the door! What did you do?" Anna wasn't letting it drop.

"Nothing."

"I've known you your whole life. When you say *nothing* like that, it isn't nothing."

"So close to nothing *you'll* never know the difference," said Rose, as if they were ten years old again. Jane almost expected her to stick out her tongue.

Jane was in a rare moment of charity with Anna's propriety. "Then did you do something back by the ovens with Emery?" Jane narrowed her eyes. "She doesn't have any liquor back there, does she?"

"Where on earth would Emery get that? Truly, where would she? I'm interested. Wait, does drinking liquor cause men to appear?" Rose's brow knit. "How does *that* work?"

"Rose, I'm serious! How did you meet a gentleman? *Here?*"

Rose just tossed her hands out into the air on either side of her. "Here I am! People can see me here! Isn't that the point? I suppose he saw me and thought, *hmm, well-baked!*"

"Rose!!"

"Jane," Rose pointedly ignored their oldest sister, "do you two actually need something? Because Emery has a plan of setting all the evening bread to rise, then sleeping for a bit."

Anna hadn't dropped the matter. "I don't know what to say to you."

"What would Mother say?" asked Rose in a tone that was half-serious and half-bitter.

It seemed something weighty had arrived in the room when the extraordinary man stuck his head in again.

"Good morning!" he said in cheery tones, making Rose flush again, which was odd, as the ovens were in back.

"Oh. Mr. Russell. Good morning."

"And I ought to greet you properly too; it must be Miss..."

"Yes, it must be, as she's very young and not out," Anna said crisply. "Mr. Russell, thank you, but we must be going."

"Out?" Mr. Russell cast his eyes around the shop. "Out of your own shop?"

"It's not a parlor, Anna," Rose said under her breath.

"Miss Rose," said Jane quietly, "I believe this is Mr. Russell, of our new neighborhood. Mr. Russell, I'm afraid I am not familiar with your family. Do they live here?"

"Oh, no!... Miss Jane." Anna looked ready to slap herself in the forehead and very begrudging of the formal title.

"It's a proper introduction or none, and we're doing the best we can," Jane told her with the brittle solidity of a Roman statue.

"They don't, Miss Jane," said Mr. Russell with the same game cheerfulness, "but I'll be glad to tell you more of them. I'm sure I'll be around."

"Around *what*? You haven't even fully entered the shop once!" Anna clearly wanted nothing more than to slam the door in his face, and was stopped primarily because that door wouldn't slam.

"I'll be back later to fetch something for my supper. And perhaps it will be quiet enough to talk. Ladies." The man doffed his hat again and nodded, then left.

"This is unacceptable," said Anna.

"Fine. I'm going back to kneading dough." And Rose disappeared to the back.

Jane wasn't quite sure what had Anna so much in a froth. Surely it would be nice for Rose to meet a nice man? Of course, they didn't yet know for sure he was a nice man; but when did they ever? Her experiences had been with men to whom she'd been introduced—perfectly properly—and they'd still wound up being perfectly dreadful.

Not that she wasn't just as worried about their little sister as Anna was. This was what they got, she supposed, for being on display in a shop. It was becoming clear why nice ladies didn't do this, and exactly why doing this would shut them out of any opportunity for a good marriage.

As society measured a good marriage.

EMERY SLIPPED OUT THE BACK DOOR OF THE BAKERY WITH arms that felt like wet stockings. She'd never used her muscles so vigorously before, and she still had half a day!

She didn't quite have new bread ready when the old came out, and she worried she was wasting wood keeping the oven hot in between. It took longer than she'd expected even to load all the pans into the oven, and take them out again; one pan near the back had almost burnt before she was done. She could see that organizing the production of bread would require further thought.

A smile spread over her face and she let her head fall back against the little door. But she had done it. They had bread, and people were buying it. People were buying *her* bread!

Arms that wibbled like empty stockings were a small price to pay.

The cool spring air brought some noxious fumes her way from the sewer drain in back, and Emery decided to step down their little stone yard to the alleyway proper.

Cobblestones stretched all across the space within the enclosed yard shared by all the houses on the block. Horse stalls studded the walls here and there, with little apartments clapped on above them for groomsmen; they created nooks and crannies all around the yard. Greenery, determined to live, climbed up wood and stone walls alike where it could, or where no one had pulled it down. Halfway down she could see a larger stable, with a pressed-earth drive beside it that likely led to the street. It had been a mews, she decided, all this; a garden or a mews, with hawks or something like, back when only lords and ladies lived in these houses.

Barely a hundred years ago, Anna had told her, this had all been grazing land. Then titled men had covered it with houses great and small, divided it with roads, filled it with people. Such a short time, really, for such a whirling collection of people to come together and decide to live all within a quarter mile of each other.

Walking toward the stable with its alleyway to the street, she could breathe a bit better. Beyond it she could see the larger thoroughfare; she didn't intend to go that far, she just wanted a few free breaths.

Across the mews a woman let herself out of a small door; she was closer to the street. Her honey-colored curls were all askew, and she had bright pink cheeks and lips, and a blue satin skirt that looked more like evening gowns than anything for daytime.

She buttoned her little spencer jacket as she came, then pulled on her gloves. Why hadn't she finished dressing indoors?

Then she looked across the cobblestones and saw Emery approach.

The woman's slow, appraising smile felt odd, even yards away. Emery could feel it, on her skin, on the backs of her hands and in the hollow of her throat. Emery was being *measured* somehow, and it made Emery notice the little beads of sweat at her own temples and trickling down the small of her back.

Emery couldn't think of anything to say. She just stopped, outside of arm's reach. The woman in the fancy dress hadn't moved.

"I must have been a good girl last night to wake up to this," said the woman in a voice that caught and slipped like silk on raw wood.

Emery felt much younger for some reason.

"I, uh, I work in the bakery... our bakery..." She pointed behind her as if that made sense.

The woman didn't care about the bakery. "The thing is, I *wasn't* a good girl last night. So I can only assume I'm going to have to be good for some time now."

Emery's hands stilled. "Should I know what that means?"

"Not really, deary. Just a compliment. Take them when they come. The world is hard and few people get them. It's a pleasure seeing you, that's all."

"You don't even know me."

"Deary, I wouldn't have to." But the woman nodded, as if they'd just been formally introduced. "I'm Jasmine Hayes."

"Miss, or Mrs....?"

The woman just threw back her head and laughed. "You're *adorable*! You can call me Miss Hayes, if you like. Just tell me your name."

"Oh, uh," as if Emery had forgotten that she even had a name, "Emery, uh, Miss Emery Bickering."

"Now that doesn't really suit you. Not the Miss or the Bickering part. I like Emery, though. I'll remember that. And it's really your name? Mm, mm, mm." She made a little curtsey, right there in the alley, and her smiling eyes said that she meant it. At least a little. "I hope to see you again, Miss Emery Bickering. Right now, I must dash."

Emery watched her sway down the alleyway, the shimmering blue satin of her skirts making small *swishing* noises and reflecting the tiny amount of light there was in the close little yard.

It was a good thing she'd gone, because Emery had *no* idea what to say.

EMERY'S DESIRE FOR SOME SLEEP HAD FADED. SHE WALKED back through the bakery proper and passed Rose, still shaping big loaves and setting them to rise.

She had questions, and who was there to ask but Anna?

Not that Anna knew that much more than the rest of them. It was just that Mother was gone, and Anna was all there was.

No, what could she ask Anna? She'd have to think far more before she even had *questions*.

She hesitated, wondering if she should simply slip through the shop and upstairs after all.

Before she could decide, a blood-curdling scream came from the shop proper.

Emery grabbed a bread paddle and charged.

JANE BURST FROM THE BASEMENT STRAIGHT INTO THE SHOP.

At the door to the bakery, Anna had her arms spread in front of Emery as if to protect her. Little Anna, protecting tall strong Emery and her bread paddle.

Apparently, Anna was determined to protect her sister from the apparition in the middle of the store, a black-haired man in a long black cape, one that swirled around him as if the very devil had arrived.

A devil with a motherly maid.

Emery tried to move forward. "What the—" Anna kept her back.

Rose had shoved through from the bakery and was stopped against Emery's back. She stuck her head past her sister. "What *is* it?"

Jane's eyes flicked around the room. "It would take a minute to explain."

"You!" Anna pointed a finger, sparks nearly snapping from her eyes. "What are you doing back here?"

"I still wish to *buy some bread*," the man said, tossing the long black cape back from his side to show his leather purse slung at his side—and his sword.

"How *dare* you harass us in this fashion!"

"How dare you post a sign that you sell bread when you clearly *won't*?"

"Now there's no worries here, sir," the woman with him soothed him. His maid? His cook? Housekeeper? Not mother, as his odd accent differed greatly from hers. "Just as I said. There's the scales, you buy a pound or two of the bread, right as everything can be. There's nothing to it."

She was wagging her finger toward the scales on the counter, to which Jane was the closest. The man's dark eyes swept over Jane, and she moved sideways a little, the better to protect the till.

"That's the one who tried to kill me," the man said, "she won't be selling me any bread."

"Oh, sir, I doubt—"

"What are you coming back here for? Shouting in here for?" Anna looked ready to pop, her face was so red, while heat-sprung curls hung around her face. She pushed her hair back with her hands, not taking her eyes off him. "You have no *business* coming in here to frighten us all!"

"Ma'am, I assure you, I was as frightened as anybody."

"Hmph," said Emery, narrowing her eyes and hefting her bread paddle.

"It's a wee bit dramatic in here for a bread shop, isn't it?" the older woman said, folding her hands together.

It made them all fall quiet.

And in the quiet, the door scraped open.

"Oh my," said the woman who'd entered, turning to take

in the whole tableau even given the limited view afforded by her bonnet.

"How may I help you?" Jane stepped behind the counter. She wasn't about to miss a sale.

"A—a pound of the whole, thank you."

"Not the maslin we have out today? Ours has onion in it."

The woman looked at the cut surface of one of the huge rounds, studded with pieces of onion. It smelled heavenly and Jane well knew it tasted even better. She longed for the days when the caraway seeds that speckled it had only been a treat. Now she couldn't look at them without seeing pennies.

"No, thank you." The woman's voice was soft, no doubt from the tension in the room.

Jane cut her the piece, weighed it on the scale, and took her coins, then returned the change. The woman tucked the bread into a napkin in her shopping basket and, with one last look around at all of them standing in their spots, left.

"There." Anna swept an arm towards Jane at the counter. "That is how one buys bread. One doesn't leap in to a place and demand to be served before the other customers and scream about how the seller has to *hurry*!"

"There *were* no other customers, and you *didn't* hurry, so—"

"What *was* the hurry, Captain Brice?" the woman with him asked, before the man could get up a head of steam.

"Come here." The man crooked his finger at Anna, who drew back, pressing into Emery behind her, as if the devil had a contract and wanted her to sign it.

"I *will not!*"

His eyes swept around land landed on Jane. "You, you were the one willing to beat me to death with a sausage. You can't be scared to come over here."

It was a challenge as much as a question and though some part of her thought she *was* scared, her sensible head took over. The man would not kill all four of them in broad daylight in a bakery, after all.

Head high, Jane stalked over to face him, nearly nose to nose.

Now that she wasn't trying to beat him with sausage, she could see that his shaggy hair had some shiny glints in it, and his eyes weren't that far above her own. She was tall, like Emery.

And she wouldn't be cowed by a man with no hat who didn't know how to buy bread.

He crooked that finger at her, as if to say she should draw even closer, and Jane wavered. She already was quite close.

Then he pointed. Out the window.

"You see those two? They've been around the square every day. They don't beg, but they'll take what you give them. And they look thin enough to eat their own shoes. I can't catch them, but if I had some bread I bet I could feed them."

Jane looked.

His description would have suited wild cats. It was children.

Through the panes of the shop window she could see them, across the street and through the coattails and skirts of the men and women hurrying about their business. They were small. Not tiny children, but not big. A boy, it looked like, and a girl. Though both sufficiently ragged in their clothing that there was not much difference to see.

Jane looked back at Anna and nodded. "There are children out there."

Anna deflated. "Why didn't you buy the whole loaf, then? The onion bread, Jane, it will keep for days, they ought to have that."

"You quoted me a price for the whole loaf that was madness!"

"Ah, I can explain that, sir." The housekeeper shook her

shawl and skirts a little, as if preparing to lecture him. "You've not done any of your own shopping on land, sir, not ever. The law sets the prices. Britain has to grow her own corn since the wars, you know."

"Corn?"

Anna flapped her apron, clearly hoping it would make him go away. "Yes, of course corn!"

Which only made the housekeeper turn sad eyes to her. "He's American, ma'am, he don't call it corn."

"Oh. Wheat, then," the man said grudgingly.

"American?" Rose put her hand on the counter to step forward. "From a ship?"

"Half," but before the man could explain whether he meant half an American or half a ship, the bell rung again.

"*What?*" Anna pushed back her hair again and whipped her head around to see. She looked as though she had been lifting heavy weights.

Mrs. Scrope's white hair just showed under the brim of her bonnet. "Ladies. The matter of the countertops…"

A carpenter was standing behind her. With a box of tools.

"If you please, Mrs. Scrope," said Anna as sweetly as anyone could while covered with flour and shooing off devils, "this might not be the best time to conclude our business regarding refinishing the countertops."

Shrugging, Mrs. Scrope turned straight back for the door.

But the carpenter, a calm-faced young fellow with thick corded arms, took in the tension around the shop, the tall man in the black cape at the center of the ring of suspicious looking young women, and folded his arms across his chest, his toolbox thudding against his back. "Oh, I can stay," he said cheerfully.

The arms, folded, looked even more massive.

"If you don't mind, Mr.…." The carpenter didn't have the expression of a man who regularly resorted to violence, but he also didn't look inclined to move. Surely Jane could sort out this bread sale on her own. Without resorting to violence. Or sausage.

But the carpenter didn't give his name, and he didn't move. "I don't mind at all," he said just as cheerfully, but there was a little force to it this time.

Jane looked back at the man in the black cape. Whatever he intended to do, he'd have to do it with an audience.

The captain, as his housekeeper called him, saw the look in Jane's eye and started to sputter. "Ma'am, you must understand a man might rightfully question a price that seems so absurd."

"Price for what?" asked the carpenter.

"Bread," Rose answered him.

"It is mighty high," he agreed, leaning on the counter.

"You see how those need smoothing," Jane pointed out where he leaned.

"Jane, not now." Anna wouldn't be calm until everything was under control. Her control.

"The divots are practically under his elbow." Jane shrugged.

"So they are," the carpenter agreed, looking down.

"*Give me some bread*," the man in the black cape was practically grinding his own teeth together. "I intend those children to have it."

"If *that's* all you want."

That was Emery.

Emery, who had said nothing the whole time, suddenly handed the bread paddle to Anna and marched across the entire shop floor and out the door.

"What the—" The man in the cape moved as if he might follow her, but Anna just poked the bread paddle in his direction.

He raised a black slash of an eyebrow. "Ma'am, are you threatening me with a bread paddle now?"

"You two. Come here." The tall lady's voice drifted through the passing horses, carriages, and people.

It was a precarious spot; it was dangerous to stay so close to a fence that shut them out of the square's green overgrowth, where they might otherwise hide, especially when carriages passed constantly.

Jordan grabbed Sal's hand. If they had to run, it was the easiest way to keep together.

"Wait," Sal whispered. "She came out of the bakery."

The two of them had been staring at the bakery for days. There had to be some way to get some of that bread. It was just staring at them, right on the other side of all that fragile, fragile glass.

Neither Jordan nor Sal liked the idea of just smashing the glass to get to the bread. That was a type of crime one couldn't walk away from. It was bad, way worse than picking up things people dropped and selling them to the rag-picker.

The problem was, it was right there.

And when the door opened, it smelled like heaven.

The tall woman in a fine dress was stalking toward them, ignoring the crowd. Pedestrians walked around her, letting her make a straight line across the street—even the carriages seemed to bend to her will—to where they backed against the shop wall behind them.

There was no good place to hide.

"She's coming at us!"

"She came out of the *bakery*," Sal said again. "Where there's *bread*."

They didn't have to discuss it; that was one benefit of being twins. The only one, some days.

No, it was never the only benefit. There was always someone to watch your back.

"You two." The woman had hair the color of bread, too, the light kind, and she was waving her big hands in their direction, beckoning them closer.

Jordan looked at Sal, who nodded. They'd stay right here.

Finally, she was right near them. They hadn't made it easier for her by going closer.

She squatted right down in front of them, in front of the fancy people and everybody, right on the pavement. Her knees stayed tight together under her skirt, but she was still squatting down. They'd never seen anything like her.

"You're hungry?"

Jordan didn't have to look at Sal for that one. He knew they'd both nodded furiously.

"Can you work?"

Jordan shrugged, looked at his sister. She nodded, less enthusiastically.

They weren't stupid. Not everything they were asked to do was something they were willing to do.

"Let me see your hands."

That was new.

Reluctantly, Jordan put out both his hands, palms down; Sal followed.

"Palms?"

They flipped their hands up.

"You haven't done regular hard work, but you look strong. Bet you'd be stronger with some food in you. If you help me keep the bakery clean, I'll show you how to make bread."

Jordan sucked in a breath. It sounded to him like she had offered to make him angel's wings.

He grabbed Sal's hand and squeezed it.

They didn't have to talk about it.

Sal said it for both of them. "Sure we will, lady!"

But the woman didn't just get up and get on with it. She narrowed her eyes, which had a look to them—there was gold in their depths, and something about them reminded Jordan of a cat.

"We will try it. First come in, and we'll wash your hands and get you some food."

"*Wash?*"

When Jordan couldn't help that word coming out quite that way, the lady smiled. And stood.

"If you want to make the kitchen clean, you'll have to *be* clean. Don't worry, it won't hurt."

EVERYONE IN THE SHOP WAS STILL STANDING IN EXACTLY the same place when Emery strode back in, this time with two children in tow.

"Was that all the whole fuss was about?" was all Emery said, looking at every one of them as if they were soft in the head, most especially her sisters.

And disappeared back into the bakery proper, the two wide-eyed, too-thin children following behind her.

ANNA WAVED A HAND TOWARD THE MAN IN THE CAPE WITH the air of a dismissive queen. "As you see, sir, your help is not needed."

"But I..." This time, no one interrupted him. His words just trailed off.

And his housekeeper had already bought a hunk of the onion-studded bread, handing her coin silently to Jane and tucking the bread in her basket. "We've no more questions, do we, Captain Brice?"

The Captain looked at Rose, waiting by the counter with parted lips for whatever happened next, Anna with her spread hands as if prepared to shoo again, and Jane with her arms folded across her chest, apparently willing him out the door.

"No," said the man in the black cloak, "thank you for coming with me, Mrs. Parker…"

Anna clearly wanted the carpenter gone as well. Everyone, if she could. "And I'm so glad to see *you*, sir," she said, nodding to the carpenter, since he hadn't given his name, "but please, do come back tomorrow."

The carpenter looked over at Anna, clearly vastly amused. "You sure you don't want me to stay?"

"Tomorrow. I would beg you, if I had the energy left."

The bell rang, and a young woman with two small children clinging to her skirts and a baby in her arms walked in.

Everyone stared at her.

She stared at them.

She put down the baby, where it immediately failed at standing and fell, *plop,* on its rear end. It began examining the floorboards. Its mother let out a long, low groan that made her seem twice her age. "It doesn't matter if you want me in here or not, I've got to put down the baby."

Rose moved to help her, either with the baby or bread or both, and Anna turned back to the carpenter. "Tomorrow?"

"We shall return tomorrow, Miss Bickering; it is no trouble at all," said Mrs. Scrope, the landlord's wife, nodding her head and waiting for the captain to open the door. The carpenter shrugged and fell into step with her.

Captain Brice held the door for them.

It was a tricky business, living on land. It wasn't his first choice, but one couldn't be at sea all the time. And especially in the business he was in now, where it was up to him to go from official to official seeking decisions. He could only hope his ship still floated when it was time to leave.

He peered back through the window, but he couldn't catch sight of the children. Well, he'd wanted them fed, hadn't he? And surely, they wouldn't starve in a bakery.

As he turned away, he pulled the sticky door finally, if partially, closed behind him.

Apparently just at the wrong time, because before he'd gone two steps, he heard someone banging on it, trying to open it again. "Why do I have to work so hard to get in? I've got bunions, you know!"

Brice just kept walking.

Ahead of Brice, the carpenter was talking to that woman. "You sure you don't want me to just come back a little later today and see to those countertops when the little ladies aren't so wrought up?" His voice carried, and he was clearly quite interested in spending more time in the entertaining bakery.

"There's really no need, Mr. Harding. You can refinish the counters at any time. They'll likely be out of business in a month. I'd just like them done before I have to show it to new tenants."

"I thought you said they had a lease."

"They do," Mrs. Scrope said, as if she had no cares in the world, "but obviously. I mean to say. Four young women trying to run a business. It's some sort of lark, and if they don't tire of it, they'll simply fail, as businesses do." She sighed. "Bakeries change hands in London every day. Everyone needs bread, but making it work as a business isn't easy. Those girls won't manage it."

"Why did *you* lease, then?" The carpenter, to his credit,

Captain Brice thought, sounded just as unimpressed by Mrs. Scrope's attitude as the Captain was.

"Oh, *I* didn't lease. It was my husband, of course. This is truly his business. But I mean. Better a few months in rents than nothing." Captain Brice could almost hear Mrs. Scrope's shrug. "And whatever I will make in the settlement when they can't pay."

"What settlement?"

"Oh, you know. In court, when they can't pay out the contract."

Captain Brice drew aside into a shop's doorway. Mrs. Parker, his housekeeper even when he wasn't in a house, went on without him, but that was fine; she knew the way.

He felt a need to see where this Scrope person went off to.

Those children from the park weren't the only ones in trouble.

Episode 4: Everything looks good at a distance

Anna could just see the shape of Lord Zachary's shoulder and the color of his hair as he stood outside the bakery, waiting for something.

The window definitely needed to be cleaned. She *needed* to wipe the glass panes with the scrap of linen in her hand. Yes, it needed to be done.

She sighed.

It wasn't that his were the broadest, most manly shoulders she had ever seen, or his hair the fairest. All right, they were. It was the whole of him, put together in such a perfect way, all his perfect parts coming together to form a gentleman who was complete.

"Are you sighing at the window?"

Anna frowned at her sister. Why didn't Jane have the good sense to leave Anna her few moments of peace and quiet? "Of course not."

"Good, because I do not wish to come over there and see what you are sighing about."

"I wasn't sighing," muttered Anna as she turned back toward the cut panes. He was still out there.

"Mrs. Bunions is going to come in today and ask after buns. At least we can offer her bread. Ought we bake rolls?" Jane laid a big half-peck loaf into one of the display baskets with both hands. "Rolls are small and they bake fast, but they take time to form and dry out so quickly. And filling an oven with them means we bake half the bread that we do with taller loaves, with the same amount of wood. They might be too expensive for us to make every day. Is it fair if we only make a few, and save them for her? I don't know."

"We don't need to make them *every* day."

"Mrs. Bunions asks after them every day."

"Mrs. Bunions clearly has nothing else to do," Anna pointed out, and they both knew she was right.

"But we haven't told her we have no intention of baking buns, or anything sugared. That is not the right attitude for a shopkeeper. We must be always thinking of what your customers want, how many of them want it, and what we can sell, if we wish to stay in business."

"If you are so practiced at business, Jane, I am happy to let you worry about all of those things, including buns for Mrs. Bunions."

Jane absorbed this in silence for several moments.

"I never thought," she finally said, "when we were in school together, supposedly learning how to be fine wives, that you would one day relegate me to discussing buns with Mrs. Bunions."

"Mrs. Bunions wouldn't eat enough buns to keep us in business, even if we were going to bake buns."

"I suspect if I could have said that ten times quickly enough, someone might have married me," mused Jane.

The door squeaked, stuck, and then was shoved open with enough force to hit the wall.

A square masculine hand caught it before it did, and that forward man, Mr. Russell, appeared in the door.

Anna turned to face him in her drawing-room pose, her hands clasped. "Sir, I know you must be here to purchase your daily bread and not to ask after our sister, which would be improper in the extreme."

Thus faced with a speech insisting he was not here for the purpose for which he was here, the man seemed unsure what to do next.

After so long not-staring at Lord Zachary, Anna found this fellow...ordinary. His dark, serviceable suit was not fashionable, his heavy shoes had no shine, and his earlobes were too long. No desirable man had earlobes like that.

He jerked a little forward, as if intending to move toward the counter where Jane had the bread and the scales and the till, then stopped. Started again, then stopped again.

"Perhaps you would be so kind as to tell me the proper way to ask after your sister," he finally said.

"I cannot think of a way to make a proper social call in a bakery," said Anna, drawing herself up to her full height, which wasn't much.

The fellow considered this. "But she's *in* a bakery."

"Hardly the point."

He looked over toward Jane, who gave him no help, then back towards Anna. "Forgive me for saying it, miss, but *you're* in a bakery, too."

Reality flummoxed Anna for a moment.

"You cannot deny the man there, Miss Bickering, that's where you are," Jane put in from behind the counter.

"Miss Jane." Mr. Russell seemed to give up on the eldest sister for the moment and look for greener pastures, in the form of Jane's less disapproving look. "I don't wish to concern you, of course. I only wished to invite Miss Rose to a political speech this evening."

"A *political* speech?" Anna, still by the window, could not look more shocked.

"Quite." He was unrepentant.

"A political speech by whom, Mr. Russell?" asked Jane.

"Erm,... by me, I'm afraid."

That raised Jane's eyebrows as well. "By you?"

"Yes, I am a partner in the event, but I will be speaking."

Why didn't he just get on with it? Must she ask him about every little thing? "Mr. Russell," said Anna, "I am delighted to hear whatever you've come here to say, but you must not make me pull it out of you like a sick tooth."

"Yes, yes. I do see, I see your point, of course. I don't have any larger speech to make, that's all—at least, not here. Not to you ladies, I mean. That is, not here. And not now." Clearly trying to get hold of himself with a deep, slow breath, Mr. Russell made another go of it. "I would like to make Miss Rose's acquaintance. Of course, I know she is young, and you made that very clear the last time I was here, as well, but I do believe that accomplishment requires effort. So I put myself in your hands, ladies, to ask if there is a way that Miss Rose might accompany me—us, all of us, perhaps—" he added quickly at the look in Anna's eye, "to the speech I am giving later this week."

"What is the topic of the speech?" Anna had many more questions, but that seemed the most obvious.

"The abolishment of slavery, Miss Bickering."

"Oh." Anna appeared to shrink in her shoes.

Jane just closed her eyes. "Oh."

Mr. Russell's bravado trickled slowly out of him, too. "Not a topic that would interest Miss Rose? Or you ladies?" He'd clearly had hopes, but this reception crushed them.

"It isn't that..." Jane looked toward Anna, who gave the tiniest shrug. It was a massive capitulation. Jane took it as permission to tell the truth. "The fact is, you could hardly have found a topic that would interest Rose more."

The effect of that on Mr. Russell was like that of a dozen candles. His very hair seemed to grow brighter. "Not really."

What a wide smile he had. Not appropriate at all.

Jane answered. "Yes, our mother was an avid campaigner against slavery in the sugar boycotts when we were young, Mr. Russell."

"Miss Rose has been interested in the subject almost as long as she could talk." Anna's eyes were trying to catch Jane's. Surely they ought to stop encouraging this person?

Jane ignored her. "It is only the truth that Miss Rose would hardly like anything else better."

"Oh!" Mr. Russell seemed to grow an inch or two in height, which made quite a difference; he wasn't tall. His smile was artless. "Then I might escort all of you ladies to the event?"

"That cannot be appropriate," Anna said immediately. "Nor will there be a moment when all four of us might leave the shop."

"Four?"

JANE DIDN'T FEEL THIS WAS THE RIGHT MOMENT TO introduce Emery. "I will accompany you and Miss Rose, Mr. Russell. I'm sure we support your goals with the topic, but you must understand that I have a great many more questions about your family and background."

"Yes, I do see. Thank you, Miss Jane, and I will return Thursday evening. The speech itself is set for eight o'clock."

Anna almost gasped at the mention of the time. They would no doubt be out until ten o'clock or later. For social affairs of the gentry, and apparently for speech-makers, it was a reasonable hour. For the four of them, working the way they had been, it would be a terribly late night.

"If Miss Rose wishes to come," Jane added quickly.

"Of course. Of course. Good day, Miss Jane, Miss Bickering, I will not keep you any longer, good day," said Mr. Russell, tipping his hat so they could see his bristling red-brown hair again, and then he bowed, and left.

Standing outside, he made sure to yank the door all the way shut.

"Jane, why ever did you—"

"Anna." Jane addressed her oldest sister, whom she loved very much, and often wanted to strangle.

The oldest sister, who was just now attempting to open the door again.

That Jane ignored. "If you are about to say something about how to behave appropriately, I already know it. Save it. If you are about to say something about how Rose ought not to have gentleman callers, then I'm ashamed of you. She's twenty. Just because she never had a season, it doesn't mean she can't wish to be married."

"*Does* she wish to be married?" The door squeaked loudly as Anna made it move an inch before it stuck again in its frame. She curled her fingertips around its edge and tried to budge it.

"Why don't you ask her? In any event, if she wishes to go, I'll go with her."

"I'm not trying to be Mother, or, heaven forbid, Aunt Eden—"

"Heaven forbid," said Jane with real emotion.

"—I only feel that I must look after her, of course I must. Since if I do not, then who will?"

The door finally gave to Anna's scrabbling.

"Emery and I will?" Jane said, half-under her breath, as Anna wasn't listening.

That blue-coated swan of a man was still standing outside.

Why was he standing outside a bakery and not coming in or going away, wondered Jane?

Anna just stood there in the half-open door, staring at him. Jane couldn't see her face, but she suspected it was lovesick and appalling.

Jane came over to the door.

Carefully circling so she could see her sister, Jane found Anna did, in fact, look a little lovesick, and slightly appalling.

"If he turns and sees you looking at him like this, how appropriate would that be?" hissed Jane.

"I don't know what you mean! Look what a lovely day it is out. We ought to open this door and leave it open more often. Do you know, I think the fresh air would do us all good."

"We cannot shut it. Anna, do come away. Now I will be embarrassed."

"But why? A beautiful day, and the square looks so green, and isn't that one of Mother's friends?" She nodded toward someone who wasn't there, somewhere on the other side of the road.

It certainly was not, but it looked as though the young gentleman was about to turn. Anna leaned forward out of the door of the bakery and waved to someone imaginary across the street in the square.

The gentleman she'd been watching? Didn't see. He stepped out into the road, steering towards a carriage that had paused, presumably to let him climb in.

Passing by just at that moment, in an open barouche, another gentleman, *did* see. That gentleman, twice the age and wearing a starched ruffled neckcloth, turned to look at fetching Anna framed in the door of a bakery and waving to him.

"Oh my goodness."

Anna, cheeks flaming red, whirled and tried to slam the door shut after her.

Of course, it wouldn't slam.

"Lecture me more about how to behave appropriately in business, Miss Bickering." Jane was not gracious in others' defeat. "Do you think that gentleman might have taken you for a countess, or even a duchess? Or perhaps a Covent Garden nun, the way you were standing in the door and waving?" The local term for ladies of the evening made Anna whimper.

"Surely he didn't see me. He didn't, did he? Oh, you go look."

"Why, so he can see *me* standing in the door waving to him like a strumpet?"

"Oh my stars, oh my stars and heavens above." Anna stood in place rocking, her hands wringing.

Jane just rolled her eyes. "I really don't think you have anything to worry about until he comes in to ask if he may accompany you to a political speech."

THE MEWS IN BACK SUITED EMERY BETTER THAN THE street out front, she thought, but it was good to be in the fresh air. She and Jane were soon at the corner, waiting for a break in the flood of people to cross to the square.

Emery's hair was a little disheveled, and she had flour on her dress here and there, but they couldn't pretend to be ladies any longer. She worked in a bakery, and she smelled of rising dough. It was a smell she adored, and she wouldn't worry about anyone who didn't like it.

"You smell like ale," muttered Jane, as they crossed on the other side.

Well, there was that.

"I don't smell drunk, do I?"

"How would I know? I've never smelled anyone drunk."

Emery thought about the gentleman she'd seen that first morning. He'd smelled drunk. Emery knew what it smelled like *now*.

Fortunately, he'd been as quiet as a mouse since, and neither she nor any of her sisters had tripped over him in the hall, literally or figuratively.

She turned down an alley.

Jane's dark head swivelled from side to side in her plain gray bonnet. If anyone was lurking in any doorway, she'd see it. "You're sure we're going to the correct direction?"

"How far away do you think the children walk? They said their father had a room down here, and we ought to speak to him."

"I don't know why. We are paying the children for their work, and what they do with the money is no business of ours."

"Jane. I don't think you mean that."

"I mean it enough," but Jane followed Emery down the tiny stairs. "This is it?"

At least Jordan and Sal hadn't been secretive about it. They gave the direction of their lodging readily, along with assurances that there was no need to go there. They hadn't seemed *frightened* of their home; but they had been completely disinterested in it, and couldn't imagine anyone else's interest in it either.

As they clearly did not have the money for school, the Bickering sisters fully understood why they were not attending any; but it wasn't clear why no one at home seemed to miss them all day while they wandered Leicester Square and the surrounding streets...and clearly did not eat enough.

Emery studied the iron-grate-covered door. "It looks just as the children described it."

An iron grate that creaked open as Emery pushed it with a finger.

"This could be quite formidable, if locked," said Jane, following Emery still as her sister pushed the grate wide. Behind it was a heavy door, grooved with age and old green paint; it wasn't latched either.

The room inside wasn't tidy; there were dishes scattered about, but they looked mostly clean. There were two mattresses covered in ticking and lying directly on the floor, and a wooden crate against one wall with a water ewer and bowl on it. Jane looked with longing at the table and chairs. But aside from laundry heaps about a small washtub and a few more kitchen items near the stove, there wasn't much else.

The place looked temporary. As temporary as theirs did at the moment.

"Where is the drying linen? There must be some." Emery looked as if she were about to launch a complete search.

"Drying linen? You want to know about the linens? Where are their *parents*?"

The children wouldn't give up any further information than that this was where they lived, and that Emery could go there if she liked, but she needn't.

Sal had been particularly uninterested in their interest. "Aren't we here like we said we would be, every day?" Her long pigtail swung behind her with the force of her motion, and it irritated her that Emery even cared where they lived.

"And we washed!" Jordan still considered this the largest affront. Behind its grime, his still-chubby cheeks were a bit sallow for the sisters' liking.

"Yes," said Anna, "but we need to know from where you've come."

"What for?" asked Sal very reasonably, "we don't know

where you come from," and Anna had to stop that line of conversation pretty quickly, as it appeared dangerous.

"We need to know they've got a decent place to sleep, that's what we need to know, and they have." Jane stayed by the door. "So we needn't poke around. It's—surely looking around more would not be..."

"If you say *appropriate,* I will do my best to kill you with a mattress," and Emery looked as if she meant it.

She picked things up and put them down with her long, strong hands. There was something not quite right here, but she wasn't sure what it was. If their father was out working to put bread on the table, where was their mother?

And if there was a father working to put bread on the table, then why weren't the children fed?

"We will come back again. It isn't far to go." Jane kept glancing out into the street, which was level with her eyes. "Surely we don't want a neighbor to see us? Who knows what we might be accused of doing in here."

"No, it's not far." Emery put down a cup. She looked in the water pitcher; it was empty and dry.

"We still have some errands."

IN BERLINTEN'S BUTCHER SHOP NEARBY, BOTH SISTERS, ONE dark head and one light, bunched up close to one another to stare at a fresh roast of beef about to be carried out of the shop by a woman who wasn't them. Both sisters silently sighed.

"One day," said Jane, before turning to the counter.

It was a little like theirs, with a deep wooden counter pocked with thousands of knife gauges, and a scale. Unlike theirs, it was stained with years of blood and nameless meats.

Jane took the little plate from her shopping basket. "Half a pound of kidney, please."

The shop assistant bobbed his head. He had the face of a little boy who'd just had cake, but his arms, when he lifted one of the heavy trays, looked carved from knotted oak.

He smiled at Jane before lifting the kidney up to slice it. His smile didn't leer. He looked at her rather as they'd looked at the roast: as a dream of something far away.

Emery considered breaking out in song, just to see if it pulled his attention from her sister.

"Thank you," Jane said without feeling as she handed over the coin.

The assistant wasn't watching his own coins as he handed them back. Emery half-hoped he'd miscounted in their favor. It was only right, since he couldn't watch what he was doing. "Please do come again, miss," he said with another bob of his head.

"I cannot tell if it is to our benefit or not when the shop-keepers are smitten," Emery said, as the butcher shop door closed after them. Such luxury, a door that actually closed.

"I cannot imagine how it benefits us, if I don't talk to them."

Emery watched Jane settle the basket. Her sister had a slightly pointed chin and slightly tilted eyes that spoke of mysteries and suspicion. The daylight shone on each twist of dark curl arranged on the back of her head, just visible under her bonnet. She looked as if she would gleam in the dark.

"What are you staring at?" Jane asked as she finally realized she was walking, but Emery wasn't with her.

"Nothing." Emery trotted to keep up. This plan of always going out in twos was unwieldy, but undoubtedly one of Anna's better ideas. "I hate to be entirely mercenary, just wondering if that butcher boy would cut his price in exchange for a smile."

"If so, start smiling."

"Oh, I—" But there wasn't time to claim that she hadn't meant what she said, as Jane began walking again.

THE SIGN SWINGING OVER THE LADIES' OWN BAKERY HAD a simple brown circle on it with an X carved in it, presumably to resemble bread. It would be a little while, they'd decided, till they could spare coins for a new sign that actually said *Ladies' Own Bakery*.

So the name of the shop was, for now, secret.

Her shopping basket dragging on her arm, Jane pushed back at her hair as she laid her shoulder to the bakery door. Emery let her try first and see if it would take both of them to get it open.

"Surely that carpenter will come back?" Jane asked over her shoulder. "Mrs. Scrope isn't just being cruel by keeping him away, was she?"

"Here," said a man's voice, "let me help you."

The voice was smooth, accented as schoolboys learned to speak at places like Eton. And Oxford. Jane turned.

Had she already forgotten what it looked like to be clean and polished? The gentleman did not have a fair hair out of place. Nor was there a speck of ash on his dark blue coat, or the edges of his beaver hat.

His smile might have been wide just because of his square jaw.

It was the man Anna had been sighing at through the window.

"Thank you," Jane said absently, as the fellow gave the bakery door a sharp push and forced it open.

Emery stood silently by, wondering if she should do, or say, anything at all.

Jane would stop looking in a moment. It had simply been awhile since she had seen anyone so clearly of the upper echelons of society. That was why she was staring at him.

Well, that and because he *was* uncommonly good-looking.

"Things are easy for you, aren't they?" The words were out of her mouth before she even realized she'd thought them.

And, she realized, because he was staring back at her.

In fact, his eyes roamed all over her, taking more liberties than eyes had ever taken with her before, not even when she had been the target of street whistles. He didn't look smitten; he looked *searching*.

"Opening the door isn't *that* difficult. You would be extraordinary to paint," he said.

"I beg your pardon?"

"You would be wonderful to paint," said the gentleman a little more slowly, as if he thought she simply hadn't understood his words. "I would like to paint you, if you have the time at some point. I would pay you, of course."

Jane had thought she was far more comfortable with their new social situation than Anna. But now that she was being offered money to let a stranger in the street stare at her, she wasn't comfortable with it. Not at all.

But she wasn't inclined to explain to this man that she deserved the consideration due to fine ladies, because she was painfully aware that she no longer had any sort of claim to the category.

"I won't," she said shortly, putting her foot on the step.

"Oh—"

When his hand made a half-formed motion toward her, Jane thought he might grab her. Or, part of her mind said in a quick flash, she thought he might explain that he rarely accosted ladies in the street or asked to paint them. Or he might even just ask her name.

Instead he said, "Don't give it a second thought, then."

And didn't even tip his hat as he turned back toward the road.

Emery silently followed Jane in, then went on through the shop and into the bakery.

Sal was sitting on an overturned half-barrel, and jumped up as soon as she saw Emery. "We did everything!" she called out, which was, Emery suspected, likely not true.

Jordan was simply stirring a wad of bread dough she had set for him. Too wet to set properly, Emery thought, but if he had stirred it the entire time they'd been out, it might form a loaf.

Emery just nodded and passed him. As she reached the door to the mews, she placed her bonnet on one of the pegs there, and tossed her gloves on the windowsill. She'd have to pay attention to see that Jordan didn't bake them in any bread.

Jane had always been striking. Emery had never been so.

So why did it itch, for Jane to be so obviously admired and by a man who didn't even know her?

By all appearances, Jane hadn't enjoyed it.

Instead of settling in to shape loaves, Emery picked up her gloves and bonnet again and went out.

The cobblestones in the mews were rounded and pushed against her feet, far less easy to walk on than the flat paving stones in front. But it was cool and quiet there. Emery walked down to the alley and out to Castle Street.

The buildings here were less grand, the pavement more crowded. As she walked, she looked up and down the street, and peered down the corridors and alleyways that turned off the thoroughfare.

Emery was no longer a gangly social failure who spent her

days in a boring drawing room. She had the pale green dress, but it was smudged with flour and dough, and she liked her life better this way. What else was she looking for?

She didn't expect light women who paid compliments to be stationed there day and night, did she? Like soldiers? In what sort of army?

She didn't. Of course not.

Yet, as she was turning to get back to her work, she saw a flicker of that bright skirt, and it was coming her way.

She took a step in that direction. Then another.

Was that the same woman?

"It's chance," she said, louder, brighter than she'd meant to, as she drew near. The sound of her voice made Miss Hayes look up in surprise.

And smile, just for Emery.

"No, it isn't, you're looking for me," Miss Hayes said.

They stood and stared at one another, Emery wondering what to say, wondering if the other woman knew what to say, wondering if she'd say it. She looked as though she knew everything. Surely she'd say something?

Eventually, she did. She said, "We're neighbors, in a way, aren't we?"

"In a way." Emery looked about. They were standing on the Castle Street pavement. The woman likely didn't even know where Emery lived. But they were standing here, seeing each other, for the second time.

"And you'd like to talk more," Miss Hayes said, more softly.

A horrible thought came to Emery from nowhere, that if this woman sold her time, she might want Emery to pay something.

It must have shown on her face, because the woman just shook her head, the tiniest shake of the head *no*, and brushed a gloved hand down her skirt, showing that it wasn't dirty.

"Not about money. You don't want to give me money. I think you'd just like to talk. Unless... unless I'm wrong?"

"No!" Emery had to stop herself from darting forward. In her flour-covered apron. What would that accomplish? "No. You have it right."

"Well. Perhaps we can find a place to talk. One night soon. If you would like."

"Perhaps we can." Why *now* did Emery notice that the backs of her knees were sweating? "I'll... we'll talk again. We will decide on an evening."

"Yes," the woman said with a most fetching dimple, "we will."

And then she saluted Emery with her folded fan and swung down an alleyway and was gone.

ANNA NEEDED TO PULL THE SHOP DOOR OPEN. BUT SHE hesitated. No, she leaned. Leaned her forehead into the wood of the door, she was still too ladylike to curse, even silently. Though she felt that dam would soon crumble.

She thought through the open crack of the door she saw a flash of blue, like Lord Zachary's coat. But what would it matter if he *were* there? She'd spent far too much time staring at his back already.

She had to finish sweeping the floor to close the shop. Just sweep the floor, out the door. She couldn't call for a sister to be there with her every time she opened the *door*, could she?

It was late, though the sun had not yet gone down, and every part of Anna was tired, in ways she had never been tired before. Every step hurt like walking on nails, the skin on her hands was parched with washing, and her neck felt bent. Could a person become hump-backed from only a few weeks of working in a shop?

She'd find out, she supposed.

Grasping the broom, she brushed the crumbs out of the door, watching the little brown specks jump over the door sill. Then she looked up.

She forgot to breathe. There *was* Lord Zachary, face reddened with exertion as he darted between carriages, across the road with a vast bouquet of flowers in his arms.

He looked so beautiful, coming right towards her with that great bouquet of red, purple, and white flowers, that Anna just stood and watched him come. She forgot she was standing out where anyone could see her.

He was coming to see her; he was bringing flowers for *her*, she knew it. The tired feet and cracked hands would be no more, because he was going to whisk her away into a life of luxury, where titles like *lord* and *lady* were used every day. And flowers. And there were servants to bake the bread.

Lord Zachary reached the pavement. "Miss," he said briefly, and half-tipped his hat with politeness, without even a true smile.

Just like that, he was gone, past her and into the door that led up to the various apartments. Including his, directly under the roof.

What was she thinking? Why did she still think it? She had to *stop*.

Anna pressed her hand to her cheek, hoped that embarrassment hadn't made her blush.

The same open barouche that passed earlier, containing the same large man with a broad ruffled neckcloth, stopped just in front of the bakery. The man didn't get out. But he looked at her, standing as she was in the doorway holding a broom. And he tipped his hat, with a very broad smile.

Flustered, hands fluttering, Anna backed into the shop, dragging the broom with her, and shut the door as best she could.

Yes, she had better call one of her sisters every time she opened the door. And stop sweeping. She *must* stop sweeping the floors. Let them all be ankle-deep in bread crumbs. It would be better.

STILL, ANNA COULDN'T STOP WONDERING. WHY HAD LORD Zachary brought flowers? Surely he didn't have a wife up there in the attic. Anna had seen no evidence of a wife.

But then what *would* show that he had a wife locked up there?

It was no affair of hers. She ought to finish cleaning the shop itself. If Jane had done all she promised, supper was waiting upstairs. She'd eat with her sisters.

She should hurry for her supper.

Instead, she went slowly.

She made sure the lock was thrown on the back door, then checked the level of the banked hearth in the oven. Sal and Jordan had gone home, holding each other's hands. Anna closed the bakery door and went to throw her hip, without propriety, hard against the front door.

Two, three times till it finally shut. And she could lock it.

It felt a little eerie, standing alone in the closed shop, where she could hear only the rustle of her own skirts. There was no one around to blame for her actions, only herself. Slowly, Anna walked up the stairs to the rooms she shared with her sisters.

Was it too much to hope that if she just kept climbing, she might find a whole different life?

Still slowly, Anna kept going.

She turned at the far end of the corridor and tried to put each foot down silently.

Anna didn't have three sisters for nothing; she knew to walk on the outer edge of the stair so it would not creak.

Step by step she moved up the narrow little wooden stairs, each one nothing but a raw, unpainted board.

There was an empty floor above them, likely why none of her sisters had noticed the man living in the garret. Why did he choose to live in a garret?

Anna should have turned back before the top of the stairs.

Anna crept slowly, slowly ever upward, step by higher step, craning her head to see what was happening up there in the little globe of golden light whose edge glimmered just within view. Lord Zachary had lit a candle.

One more step and her eyes would just peep over the top of the floor. With luck, he wouldn't see her head emerging behind him.

She stepped.

She was right. He wouldn't see her. In the golden orb of candlelight, he had arranged the flowers in a plain pottery urn. The lilacs had opened, and the room was full of their smell, like beautiful cold rain.

Bare wood sloped down all over, it seemed, making a warm golden cave of the space, even with the light from just one candle and the last of the summer sun.

And there was a canvas standing next to him. Lord Zachary, his coat gone and shirtsleeves rolled up till Anna could almost see the hair on his muscled forearms, was painting the flowers.

Why didn't he turn around and see her? *Notice* her? *Why didn't he love her?* He was so perfect, everything she had dreamed of when she was a little girl, dreaming of the day she'd be married and taken off to a home of her own. Someone of the gentry, rich, refined, educated, and possessed of finer feeling. The kind of fine feeling required to paint the petal of a lilac with such an honest, delicate touch.

He only lacked the ability to see her.

She could do it. She wasn't fine Miss Bickering any longer, attending balls all night and dancing in kidskin slippers. She had a shop; she made money. It couldn't be too far a step to being brazen enough to catch a man's eye on purpose. Stroll in, smile, perhaps make a witty remark.

She couldn't even lift her foot one more step.

Slowly, just as carefully, Anna reversed her course, moving step by tiny step back down the staircase, back to where her supper and her sisters were waiting.

"If you see any inexpensive hair ribbons, Jane, do tell me so!" Rose had greeted last night's news of Mr. Russell's invitation with a storm of preparation, including a great deal of hair-brushing. The topic of hair ribbons threatened to become all-consuming.

Pleas for hair ribbons did not assuage Jane's mixed feelings about Mr. Russell. "Rose, you needn't buy a new hair ribbon to hear Mr. Russell give a political speech. And I am going to buy necessities, not hair ribbons."

"Hair ribbons are a *type* of necessity," Rose called after her as Jane stepped out the front door, wrestling it shut behind her, into the cool morning air.

It was early, too early for people to be buying hats.

But the tailor whose shop faced into theirs across one street was waving wildly in her direction.

Jane meant to ignore him. Her sisters were all busy, baking or selling. She had to get back, herself. She was only running the few errands they needed because there was no one else to run them.

"Miss Bickering!" The neighbor tailor, who was several inches shorter than she and twice as dour, came out to the pavement and called after her when he saw her pass his shop.

The rudeness only angered her. Jane turned on her heel. "Must you shout after me in the street, Mr. Morley? I apologize, but I have errands I must attend to, and quickly."

"Miss Bickering, I really must protest." The fellow's jowls were nearly shivering with emotion. "Did I complain when four young ladies opened a business inches from mine? I did not."

"You did." Jane had only spoken with the gentleman a few times, but he'd complained every time to *her*, and she doubted he saved his opinions for their conversations.

"Did I make a comparison between young ladies with *no* chaperone, doing business a stone's throw from my own very respectable shop, where gentlemen wish to purchase fine clothing in a neighborhood of good repute, and the ladies of the evening who are showing themselves day and night on this square?"

"I am sure you did not, sir," and Jane's eyes were shooting sparks. He'd better *not* make such a comparison.

"I am a calm man, a good man, and gentle with you young ladies. You know I am. But I will not hesitate to complain to your landlord if I see any more untoward behavior above that bakery."

"Mr. Morley, there has *been* no untoward behavior over that bakery."

"I have eyes. I live right across from you, girl!" Mr. Morley's temper was rising. "I saw one of you going up the stairs to the rooms of that rake, that fellow who says he does art. *Beh.* Art is what you see at church."

"There's no rake upstairs, nor artist either. Really, sir, I must be going."

"I'm telling you. Any more unseemly episodes, and I *will*

complain."

Jane turned and looked over her shoulder at their building. It jutted into the intersection, making an awkward and abrupt turn even more difficult.

There were the windows in the building's front, above the shop, that she knew faced into their sitting room. In the daylight, she could not see in. Above them the empty apartment, and above those the garret.

"Mr. Morley, how did you see what you say you think you saw? The staircase travels up the inside wall. There are no windows in it."

"Well." Mr. Morley tugged down on his coat. It fitted perfectly, but he tugged it. "I saw a young lady leave the rooms on the second floor, and no other windows showed light but the garret."

"And how do you know one of us did not go out?" Jane had a flush of misgiving. No one could have done what this fellow claimed to have seen, surely.

"I can see the front door from here, miss!"

"Mr. Morley," Jane said, drawing herself up to her full height, "You've convinced me of two things. One is that you do not grasp that the building has a rear exit. The other is that even if it takes the last of my strength, I must close the curtains when we retire. Good day, sir."

She held her head high as she walked away, determined not to show any misgiving in front of a mortally nosy neighbor. She wasn't sure *what* was going on above the bakery, but she was sure that showing any sign of fear would only make the neighbors stare harder at their windows. The idea! Staring at her windows! Leicester Square was full of entirely too much staring of too many kinds. She refused to turn back, too, but if she had been willing to spin round, she would have contemplated how to paint "Stop Staring" on their sign rather than "Ladies' Own Bakery."

Episode 5: The difficulty of success

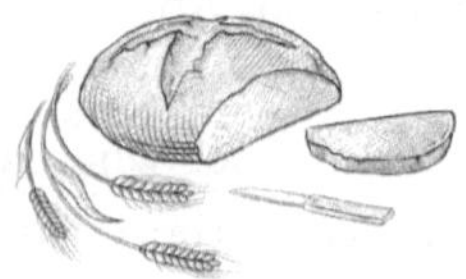

"May I serve you, please?" said the young lady behind the pitted counter.

The crowd inside the bakery of women of all ages and sizes looked motley enough, but they seemed to have some sort of order; and in the order he couldn't discern, it seemed to be his turn.

The Honorable Augustus Murgatroyd, Viscount Boislegrand, known as Puffy to his friends (especially the ones too lazy to say *Bwah-luh-grand*), couldn't decide whether one took one's hat off in a bakery, or not.

It seemed the young lady couldn't see him; even so, one wanted to do the right thing with one's hat. "I don't wish to purchase any bread, miss."

She blew a stray curl away from her nose. "Then would you mind stepping aside and letting others make their purchases?" she said in a voice that spoke to him of his own circle, and even his own neighborhood.

But he certainly didn't know *this* girl.

"Did I see you sweeping up at the door a few days ago?"

"I've no idea, sir; I didn't see you. Next?"

Was she the girl he'd seen? He didn't have the same thrill of excitement when he looked at her, and why would a blind girl wave?

Circling, mumbling ladies filled the shop. Puffy worried he would regret it if he stayed here much longer.

He tried again. "The young lady at the door, she, she looked a bit like you?"

"I have sisters," the girl at the counter said, just as briefly. "This is a bakery. If you don't wish to purchase bread, perhaps you'd step aside?"

He couldn't ignore the request; he stepped aside.

The woman behind him settled her shopping basket on her hip in a noticeably aggressive fashion. "Finally. Quartern, please."

"The quartern loaves are gone for the day, ma'am, I'm so sorry."

"Two penny loaves? I'll come back tomorrow for more."

"I'm so sorry," said the girl behind the counter, as if she had already said it a hundred times that day. "We did sell out of the morning bread, but I can weigh you a piece of the half-peck."

"Bother. If you must."

"Four pounds, or just one?"

"Just the one. I don't like the cut bread, it does get dry on the edges."

"I quite understand, ma'am," but that was all the consolation the customer would get.

The shop assistant swung a knife a yard long over a partially dismembered bread loaf. Puffy would have struggled to get his arms round that loaf. He felt a real twinge of fear, but the young lady knew exactly how to find a spot, cut the piece, and moved it to the scale quickly.

Reading the needle on the balance scale with her fingers, she said, "It's a bit under. Thruppence halfpenny, please."

The customer laid her little coins on the vast counter and took the bread.

"I say, how do you know she didn't cheat you?" Puffy exclaimed before he thought.

The room took a collective gasp, and silence fell.

"If you'll excuse me, sir." The frosty tones of the customer could have iced over the Thames. She moved her skirts so as not to brush the gentleman on her way out.

"Sir," said the young lady running the affair, "anyone can feel the difference in the coins. Also, our customers don't cheat us, as we don't cheat them."

"But how can you be sure?"

The girl put her hands on her hips. "If you're planning to cheat me, please leave. May I wait upon our next customer? Ma'am?"

He wondered, too, how she knew it was a *ma'am*, but that was just a wise guess. There were no other men in the shop.

"So, do any of your sisters look like you, miss?"

Another collective gasp, this time followed by murmurs that rose in volume.

There were those who would say a bakery on the street was a very different place from a drawing room full of fine ladies. Puffy didn't find it so, in a moment like this. The discomfiting feeling of putting a foot wrong, knowing he would pay for it socially, was oddly familiar.

"If you will excuse me, sir," said the young lady at the counter, not so differently from the affronted customer who had just left, though she stayed right where she was.

"Yes, yes," said Puffy, exiting the shop and never realizing that the rising hubbub of conversation after he left, which he could hear through the partially open door, was commenting not on the excesses of his striped trousers and ruffled neckcloth, or his extraordinary accusations of cheating, but on the fact that, after all that, he had bought no bread.

Puffy did have feelings, though, and he put his hand on the door, almost going back in. He heard the young woman behind the counter say, "We don't have buns in this shop, ma'am; we bake nothing here with sugar, as you know."

It was one blow after another. Puffy loved sweet buns.

It must have been her sister Puffy had seen standing in the doorway; he was sure of it. She had been the prettiest thing he'd ever seen, and that included several palace gardens, which Puffy considered the height of sophistication and beauty. But she wasn't in, she had a sister who hadn't cared a twig that a fine gentleman had visited their shop, and apparently they were against *sugar*. The sugar boycotts had died down twenty years ago; what did they have against sugar?

Feeling uneasily guilty about the amount of sugar he'd had in his chocolate just that morning, Puffy nonetheless walked away with the feeling that he'd be back.

Rose knew her trembling knees didn't show, but hoped no one could see the shivering in her hands, either.

"One and six, ma'am," and she served the last customer of the late morning and listened to the door scrape half-closed with relief. It wasn't uppermost in her mind this morning.

She pulled open the door to the bakery proper. "I *must* have a moment's rest! How am I to know what to say to everyone?"

"Sal, go and watch the shop for a moment, would you?" Anna was over by the tables farthest from the ovens. She didn't like the heat working closer to the ovens, but that just meant her work was much of the heavy initial mixing.

"Sure!"

Rose heard the girl skip across the bakery. "Just call out if anyone comes in. I cannot always say the right thing, I cannot."

They still had no chairs, but Rose made her way to the coolest corner, the one where she could huddle closest to the shop door without being behind it.

"Why, whatever did you say?" asked Anna.

Rose would not admit her racing thoughts to Anna. Rose was revisiting every conversation in her mind, every customer. If only she hadn't been so saucy with that gentleman! "I don't wish to tell you."

"I can get you a half-barrel to sit on!" called Jordan, Sal's brother.

To Rose's relief, Anna approved. "Jordan, that's a good idea."

As Emery chimed in with a "You'll feel better if you rest your feet, Rose," Jordan rolled one half-barrel toward Rose and helped her settle it into the corner.

"Thank you, Jordan," Rose said with as much dignity as she could while almost tearfully grateful for the seat. Her knees were tired, she noticed as she sank down. Tired from trembling? She muttered under her breath, "How do you all do it? I am wrung out, and it is only from talking to people." Then, louder, "I'll come shape loaves in a minute!"

"You didn't scrape yourself on the counter? Or with the knife?" It sounded like Jane was over by the oven, poking at the coals. Jane didn't mind the heat.

"No, of course not."

Anna gave a squeak of frustration. "I wonder what the word *tomorrow* means to that carpenter. I bet he never crosses our threshold again."

"We just have a batch going in... And there!" Emery made that sigh of half-satisfaction, half-effort, as the last pan scraped along the bottom of the oven.

Rose was beginning to see Emery's preference for staying

by the oven and baking all day. "Bread. Bread is glorious, you know. It doesn't speak at all. I asked one fellow to leave if he were planning to cheat me! I cannot possibly attend this meeting tonight with Mr. Russell."

The banging of water pitchers, bread peels, and fire irons stopped.

"Did he cheat you?" Anna sounded more astonished than sharp.

"No, I told him to leave if he planned to do it. What might I say to Mr. Russell? What might I say to other people there? Would it reflect poorly on Mr. Russell? I simply cannot go. I ought to have told him no."

"Nothing requires you to go," Anna put in quickly, just as Rose knew she would.

And that, just that, stiffened her spine. Anna was so eager that Rose not have any fun. It made Rose so much more determined to do it.

"I am going," she said, contradicting her statement of just the moment before. "But what do I wear? How shall I look? I should cut my hair." If her hair was right, she'd say the right things, she just knew it.

What would Anna say if she knew exactly how curtly Rose had spoken to the gentleman? Because Rose was sure he was a gentleman.

"Rose, *no!*" Anna's anguished response confused Rose for a second—she hadn't even been there!—until Rose recalled she had just suggested cutting her hair.

"You can certainly cut your hair if you wish, but why?" Jane had put down the fire irons and come to stand by Rose. "Not for some man, and one you've barely met."

"I agree." Emery opened the water pipe, and the water began sluicing in. "It takes so long to grow back. Cut it if you like, but not for tonight. What if it makes you *less* attractive?"

"Oh Anna!" As always when she felt truly pressed, Rose

called for Anna. Had she been thinking badly of Anna? Anna would save her from Emery; Emery was the one Rose didn't like. "Honestly, Emery! Anna would never say such a thing!"

Anna shushed their sister. "Emery, I hope you didn't imagine that would really help."

"What if I *did?*" Emery thumped a loaf, checking to see if it was done.

Anna made another shushing noise. "Emery does not mean that you're unattractive. Nor would cutting your hair affect it. It's lovely hair, that's all."

"It's the same as *your* hair, and yours is shorter."

When Anna didn't answer, Jane spoke up. "Anna had to wear the fashionable hairstyles expected at court, Rose, you know that. Aunt Eden would not have paid for her social season if she didn't look just as Aunt Eden wanted."

"At least Aunt Eden's taste is some sort of *guide*!"

"Rose, do you want to go this evening, or do you not? You have the rest of the day to decide."

"I don't, I must wait on the customers!" Rose was tired, that was all. It was so exhausting talking to the customers, and some of them wanted to chat. She had to decide all on her own when it was all right to listen to their gossip or complaints—husbands sounded like extremely unsatisfactory things—and when she had to politely usher them through the line and wait on more people. And all she wanted was a nap.

"Do you want to change places with me, darling?" Anna *was* sweet. She was also just annoying, as oldest sisters were.

"Perhaps Sal can watch the counter." Emery's tone said she wasn't sure of her own suggestion.

"Sal cannot do sums. She cannot take the money," Anna pointed out. "Which reminds me. If the children are to work here, we must make sure they are educated."

"What's educated?" asked Jordan, over by the dish tubs.

"School, dear," said Anna, without stopping. The loaf in her hands flipped over and hit the table with a *slap*.

"Oh no! That ain't necessary. We don't need it. I don't and Sal don't either."

Jordan's quick response just made Anna more adamant. "It's an ethical matter, Jordan. If you wish to learn the trade, we're glad to have you; we need the help. But you should be able to read, and do arithmetic, and learn something of the world."

"Why?"

Anna was silent at that one, and Rose wondered if it was because she didn't have an answer, or because she didn't wish to give it.

It was hard to imagine why Sal or Jordan would need to know all of those things, and Rose wondered if it was simply their mother's words coming out of Anna. Her mother had always said education was important, but she had never really made clear why, either.

"The shortest answer is that Sal must have the ability to take money and give change, and so should you, Jordan," Emery said in that firm way she had. How was she so good with the children? For a woman who insisted she'd never marry, she was so calm with them, and so easy. Rose never felt that easy with children, Sal and Jordan included, though she was getting easier day by day. But that was simple exposure, she thought. Like the ability to tell when bread was done.

Sal popped in right next to her elbow as if she'd heard Rose thinking her name. "There's a customer waiting, Miss Rose."

That was shockingly polite from Sal, who usually had no time for nicety. "Of course, Sal, thank you," said Rose and, after a bare moment's hesitation, pushed herself to her feet. She was the youngest sister. It should be *easiest* for her to work like this!

"Come back in an hour, muffin, and I'll watch the counter while you nap a little." Oh, Anna was her very favorite sister.

"I will, and remind me to tell you of the gentleman who stopped in this morning! He didn't even buy bread!"

AT THE END OF A LONG, LONG DAY, ROSE FINALLY recounted the story, over supper. "He must have meant you, Anna."

"Oh, I hope not!"

"Why ever not? Oh, you did say you weren't still searching for a husband."

There was a sly chuckle in Jane's voice. "That's not why, muffin."

"What? Then why?"

Jane spoke before Anna could answer. "She can't ask you what the gentleman looked like, and without that she can't tell if she was flattered or not."

"Jane, don't talk that way! I don't know any gentlemen who would call on me here." Anna did not add *or ever again*, but the words were there.

Rose found Anna's concern about the gentleman's looks a nebulous, mysterious problem compared to the reality of things like bread and money. At the same time, Rose herself had a worry that she wouldn't look nice enough for Mr. Russell this evening. It was very complicated. She wondered if it was as complicated for her sighted sisters. "I think you can ask any of the regular customers, they could tell you."

Anna was uncharacteristically dry at that suggestion. "I think I will not ask our customers what they thought of the looks of the gentleman who failed to buy bread earlier today."

Rose would have preferred to eat all her spot of butter in one bite, and have the rich salty flavor of the butter on her tongue all at once, to *luxuriate* in it, and eat the rest of her bread dry; but someone had spread her share of butter thin, so she took what she had. "I do need a new hair-ribbon." She *needed* it, like she needed food to live.

"There isn't even time to get one," Emery reminded her. The shops were closed, and Mr. Russell would be there in two hours. "You know you can borrow mine."

"Have they been dunked in yeast?"

"Not lately."

To Rose, that ribbon was the last idea of a possible married life. She had never expected to simply walk out of doors and meet a man who liked her well enough to call on her. She wanted to look her best, and to her, that meant ribbons.

Well, and perhaps not falling asleep while the gentleman addressed the crowd.

"Thank you, Emery."

All four of them still sat on the floor. After a day of work like theirs, it was increasingly necessary to lean against the walls. They passed their few plates back and forth over the wider space between them.

After hair ribbons, Rose would like a table.

She stirred. "I must rest. I want to look fresh when Mr. Russell arrives."

"It's going to be a tiresome litany of Mr. Russell's name from now on, isn't it?" Jane didn't sound interested.

"Don't you want to look fresh, too?" Rose half-wanted her sister to feel as excited about this evening as Rose did. It was Rose's coming-out party, in a way.

But she would be perfectly happy if Jane didn't look too pretty. It was nice having the gentleman's attention to herself.

"No." That was Jane's only word on the subject. "All of you, we must have a talk about the money."

Rose and Emery both groaned, although in ladylike tones. Anna likely wished to join them.

"I wouldn't bother you if this weren't important, you know that."

"I should sleep for a bit before Mr. Russell comes."

"Rose, this is about the survival of the bakery."

In a hard-edged tone that was more like Jane than herself, Rose said, "If the bakery won't survive, Mr. Russell's calling will become of the utmost importance, won't it?"

The resulting silence was tense.

ANNA FELT IT WAS HER RESPONSIBILITY TO SMOOTH OVER the wrinkles in the room. "Of course you should sleep, Rose, and Emery will fall asleep on the floor in a few moments. Jane, everyone is tired, including you; I'm sure you'll make this as quick as you can."

In front of all of them, and without further conversation, Jane counted out the contents of the till. Emery, eyes sleepy from supper after a long day's bread-making, sat with her legs straight out in front of her, stockinged ankles sticking out from the bottom of her skirt, leaned against the wall. Her hands folded over her stomach.

When they claimed their baker's share of their own bread, they took the darker brown maselin, because it was cheaper. In general, though, the poorer the customer, the less they wanted the darker bread; customers looked down on it. But the Bickerings' maselin was rich, chewy, and delicious. Running a bakery, one *did* get good bread for supper. No doubt Emery felt sated and sleepy on her own bread; Anna did.

The little stacks of coins clinked into place and stood there after Jane's last touch, their worn and slightly dingy portraits of the King facing up or down; they were worth the same either way.

"I've never seen so much money in one place," Emery admitted.

"It isn't enough." Everyone made noises of surprise; Jane just nodded. "Nowhere near enough. We need more than this just to live." Jane was not ready to celebrate. "And then also, we need to pay Widow Hampton for the raising and the first batch of flour."

"Oh no, she said that was a gift in honor of Mother!" Anna did not like treating a gift that way.

Jane just shook her head. "It let us buy our first few batches, to make enough money to buy more flour. We must give her *some*thing. We cannot start a business by taking advantage of friendships."

"And I think her raising has a particularly good flavor to it." Emery was sliding a little down the wall, but wanted to point it out. They could buy yeast, but Emery had made the first few batches with the raising she'd carried in a pint pot with her own two hands. That raising was in every batch they made now; it was in the very air of the bakery, according to their mother's explanations of baking bread, and they all felt they could taste it.

Jane nodded. "I think our bread is particularly good." On *that*, Jane had no contradiction to offer. "Good quality is not why people buy our bread, however. The square is simply full of people, and many of them want the convenience of buying bread or have no ovens and no choice. We could sell much worse bread and do as well. But we won't!" she added quickly, as the others made disagreeable noises.

"I agree we should pay Widow Hampton back," Emery put in from a few inches lower towards the floor.

"Well." Anna was still doubtful. "We'll see if she will accept it."

Jane didn't let it go. "If she won't take it, we must use it for more half-barrels."

"What for?" Emery, almost asleep, was determined to keep her hand in. Making the bread was *her* problem.

"We sold out of everything we had today."

"Yes, wasn't it lovely?" Anna almost sighed with pleasure.

"No, it was not," Rose put in quite tartly. Well, she'd waited on nearly every customer all day, and it wasn't her favorite task.

"It wasn't lovely," Jane agreed. "We could have sold more if we had more. But we had no more tubs in which to let the dough rise. Plus the wood for baking." She was setting aside little pile of coins after little pile of coins and making Anna's store of warm happiness smaller and smaller.

"Why must you make things unhappy, Jane?" Anna didn't like to pout. She was the oldest. She shouldn't pout. But she could feel herself pouting. She'd been so *happy*, with such a large pile of money, and here was Jane making it bad!

"Because I don't wish to have to sell our mother's candlesticks. I am making our situation clear, big sister, which you might not like but which someone must do." And Jane's dark eyes, serious in her pale face, looked so much like their father that Anna felt terrible.

"You are, and thank you, little sister. You are quite right, of course."

As she always was, went unsaid; no one would gainsay Jane about money. Not of the four of them.

But Emery wasn't going down without a fight. "But if Widow Hampton won't accept money for her present, we spend it all on barrels?"

"That, and far more flour. There, you know, the prices are set, and there is nothing we can do about it."

The prices *were* set. Britain, cut off for so long from the Continent, had fenced in ever more of her land to grow her grain, and the Corn Laws set the price farmers would earn, to encourage them to grow it. Otherwise, the country could fall short of bread in wartime.

It made bread expensive. Besides freshness, it was the other reason bread was sold by the pound. Seldom could people afford to buy much bread at once.

"I told you, we have picked the worst possible time to start a bakery." Jane would not be swayed when she was in this mood, and she was in this mood. Anna knew the only way to get to the end of it was to let her have her way all the way down it and reach the end. "The corn prices spiked so high last year that everyone cut back. Even the King ate brown bread to encourage people to buy it instead of the finer flour."

"And all he got for his trouble was that people called him Brown George." That lightened Rose's mood a little.

Jane *hmm*'d her agreement. "People are glad prices have come down from last year, but they're still far higher than two years ago. Again, no one in our neighborhood is complaining because without us, they wouldn't *have* bread. They'd have to walk all the way to Sennet's, and they don't wish to do that."

"Then if people want a bakery here, and we have one, we will be fine. If we must make more bread, we must find a way. Emery has almost fallen asleep on the floor." Rose said it just as Emery's head reached her shoulder.

"I have not!" said Emery. Rose was shorter than she; Emery's head drooped forward a little.

"And I helped customers as fast as I could, but some were waiting far too long. Perhaps ten minutes, perhaps more. Someone must help more in the shop's front."

"Rose, we know. You don't wish to talk to the customers," Anna reminded her quietly.

"When I think of how I used to *long* for conversation.

One must be careful what one wishes for. We *will* need more help, though. You do see what I mean, don't you?"

"No one is arguing." Emery shoved herself upward before her head slid off Rose's shoulder altogether. She still leaned her head back against the wall. It made an audible *thump*.

An answering *thump* happened only half an instant later, against the far back wall.

"What was that?" Anna turned where she sat, as though there must be something to see when it was clear in their bare little apartment that there was nothing.

"Very fat mice here," murmured Emery, with her eyes closed. "It heard my head."

"Why would fat mice do anything because they heard your head?" Anna squinted at Emery. Perhaps her sister was over-tired.

Jane wanted the conversation back on track. "If mice love flour, they're bound to love Emery's head. Just a moment, everyone. Rose can go nap in a moment. My point is, if we keep on with what we are doing, we will have no money left at all by December."

That made everyone sit upright.

"Surely not." Emery pointed a finger at the coins. There they were. "Those are real. Solid. Tradable. Even the merchant's conder token." Emery lifted the single wide coin, a private minting from almost twenty years ago, and brought it closer; she could just make out a carving of a gazebo on one side. "It's quite pretty."

"We can only spend it at an inn. I'm not trying to be right, though I am. I haven't a good answer. But we must do something different." Jane took a deep breath. "We must raise the prices."

"Oh no," said Emery, just as Anna said, "Absolutely *not*," and even Rose put in, "Oh Jane. No."

"The thing about arithmetic," Jane said as if explaining to

very small children, "is that it doesn't care if you like the answer."

"That would risk everything. How would we pay a fine if anyone complained? It would take everything we have." Anna wrapped her arms around her waist.

"Emery said Mr. Gruninger from the baker's guild said that no one ever went to jail over such things anymore."

"But there's a chance. Especially if someone doesn't like us. It's not worth it, Jane." Emery looked awake and sober.

JANE SAT BACK. SHE COULD WAIT TILL EMERY SAW REASON, and if Emery joined her side, Rose would too; then they would just have to get Anna over her wibbling. "You do know the harvest last year was awful, and that we have been at war almost twenty years, and bread prices are brushing the top of the sky now."

"And we must work within those rules. We knew that when we planned the bakery," Anna reminded them all.

Jane did not bother to remind them again that she had not been cheerful about the prospect of running a bakery. "My point is only that the prices are already high, and the amount of that price we can reserve for ourselves is set by law. So we must pay the high prices to eat, but have our wages set as they would be a decade ago."

"We've only just begun, Jane, and we have made large outlays to begin." Anna had recovered her breath and had some calm now. "Let us return to this problem in a few days, and see what other solutions present themselves."

"We are going to *have* to—"

"Jane," her sister interrupted her, though in a quiet voice, "I am leading this family from society into trade. We may yet go from trade to the street. I won't disappoint our parents further by leading us to gaol."

At that, Rose stood. "Prison sounds terribly uncomfortable. I really do wish to be fresh for this evening. It is my first social occasion of any sort, you know. I want it to go well."

"You needn't impress Mr. Russell if you don't wish, muffin." Jane seldom used the childhood nickname.

"But I *want* to. Don't you see? You've had balls and musicales, and so has Anna. Emery might not care for such things, but I *do*. I might have, anyway. This is what I will have instead. I *do* want it to be nice."

Abashed, Jane looked to Anna, who just said, "Of course you do, darling. Shall Jane walk in with you? And we will be quiet."

She looked over to where Emery had fallen asleep, leaning against the wall. "Very quiet."

JANE HELPED ROSE OUT OF HER GOWN. THE EVENING WAS cool, but the windows were closed, and the oven below and the day's baking made the air in the room as warm and welcoming as a quilt.

"What if I say the wrong thing to Mr. Russell?" Rose kept her voice so quiet that no one but Jane could hear her. "What if..."

"What if you fail to get married? Is that what you mean? Take my word for it, muffin, one survives." And Jane pressed a fingertip against the end of Rose's nose, just the way she had when Rose was tiny. "Perhaps Mr. Russell is worrying what to say to *you* to make you like him. Have you thought of that?"

"No! You don't mean it, not really?"

"Really. Sleep a little, and I'll wake you."

"Jane..." Rose reached for her sister's hand before Jane stood. Jane settled back on the bed next to her. "Is it all right, do you think, that I am tired all the time?"

Jane laid her hand against Rose's forehead. "I think so. You are working hard, and people forget how much sleep young people need. Get a little rest."

So Rose did, drifting away, wondering why Jane never mentioned the loss of their mother.

"He's here! Why didn't you wake me earlier?"

Emery was glad no men were calling for her. Her darling baby sister was leaping about like a crazed kitten.

Anna made her *shh-shh* noise. "Your voice will travel. There is no hallway! I must answer the door."

"Jane! Come help dress my hair! Do we have any scissors?"

"No!" All three sisters in unison.

"I won't cut all of it! I thought perhaps just a little curl, around the face?"

After a moment's silence, Jane answered. "All right. Go into your bedroom. I'll bring a knife. I can trim a few curls. Anna, she'll be ready in just five minutes."

Emery just watched Anna smooth her skirt. "Aren't you answering the door?"

"He must wait for a moment."

Emery just stared into her sister's eyes. "You don't know how to do this any more than any of us."

"I can't explain it. Why don't you go with Rose and Mr. Russell tonight?"

"Why don't *you* go with them?" When Anna didn't answer, Emery let it drop. She did not want to believe of her own sister that Anna was still nursing a hope that she would marry into society and didn't want to be seen at a common gathering. "Anyway, I intend to sleep early."

Anna didn't challenge this, when Emery had just spent the last hour sleeping, right on the floor where they left her.

When she opened the door, there was Mr. Russell, fumbling about with his hat. He looked up so fast that Emery caught the look of startled hope that had leaped to his eyes when the door opened, and the way it faded when he caught sight of Anna rather than Rose.

Points for him, thought Emery. Clearly, it was only Rose he wished to see.

"My sisters will be happy to accompany you, Mr. Russell, do come in; they'll be ready to leave in just a moment."

When the party had gone, it wasn't hard for Emery to yawn again. "I must sleep."

"I could not agree more," Anna yawned too, since Emery had started it; she covered it with her hand. "You won't mind if I retire too?"

No, Emery wouldn't mind; it was exactly what she wanted. Anna would go to the room she shared with Jane, and Emery could sneak out unseen. "You don't need a candle?"

"I barely need a bed!"

If Emery laid down again, would she fall asleep again? Her muscles were still tired, tired right down to her bones. But her mind was spinning, and she found that even with her head on her pillow, she had no desire to close her eyes.

Miss Hayes clearly visited that house down the lane regularly. What if Emery just... went to the door?

Once down the stairs and in the open air, among Mr. Russell, Jane, and Rose, there was a little game of steps.

Mr. Russell tried to give Rose his arm. While he stood, confused as to how to address her, since she didn't see it offered, Jane took Rose's arm instead. And set off down the pavement with Rose on the inside, in the lady's position.

Mr. Russell had no choice but to follow.

He said nothing of the maneuvering, only said as he reached the sisters, "Do you follow the newspapers, Miss Rose?"

"No."

He glanced at Jane, but she had no intention of helping him. He could carry this interaction on his own merits, or sink. Jane had no opinions either way, and that was practically written on her face. She walked, and looked, straight ahead. Her feet were fast and her profile unforgiving.

Mr. Russell glanced again at Rose, where a flush was coming over her cheeks, either from the exercise of walking or, he could hope, because he was near. "Perhaps you, or your family, subscribe to one of the books being written against the enslavement of African peoples?"

The flush grew deeper. "No," said Rose.

"Mr. Russell," said Jane, "you might wish to discuss something that does not require money."

"Ah yes! Quite! Unfeeling of me. I do apologize." The young man's stammers ran in staccato opposition to the sound of his feet. "I, ah... Have you attended any meetings of the Society of Friends in this neighborhood, Miss Rose? As they have been the staunchest supporters of the organization for whom I work."

"I haven't, no. Not yet." Rose's voice trailed away.

"Well, you will meet some tonight."

And with that, Mr. Russell appeared to have fired all his conversational cannons.

Jane simply stayed between him and Rose and continued on.

The hall was full of murmuring voices, the smell of lit tobacco, sweat and wool from warm bodies and dust from the roadways.

Mr. Russell abandoned them as soon as they arrived. "I must prepare to speak; I am a few minutes late. Please forgive me," he said before he dashed away.

Rose's head was hunched between her shoulders. "And we have made him late! This is awful."

"We've done nothing wrong, Rose, try to keep your head."

Just as Jane said it, she tripped over someone's boot. Either maliciously or carelessly placed in her path as she led Rose around the edge of the room, looking for a quiet place to stand, Jane staggered forward, both arms flailing high.

Everyone around them turned to look.

Through force of will and the practice of muscles now well-worked by bread kneading, Jane caught herself. Her pose, a frozen instant of wildly waving arms and weirdly twisted torso, would have been peculiar in the extreme had it lasted more than a moment.

Rose just saved herself from pitching forward by letting Jane's arm go at the right moment. Her cheeks had flushed full-blown red by the time Jane regained her balance.

Jane did not even glare around her, only took Rose's hand and walked on. "Still have done nothing wrong." She was trying to sound careless about the thing.

Rose hissed at her. "Can you *not* be one of those women who must have all eyes on her at all times?"

Jane, who in brighter light might have been seen to be flushed herself, as if mortification had made the blood rise,

"Don't *you* be one of those women, Rose. Don't attribute maliciousness where it is simple clumsiness. Or, in this case, a vicious boot."

Rose only squeezed Jane's arm in apology.

This evening was not at all as she had imagined it. She had imagined some quiet conversation where she could say something witty, something fun, to Mr. Russell and keep his attention on her. She had many questions she wished to find out, Anna-type questions about his family as well as questions about his thoughts, but hadn't been able to bring herself to ask any of them with Jane nearby.

She'd likely never get a chance to ask them now. This hall was full of shuffling bodies and feet, not at all the place to get to know Mr. Russell, and given how dull she had been so far this evening, the gentleman would likely never call again.

In only a few moments, she heard Mr. Russell start to speak. The room was large and full, but he had a voice that carried well, despite the way people *would* shuffle about. She liked his voice. It made her think of apples. Something about the way he spoke was round and sweet, and she thought perhaps Mr. Russell could eat a whole apple with one bite, like some mythical creature of old.

Or a horse.

The shuffling slowed and murmuring stopped as Mr. Russell continued to speak. He said he was only there to introduce a fellow speaker, someone whose name escaped Rose the moment she heard it.

And he spoke just as plainly and directly to the audience as he had to Rose when he'd made space for her on the pavement. The emotion in his voice as he described the horrors of slavery was real, but he did not let it collapse him; instead, he encouraged everyone in the room to stand up and do what they could to convince their government to abolish every aspect of the slave trade.

"For if we stand together, we will be heard. It is unavoidable. Many of us in this room do not agree on what must be done to repair the harm done to those who have been ripped from their homes, enslaved against their will, and taken here, to our United Kingdom, or her colonies. Yet we do all agree that this enslavement is an affront to all the laws of God and man, and must be stopped. Therefore, we must have one voice in our complaint to our King and our Parliament."

Listening to Mr. Russell's round, sweet voice, a manly declaration of justice in a world that Rose felt was very unjust, pushed aside something that had been weighing her down. She still wished she could talk to her mother more than anything. But she knew without a doubt that her mother had agreed with every word of this, and it made her feel closer to her memory to agree, too.

"How shall we do this, Mr. Russell?"

Rose said it before she even realized the words were out of her mouth.

Not only said it, but said it loudly. Of course it must be loud, to reach him all the way at the front of the room. But also quite loudly enough to reach the ears of every person standing between the two of them.

All of whom grew silent, except for the noise of them looking around to see what person—what *woman*—was so bold that she interrupted the speaker.

Rose felt her flush returning, but she held her head high.

"I am so glad you asked, Miss Bickering," said Mr. Russell, "as we need the suggestions of women as much as men. Have you an idea to share?"

Perhaps he thought she would say *no*, as she had to all his questions on the walk here. But Rose felt much more awake now, and much less nervous, oddly, now that there were many people listening, and not just one possibly attentive Mr. Russell.

"I would suggest that there is no time to waste, as my mother listened to this same discussion decades ago, and would tell us, if she were here, that we must not let more decades pass without action. We have had some small success with the abolition of the trade; we must petition for the abolition of the institution."

"I could not agree more," came his voice, and Rose felt like he was standing right next to her, with his arms spread to make sure no one harmed her, even though he was all the way across the hall. "So let me introduce Mr. Thomas Clarkson, who is so well known to so many of you, and whose rare appearance here should inspire us all to make every effort, just as Miss Bickering suggests."

The resumption of normal rustling and murmuring, and then the new speaker at the front of the room, who must be very grand but whose name Rose did not know, caused her to settle back on her heels. What had she done?

But no, she squashed the thought. She'd done just as she pleased. And Mr. Russell seemed to like it.

"I'm glad Anna is not here," Jane murmured at her elbow. "When you decide to do something, you do it properly." But Jane sounded as if she were proud.

Afterwards, Mr. Russell brought the speaker over to meet Rose, and the rest of her misgivings blew away. He could have belittled her or scolded her for speaking.

Instead, "Mr. Clarkson, may I present Miss Jane Bickering and her sister Miss Rose Bickering. Miss Rose is, as you can tell, a supporter of our cause."

"We all are, in fact, only I took the moment to speak. Which I should not have done. My apologies, Mr. Russell."

"Not at all, not at all." It wasn't Mr. Russell, but the other man who answered. "These people care, but they need to be stirred, and after twenty-odd years, they are tired of my voice. And it is a pleasure to hear from a young lady on a night of old men. Not that Mr. Russell is old, far from it."

"Thank you, Mr. Clarkson." Rose meant every word. Hopefully Anna *wouldn't* hear about this, but this room was full of their neighbors, and Rose couldn't guarantee that no one would complain to her. Perhaps they might not even come to the bakery any more, and as Jane had just laid out for them, they couldn't afford to lose a customer.

But if this gentleman—all right, if *Mr. Russell*—approved of her speech, she was glad she'd spoken up.

"Do you mind if I ask you—both of you," he politely included Jane as well, "what motivates ladies of your station to attend a meeting like this?"

"We live here, sir, our bakery is on the square." Jane made it sound... not respectable, but obvious. Easy. Businesslike.

Rose would endeavor to speak like that. "The question in my mind is why every person here does not feel the same sense of urgency Mr. Russell mentioned. Because enslavement based on such a thin division of humanity—and I can assure you how meaningless it is—is the mark of a society that will not stop at dividing people only based on the color of their skin. If we are a nation that allows it, we will not stop at treating anyone inhumanely. And who among us is safe then? If justice does not appeal to them, surely they ought to be moved by their own self-interest."

Everyone around them again was silent, and Mr. Clarkson, when he spoke again, had a voice that apparently had filled with energy again from Rose's words. "Exactly so! And it is the pre-eminent problem of our day. When the newspapers speak of slavery, they speak of Napoleon, and how we must not let the French take us over. And yet we have thousands of lives taken over by the needs of Great Britain, and how are their lives different from ours? If some men should be free, should not all be free?"

"I agree," and Rose felt quite calm now, "and of course women."

At that, the man laughed, which irritated Rose, who had been quite serious. She tried to keep hold of the compliment and let go the insult, but found it to require effort.

He went on, "Miss Bickering, a pleasure, I assure you! Mr. Russell, you promised me a pleasant evening if I would speak, and this has been so. Excuse me, ladies, I must meet some gentlemen in the front of the room."

Once he was gone, Rose waited to see if she would feel just as awkward if Mr. Russell spoke to her. Jane, she knew, was still a hands' breadth away.

But Rose didn't feel awkward now.

And she didn't feel so tired. She felt closer to her mother than she had felt in weeks. And more alive, and more awake.

Mr. Russell said, "Your sisters told me you wouldn't care for any other entertainment more than this, and I thought they must be exaggerating. But I can see that it's true. I'm so glad you decided to attend, Miss Rose."

"And I, Mr. Russell," said Rose, letting her smile show.

THE WALK BACK TO THE BAKERY WAS ENTIRELY DIFFERENT from their walk earlier. Jane had no further opportunity to ask Mr. Russell about his family, his fortune, or his intentions. Rose and Mr. Russell traded favorite phrases from the evening like jewels. Jane might not even have been between them, for all the notice they took of her.

"Mr. Russell, here we are." Jane had to draw their attention to the fact that they'd arrived.

"I thought it was a longer walk." The gentleman seemed confused.

"It was, the first time."

All three of them stood there in silence for a moment. Then a moment longer. And another.

"Thank you for the invitation, Mr. Russell. It was a reviving evening."

"Thank you for attending, Miss Rose. I hope to see you again."

Another awkward moment of silence, and then he tipped his hat and was gone.

"He tipped his hat, didn't he?" Rose wanted to know.

"Yes, he did." Jane's voice was a little gentler than usual.

"I like him, Jane."

JANE FELT WEIGHED DOWN BY WORRIES ABOUT MONEY. HER sisters hadn't grasped the danger, not at all.

She could be just as anxious over a stranger calling for Rose, one whom she didn't know at all.

But Rose deserved this. Jane squashed those doubts deep inside and spent her breath on happiness for Rose, who had never expected to be part of a social season through no fault of her own.

"You were the diamond of the evening, and I'm glad Mr. Russell is wise enough to appreciate that," Jane told Rose before giving her a hug.

She was the older sister, and a good deal less trusting; she'd have to keep an eye on that Mr. Russell.

Episode 6: The problems of cake and sugar

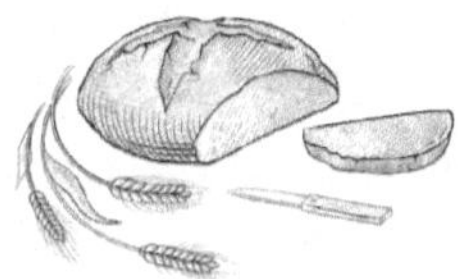

Captain Brice pushed open the door of the ladies' bakery with conviction. Speed. Determination.

Surely they had reached a truce and this visit wouldn't be a disaster.

There were four customers in there, of varying ages, mostly women, one old man; there was only one sister to wait on all four.

The cranky one.

She turned at the sound of the bell, putting on the welcoming face of a person in a shop, then saw it was him.

"Oh, no!" she said at the top of her voice.

All the customers turned and looked at him as if he might be a Viking come to pillage.

What had the landlord called her—Miss Bickering? Assuming it was her name and not just an insult, she must be the oldest of the four.

Didn't look it.

"Miss Bickering." The Captain tipped his hat. "Never you mind, I've just come to see how my orphans are getting on."

"They aren't orphans!"

"I'll just have my bread," said the woman whose cut portion of bread Miss Bickering was presumably holding.

"Oh yes, Mrs. Simpson, here you are. Let me get you the rest of your money."

"And I must dash, Miss Anna, I'm so sorry!" A young woman with a baby on her hip. Probably about to explode or something. The baby, not the woman.

Captain Brice didn't have any direct experience of children, but he regarded them as roughly the same sort of danger as open powder kegs, or cutlasses.

"Sorry, should I have said Miss Anna?"

The lady in question shot him a look over the heads of her customers. "*You* should not."

Brice squared his shoulders. If he could command men in battle, he could handle a bakery.

"Miss Bickering. Your animosity is unreasonable. I haven't done a thing to frighten you today."

That said, he charged toward the door to the back of the shop.

EMERY DROPPED THE ENORMOUS BALL OF DOUGH. "NOT you."

"What?" Rose, kneading at the next table, straightened.

"That American captain fellow, the one who can't buy bread. Do we need to hire a soldier to keep people out of here?"

The marauder stood inside the bakery, taking it all in. Wide tables, Emery, Rose, and half-barrels full of dough beside them and everywhere. The hot oven's door showed glowing coals deep inside, and the place was steaming. The American captain fellow tugged at his collar.

Jordan stopped scrubbing out a half-barrel, and whirled at

his washbasin post. Sal stopped folding white ironed linens into a basket near a window.

Both children advanced on him, the boy with folded arms, the girl with a rolling pin almost as big as she was.

"Oh good, it's handled then," Emery shrugged and leaned back into her dough.

THE ONE WHO'D GONE AND DEALT WITH THE CHILDREN WAS paying Captain Brice no mind at all. She was one of the tall ones, with wheat-colored hair, but it didn't curl around her face in the heat the way it did around her smaller, angrier, older sister.

If he'd had to choose the oldest, he would have chosen her, not Miss Anna. But it was only because she had a slightly sallow sunkenness to her cheeks that spoke of a little too much hard work. And perhaps not enough joy.

She was far easier to deal with, to his way of thinking, than any of her dramatic sisters.

He addressed her directly. "How are your charges?"

She pointed a floury finger at the children holding him at bay. "Sir and madam?"

"We're good!" said the girl. Her brother added, "*Real* good!"

The shortest sister, the blind one, just kept her head down. She wasn't interested in him either.

But he really needed to speak with them.

"Invite me to supper," he entreated the tall one.

The lady's eyebrows climbed up her forehead. "*Anna!*" she shouted at the door.

The original Miss Bickering put in her head from the front of the store. "Really, you *must* leave!"

"Miss Anna, I have to run away, truly!" A young mother

with two children clinging to her skirts tugged at Miss Bickering's apron strings.

"Oh yes, Mrs. Wallace, I—" Miss Bickering did a little pantomime, stretching towards the shop as if she intended to go there, then back into the bakery proper as if someone were pulling on her arm, then back towards the shop, then back to the bakery. "Captain. I must ask you to leave."

"You should *bring* supper!" The little boy, covered in flour and water, no doubt currently forming a cement that would rival what the Romans had used to build thousand-year-old roads, held his position like a soldier, but clearly wanted to talk more about food.

But the Captain wasn't so foolish as to try to invite the young ladies to dine with him.

Captain Brice tried to make his look at the tallest sister imploring. "Truly, I would not impose if it were not important."

She was neither moved nor interested. "We don't know you, it *is* imposing, and I doubt we would judge it important."

"Miss Bickering!" a customer wailed, her clinging child wailing in turn.

The oldest Miss Bickering pointed a very rude finger straight at Captain Brice's face, rather as if it were loaded— the finger, not his face—and dashed out.

He wasn't done. Perhaps the littlest one would yield if the tallest would not. "Miss, if you could take a little pity, this is truly important to your family."

That one too went back to kneading bread. "If you are addressing me, sir, I'll let my family judge what is important."

The door opened again and the one with the darkest hair, the one with the flames in her eyes, stalked in.

"*What* is going on in here? Anna is acting as though the French have landed."

He swung towards her. "Ask me to supper."

She drew back, moving her shopping basket protectively in front of her. "*Sir.* You *cannot* be asking me for a supper invitation. I walloped you with a sausage."

"Not your oddest social engagement, Jane," said the short one, and the tallest one shushed her with a "*Rose.*"

This wasn't going to work. He needed to change course.

"You're quite right." He nodded in a way he hoped would reassure the one who'd walloped him. "I should like for all of you to take supper with me."

He needed to see them, and he couldn't interrupt their work. He wouldn't mention yet that he lived in one of the hotels down the street and that supper would have to be there, at Jacquier's. He had no cook. He didn't even have enough chairs for them to sit, if they brought the children, and he'd bet they'd bring the children.

He hoped they would—he'd like to see those urchins eat, and they didn't seem as dangerous as actual small babies—but there was serious business to discuss.

"Please, Miss Bickering." He was standing the closest to the dark-haired one. It wasn't clear sailing. She had a basket.

"What *is* your concern this time, Captain Brice? Can you not simply say what worries you without issuing orders? This is not your ship."

That reefed his sails. She was right. This wasn't the *Halia*, and he was barking orders. And it hadn't gone well the last time, so why was he doing it again?

"You are right. Very right. So, Miss Bickering. I extend a more appropriate invitation. I do wish all of you—all of you —" he rounded to take in both the boy and the girl with a swing of his arm, "—to visit me this evening. I shall call for you. I look forward to it."

"But please," he stepped toward the dark-haired Miss Bickering again, "we must have some time to speak. There *are* things I cannot simply announce in the center of your shop. Or your bakery either."

Jane cocked her head. The man seemed to interact entirely in spasms, leaping in and demanding things.

But he had a good heart when it came to Sal and Jordan, and he likely wasn't agitated about nothing. She had no experience of sea captains, but they couldn't run a ship if they fainted every time they ran out of sugar.

Could they?

"I'll let my sister know and we will respond accordingly," Jane found herself telling him.

He nodded, quickly, and whirled around one more time, taking in the warding children, all the sacks of flour, the tables covered with rising loaves under clean cloths, the three Bickering sisters.

And without another word, swept out.

Anna still hadn't recovered by the time she changed places with Rose.

It would be a relief to slap bread around today.

"We aren't going to supper with him. That's all there is to that."

"That stew is on its third day." Emery's hands stretched the dough into a rounded loaf with motions that were strong and subtle at the same time. "I don't think you really want to refuse."

"Alone with him? In his house? Perish that. You know what people will think."

"Anna, the people who live on this square don't even see

us. Their servants see us because we are exactly the same as they are. Working for our daily bread."

Anna made a *puh* noise and tossed Emery a sour look. "No one judges others like servants."

Emery was still trying to think of a rejoinder when Rose opened the shop door. "Mrs. Parker just stepped in. She bought two pounds of bread and gave the direction of Captain Brice's residence."

"He doesn't live on the square proper, does he?" Anna was sure he didn't.

Emery didn't let it rest. "Would you change your opinion of him if he did? I'm sure he lives somewhere along Lisle or Castle Street."

Rose looked solemn. "Captain Brice resides at Jacquier's Hotel."

Anna just closed her eyes. "Oh, no."

Even Emery looked doubtful. "We cannot visit a hotel. Can we?"

Rose folded her arms about her waist. "I was so eager to eat something that wasn't our bread. But. What would Mother say?"

"It settles the matter. We cannot." Anna slapped her massive armful of dough on the table.

Jane came in from the back door. "Cannot what?"

"We are not visiting Captain Brice in a hotel."

Jane turned in the middle of removing her gloves. "He resides in a hotel?"

"Jacquier's. Just down the street."

"Ah." She removed her other glove. "We must go, then."

"Jane, I cannot—"

"Then stay home, Anna. Don't you see? This is our chance to see what type of bread they serve. It is one of the most famous French restaurants in London. They're not in competition with us, a meal there costs three or four pounds."

"*POUNDS??*" Anna braced herself on the table with both hands, dough forgotten. The word *pounds* seemed likely to blow her over.

"He didn't mean for us all to come, did he?" When Emery looked uncertain, things were uncertain.

Rose shrugged. "He said to come and to bring the children."

Jane nodded. "Then I certainly will, at least. Ladies, what if we were to supply bread to Jacquier's hotel?"

ANNA WAS STILL THINKING ABOUT THAT QUESTION LATER IN the shop as she watched the sun fall slowly down in the sky, and her legs were heavy with weariness.

This would ruin them. It was bad enough that Rose and Jane had gone to that political meeting. They'd all be lucky not to be arrested and thrown in London Tower. Or transported!

She hoped they wouldn't be transported. Anna couldn't survive for weeks on end at sea, she was sure of that. Perhaps they'd have time to ask Captain Brice for some tips before they were taken away.

The fine woolen coat and immaculate hat that she was always alert for passed the window.

No one could dart like Anna and just appear to be opening the door.

Well, it would be easier if it didn't stick.

Rather than an easy "Good afternoon, Lord Zachary," it was *yank, yank,* pushing her hair back into place, and then saying it.

He nodded without looking at her. "Good afternoon."

He had his hand on the door to go upstairs, just beside

the shop door. He wasn't going to speak to her. He wasn't even going to *see* her.

"Lord Zachary," Anna burst out, "I wonder if you... give business advice."

His eyes were unfocused when he looked up. He had been far away. He focused on her with some irritation. "Pardon me, miss?"

"Business advice." It was incredibly forward, but she needed help. Someone should help her! She oughtn't to have to do all this eldest-sister business by herself. "We... are concerned about our business investment in the long term."

Lord Zachary seemed to awaken. His eyes were a curious swirl of green and brown, Anna realized, neither one nor the other.

He looked at the door of the shop in which Anna stood, then around the pavement, as if he might read it.

"Are things not well? I have no great business sense, miss, even if I knew something about baking."

It was the way he said *baking*, as if it were the least notable activity in the world, that tightened Anna's stomach like a cold belt.

He'd never noticed her, unless it was to be introduced while she held a slop jar. He'd never really even seen her. He'd never seen her *bakery*, for all he lived above it.

"You know, our oven likely keeps your garret warm."

"Does it?" He looked startled again. He could blink a great deal.

"If our doors close this winter, it will be cold for you, I imagine. You'll be forced to go elsewhere. Wherever your family home is, I suppose. Wherever you don't wish to be, as it's absurd for a man of your wealth to live in a garret. It will be cold, possibly as cold as it was last year. Our mother caught croup and died, it was so cold. But I imagine that business sense, even as it affects you, isn't something you have."

The door didn't slam, but Anna shut it all the same.

THE HUBBUB REGARDING WHAT TO WEAR WAS SIMPLY indescribable.

"What will I do with my hair? I can't wear it down!" Rose wailed.

"Don't expect me to primp, other than to put on my nicer dress," warned Emery. "I'll do your hair, Rose."

"Are we even *going*, Anna?" Jane was watching her sister.

"Why ask *me*? You all seem quite ready to march off to the fires of hell, whether I wish to go or not!"

Anna dropped to the edge of her bed and let her hands fall at her sides. She wished that was all it took to drop the whole thing.

But she did not wish to anger the Captain. She did not wish to anger anyone. And if he truly intended to feed them all...

"The relief to our budget for food is reason enough to go," Jane said softly.

"A reason I'd expect from you. Why are you never more concerned by him?" Anna felt betrayed that she had left him in Jane's care, and Jane had given the horrid man the idea that they would socialize with him.

"Honestly, Anna, I know he startled you at first and I believe we startled him right back. But he doesn't alarm me as he does you. Why *do* you persist in being alarmed?"

Rose and Emery had fallen silent on the question of hair arrangement; they stood just outside the bedroom door, listening.

"Why must I justify my alarm at a horrid man who leaps into our shop and issues orders?"

"Fair point," put in Emery.

"He's a man, after all!"

"Rose, that doesn't make him able to do just as he likes!"

"Doesn't it?" Rose turned toward where Jane sat. "You know the most about men, Jane, don't they all leap about like that?"

"*Rose!*"

"Don't scold her, Anna, when you have taught her to talk like that." Jane had that forbidding look on her face that she had when her feelings were truly hurt.

"I didn't!"

"We all know how often you have tried to be married, Jane," Emery added, all matter-of-fact. "We're not judging you for knowing something of men. We *need* you."

"For information about men? I doubt it." Jane's quelling tone matched her face. If she was trying to point out that none of them were likely to need information about men, it showed.

But then she added, "I don't think they all leap about, but they are abrupt. At least some of them. Honestly, you can't all keep acting like schoolgirls now that we are out in the world."

"Some of us never got to be schoolgirls," Rose put in with her usual pout over the lack of schooling for her and Emery, but her heart wasn't really in it.

"Anna, you must get hold of yourself. Captain Brice has done nothing to you but startle you." Jane's tone had softened a little, but her words were firm.

"And saddled me with two orphans to feed!"

"Not orphans," Emery reminded them from where she'd slid to the floor. She liked to lie on her back when she wasn't kneading bread.

"Fine. Starving children, then."

Emery's shoulders shrugged against the floor. "And now he is offering to feed them. And us."

"For one meal!"

Anna knew she was going to lose. It wouldn't be awful. She wanted to dine somewhere, anywhere, that wasn't right in this room. She wanted to eat something more interesting than an egg.

But she didn't want to become the sort of person who let men like Captain Brice order them around.

And she never would.

Well. At least she could organize them a little.

"I'll wear the striped cream dress. Jane should wear the dotted pink one. Emery must wear her best gown, the pale green, as nothing else is long enough for her, which means Rose will wear the flowered one. The roses on blue."

"Predictable," murmured Rose, tapping her lip with one finger, "but appropriate."

"I don't know why Captain Brice finds it such a desperate matter to entertain us. But I doubt it is for *our* benefit. Let us use this as a chance to see something new, eat our fill, perhaps learn a little something."

"Learn a great deal." Jane had a fixed purpose. "Peers close to the *Crown* dine at Jacquier's. We'll never have a better chance to see what money buys for the table."

Anna had a different purpose. "And *don't* let us talk about marriage prospects, before *or* afterwards. Captain Brice isn't anyone any of us ought to want to marry."

Having drawn lines, Anna leaned back where she sat and let Rose and Emery chatter on about hairstyles. They only had their mother's combs, and Emery and Rose would be wearing them out of necessity, with their long hair. She and Jane would need to make some sort of arrangement with the ribbons they had left.

She must find them and iron them.

Jane was suddenly kneeling right in front of her, leaning in to pat her knee.

"It's all right, Anna. He's not going to kill and eat us. We'll do up our hair and have a supper and it will be fine. You mustn't treat *everything* as a crisis."

As usual in a crisis, Rose retired to her room to brush her hair.

That left three older sisters in the sitting room, standing about on tired feet and trying not to wrinkle their skirts.

"Perhaps Captain Brice will have some thoughts about how to address the state of our funds," said Anna, standing by the window and looking out over the square.

Jane turned to see if her sister had come down ill. "That is the first time you've given Captain Brice any benefit of any doubt."

"Someone must be willing to help," sighed Anna. "The world cannot be full of unfeeling men."

"Yes, it can." Jane turned back to the button she was sewing on to her glove. "We must solve this problem ourselves. And we can. We simply must."

"We can sell more bread." Emery wasn't giving up lying on the floor just because she had to be a lady in a quarter of an hour. "We may need to make up the difference in sheer volume."

"That is not how arithmetic works. If we make more bread, we must buy more flour. Our portion remains the same, by law. I wonder," Jane added thoughtfully, "if we ought to bake some sweet buns, like Mrs. Bunions wants. And perhaps even some type of cake."

The word *cake* went round the room like chain lightning, even Emery sitting straight up.

The fights they had all had about cake had nearly derailed their whole plan. Once they'd seen the advertisement for a bakery to let, the idea of running one themselves had started with Emery. They all knew how good a baker she was, but bread prices were indeed set by law.

There was much more money to be had in cake.

But cakes were more difficult to make, with much more expensive ingredients, including eggs, butter, and the problematic difficulty of sugar.

"She won't like sugar any more than ever," warned Emery, meaning Rose. They all knew that their mother's words had struck home with Rose. Sugar meant slavery, and Rose could never overlook it. Even Mr. Russell, who likely had only exchanged twenty words with Rose, knew how she felt about that. How they all felt about it, but it was Rose who drew firm lines on that.

For all Rose could be listless these days, she could take a position and insist upon it like any other Bickering sister.

"But she loves cake," whispered Anna. For she did. So did Anna. Anna's mouth was watering just thinking about it.

"Everyone loves cake," said Emery, "but what of the costs?"

"We must at least consider the idea." Jane kept her face immobile and pretended her emotions were just as unmoved. "We could charge so much more, if we can make a good cake. And we *can*. Mother's receipt book has so many good prescriptions for cake. Mother *did* make cake."

"And they are things we can make, Jane and I and Rose, just as well, and not make all the work on you, Emery," Anna reminded her sister. "But..."

Emery shrugged off all the incredibly hard work she had done today, lifting pounds and pounds of dough, kneading it endlessly. And she'd begun in the middle of the night and worked through the day. "I only mean, it's one thing to survive; it's another thing to survive at the expense of others. And this isn't even our survival. We're talking about unnecessary cake."

Anna did not look at Jane. She didn't want Emery to feel outnumbered, especially without Rose to support her. It was touchy, when the older sisters were in rare agreement against something that the younger sisters wanted.

"Jane, hadn't we better stick to bread for now?"

Her sister shrugged. "It's only more money for wheat."

Rose emerged from her bedroom. "Monsieur Jacquier's Hotel is, what, fifteen steps from our door? I intend to count them!"

"Are we late?" Anna looked round.

"We don't have a clock," pointed out Emery from the floor.

"It is such a different matter, needing to be punctual when one doesn't have a clock, than it is when one *has* a clock and punctuality at social affairs is so much less important." Anna looked out the window again, perhaps for a clock. Or a captain.

"My assumption," said Jane, "is that Jordan and Sal will not arrive as clean as we would like them to be. Let us go down and see, Anna, and escort them to the washtub if necessary." In preparation for which, she held her gloves in her hand without pulling them on.

EMERY WAITED UNTIL SHE HEARD THE DOOR AT THE bottom of the stairs close before she said, "They're talking about cake, you know."

"Oh, no!" Rose's cheerful smile faded away. "What *is* the use of persuading someone when they won't stay persuaded? It was Jane, wasn't it?"

Emery's shrug was audible, her shoulders rustling in her brown linen gown. "It's not just Jane. We all need the shop to make enough money so that we can eat. You eat the same food we all do."

"But my voice counts less than everyone else's, I suppose, because I am blind."

"Rose." The drawback of having a sister was that they knew you your whole lives, and recognized your sulks when they heard them.

"Very well then, because I am the youngest."

"*Rose.* I will say I don't think you ought to be left out of the discussions about money. We *are* all in this together, and if you are old enough to work and tend the shop, you are old enough to worry with us about the money."

"I thought that our bread is selling quite well!"

"It is. Look, you know I'm not the person to argue about money, Jane is."

"But I thought Anna would argue with her *for* me!"

"You can argue for yourself. Truthfully," Emery added, "I'd rather have hands to help than cake."

"Oh, I'm sorry!" They all knew what hard, heavy work Emery was doing day after day. She had a relationship with the bread that the rest of them didn't quite have. But it meant that she checked every loaf going in and out of the oven, even when the rest of them stirred and kneaded and lifted.

"I didn't mean that you're shirking, you goose. It's just, there's always a lot to be done. A few more hands wouldn't hurt."

"But..." More hands would mean more outlay of money, not more money.

Emery understood her. "If we could make more bread each day, we could have help. But I can't make more bread without the help. And frankly, there's only so much kneading

I can do along with everything it takes to keep the place clean."

Rose nodded. It had been impressed upon all four of them from a very young age that a clean kitchen was a tasty kitchen. "But what can I tell Anna about cake that I haven't before?"

"Just say all the same things over again," Emery grunted. "That's what Jane does."

BYPASSING THE *CLOSED* CARD IN THE WINDOW, CAPTAIN Brice wondered if he would be able to tell if the door to the ladies' bakery were locked or not. He put his shoulder to it; one shove pushed it open and settled the question.

Inside, he was astonished to find the entire crew assembled.

"Have you been introduced, Captain? This is Jordan Collier and his sister Sarah Collier, who is called Sally."

"Sal," said the young lady, which the eldest Miss Bickering pretended not to hear.

Jordan and Sal had matching damp heads, Sal's hair combed and tightly braided, Jordan's just as tightly combed. They both looked angered by these developments.

Around them the various Misses Bickering stood arrayed in dresses without aprons. It was a surprising event.

And the eldest one was staring at him.

No, waiting.

"Oh, ah... Captain Joshua Brice. I'm very pleased to make your acquaintance, madame."

Her lips folded together a little more tightly. "Thank you, sir; I am Miss Anna Bickering, and may I present my sisters? Miss Jane Bickering, Miss Emery Bickering, and Miss Rose Bickering."

Brice hadn't spent many of his years in the Britain of his mother, but he knew perfectly well that all women of a certain age were called Mistress as a courtesy. If this Miss Bickering refused to write *Mrs. Bickering* on her calling cards, she was clinging to her unmarried state, despite the fact that she was no longer all that young.

Or she was clinging to being a member of the gentry, which she clearly wasn't, as she stood in the bakery in which she worked.

Well, that was none of his affair. Better she think herself too good for the neighborhood than bat her eyes at him. He had to keep the names all straight.

"If I may escort you all," he said most solemnly, then paused before turning and opening the door for them all.

Once they were all out, he also yanked the door shut so that the eldest Miss Bickering could lock it.

He had the feeling that if he offered her his arm, she'd stab him in some soft place with that key, and he didn't want to insult the other young ladies; so he merely bowed. "How shall we go, ladies?"

"I'm going to count the steps," the littlest Bickering—Rose—said, and the tallest one nudged her with an elbow.

After some moments of shuffling and polite murmuring, they were arranged so that those two led in front, followed by the children, followed by the Captain with one of the two elder sisters on either side.

This made it impossible for him to give both sisters the spot farther from the noise and dust of the street, but he put the cranky one on the inside and hoped for the best.

The whole procession slowed when a very high-nosed young maid in a fine linen cap crossed their path. She nodded to the ladies, a nod so dripping with condescension that he supposed the girl thought herself a duchess in disguise.

And it stopped altogether when a little woman wrapped

in a shawl, even in the summer evening, walked straight up to their little party and said, "Amazing strength, all of you Misses Bickering. I could never spend so much of my day on my feet. Bunions, you know."

"We know," said Miss Rose, not unkindly. She'd been so quiet on Brice's visits to the shop, he'd barely heard her voice. She must be different with the customers.

Brice growled a little inside when he realized these must all be customers, the people who acknowledged the Misses Bickering in the street. This little bakery didn't just concern these young women. All the rest of these women relied on it, too.

Dammit.

Progress was easier, once they reached the establishment. He had, of course, reserved a dining room and the staff were alert as hunting hounds.

The Hotel Jacquier emulated elite dining rooms for their guests in every way they could. The table was already groaning under all the dishes of the first course, arranged in rectangular fashion around a central bowl of dried fruit; it could not look more French, and it waited only for them to sit and enjoy it.

"Monsieur," said a young fellow, handing him a printed menu as he entered.

Brice didn't care about the menu. There was simply no other place for him to converse with the Misses Bickering in private, and this one offered him the pleasure of making sure they had a full meal as well.

He handed the menu across the table to the tallest one.

Other servants whisked about, relieving him of the hat he'd worn for the entire walk of dozens of feet and taking the ladies' bonnets as well. It was practically as efficient as his ship's crew as they poured wine, moved chairs for the ladies, and never brushed a single piece of china accidentally.

What he hadn't expected was that efficiency wouldn't start this conversation.

The children's eyes were wide over the gilt chairs, thick carpet, blue figured wallpaper; the tall one, Miss Emery, also had wide eyes as she ran her fingertip over the fine embroidered linen, delicate porcelain, and shining silver before her. The elder two seated themselves easily, with the help of footmen; this was not their first time at such a table. Miss Rose, of course, paid all the fanciness no mind.

He'd bribed the servants not to fuss about the children; it was his dining room for the moment; he could do as he pleased. He seldom ate in the restaurant, not only because of the price of a meal, but because he had no one to dine with. Now he had months' worth of guests all at once.

Jordan was leaning over Miss Emery's arm and pointing at the dishes. "What's that? What's that? What's that?"

"I have no idea. I don't read French." With that, she handed the menu over to Jordan, who handed it to Sal, who handed it to Miss Rose.

"I don't read French either," said Miss Rose, handing it to her sister Jane on his left.

Miss Jane raised an eyebrow as she ran her eye down the page, and handed it past the Captain, very rudely, to her eldest sister.

Who began the meal, of course, with a complaint. "Captain. You don't plan to serve everything on this menu to the children?"

He took the page from her and rolled his eyes down it, glancing at the dishes on the table to confirm their contents. Paté—didn't children love rich meat? Butter cake; fish stew; slices of deer breasts fried in—

Coughing to clear whatever was suddenly stuck in his throat, Brice rose. "If you'll excuse me. I must just speak to the chef."

It took only minutes and a hurried conversation with a footman, who went in and whisked the dish away. Brice had no doubt that it was delicious; he simply didn't want to explain it to the children. Or for that matter, to the younger Misses Bickering.

As he returned, he heard a lively discussion. Apparently, all it took to start the conversation was for him to leave.

"The children will make themselves sick."

"We won't! We're going to eat *everything they have!*"

"We ought to have discussed it with him."

"He ought to have discussed it with *us!*"

"It makes me ill to think of any of this going to waste, and the cost."

"He said we're going to eat it all. We *will.*"

"Really?" The dark-haired sister's dry tone was easier to pick out than the rest. And she apparently had no qualms about discomfort at the dinner table. "How do you feel about eating—"

"I hope no one is disappointed. The chef has had to make a last-minute change, and that dish will be mutton. Mr. Collier. Miss Collier."

Both the chairs nearly fell over as the children turned immediately to see him over their shoulders.

"You have two tasks tonight. Not to overeat. And not to repeat whatever you hear. Can you do it?"

Jordan, his eyes huge, nodded violently.

Sal just narrowed her eyes. "We don't have to prove it to *you.*"

Brice had stared down sea captains over cannon. He didn't waver.

Finally, Sal nodded. "We can."

"Good. Ladies, your landlord does not expect you to be able to pay your lease. He *will* bring you before the magistrate to collect the debt. He will take everything you have."

The chill of silence filled the room from the floor up.

Then all the voices started going at once.

"If you were going to blurt it all out like that, why didn't you just do it?" The eldest Miss Bickering, it seemed, would begin every conversation with a criticism of him.

The younger two and the children talked over each other.

"We still get supper, don't we?"

"I never trusted Mr. Scrope."

"Why would they plan such a thing? We *have* nothing!"

"What was the thing you didn't want us to eat?"

"Oh Emery, all your work. *All* our work!"

"All of you, we must discuss this at home." But Miss Bickering's warning didn't work.

The voices continued to cut across each other. The dark-haired one—Miss Jane—rolled her eyes at one or all of them, he couldn't tell, and said, "Captain, what do you suggest we do about it?"

She was sensible. She reminded him of his sister at home. Though he must think of Britain as home now.

Sitting at the table again, Brice surveyed all the eyes turned toward him. It ought to be comfortable enough; the men of his ship looked to him all the time. This collection of eyes was more daunting.

"I don't know what you can do but pay it."

At that, Miss Bickering's chair jerked back in an appallingly undignified way.

"This is what one gets from men. Everything is so easy for you. Easy answers! That's all you have in your hats. Easy answers and not one bit of *help!*"

Rising, Brice pulled her chair out over the carpet for her.

After a moment, still glaring and catching her breath, she slowly sat back down.

Brice sat too. "I thought it was better to know than *not* know."

"We knew we had signed paperwork. We must make the bakery pay." The littlest one, Rose, locked her jaw in a way that wouldn't have looked out of place on his ship.

"But we are *not* making the bakery pay." Miss Jane's voice fell across the table so hard it surprised him that the crystal didn't break.

The silence now pressed everyone down into their seats.

"Miss Jane," said Miss Bickering quietly, "our circumstances are not such that we need tell strangers about our affairs."

"Miss Anna," said her sister, "they very much *are*."

Two servers swept in past the gold brocade curtains; crystal decanters of port sparkled in both their hands. Along with the wine already on the table.

It was a good plan, thought Brice. Everyone needed a drink.

Except the children. "*I don't think so,*" he said in French as one approached a crystal tumbler at Jordan's place.

"*Of course, sir. We are unaccustomed to serving children,*" the man said with a sniff, and was gone.

"Ladies," he said, "I don't have any good answers. But I want you to find one. You deserve to make that bakery pay you enough to live."

It was the first thing he'd ever said to her that took some of the starch out of Miss Bickering's spine. "Thank you," and her eyes showed she meant it. "It is good to hear that, today."

"We're not selling cake."

All eyes turned to Rose.

"We're not selling cake, and that's it."

And for the first time, Brice felt something other than worried responsibility for this collection of unprotected women and children. He saw the way *her* spine was set, and it was very, very familiar to him. "Pray tell me why, Miss Rose."

"Because it funds slavery on those islands where the sugar cane is grown, as my sisters know very well."

"You're quite right." Brice settled back into his chair, picked up his fine crystal goblet and took a mouthful of wine before he went on. All too soon he'd be back aboard ship and though he didn't indulge in these sorts of pleasures often, he wanted them while he could have them. "The war over slavery is funded by sugar. The French plantation owners complained that Napoleon's abolishment of slavery had made their work impossible, and slavery was re-established. Oh, I'm sure it's more complicated than that, but there it is."

"Finish the story, Captain Brice. That the British Parliament considered abolishing the institution of slavery altogether but backed away because of the *British* plantation owners on those islands. Who said they couldn't compete with French sugar if they didn't have slave labor." Now Rose was sitting back in her chair as well, and though her face was not as expressive as her sisters', he could read her disgust quite well. "All to make sugar so cheap that everyone eats cake for breakfast and no one bothers themselves about it."

Jordan looked longingly at the golden cake at the table among all the other dishes. "Does this mean we can't have the cake?"

Brice breathed in, slowly. This supper was more like a night aboard ship than he'd expected. "If I may?" he asked Miss Bickering, if only to appease her beforehand.

"By all means. Do *something*."

"Mr. Collier. We are here to enjoy ourselves tonight. Remember, your task at hand is not to overeat and make yourself ill. Other than that, I expect you to enjoy every plate. There is a moment before battle when one must gather knowledge of the enemy."

"This is that moment in many ways," Miss Jane muttered to herself.

"However," Brice went on. He nodded across the table at Rose. "You are quite right, Miss Rose. I admire your knowledge, and your principles. Surely you can save your business *and* step out of the bloody sugar business."

"How?" The tallest one, who'd said nothing, slumped a little. She looked tired, he thought; he could see dark crescents underneath her eyes, which might otherwise be quite fine. She had lighter eyes than her sisters, as well as lighter hair. And she looked at the cake on the table as if it were a bowl of serpents. "You might as well know, Captain Brice, that you see before you our entire family. We have no other resources, no one upon whom to draw if there is a crisis."

"Well." The eldest Miss Bickering shifted in her chair. "There is our Aunt Eden."

Another round of remarks went off like gunfire.

"I will *not* ask Aunt Eden for anything."

"What is she going to do with *me*? Marry me away?"

"We didn't part with Aunt Eden on the best terms, you know."

"I don't have an Aunt Eden," Jordan said calmly, and reached for Emery's wine.

"You can have mine," Emery said sourly, and moved the glass. "My aunt, not my wine. We are grateful for your concern, Captain Brice. We have come this far together and we will continue on. I know," she raised a hand before anyone could interrupt, "we have to do *something* different. But stubbornness is worth something, and we have that."

"We do," said Jane, and raised her glass, and then Anna and Rose lifted theirs too. Sal lifted hers, sipped from it, and put it back down, not quite grasping the spirit of the thing. But overall, the feeling around the table was clear.

So Brice lifted a glass to stubbornness.

Miss Anna paused, and then lifted her glass too. "I too can be stubborn. And I am going to have cake."

"Hurrah!" said Jordan, and Sal sat up straight.

"Before you harangue me," said the lady, interrupting her sisters, "we are in Monsieur Jacquier's *hotel*. Have any of you eaten in that gentleman's coffee house? No, I don't mean you, Captain Brice. We are eating here and we may never eat here again. Miss Rose, you know I agree with your principles. I am still looking for a solution. I will not miss this opportunity to understand what the French can do with cake. I am going to eat some of that cake, and in fact any cake they put before us. In fact, we should ask for every cake they have."

"I won't," said Miss Rose instantly. "You are turning your back on the problem."

"No, I am looking very squarely at the problem," her sister responded just as swiftly. "You know how well I make cakes. If we are to find a solution to our dilemma—"

"Which of your dilemmas?" asked the Captain, but Her Majesty, as he was coming to think of her, ignored him.

"—I shall only point out that this sugar is already sold and baked in this hotel, today, and we are in no position to persuade them to stop using sugar. Not right now. Not today. If we wish to find pastries we might sell, we must know what people like. And this opportunity may never come again. We are only doing this once."

All around the table, glasses were held aloft, no one moving. Then the eldest Miss Bickering drank. "To stubbornness," she said, and there were murmurs all around the table till Brice couldn't quite tell who felt good about stubbornness and who didn't. Everyone but the children toasted anyway.

Episode 7: The triumph of pure flour

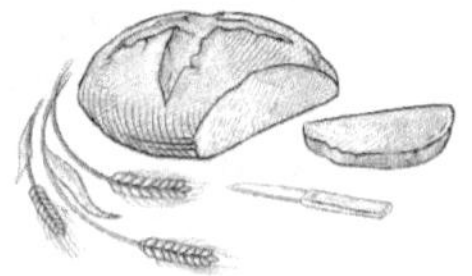

As happened in the wee hours of every morning, Emery woke at the fall of a spoon.

It clanged on the floor, and the string that had held it suspended under the window-sill slipped away.

"I hate it," said Rose in her sleep, and turned over.

They weren't the only ones to give Mr. Macaulay, the night watchman, a few pennies to pull a string, or throw a rock, or tap on a window, and wake them even while the rest of London was still asleep.

Emery felt the short hours, and the rich French food from the Captain's long dinner felt like it still lay on her stomach several days later. Once the stiffness around the table had worn down a little, the evening had been very pleasant.

Anna had asked for every possible cake, and had tasted everything, no matter from whose plate. Captain Brice never said a word. Emery was fairly sure Anna had eaten half the *gâteau Breton*.

The Captain looked out of place in that dining room padded with paisley wallpaper and gilt chairs. His hair was perpetually tangled, as if a sea wind had caught it. He had black eyes that snapped, but they didn't bother Emery. He had wanted Sal and Jordan fed, and that made any person acceptable to Emery.

She slid out of bed, careful not to jostle Rose, and slipped on her shift and favorite dress. The printed cotton had been one of her nicest. Its swirling leaf pattern was getting worn with constant washing and ironing. Well, that too was becoming familiar.

When she opened the door to their rooms, she glanced left, then reminded herself not to look guilty. The disreputable neighbor hadn't reappeared; perhaps his drunken night out had been an anomaly? Or perhaps there really were mice. She sometimes heard distant sounds overhead that couldn't be from him.

The moon cast a glow through the narrow window atop the door at the bottom of the stairs. Emery stopped short of venturing out into the night air—she couldn't think of it as morning yet—and instead turned into the shop.

The shop itself was full of moonglow. Number 17, Leicester Square was a funny little building that came to a point with windows on both sides. With the bread counter at her back, she could peer out onto Leicester Square on one side and Bear Street on the other. Bear Street's buildings were gray and cut off the sky, but there was still room for the silvery light to work through the twisting runnels of cobblestone streets into their little shop.

Alone at night like this, Emery's world was full of possibilities. She had dreams, she had plans, she had...

She had little people under her feet.

She nearly tripped over them, lying across the doorway to the bakery proper.

"What are you two doing here?" Emery doubted Jordan and Sal could keep secrets. And they ought to be sleeping. Of course, they had been, till she bumped into them.

Uncharacteristically, Sal spoke. Rubbing one eye with her fist, she yawned, but looked as cheerful as ever, which was to say not very. But she was awake. Emery still felt a powerful pull to her own bed, and she was full-grown; Sal must be awake through sheer determination. "We knew you had something to do in the morning and we wanted to help."

"We don't want to miss anything important." Jordan was standing up too, though behind his sister. His cap had fallen off and lay on the floor by his heavy shoes.

Though Sal wore a linen dress and petticoat that was just a small copy of Emery's own, and quite different from Jordan's breeches, shirt, and open hanging vest, she planted her feet more sturdily than he. She would not be moved. "We reckoned you needed more hands."

"Now, how did you know I had some plans for this morning?" Emery held the door open and shooed them in. Ghostly tubs draped in snowy white sat in huddles on every table, the late orange glow of the oven embers mixing with the moonlight to make the shapes neither warm nor cold, but gray.

"You always have plans for the morning," Jordan said, and she couldn't argue, because that was true, she baked every morning but Sunday, "but we knew you were up to something different because you made more barrels than usual. And some of them are wearing dresses."

That was true too. When she'd used all the linen toweling, Emery had draped the last few tubs with clean, ironed petticoats from her sisters. Hopefully, they wouldn't notice.

Well, they certainly wouldn't notice till they woke up.

"All right, you can help. Remember a few weeks ago, Jordan, when you stirred that dough forever, and I had to make you stop?"

"I was bored," said Jordan with a fond remembering smile, like a young man remembering his bachelor days.

"Yes. Remember what happened when we baked it?"

"It was *good*." He patted his stomach as he tried to see into the barrel. "But bread's always good." Sal stood on her other side; Emery lifted off the ironed petticoat.

The dough inside had wet, half-blown bubbles in it. The children hadn't baked as long as Emery, but they knew the bread dough Emery baked in the morning didn't look like *that*.

"We're going to punch this batch down gently and make gentle loaves," said Emery as she tied on her apron.

Sal squinted at her. "What the devil is a gentle loaf?"

Emery looked down at her skinny young apprentice. "Who taught you to talk like that?"

The girl rolled her eyes, but pressed her lips together as if sorry she'd let the words out. "Everyone talks like that."

"I don't and my sisters don't."

"I don't want to grow up to be one of your sisters. Miss Anna says I must learn to read, and Jane keeps showing me numbers and they're wrong."

"Hm." Emery went over to the pump and washed her hands, reminding the children by example what they must *always* do before touching dough. She could tell them something over and over, but they remembered better when they watched her do it. "Jane is very good with numbers. I doubt hers are wrong."

"They are, though." Sal didn't much care.

By the time she and Jordan had finished shoving each other, washed, and dried their hands, Emery already had two loaves done.

She cut through the wet dough with the blade of her hand and pulled up a wad. "See how it's stretchy? It's changed like it should. We didn't knead it, but it's stretchy. It's just a little wet, that's all. Pull the sides down and around—yes, Jordan, like that—and make a ball. Tuck the bottom under. Yes, then shape the loaf."

They had to work quickly, and it wasn't easy not to just let the wet dough sag right through one's fingers. Jordan learned the trick after a few tries and soon managed as well as Emery. Sal scowled at the uncooperative wads of saggy dough, but she pulled a few into shape.

Morning was Emery's quiet time, but she found she didn't mind sharing it. With the children helping her, though she had prepared twice the dough, she had it in the pans in much less time. The room was warm, almost too close; July was warm in the city, and the oven had settled into coals.

This was going to work. Emery could just imagine the faces of her sisters when she showed them how much bread she'd been able to make by leaving it wet and letting it somehow knead itself.

Oh no, it was nothing. Anna would look impressed—they *all* would. What would Jane look like if it impressed her? Emery imagined all three sisters smiling, perhaps their mouths gaping open a little in surprise, astonished by Emery's ability to solve their problems all by herself.

It was nothing. Yes, of course we will be able to do it every day. Oh Rose, your favorite hair ribbon? I couldn't possibly. Yes, Anna, I was right. Well, it was bound to happen someday. Should have listened to me before? Of course I forgive you, Jane, of course. We were like twins, you remember, before you went off to that fancy school with Anna. Ha ha ha, never say so! I'll never mention it again. It's forgotten!

"What's forgotten?" Jordan's voice pulled her out of her reverie of ribbons and adulation.

Had she said any of it out loud? "Don't know, I forgot it."

Emery dabbed at a drop of sweat on her brow with the tip of her apron. All the loaves were covered again, proofing in the room's warmth. It would be a little while before they had grown enough to put in the oven.

Once there, she'd have to watch them carefully, turning

and rotating them to fill up the entire space, and making sure that they baked evenly. Their customers appreciated the look of their bread.

Would they like the taste? Emery wasn't sure. When she'd tried baking Jordan's wet dough, she'd thought it heavenly. It let off steam as it baked, even without her adding water to the oven. The crust was brown, and it crackled, yet inside the bread was tender, with larger holes but a flavor like nothing she'd ever tried.

She'd used less rising, as the first rise had started around noon when she'd begun putting the dough together. She had a feeling she could use less and let it go longer. But even if they didn't rise as much as usual, they'd taste good. She thought.

"All right, now I will come back and put them in the oven when they're ready. Meanwhile, I must walk you home."

"We don't want to go home!"

Sal's quick words squashed Emery's half-formed idea that the night watchman could walk them all to the children's home, then see Emery back safe. It wouldn't exactly be breaking Anna's rule that they not go out alone.

But if the children didn't wish to go?

Emery looked at the little dark heads. She was good at showing them what to do, and they liked her. They liked her primarily for not forcing them to learn to read, these days. What she wasn't sure about was whether they needed hugs right now, or something like that. Not Emery's strongest skill.

She'd have to coax some sister better at talking to find out if the children only wished to help, or if something else was bothering them.

Thinking of her sisters in reality, *not* dreams of admiration, reminded Emery of the arguments at the Captain's table, and that made her stomach clench. Jane was good with numbers, but more bread simply had to be better than less bread. Why were Anna and Jane even entertaining the idea of cake? Was it just the memory of all those years when cake was the one treat they had?

And Emery couldn't believe she'd never thought of it before, but how had her mother spent all that time showing them how to bake cake, when the sugar trade appalled her?

Still. Her helpers. "There's a heap of flour sacks below, and it's cooler there. You can go sleep, if you want." She did not even raise the question of why they didn't want to go home. She felt like she was entitled to her own secrets and they were entitled to theirs.

"I'm not sleepy!" Jordan looked as entranced by the dough as Emery felt. It wasn't the usual silky dry stuff they kneaded into submission. It was wild-looking, and rough. He wanted to see how it baked as much as she did.

"Fine." Emery shrugged. "Bring me that book Anna is showing you how to read. You can practice with me."

"I'm awful sleepy," Jordan said instead of complying, and seizing Sal's hand, disappeared through the door to the shop where they could go down to the cool basement.

Emery smiled to herself and bent low over the nearest bread pan. The dough was growing, breathing. She loved this stage. It magically became more bread, and if she did what she should all the way through, it would become delicious dinners, breakfasts, suppers for all the people around Leicester Square who shopped at the Ladies' Own Bakery.

There were a few smaller buildings, like theirs, where the master or mistress sent the cook over to simply buy the daily bread. It was so much easier for a small household. But there were also families over the shops, as they were: young couples in garrets; working people like the tailor across the way; even Mrs. Macaulay, the wife of the night watchman, would be in later to buy their daily bread.

Leicester Square still had many large fine homes where moneyed people had servants everywhere, including a cook who baked bread perhaps every other day, maybe even every day. No one would come from those houses, unless it was the cook's day off that month. But Leicester Square also had physicians who might come and go by themselves; the hotels that shared their side of the square; and a growing group of night ladies who, in their own way, served the same purpose as the bakery sisters did, fulfilling the needs of people without full homes of their own.

Emery had only the faintest idea what the night ladies did. She knew men paid for their company. She wasn't entirely sure what the two people then did together. She suspected it wasn't just reading. When she thought about pretty Miss Hayes, she suspected men felt about her as Emery did. The suspicion that she would look even prettier without her shiny clothing, and the need to see it.

Beyond that, she didn't wish to think about whatever Miss Hayes did with her customers, but it made sense to think of her trading something they needed for coins, just like they did in the bakery.

Emery let out a huff. She mustn't let Anna catch her thinking that way.

Nor would Anna catch her if she managed her plans today. She was going to produce the largest batches of bread the Ladies' Own Bakery had ever baked. And, with any luck at all, the tastiest.

They wouldn't have to buy sugar because Emery could make the bakery profitable through sheer act of will, and muscles. And Jordan's wet dough. And the ability to get up early, thanks to a spoon that fell on the floor when the night watchman pulled a string from Bear Street.

They didn't need anything but flour, water, salt, and yeast. Flour was all a meal needed. Flour made a bread that was pleasant to chew, meaty and rich on the tongue, brown and toasted on the outside with that crackle that made people hungry. Flour was all that was really needed.

Emery was going to solve their problems through the triumph of pure flour.

ANNA WOULD NEVER AGAIN LOOK OUT OF THEIR WINDOWS for some handsome man who would notice her and offer her a solution for her problems. She told herself that as she swept the bakery floor. And throughout the ten minutes that it took to sweep the last crumbs out over the threshold, she swore to herself that she was no longer looking for Lord Zachary.

It was a complete surprise when, not a quarter of an hour later, Lord Zachary actually arrived in a carriage, one covered in elegant black lacquer and chased with gold leaves round the top.

He looked so good, so *right* climbing out of that carriage in boots as shiny as the carriage and hair as gold as its laurel leaves. Anna couldn't help but stand foolishly close to the window. He was *so* close.

It was a more unpleasant surprise when he turned back to the carriage and handed out a lady in a fluttering day dress—was that silk?—and wearing a summer bonnet trimmed with expensive silk roses. The gold of a blue ring winked on her hand.

The second her feet reached the pavement, she turned to Lord Zachary. "You can't imagine that we want to live in this neighborhood."

Anna caught her breath and pretended very hard not to listen.

The young lady went on. "As much as I wish to see more of you, I am not beginning my married life in a house this tiny. And look, next to a bakery, and with a tailor across the way. I'm not a tailor, Zachary."

Anna peeped around the broom handle.

"By definition, unless you are in the building that says Tailor, no one has reason to think you a Tailor." Lord Zachary didn't look the least bit alarmed by a woman that Anna could only assume was his betrothed reacting to the site of his home with horror. "Honestly, Cecily. You are steps away from where the Prince of Wales once lived. Look out over the park. That gilt statue of George the First is keeping watch over all the square, bakers, tailors, and all."

"That's the kind of fantasy you like, Zachary, but it does nothing for me." The young lady turned her back on the wild growth of the square and fixed her attention on the entirely unsatisfactory building next to the bakery.

It had never occurred to Anna to find out who the tenant of that building was. It had never occurred to her it was empty, or that if it were empty, someone might come to claim it. It had certainly never occurred to her that Lord Zachary would wish to move next door.

Why was she even thinking about this? Wasn't she done worrying about him? He had no interest in her or her problems, and she needed to get over this infatuation of hers. She didn't even know him.

Why was she opening the door?

It was warm enough to leave it open, and Anna stood inside, broom in hand.

All she knew was that Lord Zachary was a well mannered, beautiful man in fine clothes, who lived above her and painted exquisite paintings of flowers. They had no interaction, no reason to know one another other than that.

So the next moment should have made no difference to her, when the woman beside him made another complaint. "Zachary, why would you subject a sister that you claim to love to a place like this? Lord Milbray wishes to get away from the bustle of Grosvenor Square. He didn't say he wanted to move to a cow field."

Anna felt her shoulders fall away from where they had been trying to crawl into her ears. She was his sister. Of course, that made perfect sense.

She was his sister, and he was showing her the house next to the one where he lived. That was all.

Leaning a little out the bakery door, Anna waved the handle of her broom and curtsied. "The frontage of the house looks narrow, but it does extend quite a long way back."

The woman with the silk roses spun in a circle, as if voices had come at her from the disembodied air. She finally noticed Anna. "Excuse me?"

Anna felt good enough to excuse her. His *sister*. "The houses, they're quite deep. I imagine you plan to take the entire house?" The young lady's sweeping eyes took in every detail of Anna, from the top of her hair, curling wildly and daubed with flour, all the way down to the worn toes of her slippers underneath the hem of a gown that grew more ragged every day. Jane insisted that they still did not have the money for anything other than the bare necessities of survival. And dresses did not qualify as the bare necessities of survival.

The dotted lawn dress had once been perfectly suitable for an afternoon call to a drawing room. But now it looked ragged. More so next to a perfect fluttering silk.

The young lady did not answer her, but turned to Lord Zachary.

"I did not venture here to be addressed by such a person. You cannot imagine that I intend to begin my life with my new husband in a place such as this with French hotels, Zachary, French hotels, mere steps away, and common working people of every sort. In every direction. Look how that building comes to a point. Even the streets are crooked. There is no mews or carriage-house in back either, is there?"

Anna's good mood crumbled away, like the crust of a dry loaf. Underneath she felt warm and pure, but pure what, she couldn't quite say. The moment of illusion that she was still part of this woman's society had faded, and she should feel foolish. But she didn't.

She knew exactly what she was saying when she opened her mouth and spoke loudly enough for a lady to hear, even while ignoring her. "There are carriage houses in the mews, but not for you."

"Excuse me?" The young lady said again, turning back to stare at Anna.

"Just what I say. There are carriage houses in the mews, but not attached to that house, and not for you." Anna left it up to wordless, useless Lord Zachary to explain to his sister.

"Zachary, who is this person?" the lady asked. "Do you know her?"

And then Lord Zachary put himself in the category of people like his sister.

"No, I don't know her. Someone who lives nearby."

Anna stood up straight and gripped the broom like a spear. She didn't curtsey, she didn't wave, she didn't bob her head, and she didn't use any polite form of address.

She just said, "I am one proprietor of the Ladies' Own Bakery." And turning her back on them both, she marched inside.

The door wouldn't let her slam it, but the effect was sufficiently similar.

JANE AND ANNA WERE LAUGHING BEHIND THE COUNTER when Rose tapped on the door from the bakery to the shop proper.

Well, kicked the door. Rose's hands were full of bread.

How could they be laughing? She was still simmering from their argument at the Captain's dinner, while her sisters laughed and pretended it had never happened. She followed the shop wall around with her shoulder, bumping into it occasionally; it wasn't comfortable, but it let her walk with both hands full of the tray.

Jane noticed and spoke up. "Oh, just the right moment, Rose, let me take those for you."

"I'll put them down." Rose followed the wall around to the right; it was getting to be quite familiar. It felt like she'd brought more trays out today than ever before. Well, perhaps that was her temper getting the better of her.

Also familiar now were the deep empty counters on that side of the room.

Where no doubt Jane had villainous plans to put cake.

"Why, Rose, shouldn't we keep it all on one side of the room where the till is? Why so far away?"

Because if I get any closer, I will beat you to death with bread, Rose thought to herself. "I'm stepping outside," was all she said, continuing along that wall to the door.

She needed a breath of fresh air. She'd been too tired to think this morning, and she still couldn't. If she could just breathe and think for a moment, perhaps she'd think of what to say.

She *wanted* to know her own mind, and say what *she* thought. Not Anna, not Emery, herself. But for that, she had to think for a moment and not throw any bread at Jane.

JANE HOPED ROSE WASN'T STANDING OUTSIDE WAITING FOR Mr. Russell to just appear. It would be awful if he didn't and worse if he did. She suspected that the way to handle that awkward situation was not to order it away, as Anna hoped to do. But she didn't trust Mr. Russell, not for any reason, and certainly not with her littlest sister.

If an encounter with Mr. Russell was Rose's goal, she dropped it soon enough; in minutes, she came back in and wrestled the door mostly closed behind her.

"Oh, hello, Rose." Anna's tone was familiar to Jane; it was Anna's fake *I was very worried about you but I know I am not supposed to hover over you* tone.

She knew Rose recognized the tone, too.

Rose was smiling now, though. "A minute of air did me a world of good. Is Jane here?"

"Yes." Jane added nothing. Rose complained that Jane talked too much, that Jane talked when Rose wanted to talk, that Jane didn't talk when Rose wanted to hear. She'd heard every form of complaint from Rose about how to talk and had come to the conclusion that there was no right way.

"Jane, may I speak with you?"

Huh. That wasn't how this was supposed to go.

"Ah—of course. I'm right here...?"

"Come down to the basement with me, and fetch another sack of salt. It's easier if we do it together."

It wasn't. The slippery sacks worked well enough slung over one shoulder; when one tried to grasp them in the hands, they were too hard to hold.

But she followed Rose down the basement stairs.

"I want to talk to you." Rose was standing tall in that way their mother had always told her to stand. As if it would make her look less short. "Are we alone?"

"Fairly. I've left the door open at the top of the stairs."

"Why?"

"Because there is no light down here."

"Ah." Rose didn't always remember that her sisters needed silly old light, but she remembered not to argue with them about it. She got right to her point. "I must know. Why is it so important to you that we sell cake?"

That was new. Well, not a new topic, but a new way of arguing. Rose knew the rules; she complained to Anna, Jane complained to Anna, and Anna tried to figure out a way to have them all agree on something.

That was how they had always done it.

Jane shrugged; it was reflexive, she knew Rose couldn't see it. "I agree with your objections to sugar."

"Not what I asked." Rose was still standing tall, as if two minutes out of doors had given her a new grip on life. "No reasonable person can be comfortable selling food made with sugar, not knowing its relationship to the enslavement of others. I'd like to know why you wish to do it anyway."

Whatever had given Rose this idea, it was working. Jane felt quite off-balance and put in the wrong.

"I don't have a lecture prepared, Rose. I sum up the numbers, as you know. Cakes are popular, and not everyone can make them well, just like bread. And they take much more expensive ingredients but we can *charge* so much more for them. It's just an example, but imagine we spent a pound now to make two pounds when we sell a loaf of bread. It would be more like spending two pounds to make six. We can charge much more for them."

"And how much can we charge in order to redeem our souls?"

Souls? Rose never talked of souls. None of them did. "Oh, now *don't* start that. Our vicar never preached a sermon against slavery *or* sugar."

"And why is that? Why doesn't our church preach against both of them all the time? The Quaker houses do."

"Quakers are quite odd, Rose, even you know that."

Rose pulled herself up even taller. In the gloom at the bottom of the basement stairs, with her head held high, she quite reminded Jane of their mother. "I find nothing odd in the sermons or the people. Moreover, you know that every sack of sugar we would buy might as well be soaked in blood. How can you pretend not to know it?"

"Because everyone around me pretends not to know it!" Seized with the urge to shake Rose until her teeth rattled, Jane clenched her fists. "Everyone in London eats sugar all day, and we cannot change that by ourselves. I *do* remember the boycotts, and Mother was always so discouraged. She couldn't even get her best friends to join in. My care for my soul is to keep it in my body, and yours too. Any number of other shops may not have to worry; they aren't bakeries. Run by ladies. With no *husbands*."

"I find it curious that you would rather sell sugar and contribute to the suffering of thousands than find a husband and just contribute to *his* suffering."

That was cruel.

"You aren't usually cruel," Jane said, a little quietly. They had all stopped hitting each other as tiny children; their mother wouldn't stand for it. The words, however, hit harder.

She thought Rose knew perfectly well that Jane had gone to every effort to convince several young men to marry her. *Jane* wasn't fussy. Men were fussy.

And Rose was fussy, about the damn sugar. She wore cotton that came from Indian workers that had no choices either, and drank tea from the Chinese who were forced to take opium in trade. It was all quite well known; it was simply also well ignored. The world was full of evils and Rose knew it just as well as Jane did. People who claimed not to know must shut their eyes very tightly.

They had to pick their evils, and Jane picked survival.

"I'm sorry." Rose did look a little sorry. "I should not have said that. But I must tell you, Jane, I am not giving in on this sugar business. You read me the pamphlet, for pity's sake! You read me the story of the slaves still living on those islands, and how they are treated in the name of the sugar trade. You were the one who said we ought to have a way to stop it."

"Well, *we don't!*" Jane took a deep breath. Let it out, slowly. Just as their mother had always told her to do. "I don't think about changing the world any more, Rose. I don't even think about getting married and having a home of my own. I think about weighing out our porridge to the last ounce and how thin we will be when the last grain in the pail is gone. I think about how hard Emery is working and how thin she is already becoming. I worry about our contract to pay our lease. Why don't you join me in worrying about *those?*"

Jane hadn't expected any of those words to tumble out. She'd been full of them all along and never said them. Now that she heard them herself, she could hear the fear in them. She was afraid.

Of course, Rose was right. Rose had always been right. And Jane didn't want to give up her own principles out of fear. She didn't want Rose to be afraid, either.

Rose stood for a moment, head still pointed down; she looked as though she was looking at the floor. The way she did sometimes when she was thinking.

"All right," she said, coming forward to find Jane by touch, and then squeeze her arm with one hand. It wasn't a hug, but it was some sort of signal of peace. "I will join you in that. You shouldn't have to do it alone. I didn't think about how it was weighing on you."

Jane opened her mouth to say that it wasn't. But it was. She did the sums over and over again every night, adjusting this number and that, trying to find a combination of figures that resulted in them having slightly more money for food.

Thank goodness there *was* no money for dresses, or entertainments, or anything special of that sort. Had she one decent pair of gloves, she might try again to find a husband.

And that would be foolish. Men were weak reeds. She and her sisters needed to rely upon themselves.

But Rose apparently understood the snort. "I don't wish to fight, Jane. Not with you. We ought to stick together, as Mother always said. But I'm not giving up. Just as you say, I'll join you in worrying about the money."

Rose wasn't good with math. It hampered her a little, not being able to write it down, and she had no patience for doing sums with pebbles the way their mother had devised.

But wouldn't anything be better than losing themselves in a pool of fear? Jane was drowning in it. She didn't want Rose in it with her, but perhaps together they could find a way out.

"Honestly," said Jane, "I would welcome the company."

THE CUSTOMER THE BICKERINGS ALL REFERRED TO AS MRS. Baby finally gathered up her strength and her children. "Thank you, Miss Bickering, you know I'll be back."

She was always tired, always had children clinging to her skirts as well as the baby who toddled around the shop with great delight. Fortunately, the baby was too short to reach any of the counters, Anna thought, or all the loaves would be sticky.

"Yes, of course, come again," Anna was saying when the miracle occurred.

A man finally offered her some help.

"Miss Bickering." His bulging arms and rattling toolbox shoved his way through the door.

Anna had come a long way from being alarmed whenever a man came in, and this one made her heart sing. It was the carpenter, the legendary carpenter! He'd finally returned.

"Oh! Don't leave! Don't move!" Then a moment of remembering how many days and nights they had waited for him. "You said you would return tomorrow! You might have mentioned that *tomorrow* means something different to you!" Then, just as quickly, back to gratitude. "Come right in. Yes, please do!"

There were a few customers standing about gossiping, and Anna had half-enjoyed it just a moment before, but now she was glad of an excuse to send them packing.

When she'd bustled them all out, she nearly lay across the counter, her arms extended over it entreatingly, towards him. "You are going to refinish the counters. Oh, I cannot tell you what this means to me."

The carpenter had a thick neck, too, that contrasted with his sheepish expression. "I'm sorry to make you wait, ma'am. A floor collapsed down by the Queen's Mews, and—"

"No no, no no no! Never you mind!" Anna knew she was giddy with excitement and didn't care. "Please! Come in! Sit down! Oh no, you can't. I mean, please, be comfortable! When will you begin? Are you going to fix the door as well? My apologies, sir, did I have your name?"

"It's Mr. Harding, ma'am, and never you worry, I'll have those counters smooth before you know it. Unless there's some other floor disaster. Mrs. Scrope wasn't as excited about the fixing of the door."

Her heart was thumping for a carpenter. The giddiness was just a heartbeat away from alarm. "Wasn't excited about it? I don't need her to be excited about it, Mr. Harding, I need her to pay for it! We had a bargain!"

"I'm sure, but I only know what she said. Mrs. Scrope says the door works fine, and she's the one paying the bill."

Anna's eyes narrowed. She had been holding on to the last

vestiges of her good breeding for weeks and *weeks* and it had done nothing for her. Lord Zachary's sister had looked at her as if she were a chimney sweep. By all that was holy, she'd wrestle like one.

"I'm paying half the bill, Mr. Harding. Three and six from me, as well as Mrs. Scrope. So you have to suit me as well."

The fellow's massive shoulders just shrugged. "I'm only collecting from her." But he looked worried.

"You'll be happy to go with me, then, to meet her and sort this out."

That hit him between the eyes; apparently she wasn't the only one who found Mrs. Scrope unpleasant. "It's really not a concern, ma'am." Mr. Harding looked around the shop with eyes that saw every join of the boards. "Seven shillings *is* a good bit of money. I don't have a ladder today to look at that door, but see here." He dropped his voice as if it were a secret discussion. "I've got some wood I need to clear out. I can knock together a few stools for you, if you like."

"Chairs." She said it like *chocolate*. "Chairs. That would be glorious, Mr. Harding. Four chairs? What would it cost for a table?"

Jane would not give her a farthing for furniture. But Anna was tired of eating on the floor.

"Not chairs with a back and all, but stools. Two, though, not four. I could fit in two stools with the seven shillings, and do those shelves too. You *did* want the shelves smoothed up."

"And the door?"

He just rolled his eyes dismissively. "The door's five minutes. We'll get to it another day. It's not a problem. Say five pence more."

Anna wanted to tell *him* to try opening and closing it all day. "No, the *same price*, Mr. Harding."

"I've got to eat too. I can do the counter and shelves *and* the stools. What's a little problem with the door, as long as it closes? You don't know when I can get back here; floors collapse, you know."

Anna wanted somewhere to sit in her sitting room. Wanted it till she *dreamt* of it. But maybe wanting that equaled wanting everything that used to go with a sitting room that she no longer had.

At important moments in life, a person has to look deep inside themselves and make their own decisions about what is important. Anna had such a moment.

Two stools upstairs would be constant negotiation between the four of them.

But two stools down here...

And she *wanted* them. She was allowed to want things. She had feelings, too.

She looked toward the door where Mrs. Baby had gone.

"Do the chairs, and we'll have them down here, Mr. Harding, so make them nice. We have a few tired customers from time to time and they should be able to wait in comfort."

"Out here."

"Out here."

"For *customers*."

"For customers, yes."

He'd never heard the like. Well, Anna hadn't either. But this was her bakery and her customers and Mrs. Baby needed a chair.

And sometimes, in between customers, Anna might be able to sit like a lady again.

"Sure, I can do that," the man muttered, eyes already measuring the space to where the glass in the wall began, and Anna felt a cool sense of triumph, that one thing in her day at least responded to her control.

MISS HAYES.

Emery had slept a little and baked the afternoon bread, and she was filled with the joy of perfect crusts. None of the morning customers had complained about the look of the bread. And they'd sold so many more loaves by sheer numbers than they ever had before.

There was the sneaking danger that this new bread would dry more over the next day and fall below the weight required by law for each loaf size. But she'd already taken that chance. The others might not even think of it, as they'd let her ask the questions of their old neighborhood baker, who had unwittingly tutored her on the pertinent laws.

Sal and Jordan had fallen asleep while Jane was trying to teach them arithmetic, but that didn't worry Emery; she slept at odd times of day, so why shouldn't they?

None of them noticed Emery sliding out the back door.

Outside, there was a little breeze in the mews. Emery intended to make her day complete. All she wanted was to see Miss Hayes. She shoved her bonnet back from her face like she always did. She wore it to please propriety, but she wouldn't let it block her view.

Leaving the mews through a tiny passageway to Bear Street, she encountered...a lot of other people. The road was full of fine carriages and market carts, and on the pavements serious men, with scowling shaven faces under stovepipe hats, and ladies carrying every kind of load in their hands or on their hearts, all bustled past each other in every direction. The smells of warm bodies, horse manure, and purposeful boots all mixed.

Emery had imagined that she would just walk out the door and into the beautiful woman. She had before. That was the way her life would go now. That was the triumph of pure flour. The world was turning for *her* today. So where was Miss Hayes?

More importantly, what was she to do until the lady appeared?

Bear Street had shop windows; Emery knew them all already. She got to know them a great deal better strolling up and down the street, then up and down again, then a third time. She could see one shopkeeper, nose twitching with agitation, peering back at her and considering calling for help.

Ought she to give up, go home, come back later?

She looked up towards the rooftops. Perhaps she ought to have found a way to a roof. That was what she needed, to look down and see everything below. Miss Hayes, she felt sure, would shine like a star even in the middle of the afternoon on the Bear Street pavement.

There she was. The swinging, shining curls of golden-brown hair peeked from under her bonnet; she bounced down the steps from a red front door across the road. She paused and saw Emery. She didn't smile.

Emery tried to enjoy the look, anyway. Like her plans for the bread, this had worked too.

Then Miss Hayes crossed the street and drew closer.

Once near, she had to look up a little to meet Emery's eyes. "Oh dear," she said softly, "I've encouraged you, haven't I?"

"No, you haven't—I mean—" Why couldn't Emery be encouraged? Emery *wanted* to be encouraged.

Seeing her confusion, Miss Hayes shook that glorious head of curls, just a little. "Don't fret, I didn't mean that I didn't mean it. I mean, I meant everything I said. You know what I mean. I just meant... this is the worst conversation ever, isn't it? You want to meet the rest of the ladies in the neighborhood, that's what I mean."

"You mean, instead of visiting you?"

"Yes!" Her eyes weren't twinkling, but she nodded vehemently.

Emery narrowed her eyes a little. "No, I don't want that. I want to visit you."

"Oh, dear." Miss Hayes took in a breath as she stepped back. "I've gone and done something rash again, haven't I?"

"Nothing terrible. May I walk with you a little way, at least?" Emery had never been so willing to be seen. She had made a mountain of bread with her own two hands—well, plus Jordan and Sal. She had triumphed. She could do anything, including walking with Miss Hayes of the flirtatious curls to the end of the street.

Something startled in the back of Miss Hayes' eyes. Something glad for a response that wasn't quick to blame. "Yes, let's walk a little, Miss Bickering."

THE DOOR SCRAPED OPEN, ITS FAMILIAR WARNING THAT A customer had entered.

"We haven't any more quartern loaves or rolls, but I can sell you a slice—" Rose began the little speech reflexively now, she used it so much. Why had she ever been afraid of talking to customers?

"Thank you, Miss Rose. I've already decided what I'll have."

Mr. Russell's voice, rich with smiles, was familiar too, even as it was still new. Rose stood straighter. "Mr. Russell! I'm glad you've come in."

"Are you?" She heard him approach the counter, staying properly on his side but leaning towards her. "I haven't seen you out and about."

"You haven't called here either," Rose retorted, then wished she hadn't. What if he hadn't wanted to call?

But Mr. Russell only said, "I wanted to have a chance to talk to you without your sisters about, and buying bread seemed to be the only way to do it."

"So... you are here to buy bread?"

"I'd like a half pound of the half-peck, and slice it for me, very thinly, please." He reconsidered. "Unless it poses a difficulty."

Rose already had the massive knife lined up against her knuckles, making it impossible for her to cut herself. "Not at all! But it will dry so quickly; are you sure that's what you want?"

"Yes. I want thinly sliced bread, which I will gnaw if I have to, while you tell me something about yourself, and let you tell me something about me. Is that fair?"

Rose felt her insides warm more than the summer day allowed. "More than fair. I'm..." Why shouldn't she just say it? He was the only man she'd ever met. Perhaps he'd be the only man who ever would express any interest in her. "I'm only sorry it isn't more bread."

"The lovely thing is, when it's gone, I will come right back here for more," said Mr. Russell in a voice that shared secrets.

THAT NIGHT AFTER SUPPER, THE SISTERS SAT IN A CIRCLE ON their carpetless floor.

Jane rubbed Emery's sore feet, and Anna brushed her hair dry after her bath. Emery just lay there with a ridiculous smile on her face that made no sense, given that she was half-asleep. There was still some palpable tension in the room, but Emery's silly smile and the quiet fought against the strain.

At night, the bakery oven held only a few banked coals, but their warmth seeped upward. It was close in their sitting room, even with all the space.

Rose's head was bent, her fingers detangling Emery's long hair. "I know you heard all the same stories about the slave plantations as I did."

"The sugar protests were twenty years ago!" Jane sounded tired. They were all tired. Anna's head was worn out by a day of constantly bouncing emotions; she had a vinegar wrap for her aching head. And even if secretly pleased about something, Emery was obviously too tired to talk.

Not that Emery usually talked.

No, thought Rose, she and Emery did little the talking. They left it to their older sisters.

But Rose was through with that.

She was a grown lady; she knew not to walk into the street to be trampled by cows, and her opinion meant as much as anyone's.

It was all of them she had to talk to, not just Jane. If she could speak up in front of strangers—if she could talk to *Mr. Russell*—why couldn't she speak to her own sisters?

It was weightier. Which was why she had to do it. "Mother used to sob over those pamphlets, just sob."

Jane sighed. It wasn't a simple sigh of irritation. Her tiredness was in it, too. "The war changed things, Rose. You don't even really remember when Mother first got those pamphlets."

"But I heard them. Because she kept them. And read them. To us."

"The war, and no more money. You've made a hundred cakes, Rose, we all have."

Rose had been worrying that idea over, but hadn't intended to bring it up. Trust Jane to do it. "Father loved cake."

"No. Mother made cakes for all of us because it was all we *had*." Jane usually sounded above it all, but now she sounded bitter, openly bitter. "We couldn't go to parties anymore. We couldn't have roast beef. And then, a few years later, we couldn't see Father ever again, either."

They were all silent for a moment.

But Jane, though her voice was thick, went on. "The one thing she could afford for us was cake. Cake for our birthdays. Cake for Easter."

Anna's voice, a little thin but still strong enough to hear, piped in from where she sat leaning her head against the wall. "In ladies' houses, they have cake for breakfast, every day. All *kinds* of cake." The longing for cake was palpable.

"And people put sugar in their tea, and their coffee. Even in chocolate." Jane finished one of Emery's feet, moved on to the other; Emery smothered a little groan.

It was awful, thinking about how tired Emery was. How tired they all were.

Jane was still talking. "We won't have husbands or gowns or homes of our own. But we can still by God have cake."

"Oh, don't swear," Anna moaned from her spot.

Emery stirred. "Enough fussing, my—my chickadees. Did you not see? We sold half again as much bread as we usually do. Jane, haven't you done the totals?"

"Not yet. I'm tired of trying to make the numbers come right." She put out her hand and stroked Rose's forearm; Rose patted her hand. The other two didn't even notice.

"Do it." Emery's eyes were closed, but her voice vehement. "So much bread. Did none of you notice? The bread today was completely different!"

"I noticed, the crust crackled so. I thought it was from the heat," said Rose.

"No. The dough we sold today wasn't kneaded at all. It just rose. Since yesterday."

"Wasn't *kneaded?*" "Is that bread at all?" "I'm getting the till."

That last from Jane, and the sound of the rattling box sounded in the room's quiet.

Emery slit her eyes open to see it. And smiled.

"Why," Jane poked into the compartments, "there are many coins in here! I must take the total, but I can see from staring at them every night. This *is* more."

"I have done it, my darlings, I have done it! This is the triumph of pure flour."

Jane stared as though Emery gave *her* a head ache. "That makes no sense."

Emery just put a finger alongside her nose and winked at her sister. "Oh, yes it does."

"I'll do the totals, but... Emery! You are a genius!"

"I agree! But must admit to a happy accident. Jordan made a dough that I let stand overnight. I wasn't sure what to do with it. Finally I just baked it. It was marvellous. I went from there."

"Why didn't you tell us what you were going to do?" Anna had sat up against the wall, her vinegar wrap falling into her lap. "Honestly, are we in this together or not?"

"Isn't this together enough?" Emery tried to smile at Anna, then looked away. Anna did not like having to decide whether to be happy or annoyed.

"And we owe the twins for this. We must let them stay," Emery added. "They only eat half as much as one of us."

"The two of them together eat *twice* what you do," Jane put in her sour contradiction.

Anna wanted this situation back in hand, and Emery had certainly proved a point. "Very well, but how much more bread can you make with their help?"

Emery was silent a moment.

"They've already paid their way so far," she said slowly. "They're bright enough to clean up after me, keep things clear... We did twice the loaves today, my titmice, twice!"

"Not really!" Rose breathed out her hope.

"That is a *guess*." Jane was sharp. "And you are worn through."

"We must try it." Anna, still unhappy from the ache in her head, put an end to the discussion for now. As she always did. "We must try it because we have no choice. Once you feed a stray animal, you own an animal."

She was talking about the children, not the bread. She didn't understand the triumph of pure flour.

"They're not *animals*," Emery muttered.

"Aren't they?" Anna sighed tiredly.

Rose sat up, her fingers stilling where she braided Emery's hair. "We must try this. Because I know all of you know what Mother thought about the sugar trade. I know we all ate those cakes. I never told you how sick they made me feel. I should have told Mother. I'm telling you now. And if this is *our* business, then we can choose how to run it. We needn't give up all our principles, not now."

"Not yet," said Jane, sitting back against the wall.

"We can make this work, Jane, I know we can." Rose finished braiding Emery's hair. She rested her palm on her sister's forehead and realized that Emery had fallen asleep.

"She's going to work herself to death." Jane's voice was soft.

"No, she's not. We'll help her more. We'll help you. We can do this! We mustn't give up at the first hurdle, Jane. We have the shop. We have our lease. We have this place. We have each other. And our bread is selling. We have come so far, can't you see?"

"All right, little miss sunshine, all right." Jane's voice sounded as if she might drift away, too. Perhaps they'd all end up sleeping on the floor.

If they did, Rose would go get the quilts and bring them in here.

To prove she still had the strength, she stood and pulled Emery to her feet, walking her, still mostly asleep, to their bedroom.

"We can do this," Rose muttered, almost to herself. "We are on the verge of success, I just know it."

WHEN EMERY WOKE, HER SISTERS WERE STILL SITTING IN the front room, murmuring among themselves.

Surely it wasn't possible to put on both stockings and shoes, and make her way out the door without them noticing?

It was.

She was still so tired, tired down to the bone. But there had to be more to life than bread, even bread of triumph. And if she were to accept Miss Hayes' tentative invitation, she must go out again. Now.

Miss Hayes had the key to a secret door Emery had never thought to seek. Nothing could keep Emery away from finding it.

It helped that Rose was the one facing their room, and that Emery had had plenty of practice walking silently away from her sisters.

SHE'D WOKEN BY CHANCE, WITHOUT A FALLING SPOON, BUT surely she was still in time?

As Emery passed through the bakery, she checked the tubs for the next day. They were all full of the wet dough this time, not just half. She'd mixed them up as she'd baked the afternoon bread, and there they were! Doing their work without her!

It hadn't needed kneading. She could still bend her arms, and there was plenty of dough rising already for the next day.

She'd won.

When she slipped through the mews to meet Miss Jasmine Hayes at the corner of Bear and Castle streets, as they'd arranged, Emery felt, for the first time in her life, content. She felt tall with pride, not just too tall. She felt ready for anything. She could conquer anything.

"Well! You look bright-eyed." Miss Hayes at least did not say *eager*. Emery knew she looked eager, she did; but she didn't want to admit that, not yet.

Miss Hayes went on, in a rush. "Don't let anyone push you into anything you don't wish. Not even in conversation. You needn't tell anyone any more of your life than you wish. None of us do."

The street was still light in the summer evening, and they could hear their shoes knock against the flagstones of the pavement, so few other people were about.

"Who is we?"

"All of us, of course." Miss Hayes' eyes peeped around the edge of her bonnet with a look that was coy and sly and secretive, and Emery didn't want her to tell everything. Emery wanted to find it out for herself.

Two crossings later, down the stairs to a thickset kitchen door, she found it.

It must be the house's kitchen, thought Emery, but when the door opened to Jasmine's triple knock, it was a door to another world.

Somehow it was just what she'd expected, and yet so much more. It was women. Lots of women, a dozen or more. But they were all so different, Emery almost couldn't see them all. There were women who were elegantly dressed in evening wear, two of them holding each other's hands (*holding each other's hands*); there were washing women with hands reddened by lye. There was a woman with skin darkened by sun, and thick black hair that spoke of a Welsh background; there were two women with skin even darker, of African descent, and hair just as black but in tightly wrapped braids. There was a pale freckled lass barely out of childhood, with hair so bright an orange that it seemed to glow; there was a fat woman with gray wisps of hair escaping her linen cap that might have three score years at least. Emery couldn't take it all in. She was blinded by flashes of excitement, excitement at their very existence, and even though she'd never met them, she understood that everyone there felt the same way. Even though nothing was said, it was palpable that, in that room, they were renegades. Palpable enough almost to touch.

"Oh no, Hayes, not another panting puppy," said one woman as the door closed behind them, and Emery was afraid she was about to be sent out; but the only response was general laughter, and someone passed Emery a teacup.

"Whiskey or tea? You must drink something brown to stay," said the fat woman, and Emery thought this might be her kitchen. Surely she was not the mistress of the house? She looked like its cook.

Whiskey would put her to sleep. "Tea, thank you," said Emery gratefully, and sat next to Miss Hayes on a low stool, leaning at the edge of a massive kitchen table that bore more pits and stains even than the counter of the Ladies' Own Bakery.

"Tea drunk from Hayes' shoe, no doubt," another woman called, batting her eyes exaggeratedly, and Emery flushed, wondering if they all knew exactly how smitten she was with Miss Hayes' curls.

Likely they did. What would it matter, if they all shared the same sorts of dreams?

But were they all vying with her for Miss Hayes' attention?

Emery sipped her tea, kept her mouth shut, watched for competition, and enjoyed herself tremendously through her first evening in a whole new world she'd waited a lifetime to find.

ZACHARY HALF-CONSIDERED FINDING AN INN AND A TALL tankard as his cab pulled away, leaving him in front of number 17 in Leicester Square.

He loved his sister, of course, in the way one loved sisters. But Cecily did not understand why he lived alone in this garret and worked on his painting. And she didn't understand why her impending marriage was not the most important thought in his mind, every moment of every day, as it was for her.

He didn't want her in the square, actually. He had settled here precisely so that he could not be expected to appear each day at breakfast or nuncheon, could not be expected to eat crab biscuit or anything like it at a table that was opulent, shiny, and dull.

Zachary needed something with a little edge to it to wake up his eyes and get himself to paint. He needed flaws. He needed flower petals that had already crumbled, cracked porcelain, even torn canvas. He needed something real.

Cecily did not like flaws, and number 18 Leicester Square, though possessed of an illustrious history, was too flawed for her.

Best. He did not want his sister underfoot, or that porky earl she was marrying. He wanted to paint.

And he wanted to be free to do it by daylight. This was the last time he would let his family keep him away from his work all day, the very last time.

It was so late that it was finally full dark, and Zachary

abandoned the idea of ale. He'd do some painting and fall asleep.

He didn't expect his progress up the stairs to be blocked by a sleeping woman.

It was one of the baking sisters; it must be. He didn't really know one from the other, but there were no other ladies that would be sleeping on his stairs.

Her head was pillowed on her arm, linen skirts draping over her knees and hiding her shoes. She might be interesting to draw. But he couldn't get past her to his pencils.

She wasn't small, either.

This was difficult.

While he stood there wondering what to do, a man in a rough leather jerkin coat rounded the corner from Bear Street and stopped to stare at Zachary standing in the door.

"Are you going in or out?" said this odd apparition.

He wore a half-crushed beaver hat, had lank black curls, and contained at least four large ales himself, judging by the slight weave in his steps. No, whiskey, Zachary revised his supposition as the man grew closer and a slight sour cloud preceded him. Surely that was too pungent to be gin.

The fellow peered around the doorjamb at the sleeping woman on the stairs.

"Oh, her," he said.

"Do you know the young woman?"

"We've met," the newcomer said briefly.

Well. Did this improve the situation?

"Might you assist me in helping her upstairs?"

"Don't know. I'm pretty tight myself. She must have put away quite a bit."

Zachary looked down his nose at the other fellow. "I don't smell any liquor on *her*."

"Not like you could after I arrived," the man said cheerfully enough. "All right, get under her arms and I'll get her feet."

Zachary didn't feel right about letting a drunkard carry the woman's legs, but after all, Zachary was right there. "Very well."

He really didn't think the woman was drunk, but she certainly didn't wake as Zachary slid his hands under her armpits and tried to haul her up.

It didn't work.

Her arms just flopped.

Sighing a little and closing his eyes and grateful that his sister was not here to see this, Zachary slid his forearms under her armpits and clasped his hands just across her waist, below her.... Well, her breasts. It was still easier to paint them than say so, though Zachary was getting better. He subscribed to the school of artistic thought that believed in reality and brutal reference to it; it was just that his decades of upbringing had all been in the opposite direction.

The drunk man grabbed her knees by standing between them, and would have been scandalous had he made the least attempt to see up her dress, or feel her any farther.

No, it was already pretty scandalous, Zachary had to admit.

The fellow didn't help much, either, Zachary thought as he hauled his neighbor upwards. He went slowly, stair by stair. But the drunk fellow wasn't hurting either, and he didn't let the woman's legs bang on the steps.

"Decent of you," said the drunk man holding her knees.

"Couldn't get up the stairs otherwise," said Zachary, puffing at each step.

"Nah, you're doing something decent."

"Am I?" Awkwardly shuffling backwards, Zachary pulled the young lady along the hallway to lean against the door to the rooms shared by the baking sisters.

Then he was seized by a misgiving. "This *is* her home, isn't it?"

The drunkard rubbed the stubble on his chin. "I think so?"

Right. Zachary leaned down. "You live here, don't you, miss?"

"Pure flour," the young woman said, and turned over. "I did it with pure flour."

Zachary regarded the door for a moment. "Should we knock?"

"Best not to," his co-conspirator decided.

"Perhaps not," said Zachary in turn.

He followed the drunk man down the hall, and was surprised to see him disappear inside the tiny door that Zachary had always considered some sort of cupboard.

No, Zachary thought as he climbed the stairs to his garret. This neighborhood wouldn't suit his sister at all.

Episode 8: You can still get burned

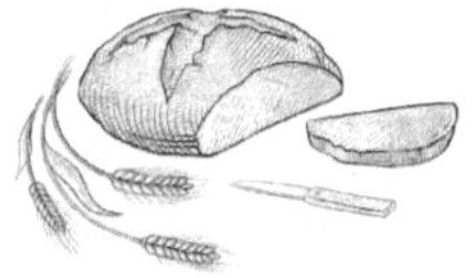

Puffy had a knack for arriving when the bakery was crowded, he reflected as he stepped down to the pavement.

It had taken him some time to come to terms with his embarrassment from his previous visit. But to his credit, he was a fellow who did not dwell on his embarrassment, though he felt it keenly. He contemplated it a little, and put it away.

He didn't learn much from it, but we all have our faults.

As soon as he pushed open the sticky door, he felt the kind of accomplishment in his chest that he had felt very few times in his life. Once, when he'd shot one more pheasant than Lord Rawleigh at his winter house party. Once when he'd won a bet with a toss-haired rapscallion at his club, when everyone had been behind the other fellow. Very satisfying. And, though we mustn't think ill of him, once the day he'd woken to find his mother had passed away in her sleep. Because she had made Puffy do exactly as she said every single day of her life until she departed this world, and Puffy had decades of thoughts of his own pent up, just waiting for an airing.

"Miss Bickering?"

"Yes?" The little goddess barely turned and looked at him, but he could still see those deep brown eyes, as warm as velvet, and the gleam of a curl tucked behind her ear, just behind a smattering of flour.

"I'd like—"

"I do apologize," she said in that way shopkeepers had that meant they didn't apologize at all, "there's a line just here if you'll wait until it is your turn?"

He waited, and when all the women in front of him had bought their halfpenny loaves or big quartern loaves, he stood at a rutted, cut-up wooden plank looking at the most lovely woman he'd ever seen, and he had to say something.

"I'm so glad it is you and not your sister."

The young lady shook her head as though not hearing him correctly. "Did you wish to buy some bread, sir?"

"Not really, no."

"This is a bakery." She let those words fall between them, hard, and waited for him to grasp that he had better do something about them.

"I have come to see you, Miss Bickering."

The little river of chatter flowing all around the room quieted a little.

Her eyes shooting about, Miss Bickering leaned over the counter. "Did those men from the hotel kitchen tell you to come in here?"

"I don't talk to men in hotel kitchens." Then Puffy felt that this might reflect poorly on the conversation he was having now. He didn't wish to be condescending. "Not usually."

"They try to pull the most terrible jokes. We are not streetwalkers, sir, we are bakers."

"Naturally."

"So if you would like some bread, please say how much you would like."

"And if I don't want some bread?"

Her cheeks flushed, which only made her prettier. Why was it that she was so much prettier than any young lady in a spotless white gown that Puffy had met at a society affair? Was it only the color in her cheeks?

No, it was also the way her eyes snapped. "Then please leave."

"Miss Bickering, I wish to pay a social call."

Then for the first time he saw her look surprised, and a little lost.

"Sir," she said, "I am in no position to receive a social call."

She could have said many other things, Puffy supposed, but that simple declaration cut it. This was a lost gem, a princess in hiding, and he was going to find out who she was.

"Is there no time I might make a visit?"

"None come to mind, sir." And then the young lady paused before gesturing to the next customer to come forward. "But...thank you."

"Yes, I see." Puffy looked about. She was a lost gem conducting pressing business. "I often drive through this neighborhood of an afternoon. I believe I will take a turn around the square this evening when you might be closed, and perhaps we will see each other."

"See each other?" She drew herself up, clearly offended. "In a carriage?"

Oh, she was magnificent.

"Perhaps our eyes will meet," said Puffy, and smiled at her.

Though he didn't realize it, that smile was transformative. Because Puffy was a middle-aged man with a man's spreading middle, disappearing hair, and skin beginning to show spots of age.

But when he smiled, all his innocent good intentions showed, and because they were real, they were persuasive.

"Perhaps not," said the gentle lady behind the pitted counter, "but...thank you for the kind thought, sir."

Breadless, Puffy walked outside and stepped up into his brougham with more than usual spring in his step. He'd actually talked to the correct young lady this time. This was progress.

He never once had a thought so common as that if he wished to do the lady a good turn, he ought to have bought some bread.

THE BICKERING SISTERS HAD LEARNED TO WATCH THE tailor's across the way to determine when it was time to close.

The tailor, Mr. Morley, hadn't bothered them about things glimpsed through windows in weeks. Jane watched to see when he would flip his card to *Closed*, and never thought that she was peeking in *his* window. He must own a clock, and she was simply taking advantage of it.

She wasn't sure, and didn't want to stare out the window at the tailor's, but she thought closing time was getting close.

Mrs. Talker, as Jane thought of her, usually spent ten minutes picking out her bread. The two of them were alone in the shop, with minutes to go until closing time, and Jane didn't think she'd make it.

"My husband does prefer the inner part of the loaf, you know, but it is so handy to have the crusts. Little Billy loves to gnaw on the crust, and that keeps him occupied, you know, for an hour or more at a time."

Jane nodded while looking over the still pockmarked counter at Little Billy. Little Billy had piggy eyes and a fat stomach, and Jane thought she could already tell what Little Billy was going to look like when he was forty.

She was trying to think of new, clever ways to say "Make your choice and move on, please," but it was difficult when the shop was empty.

"There's only so much crust on one of your twopenny loaves, you know," said Mrs. Talker.

"I do know." *I sell the bread*, she did not say. She knew everything there was to know about it. She stared at it all day.

"I'd like a loaf with just a little more crust on it, please."

Jane wondered what would happen if she beat the woman with one of the loaves she said wasn't crusty enough. But there was little Billy. Little Billy would be a witness. He'd tell.

Suddenly realizing the answer, Jane turned to a tray behind her, blocking the woman's sight.

She waggled her rear about, bending forward and back, and did everything she could think of to pretend that she was examining their last twopenny loaves very closely.

"Here you are, madame, the very crustiest loaf we have."

"Oh!" Mrs. Talker's eyes were wide. "I never thought of checking! The crustiest?"

Jane leaned an elbow on the counter. "Trust me. The very crustiest."

"I'll have it, thank you so much!"

"Not at all, madame, we want every customer to be happy at the Ladies' Own Bakery."

"Is that the name? Oh, how nice. Though the name leaves the gentlemen out, doesn't it? And nothing is ever quite complete without a gentleman."

Jane gritted her teeth. "I've never found that to be so. Two pennies, if you please."

THE NEXT MORNING, ROSE HAD SOLD THE LAST OF yesterday's twopenny loaves at half price when Mr. Russell came in.

She was full of the excitement of actually *having* day-old bread. There had been so much bread lately that not everything sold the day before. It made them all hopeful. Moreover, Jane had pronounced it financially prudent for them to eat some of the bread rather than sell it, and they'd had a filling supper.

It was all too much to blurt out to Mr. Russell. Even if Jane hadn't just come in with half-peck loaves. Rose felt better lately about having Jane for a sister, but she wasn't about to spill her innermost thoughts to Mr. Russell while Jane watched.

IT WAS TOO LATE TO BUY FOR BREAKFAST AND TOO EARLY for dinner. Jane had a deep suspicion the Russell man had been watching to see when Rose was alone in the shop, but didn't ask. Among other reasons, she did not want to hear something sticky about how the color of Rose's hair glowed across the square, or some nonsense. He looked full of nonsense.

"Oh! Miss...Bickering." He had clearly been about to say *Rose.* Jane just stared at him. "Yes?"

"I meant...yes, good morning, Miss Bickering, and the younger Miss Bickering as well. All the Misses Bickering, of course."

And then he just stood there, hat in his hand, broad shoulders climbing toward his head and face turning red.

Finally, Jane couldn't derive even the tiniest bit of amusement. "Did you want some bread, Mr. Russell?"

"Yes! Yes, and..." Was he going to do it? He was. "To see if

Miss Rose Bickering would attend a speech I am giving in the park tonight."

"The park." Jane pointedly looked toward the window. The park was an overgrown clump of trees and weeds. There was no room for speech-giving, even to such a small crowd as Mr. Russell might draw.

"Just in the park. By the gate." He wasn't giving up; Jane had to give him credit for that.

And she was taken aback when Rose answered without consulting her. "Yes, Mr. Russell, I would like that."

"Would you? Good! I mean...of course I'd like all of you to attend. We are encouraging signatures for a new petition to the Crown."

"Wonderful," said Jane, who didn't know what the petition was and didn't care. "We'll have to see how we do today, Mr. Russell."

"Oh, we have just as much bread as yesterday—today we really will sell twice as much!" Rose's smile was infectious.

Jane wished she could be infected. "I meant, you might be tired."

"I'm sure I won't. Please don't trouble to call for us, Mr. Russell, it is such a short walk."

Was that *Rose*, bolder and bolder? There wasn't much Jane could do but agree. "We shall see you this evening, Mr. Russell."

The gentleman bobbed his head and turned and left, apparently forgetting he'd claimed he wanted bread.

Well, he'd be back.

"You're not encouraging Mr. Russell, are you, Rose?"

Her youngest sister had a smile playing around the corners of her mouth that was new. "And why shouldn't I encourage him?"

"Why should you? What is he to you?"

"Jane, you've never grasped that men are *people*. If one

doesn't speak to them, how will one ever know what they might or might not be?"

"Hundreds of women avoid speaking to men in London every day. I must go out for soap. Do watch the place. I suppose your secret lover can come back if he likes."

"He's not a secret, he came in the *front door*."

But Rose was still smiling that little smile. And she hadn't denied the word *lover*.

Jane liked being more in charity with Rose, but what was she supposed to do about this?

"I'll be back," Jane said shortly.

BY THE TIME JANE HAD FETCHED HER BONNET AND GLOVES, she found that a carriage had pulled up to the pavement right in front of number 17 Leicester Square.

Just as she stepped out their door, the carriage door opened as well.

The inside was richly appointed in leather, with patterned silk curtains at its tiny window and a bearskin rug inside.

Why it needed a bearskin rug in July, she hesitated to even wonder.

"Dalby, you're a horse's ass," said that pompous blond lordling that Anna found so entrancing, just as he tripped and rolled out of the carriage.

Uproarious laughter came from its depths, and Jane swung wide to avoid it, and the lordling, before walking on her way.

She wouldn't look back. The fellow must have seen her half a dozen times since he'd asked her to pose for him, and never once gave her any sign of recognition. Jane didn't know whether it was better or worse than the noises the hotel servants made as she walked past. She disliked all of them.

When she reached the corner, she wanted to cross Green

Street, but the rain and horses' hooves had churned it up into a mess.

There were more men there, setting paving stones into the pavement itself, and one paver leaned on his shovel and yelled the same sort of words the hotel men yelled. Though not in French.

Before Jane could even lift her chin to prove his nastiness did not affect her, the paver's neighbor casually knocked his shovel away.

While the paver tried to keep from falling, his casual colleague kicked a board into place over the worst of the churned mud and horse manure in the street.

"Just a step or two, my lady," he said, and he put out his hand.

Jane took it.

His hand was hard in places, worn, dirty, and very welcome. He simply helped her over the mud.

And at the end, he didn't whistle or call, or imply she was a prostitute, or leer at her. Nor did he ignore her.

He looked right into her eyes, bold as you please, and nodded, tipping his hat. "There you are."

When he turned away and applied himself to his own shovel, Jane felt the world was a much sunnier place.

EMERY WAVED LIKE A PRINCESS IN A CARRIAGE AS SHE processed through the shop on her way to the bakery. "You may all thank me later. I imagine my birthday will be quite an affair this year! I'd like something larger than a basket to store my clothes. Perhaps also some new clothes. Yes, you're welcome, you're welcome."

Ever since the day Emery always referred to as her "triumph", Emery's time had become even more erratic. She slipped out of the bakery, and indeed out of the building, at all hours, but even Anna no longer scolded her. She had dark circles under her eyes as she made her royal wave, and at least two of her adoring subjects thought she might be wearing yesterday's dress, but she was grinning so broadly that no one could contradict her.

Even Jane just shook her head and smiled, while Rose swept the crumbs of the morning from behind the counters and Anna pretended to tap her chin with thought over the question of Emery's birthday. "Yes, I can see you need more this year than cake—"

All the sisters groaned.

Anna's eyes actually sparkled as she laughed. "What sort of jewels do you like, my lady? Pearls?"

"Pearls are for queens, and queens are no fun at all. Nor diamonds, thank you very much. Rubies? I'd like some rubies."

Jane felt her own eyes crinkle as she looked at Emery. Aunt Eden had always proclaimed her the plainest sister, but today, even with her shadowed eyes and uncombed hair, she burned with an energy that gave Aunt Eden the lie. With her hair shining, rested and fed, Emery would look spectacular in rubies.

"No lace?" Anna couldn't resist. Emery had never liked lace, not even when she was tiny.

"Of course, no lace!" Emery brushed at her skirt to get rid of even the offending idea. "Velvet, please, and satin for shine if you must."

"Certainly, if we must," said Rose, as she opened the door and swept out the crumbs.

Over the shoes of a man standing there, just about to knock.

"Oh, Miss Rose. There's a gentleman there!" called Anna. "Were you about to knock, sir?"

Rose stood back and held the door wide open. "You don't have to knock, it's a shop!"

"Is it?" The fellow seemed bemused to be surrounded by ladies. "And where is the proprietor?"

"We are the proprietors," Rose's pride showed all over her.

"Eh...of this bakery."

"Yes," said Rose.

"I'm looking for the baker," the man said, his coat flapping behind him as he bent closer. As if she couldn't hear.

"I am *the* baker," Emery assured him. "Did you wish to buy something?"

"No, I have a matter of business to attend. Seriously, girls, I must speak with the owner."

The air in the shop became noticeably cooler.

Anna went to stand before the man, with her hands clasped at her waist. "If you have a business matter, then state it, as you've found the business owners."

The man looked around at all four sisters. He still looked confused. Jane just shook her head.

He shrugged. "Whatever game this is, you won't be so amused by it when I tell you it regards the fees for your water."

A deathly pall fell over the place.

"Please excuse me, sir," Anna choked out, "what did you say?"

Jane was leaning on the counter with both hands and her face had gone grayish white.

"Your rent, as we call it, for your water service, ladies." The gentleman had several huge sheets of foolscap in his hands, folded in all directions; he ruffled through them. "It is July and I am collecting for the second quarter. Though I see in my records that you have not paid the first quarter either." He had an average face, broad cheekbones that looked a bit soft, and he glared a glare at them all that he had clearly practiced in front of a mirror. He wanted to look intimidating. "I am not one of those who lets his business accounts get in arrears, you know."

"We wouldn't know. We have no arrangement with you for water, sir." Anna was still standing tall in front of him, though she was shorter than he by several inches.

"Do you have water service?"

"Of course!"

"Have you purchased that service elsewhere?" This agitated him.

Anna felt the first flush of concern that the man would get angry. "No, of course not!"

"And did you think water was free? Your payment is due, madame, and if not arranged today, I can return at the beginning of next week to collect."

"We were not in business the first quarter." Anna kept her distance, in case he showed more temper.

"To the best of my knowledge, you were. The sign outside says Bakery, this is the bakery at the location for which we have contracted water service."

"How much?" Jane's voice was as thin and gray as her face. "How much is it?"

"Ah...your rent is based on the size of the building, with a consideration for the business you are in. Baking, I know," as if someone had said it. No one had. "It's rated here as sixteen pounds for the year, so two quarters are owing and that is eight pounds. Madame."

Anna looked around the room. Rose's head drooped toward the floor; Emery was simply frozen in place, and Jane looked as though she had died but retained the power of speech.

Anna set her shoulders. "Next week, we will be ready. Thank you, sir. Your name?"

"Mr. Babbage. Calvin Babbage."

"Thank you, Mr. Babbage. We are the Misses Bickering. Next week. We will certainly have your payment. Thank you. Next week."

Her *thank you's* were shoving him backwards somehow, and it was only three steps back out of the open door. He tripped a little, backing up over the threshold.

"Misses—"

"Thank you! Rose, close the door." Anna waved a little as Rose closed the door in the man's face.

Emery, whose arms had been aloft and full of imaginary velvet skirts the whole time, dropped them. "Well. I had thought to have some rest today, but…"

"Yes, you must show us all your new recipe for dough, Emery, we'll all help. We had been with the kneading, you know, we will with this."

"We have to make yet *more* bread?" Rose leaned the broom against the wall. "In one day?"

"Every day, I would imagine," Anna said briskly, and that was when Jane thumped against the wall.

And slid down it to disappear behind the counter.

"Jane, did you fall?" Rose followed the wall to the space behind it. Her hand slid down the wall to find Jane sitting on the floor. Rose knelt next to her. "What happened?"

"Didn't you hear?"

"Jane, don't take it so hard. We can do more bread every day. We ought to have another bake at night." Emery moved behind the counter, too. "You're on the floor, you know." She sat down next to her sister.

Anna went round to stand by Emery.

"Didn't you hear?" Jane said again. She looked ghastly. "Eight pounds. *Eight. Pounds.*"

"We weren't even here the first quarter of the year, there

is some mistake there." Anna bent closer. "I'll arrange it with the landlord, never you worry."

"Eight pounds. Four pounds a quarter. A pound and seven shillings a month. A month. Where will we get twenty-seven more shillings a month? Seven shillings a week? We can't do it. It can't be done."

"Yes it can, I just told you—"

But Jane cut Emery off. "We didn't plan for this. We didn't account for this in the reckoning. *I* didn't account for it. You don't understand. We need seven more shillings a *week*. We can't change the prices and we weren't making enough as it was."

"But have you performed all the calculations with the new bread?" Emery shuffled closer.

"Seven shillings a week. *Seven*. Every week. Every *week*. Don't you see, he will want them *every week*? Why doesn't he just take it out of us in blood?"

Rose threw her arms around Jane's shoulders. "It isn't so bad as that!"

"Yes it is. Yes it is."

Anna squashed her knees in next to Emery's and reached over her to take Jane's hand. It was cold. "Jane, don't despair. We will work this out, never fear. There were bound to be tough times, and this is one of those."

"We were already *in* the tough times!" Jane's head thumped into the wall and rocked back and forth. "We can't do this."

"Yes, we can. We can." Anna squeezed her hand. Jane's hand was never this cold.

And her eyes, when she turned to look at Anna, weren't just dark, they were hollow. "*How?*"

Anna, who was truly just grasping the magnitude of the problem, felt her stomach clench. Jane was the one of the four of them who truly grasped money, and she looked as she had when they'd buried their mother.

Well, that day had made Anna the head of the family.

"Together. We can find a way. Bakeries *do*. There are bakeries all over the city who must have the same expenses as we."

"Bakeries *fail* all over the city."

Sober now, Rose kept her arm around Jane.

"But there are bakeries that don't," objected Emery. "Mr. Gruninger who explained the law to me, his bakery has been there for ten years and more."

"What do some bakeries know that others don't?" Rose sounded surprised that there could be such a variable ground of knowledge among the same types of business.

"For one thing, that they have water charges to pay." Jane's voice had a bitter bite.

Anna was glad to hear it. She'd take a bitter Jane over a collapsed Jane any day. "Don't lose heart, Jane. This isn't the last bridge we must cross."

"Because we won't be crossing it."

"We have a roof over our heads and we're fed, Jane. Everything is not so bad as that."

"Your dress will be in *rags* soon. We are saving nothing—what if something happens to one of us? All four of us are here, all day, nearly, and Emery isn't even sleeping."

"I'll get up with Emery, and you and Rose can do the night round after supper."

"That's not the *point*. We're on the edge of disaster, all day, every day. If we fall, we cannot catch ourselves. We are still taking more out of our store of pennies than we are putting in. We cannot catch ourselves. We *will* fall. We're falling now."

All three sisters shoved themselves closer to Jane till she was more in danger of being crushed than financial ruin.

"Very well, Jane." Anna sounded more certain than she felt, but if she had learned one thing from nursing their mother through her illness, it was that a positive outlook simply helped more than gloom. "You have a little panic, and let me do some thinking. We are not finished yet."

"Seven shillings," moaned Jane, but then when Rose squeezed her again, she squeezed Rose back.

The sight of Rose and Jane with their arms around each other gave Anna more heart. In a crisis, they were still sisters.

"I have perhaps a little idea," said Anna. "I've been considering thinking about it. This might be the time."

"If you have some big plan, you ought to share." Emery clearly understood that none of them wanted to hear the word *cake*, but neither was she inclined to take Anna on faith.

Which irked her sister. "I'm not having that from you right now, Miss I Am Chancing A Day's Income On A Whole New Way of Making Bread."

"It worked!"

"But you certainly didn't share."

"Well." Emery subsided a little and leaned her shoulder into Jane's. "You have to be sure it will work."

"Oh, *do* you? Well. If you could take a little leap, perhaps I can, too."

"Why?" Jane wasn't used to seeing Anna look so thoughtful. "What are you going to do?"

"A few things, in the right order, I hope."

EMERY WAS SO ENGROSSED IN CALCULATING HOW MANY bakes she could do in a day if she had Mr. Macaulay wake her up at new times as well, she didn't notice Anna coming through the back door of the bakery with her bonnet on, carrying her shopping basket. She hadn't seen Anna venture out by herself.

And she didn't ask about it because Anna immediately distracted her with questions. "Where did the children go, Emery?"

Emery dried her hands on her skirt. They were clean, but chapped. She'd been so exultant about the wet rising bread— and here they were having to pay more money for water! It wasn't because of her bread, she knew that. It was because they hadn't known there would be rent for the water at all. But she was deflated and felt all the tiredness that she hadn't felt before.

"I sent them home. They were here early. They're too thin, Anna." Emery bit off the rest of that sentence. If the sisters couldn't feed themselves, they couldn't feed her small journeymen.

"They are avoiding Jane's arithmetic lesson." Anna didn't add that Jane was avoiding it, too. Jane was in the bakery proper as well, scrubbing barrels and saying nothing.

"We don't want them to work all day."

"No, we don't. Nor you, Emery. Get some rest. That Mr. Russell has invited us, by which he means Rose, to hear him speak this evening, but you needn't go. You ought to sleep. You look so thin."

"Is thin no longer fashionable? And my dress will soon be transparent. I will be a paragon of fashion."

Anna's soft eyes stayed on Emery's face. "Bitterness from you, I don't expect. Are you feeling well?"

No, she wasn't. Emery had such dreams, dreams about saving her sisters with bread and having an hour or two in the evenings to visit that kitchen full of remarkable women and to stare at Miss Hayes as much as she liked. Small dreams, she thought, and now they were gone. If they were to make more in the evening, she must set up more dough.

But Anna's spine only seemed to have been hardened by the blow of the water bill. "Not tonight, don't do more work tonight. We must breathe. Can you not listen to your older sister just once in your life?"

"I always listen to you, Anna." She then ignored her, but...

Anna just nodded, a firm, crisp nod. "None of you listen, but you must trust me. I have an idea. And I have already begun it. Do sleep, Emery. Sleep the night through, if you can."

"Ah, Captain Brice." On the pavement outside the bakery, Miss Bickering joined the flow of passers-by, toward the south end of the square and its gate. Miss Rose's hand was on her elbow.

"Ladies." The Captain tipped his tricorn hat. "Are you going to the speech as well? Perhaps I may walk with you."

"Yes, please do."

The pleasantness of her tone made the Captain look twice —that was Her Majesty, wasn't it?

But she really wasn't looking at him. Her thoughts were far away.

The youngest sister, however, seemed pleased to have him. "Are you interested in politics, Captain Brice? Or are you friends with Mr. Russell?"

"I know Russell a bit. Seems a good fellow. I am interested in politics, Miss Bickering, though I have no ability for it."

"That's unusual, isn't it? So many people consider it dry and boring."

He smiled, remembered to himself that she wouldn't see it, and wondered how to make himself warm with just his voice. It wasn't his habit. "But not for you, I see."

"Not for me. I find it exciting, thinking of all the different types of people who must come together and agree to do things. All the great things we have accomplished—cities, world travel, and hopefully peace—they are accomplished through politics."

That took him aback. "I'm surprised you didn't mention art as our great accomplishments. Paintings, sculpture, symphonies, that sort of thing."

Miss Rose smiled her smile with dimples. "Those aren't interests of mine, as you may imagine. Though my sister Jane is an excellent musician. Not all ladies are interested in art, Captain."

He was a sailor. He spent little time with ladies. "Thank you, I'll remember that."

He knew enough about ladies to know that Miss Anna was looking for someone. She wasn't searching the faces around them; she was watching the carriages.

Miss Rose was clearly waiting only for the speech. Remembering her question, Brice smiled a little again. "So you are going for the politics, rather than Mr. Russell himself?"

The flush on her cheeks told him everything he needed to know about her fondness for Mr. Russell versus politics.

But she said, "I consider Mr. Russell a fine thinker. He has a generous heart, and I like seeing that in a person with political inclinations. But he cannot always say what he feels. It's a shortcoming for a man with political ambitions."

"Has he political ambitions? I confess I don't know him well enough to know that."

"He does, though he worries a Quaker has never been elected to the House of Commons."

And won't be now, thought Brice, but thought it more polite to say, "You've had more chance to converse with him than I."

She blushed again. "You could speak to him after tonight. If politics interests you."

Brice had never once had occasion to say anything personal about himself to these peculiar young ladies. He was reluctant to begin. He was here, in a country not of his birth, for reasons that precluded attachment to any one young lady. A set of four might be all right—or it might be even worse. "Politics interests me in that the decisions made by the body politic must be enforced or they have no reality. I am interested in seeing politics made real."

Her widened eyes indicated her surprise, but by then they had reached the spot to cross the street into the garden, and Brice said sharply, "Careful of your steps—wake up your sister. There are many carriages still about."

Miss Anna was staring at each vehicle instead of watching her steps or anyone's, but Rose did as the Captain said and shook her elbow. "Are you leading me into traffic, Miss Anna?"

"Oh yes. We'll be careful."

Some wealthy resident of the square had opened the gate and the little crowd milled there on the walkways. The trees and shrubs inside had so grown wild in the past years that there was little room to move in the park except on the walkways.

Still, it was a pleasant spot of green among stones and packed earth.

Mr. Russell saw them immediately and politely elbowed his way through. He was a stockily built fellow, thought Brice, a bit like a wall, albeit a short wall. He ought to be good in a fight.

Instead, here he was giving a speech.

No, in fact, here he was using his shoulders to make his way through the people to get to Miss Rose.

"Miss Bickering! And another Miss Bickering. What a pleasure! I'm so glad you could attend."

His show of addressing Anna too was wasted; her eyes were still on the carriages.

"Let me bring you closer to the spot where I will stand."

"No thank you, Mr. Russell. We need to stay by the gate. Thank you," Her Majesty said absently, without ever looking at him.

Miss Rose flushed, this time with a bit of anger, Brice thought with silent amusement, but Brice didn't interfere.

MR. RUSSELL HAD WELL WARMED UP THE CROWD, BRICE thought, when Miss Anna caught sight of whoever she was looking for.

Russell's voice carried well. "We must embrace this moment! The end of our war with the Continent is in sight. The end of war will mean a new era of prosperity for our United Kingdom. The possibilities for more trade with countries previously under the Emperor's heel may make us all dream of more money. But we must also look to the effects of that growth. London will grow and our neighborhood will grow. We must choose the future we want for Leicester Square, for London, for Britain herself."

"I'll return in just a moment," said Miss Anna, and left Miss Rose standing next to him to dash over to a barouche which had stopped in the street.

Brice was taken aback. He was a rough man himself, but the Misses Bickering were *not* the sorts of ladies who accosted carriages in the street. Now here the oldest one, the stuffiest one, was doing it in view of all Leicester Square.

Talking to a middle-aged old coot leaning out the window with a sappy smile on his face.

What the devil?

"The world is a small place. We rub elbows with our neighbors every day on the world stage, just as we do here in the street in our neighborhood. How shall we get along with France now? How can all our relationships be built anew when France returns to the brotherhood of states ruled more by freedom than despotism? And how shall we extend those ideas of freedom west, into the colonies with whom we still struggle?"

Miss Anna had dimples too, like Rose. Brice had never known this before because he'd never seen them. He saw them now, because she was showing them to the old coot in the carriage. Showing them hard.

"And how shall we convince our King and our Parliament to embrace those ideas of freedom to their fullest extent, abolish slavery throughout the Kingdom and our colonies?"

Brice's ears perked up, and he stopped watching Anna to watch the crowd.

There were a good number of people nodding at Mr. Russell's words. Encouraging. Though, these were people Russell had asked to come.

Even so, some people were frowning, and one shook his head. "Too far, Mr. Russell, too far. There are those people who are naturally fit for service and we will only get into a quagmire of failure if we try to change the natural order."

Mr. Russell had an answer ready. "Napoleon has claimed all along that empire is the natural order, and that he as an emperor was only fulfilling his natural purpose and France's. Should we be persuaded by those claims? Ought we have given in?"

The murmur of dissent that went through the little crowd at this only made the interrupter turn a bit red and redouble his effort at dissent. "We don't need *chaos*. I see where that path goes, Mr. Russell, and you can't sneak it past me. You people start by claiming African men are no different from others, and you end with Catholics in Parliament. I suppose you want the Church abolished too."

And little Rose, standing next to him, *spoke up*. "Speaking only for myself, I would not abolish the Church. How does treating some people fairly mean destruction of anything?"

The interrupter looked over at Rose with a sneer on his face, and Brice felt his back muscles tighten. "We're not all as soft as women. Who also ought to know what they can do and what they can't."

Brice thought Rose would let the nasty remark pass her by, but instead she laughed. "Is that what your wife thinks?"

At that, the crowd laughed too, and the tension snapped. Mr. Russell picked up the thread of thought as if it had been unbroken. "A new day means new dreams. New dreams are built on clear-eyed understanding of the world as it is, so we can imagine what it could be. Our principles mean nothing unless we put them to work. I propose to petition the Crown to put your principles to work."

Brice was never fooled by a temporary break in tension. He cast an eye over to where Miss Anna curtsied to the man in the carriage, and leaned down to speak very quietly to Miss Rose. "I will be sure to accompany you ladies all the way back to the bakery whenever you are ready to go, Miss Rose."

"Mr. Russell has quite a bit more to say!"

"He'll be finishing it soon if he's smart, and he ought to walk with you, if he's got a care for your safety."

"Captain Brice. You don't think our neighbors would have any ill will over a few words."

"I think many of our neighbors would have lots of ill will over a few words."

He thought that would quiet her, but instead, she just pressed her lips together and looked more than ever like her oldest sister. "Then I'm glad I spoke out."

Anna was breathless when she returned. "I'm sorry I was away so long; I believe I saw an old friend."

Neither Brice nor Rose reported what she had missed. But Brice took note of the carriage as it drove away. He'd be sure to recognize it if he saw it again.

ANNA WATCHED AS ROSE NARRATED THE EVENTS OF THE evening to Jane and Emery. Rose was animated, colorful, full of optimism and youth.

Jane and Emery had never looked more alike. Both were tired, wan, one light head and one dark one leaning side by side against the far wall. But they laughed when Rose laughed, and both of them had similar looks of shining pride in their eyes as they listened to their littlest sister.

If Anna thought about what she'd done this evening, running to speak to a gentleman in a carriage like the street-walker the cleaning men called her, the shame would make her burst into flame. If she thought about what she'd *said,* she'd sink right through the earth.

But she couldn't think about that. She had too much to do.

It wasn't long before Rose and Emery went off to their bedroom, and Jane just nodded before trailing away to the one she shared with Anna.

Anna couldn't have that. Jane was their rock, their strength. She'd been Anna's strength ever since she was seven, and their governess had slapped Anna's behind. Six-year-old Jane had slapped the governess' hand, then run straight to their parents, and that governess had been gone the next day.

It wasn't easy, being the head of the family. But none of this was easy for any of them. And Anna had to do something before Jane crumbled.

It was the height of summer. The sun hadn't even gone down. In their quiet, empty parlor, Anna retrieved the shopping basket and took out the things she had bought. A sweeping turkey feather that would have been lovely on a bonnet but which had been made into a quill pen, a half-sheet of writing paper, the tiniest bottle of ink she could find.

She'd write the letter and ask the night watchman to post it for her. She knew he spoke often to Emery, who worked in the wee hours, and Emery thought well of him. She ought to have learned his name.

Anna couldn't wait for Emery to speak to the watchman. Always upright, tonight Anna sprawled on the floor; she'd write on the floorboards. She could do this downstairs in the shop, but she wanted to do it here.

It didn't take long; she had been composing the letter in her mind all afternoon.

After she folded and sealed the letter the best she could, Anna put it in her pocket, along with a coin to give the night watchman to post it. Her insides quivered when she thought of all the money she'd spent today. But she had a complete accounting of it in her head, and she'd tell it all to Jane tomorrow. Tomorrow.

She who had insisted that her sisters discuss and agree on every aspect of their little business before it began, had taken their money to put in motion a plan of her own about which they knew nothing.

But she'd grown quite a bit older in the last few months, and though she didn't think the words, there was a part of her inside that wanted all the risk to be her fault. If this went poorly, they could all blame her without blaming each other, and in a way, she'd have done her job as the head of the family.

She paused for a moment to look at their mother's silver

candlesticks on the floor, with their unlit candle stubs in the waning summer light. Then she slid the linen off her basket.

Around the basket's bottom there were a dozen and a half of eggs, cushioned with toweling she'd borrowed from the bakery proper. They kept a supply of butter in the basement, to keep it cool; she'd hope that the tiny street-level window would be enough to let her find it, if she went down before the last light was out of the sky. There was also the soft lumpiness of a bag of almonds, a pound and a half. It would take her an hour just to shell them. She ought to steam the skins away too.

It was all nestled next to a fat round pot the color of earth, with a little circle for a handle.

Anna took the pot out of the basket. She needed every speck of what was in there for what she was about to do. But nonetheless she uncorked the little pot and tipped it so that one perfect drop of golden light dripped out and on to the tip of her finger.

She put the drop on her tongue, closing her eyes and feeling it melt. It tasted of sweetness, yes, but also sunshine, open fields, flowers, and hope.

Episode 9: Too bold an assault

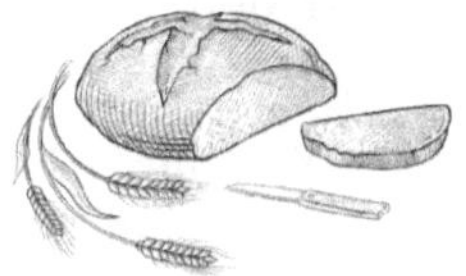

The first thing Emery saw in the dim gloom of early morning in the bakery was the glow of her mother's large porcelain dish. White and clean and tucked in between two bowls of rising bread, it outshone the snowy linen draped over it.

And at the end of that table, on all four of the plates that they owned, sat four cakes.

Emery swept her eyes over the room. There in the farthest corner slept Anna, curled up on the pile of flour sacks, as far from the oven as she could get.

"Are you hurt? Are you well? What's happened?" Emery's words and drawing closer seemed to wake her sister. And then as Anna's eyes fluttered open, "What have you done?"

"I fell asleep on the floor. Why are you down here?"

"But I mean, what have you done? You've made cake, Anna, cake. Why have you made cake?"

Anna sat up and wiped her hand on her apron before using it to scrub her eye.

"I had the idea when we ate at the Hotel Jacquier; those

cakes are soaked in sugar syrup. Why sugar syrup? Why not honey?"

Emery put out a hand and helped her sister up. Anna seemed to consider whether or not she was ready to be helped up, then took it.

"You can't bake cakes with honey. It's the way the sugar stays sugar, even mixed with butter, that makes the cake light. You can't do that with honey."

"I know." Anna was waking up fast now. She took a deep breath and shook her curls behind her. "You can't do that with honey. But the French *didn't* beat the sugar with the butter. Those cakes weren't light, weren't airy at all."

"But they were light." Emery closed her eyes and thought back to the cakes that they had all sampled that evening, at the French hotel when Captain Brice had hosted their dinner.

"Those cakes weren't sticky-heavy like a pudding, they were refreshing, but they weren't light." Anna had her feet under her now and went to bend over her treasures sitting on their plates. Emery had to follow.

Anna went on. "Those cakes were rich and very sweet. I thought, why not do the same thing with honey?"

Emery recorded the golden disks with suspicion. "But no one bakes cakes with honey."

Anna just pointed a finger at her as if she had made a deft point.

"No one bakes cakes with honey *now*. But sugar did not come into being at the dawn of the earth. Britain has only imported so much sugar for the last, what, fifty years? Yet it's not as if we have only recently discovered cake. Cake is older than sugar. And I wanted to see if I could make some."

"You've made antique cake."

"Yes, precisely. I like that description. Perhaps we can sell it by that name, antique cake."

Emery had spread both arms and thrust her chin out like

Rose did when she was stubborn. "People don't like antiques. They don't like things that are battered and pitted like our bread counters. They don't like things that are old. I certainly don't like Aunt Eden."

"But they like prestige, and in this neighborhood, they like French food. They are French cakes, Emery."

Emery bent down for a closer look.

There were two types of cake, one with delicate brittle pastry dough and one plainer; she could see the crumb.

Gently, she shaved a bit off the side of the one with the crumb, the way she used to steal bites of cake as a child, using her fingernail. She tasted it.

"It's missing something," she said immediately. "But the texture is good. That's not only flour."

"No." Anna leaned back into her own hands, stretching the small of her back. "I ground some almonds to put in it. I supposed that would break up the egg and butter texture even without the sugar."

"It does." Emery ran her tongue over her teeth. "There's another flavor missing."

"At *least* one. I had to reduce the butter and eggs a little, to account for the wetness of the honey. I think the texture is close, but I did not have apricots. It ought to be filled with jam."

"Chopped dried apricots, or plums," Emery said immediately, "or even currants. The jam would add more liquid."

"Quite. But I think there's still a flavor missing. A richness, a smokiness."

"Not tobacco." Emery's thoughtful look disappeared at the thought.

"No! I wondered if our French neighbors have a way of importing vanilla from Spain. It comes from their colonies, if I recall correctly."

"There was something else. Perhaps it *was* vanilla."

"It might have been whiskey. Or rum? I don't know." Anna was not unhappy with the cake. It was cake, and turning out a recognizable cake in the oven had been her chief worry. She had literally watched it bake every minute, turning it with the wooden paddle as it went; her nose felt baked as well.

Emery pointed to the other two cakes. "It's too warm for that pastry dough."

"I know! I didn't have money to buy ice to chill the butter. I think it will do. It will be better in winter, of course."

They'd both made the flaky dough, which involved rolling a dough made primarily of flour and butter over and over again, folding it at every step in between until it had too many layers to count.

There were almonds in these cakes too, pounded into a paste with the honey and used as a filling. The cakes themselves weren't sweet at all.

"I don't know if we can get by on a *gâteau Breton* and a *galette du Roi*," Anna's schoolgirl French accent came easily, "but given that people come even from other parts of London for the French food in Leicester Square, we might. On the other hand, we might sell them as antique cakes for a distinctly British set of patrons. With British honey."

Emery's look pierced the early morning gloom, shifted from the golden discs to her sister's face, and then back again.

"A chance. You think there's a chance. Where did you get the money for all of this? Honey? Not to mention the eggs, the cakes must have eggs."

"They have egg yolks and I assure you, we are all eating egg whites for breakfast." Anna pointed at a bowl. "I don't wish to discuss it right now. I wish to get some sleep. I had to bake the cakes overnight when the ovens were cooler. I know you are going to bank up the fires now, and the oven would be too hot for cakes."

Emery was plenty awake and ready for answers. "We're going to have to talk more about this. We must all talk more about this."

"Oh, I know. But I need sleep." She hefted a precious plate with both hands. "Let me put the cakes in a cool spot. And I will be out of your way."

Emery peered into the depths of the oven. "Rose told me to wake her. To help me shape the loaves. But I didn't wake her. I didn't have the heart. She's been more happy lately, and not so tired."

Anna looked at the cake in her hands and then back at the oven. The pull towards sleep was strong, but the pull to let Rose sleep was stronger. "Let me move the cakes, and I will help you shape the loaves for the next bake. And then we will both get some sleep while they rise."

"Don't open the door. We need to figure out what to do with this cake."

It was time for the Ladies' Own Bakery to open. The shelves held baskets full of fresh brown crusts of their best white bread, and the brown maslin they still made for the few neighbors who bought it, and themselves.

But on the counter were four plates of golden cake, and the sisters looked at them as if they were plates full of pistols about to go off.

"I can't believe you did this," Emery said again, as if they hadn't had a whole conversation about it in the wee hours.

Jane just stared down at a cake. "Of course you took the money from the till, to purchase everything."

Now that her sisters were all around her, Anna felt less certain. But she must appear more certain.

She put on what she hoped was a very certain smile. "I have a plan. Lord Boislegrand will provide the money."

"Who?" asked Rose.

"What?" asked Jane.

"Never mind. I couldn't be so bold as to ask him for money on one day's acquaintance. But he is the sort of person who has it, and will cheerfully give it. So I promised to bake him a cake."

"And yet there are four." Emery wasn't letting this go. She didn't feel threatened by the cake. Not at all.

This was a bakery, and it sold bread. As the chief bread baker, the bakery still depended upon her. She couldn't lose that, just because of the existence of some cakes.

Still, to her, they seemed sinister cakes.

Anna was still on the topic of this unknown person with money. "I promised him a cake. But I told him we are not such good friends that I could make a gift of it, even if I wished. I told him we are a bakery, and suggested that he could buy a cake. If I were to bake a special one, just for him."

Jane regarded her sister. "How expensive is this special cake?"

"It's a very special cake," Anna said grimly. "It costs as much as four and then some."

"Ah..." Rose spoke up more shyly than she had of late. "Might there be... a cake that costs as much as, for instance, half a year's water?"

"No." Anna did not dwell on Rose's sudden slide into deviousness. "You see, we need a solution that will last. We cannot simply pay this water charge; we must pay all our water charges in future."

"That's what I've been saying!" Jane threw up her hands.

Anna glared. "I will reserve one of these for his lordship. And we will not sell the other three, either."

Jane simply stood, like someone who had seen the gates of

hell, and was being asked to walk through them. "Of course we will not sell them. How foolish would that be, recovering the money that you spent making them?"

Anna flushed a bit red. "We can't sell them, don't you see? I don't know if people will purchase cakes made of honey. And if I don't know, neither will anyone else. They do taste different from cakes made of sugar. See, I sliced off a tiny bite there. It's good. I like it." It had been heart-meltingly delicious, in fact, and reminded Anna of every food she was not eating any more. "I love it. But I don't know if our neighbors will buy it. I couldn't risk our money, only to find out if they would. I am risking his lordship's money—"

"—on a slightly fraudulent transaction," Rose put in.

"—just to see if the cakes will sell at all," Anna finished as if she had not been interrupted. "Really, Rose."

"What are you going to do, then?" Emery put in from where she leaned against the wall.

"I'm going to slice them into tiny bites, and give them away. If our patrons don't like them, then we needn't pursue the idea of cakes at all. They will be paid for. We will know."

"It's clever," admitted Jane. She didn't yet look like she was on her way towards the earth's surface, but she did look as though she was at least listening.

"It's mad," said Emery. The whole idea of cakes was a bizarre risk. And these cakes were even riskier.

"It's splendid," said Rose. "We ought to try it, if there is a way to bake cakes with honey. And I agree with Anna. The cake we had—well, one of the cakes we had—well, a couple of the cakes we had at the Hotel Jacquier were quite dense and very sweet. It might just work. And it gives us something to sell at a higher price not limited by law. As long as people will buy it."

"Yes," Anna snapped her fingers in triumph. "Yes, that is exactly it. And I have lightened these a little. I have had barely a taste myself, but I think they are good. And the entire idea terrifies me so much that I am surprised my shoes don't shake off. But we must try something, my darlings, and I felt this was one idea I could contribute."

"But why not tell us about it?" Jane shook her head. "Why not simply say it?"

"We can't argue about every little thing, if we're going to survive." Anna's hands at her waist clasped and unclasped. "Someone must take the initiative. And I felt it ought to be me. It's my responsibility. I'm the oldest sister."

"No," said Rose, "that isn't true at all. We must agree on every little thing or this business won't survive. We can't stop being sisters and I don't want to try. If we are sisters first and bakers second, we must at least agree what to do with the resources we have."

"I can't do it." Again Anna's hands flew up in the air. "I can't argue about everything all the time. You don't know how it wears on me. I feel as though everything I say will be wrong to one of you. And I want all of you to be happy. If you are unhappy with me, so be it, but at least you will still be happy with each other, and we didn't have to have another argument about cake, and I'm not sorry that I've done it and I think it will go well. So don't chastise me."

Predictably, she burst into tears.

"Oh no," Rose crowded into her and put her arms around her waist, "is there a handkerchief? Surely your apron has flour on it. No. Don't cry. None of us want you to cry."

Jane patted Anna's back. "No, please don't cry. We had a difficult day yesterday, so much hope and disappointment all in one day. And it is difficult to face. Hope and disappointment again. That's all. Don't cry."

Anna daubed at her face with her sleeve. "I had a difficult day, too. And then awake all night. But I think the cakes are good. Darlings, I think they are. I had to watch them and rotate them more than I would in a small oven, but I think they baked. Well, moister than I would normally bake a cake, but I think I have a decent prescription for making them again."

"I wish we could consult a French cook, but the servants at the hotels aren't pleasant at all," Rose had the idea and discarded it immediately.

"I know. I told his lordship that I would make him a cake that I had never made before and that I wasn't sure of its concoction as I am no French chef. And he quite understood."

Emery was still standing a little apart. "Let's return to the idea of this lordship fellow. Who is he, when did you speak with him, and what does he expect for this cake?"

"I met him here. You've all seen him; he came in and spoke to Rose that time. I only had a brief conversation with him while we attended Mr Russell's speech yesterday."

"Is that what you were doing?" Rose's arms dropped. "Mr. Russell was speaking of serious topics and you left me in Captain Brice's company to bat your eyes at an earl?"

"Oh, I thought everyone adored Captain Brice now!" Bitterness was creeping into Anna's voice.

Jane's hand on on her back stilled. "You talked to an earl... in the street?"

Anna's hands went over her eyes. "He is a viscount. I spoke to him in the street and please don't bring it up again, it is mortifying, or beyond mortifying, I don't wish to discuss it. I promised him the cake. He is going to come and buy the cake. There is nothing improper about that. We are a bakery, and we are going to sell him a cake."

"You're going to marry him, aren't you?" The suspicion in Emery's voice was hard and sharp. "I didn't like to think it of you, but you're going to do it, Anna. You said you wouldn't and there you are."

"I am not going to marry him." Anna's spine straightened. "I am a baker and I baked him a cake." She said in regal tones and marched out of the room, towards the bakery.

LADY ARNOLD TRIED TO TAKE A STROLL AROUND THE square at least once a day

She took her airing in the company of her children, and their governess. It was still hard for her to absorb, after all this time, but she was a widow of considerable means. Her husband's estate had passed to their son, of course, but her dowry and widow's portion made up a fortune that exceeded the expectations of many young men in society. She was a woman of advanced years, over thirty, with two children. Moreover, she had possession of her own house on Leicester Square. Something few could say, since most of the houses were in the possession of absent owners and merely leased.

She'd noted the bakery on the corner of the square had opened again, but paid it no more mind than that. She was in possession of an excellent cook and did not need to notice them.

Nonetheless, she was fully intelligent enough to be bored with existence as a widow, and sufficiently bored to take notice of her neighborhood. She could hardly avoid noticing the bustle outside the bakery.

"What is happening at the bakery, Miss Williams?"

Miss Williams, who did not enjoy being a governess or much else, and who certainly didn't walk around the square unless required to by her employer, tried to school herself into a suitably gracious tone. "I have no idea, madam. But if you wish to find out, we can certainly walk closer." If they made an entire circuit of the square, they'd pass by, anyway.

So it was only a few more steps when they reached the

hubbub of women, young and old, all clustered outside the door of the bakery. "What is the trouble?" asked Miss Williams, politely taking on the task to spare her ladyship the need to do it.

"Well I don't know that it's a sort of a trouble," said one woman. "The Misses Bickering have baked themselves some cakes."

"Surely all this fuss isn't over the purchase of cakes." Miss Williams clearly didn't approve of fuss, or cakes, or both.

But both Lady Arnold's children stood straighter.

"They aren't selling them," said another woman, "they're giving away tiny bites but they won't give them away to everyone. Miss Anna says she has to pick who gets to taste. And it can't be everyone, I don't know why, I guess there's a lot of us. But some of us have had a taste and they say it's awful good."

Lady Arnold perked up her ears. She had little interest in affairs of the kitchen. Hers had been an extremely predictable life, from her training to be a wife to her debut in society to her marriage. Even the death of her husband had been predictable; he had been quite a bit older. And these things were to be expected, according to her mother.

The idea of giving away bites of cake was new, and Lady Arnold was ready for something new. Her children were both far too well bred to crowd around her, or beg. But clearly, both of them had heard the word *cake*.

"You like cake, madame." The young Lord Arnold, whom she still thought of as her son James, was old enough and clever enough to frame the question as an appeal for a treat for his mother, not for himself.

"I like cake too!" Alicia, two years younger, was neither so mature nor so devious.

Lady Arnold smiled at them both. "I do like cake. Miss Williams. Perhaps we should all attempt to go in."

"Of course," Miss Williams said, raising her voice a little. "If you would permit us. Her ladyship would like to enter the establishment."

The crowd didn't part gracefully, but it did part.

Inside, the shop was a little darker and a little warmer. It surprised Lady Arnold that she could see through windows on both sides. The crisp panes of glass were very clear. Beyond the milling crowd of ladies and hands, there were four young women behind the counter.

The baskets of bread on shelves behind them were nearly empty, but nobody was buying bread. The young ladies had two plates in front of them and had clearly divided each cake into tiny bite-sized morsels.

Miss Williams again cleared her throat in a punitive manner. "Lady Arnold would like to see the cakes."

All heads turned.

Lady Arnold could now see the bakers. They were women, all four of them were women, two with curly hair, one slightly darker. And one handsome woman with the kind of square shoulders that had always made Lady Arnold inclined to daydream. The woman had a look of determination that gave strength to features that would otherwise be girlish—well, some features; her nose was regal, and serious.

Lady Arnold walked through the crowd. "I did not know this bakery sold cakes."

The curly-haired woman in front curtsied. "Normally we do not, my lady. But today is a special celebration. And we are trying something new. Would you like to taste?"

It was a shame that she was talking instead of the handsome one in back.

That woman, the interesting one, folded her arms across her chest.

Her sleeve cuffs were rolled back, and Lady Arnold could just see a slight cording of muscle in those forearms, in her hands. She looked strong and capable. Those arms spoke to her.

Lady Arnold looked back at the speaker. "I would very much enjoy a taste, and perhaps one for my children." Miss Williams cleared her throat again. "And Miss Williams, of course."

The curly-haired baker swallowed and looked down at the plates, clearly considering the investment of four whole bites on this family.

"Yes, of course," she finally said, faintly. She used the tip of the knife to push one of the cake bites to the edge of the plate.

Whence Lady Arnold took it delicately between thumb and forefinger, and popped it into her mouth.

It wasn't at all as dense and chewy as she had thought it would be from its appearance. It had a lightness, a crumbling delicacy that she had not expected, and more flavor than she had expected as well. "Is that honey?"

"It is exactly that, your ladyship," said the woman in the front, and served her children, and Miss Williams, the same way.

Her daughter Alicia looked slightly troubled by the stickiness on her fingers. But the cake was popular all around. James' smile was broad.

"You may lick your fingers, Alicia." Lady Arnold was still chasing the taste of the cake and didn't really want to discuss it.

It ought to have been earthy or heavy and it wasn't. It wasn't a perfect cake, but it was a pleasant surprise for all the senses. Just like the woman in the back. "It's an achievement, Miss…"

"Miss Bickering, madame," said the baker as she curtsied. "Thank you. I hope we will have more. And you will consider purchasing them."

"I certainly will consider it," Lady Arnold smiled at her, letting the smile serve for the entire group and not allowing herself the pleasure of smiling at the woman with the alluring hands. She needed to be discreet. And it was no one's fault that seeing her was the first interesting thing that had happened to Lady Arnold in years.

CAPTAIN BRICE HAD HEARD SOME ILL-TEMPERED muttering among some servants in the *Hôtel* Jacquier, and as near as he could tell, it was about the Misses Bickering. He had learned French on an island, not in Paris like many others in this hotel, and his French sometimes did not quite fit with their words.

But he definitely heard *boulangère* mixed in with disapproving tones.

When at last he dispensed with his final letter—it seemed all he did with his time these days was write blasted letters—and made his way to the shop, it looked like any other day.

"Isn't it exciting?" said a woman in the door who kept him from going in.

"Yes," he responded, as agreement tended to bring stupid conversations to an end.

It didn't. "I was just telling my husband that this neighborhood is becoming higher and higher in the step. He said that because we're so close to Covent Garden, we must resign ourselves to the neighborhood becoming dank, but I said no, there are earls and probably viscounts about, and now the ladies' bakery is moving up in the world too!"

If stupid conversations would not end, they at least ought to be informative. "Moving up for what reason, ma'am?"

"Cake!"

"Cake?"

In a most ungallant way, Brice gripped her elbow, just lightly, and moved her forward two steps so that he could get around her and into the shop.

Mrs. Talker called back after him, "See? Cake is terribly exciting!"

Inside, all four Misses Bickering were standing around the shop, though oddly, silently.

There was only one woman left inside, and she appeared to be an actual customer. There was a quartern loaf on the counter in front of her—odd to have them so late in the day, he thought. And there was no sign of cake.

"One and six, ma'am," Miss Rose told the customer.

"Can't you make it a little less dear?"

Brice looked the woman over. She wore good solid clothes, not half as worn as the Misses Bickering wore, and looked decently fed.

Miss Rose behaved as if she expected this question. "I'm sorry, ma'am, as you know we cannot."

"It's just that it is *so* dear."

"Yes ma'am, it is."

There was a long, awkward pause while everyone stood silently.

Miss Rose had clearly had experience with her position now. She was different from when he'd first met her, Brice reflected. And she said, "One and six, ma'am," with the perfect inflection of *buy or leave*.

"Yes, of course," sighed the woman, as though they'd insisted on removing one of her kidneys and eating it for supper. She counted out the coins, and Brice was not surprised to see her make it exact.

When she'd finally left, there was a relaxation in the air that said that it was only an intimate circle now. Brice liked being included.

For the space of one breath. Then, as usual with Miss

Anna, it was "Captain Brice, we haven't time for social conversation today."

"What, didn't you bake him a *cake*?" The tallest Miss Bickering sounded as bitter as an old sailor.

Miss Anna just flapped her hands in Brice's direction. Was she trying to blow him away? "Why must you always be around when you are not wanted?"

"I consider it my most obvious talent," said Captain Brice. "*Is* there cake?"

"No," said Miss Anna.

"Yes," said Miss Emery.

"Anna made cakes with honey by promising one to a rich man in the street," said Miss Rose.

"You needn't tell *every* thing to *every* person, Miss Rose." Miss Jane sounded more defeated than Brice was accustomed to. What had gone on?

"I like Captain Brice perfectly well, and it's not as if he were in the *street*. He's standing in the shop."

The way Miss Anna flushed at this told Brice that there was some sort of truth to the story; this must be about the man she'd spoken to in the carriage.

"Thank you, Miss Rose," he said. "Though perhaps you will not like me as well when I admit that I saw Miss Anna speaking to the carriage person and did not mention it to you. Nothing untoward happened that I saw."

"Oh." Rose folded her arms across her stomach. "I did think better of you, sir, but it's clear that the whole square knows, why shouldn't I?"

"Most of the square was paying attention to Mr. Russell," muttered Anna. Then another thought came to her. "And watching you fawn over him, I'm sure!"

Attack was good defense, but Brice wondered why Miss Jane wasn't doing it. Miss Anna did not usually have to take up arms in her own defense.

He decided to fight both fronts. "I can also attest that Miss Rose's behavior was perfectly appropriate, as I stood by her side the whole time. Ladies, is there some misunderstanding here I can assist with?"

"No," Miss Emery assured him. "There is more clarity than previously."

"There's nothing to be done but—"

Whatever Miss Anna was going to say, it was cut short by the arrival of a carriage outside.

But this one was black lacquer, gilded with laurel leaves; ostentatious and *not* the barouche where Miss Anna had conducted some sort of visible business.

A young man climbed out, one wearing a perfectly tailored dark blue coat that made Brice think his eyes must be blue as well; he'd be the sort that wanted that. And yellow hair showed under the brim of his stovepipe hat.

He turned to talk to someone inside the carriage for a moment.

"Is this the fellow to whom you promised a cake?" Brice couldn't see any cake, and wondered if the cake even existed. Was that the problem?

"No, that's someone else; he lives upstairs," Miss Anna dismissed the fellow with a flick of the wrist, and then froze.

"What?" said Rose.

"*What?*" said Emery.

Then the two of them were talking over one another as, sure enough, the man outside walked up to their building and right through the door beside the shop door that led to the apartments above.

"There is a *man* living in the building and you didn't tell us?"

"How can you lecture us on propriety, knowing we are living in the same house as a bachelor? He is a bachelor, isn't he?"

"How long has he been here? How long did you know?"

"Is this another man you're planning to marry? How many men *are* you planning to marry?"

"Oh stop, *stop* that! I cannot control who leases rooms above us. I cannot control how much we are charged for water, or how much we can charge for bread. I can only control how I bake a cake. You have all forgotten that the problem isn't cake, it's *sugar*, and now I've gone and found a way to make a cake without sugar, I stayed up *all* night making *four* cakes I'd never made before and you're all *angry* and it is *not* easy, you know, it is *not* easy to be the oldest—"

Another carriage stopped just beyond the pavement. A barouche.

Brice recognized it.

He didn't know what he should do if Miss Anna went to it to deliver a cake. Something was wracking her, he could see that, and her sister Jane wasn't rushing to defend her today. And he didn't think that in the space of a day Her Majesty had become the sort of woman who hung upon carriage doors in public view.

She clenched her hands and grew a little taller. "I will *not* cry," she announced to the room at large, and she obviously meant it.

She disappeared into the bakery proper and emerged a few heartbeats later with a cake. A plain little yellow cake on a plate.

She clearly wondered too if she would be required to deliver it in the street, but by the time she looked again, the gentleman had disembarked from his carriage and was struggling to unstick the shop door.

He walked in, a soft, portly man in very shiny boots, and when he swept his hat from his head Brice could see there were sparse hairs on top of his head, showing dark against the paleness of his skin.

He wasn't a man Brice would have cared to know, but he bowed as soon as he entered the shop, and his eyes were only for Miss Anna.

"Miss Bickering, I consider it a signature honor to see you again."

Miss Anna's eyes, soft, brown, lost, cast around the room, clearly wishing that everyone else in it would disappear; but no one moved.

Her eyes closed, and Brice saw her take a deep breath. Then she curtsied.

"Lord Boislegrand, thank you for coming."

"It is almost in the nature of a social call, is it not?" He held his hat in his hand. Brice thought he hadn't even noticed he was in a bakery, not a drawing room.

"Of a sort." She tried to smile, but it didn't work. "I have..." Her eyes dropped. "Baked your cake."

"Thank you." He took the plate from her hands. Freed, her hands tangled themselves in her apron.

He smiled at her, not the cake, but then he did look at the cake.

If he made one lascivious remark, one comparison between Miss Anna and a cake, Brice would have to do something.

But he didn't.

He did say, "I'm honored to purchase your first cake, Miss Bickering, and would cheerfully have paid twice the price for the honor. I'm afraid my coins are in my pocket—"

"Oh!" Miss Anna reached out and repossessed the plate.

The Boislegrand fellow bobbed his head and fished in his pocket for a coin. Brice saw the silver flash—a pound. Someone had *polished* his pound sterling.

"Now we must exchange again," he prompted Miss Anna, who held the plate in one hand and reached for the coin with the other.

He took back his cake.

She held a pound sterling.

Miss Anna had apparently contracted to bake one cake at an exorbitant price. But there was no way, no way that Miss Anna, even in a moment of desperation, would have asked a man to pay twenty shillings for a cake that might normally be priced at two.

Indeed, Miss Anna moved to go round the counter to the till and get him coins in return, but he waved them away with his hat. "Not at all, Miss Bickering, not at all."

Brice had seen people humiliated. He doubted this fellow, generous as he clearly was, realized what he'd done. Because also clearly, Miss Anna was mortified by the need to over-charge him for one cake. But by tossing her the price of ten without a second thought, this Lord Boislegrand had unwittingly put her in her place.

If he had any serious intentions, they were dead now.

He might only think he was purchasing the favor of Miss Anna's time. But what could be more humiliating to a lady?

He showed no sign that he understood what he'd done; he only stood there, cake in one hand, hat in the other, and stared at Miss Anna like a frog at the moon.

He didn't lack persistence, though. "I wonder if I might call upon you some afternoon."

"As I've said, my lord, I am in no position to take social calls."

"I don't suppose you'll be at Lady Woolacre's musicale next week?"

"Sadly, no." Brice could see her quivering with the weight of yet more humiliation.

"Perhaps you and your sisters would take the air with me some early morning when it is cool, a drive in my carriage, perhaps."

"Lord Boislegrand," said Miss Anna, in the least regal voice Brice had ever heard from her, "I am a *baker.*"

"Miss Bickering, you're so much more."

He obviously did believe that. Thick as a bucket of water, clearly, but the man believed what he said.

And with that, the gentleman bowed again, and turned to go.

He was stopped by the need to put on his hat in order to open the door, which was its own struggle. Brice suspected that usually footmen opened all his doors.

But then he was gone.

Miss Anna, her back straight, pale, trembling, watched the gentleman reach into his carriage and put down the cake before climbing in. His driver clucked the reins, and the carriage drove off.

"Please pardon me." She turned and walked with her head held high through to the bakery itself.

Brice thought her sisters might go after her. But Miss Emery only let out a *huff* and departed through the door that led to, he thought, their rooms above.

"Ladies," he addressed Rose and Jane, "I gather that something has gone very wrong. Something other than the matter of cake, and Miss Anna speaking to a viscount in the street. Has something caused all this?"

"The water rents must be paid," Rose simply said.

"Rose."

Rose shrugged off Jane's warning. "Mr. Russell believes that problems are easier handled when shared. We are not of society, we are shopkeepers, and we have a water rent. Why be embarrassed by that?"

"I'm not embarrassed by that," said Jane, but nonetheless instead of staying to discuss it, she left. By the bakery door. Brice hoped she was going to talk to her sister.

"I would not tell anyone else, Miss Rose," Brice told the

remaining Miss Bickering as quietly as he could. He'd been on land so long now that he was learning to speak in a voice suit-able for indoor spaces.

"My sister Jane handles our books, sir, and I have every faith that she is correct when she says that we were already not profiting from our business. We must draw on our savings to pay for flour and such. Emery devised a new sort of bread and for a few hours we thought we were fine. But now there's eight pounds owed for the water—"

"*Eight!*"

Rose nodded. "And four pounds a quarter in future. And we cannot do it, not with only bread. So Anna—do you think what Anna did was wrong, Captain Brice?"

"No." A little unethical, but nothing compared with what Brice had seen of men's sins. "Is that why you're all angry with her?"

"Not really. Emery is convinced Anna intends to marry and leave us all here. But that exchange didn't strike me as Anna attempting to beguile Lord Boislegrand."

"Me either." Though Lord Boislegrand was clearly smitten.

"It's just that Anna wants us to be so proper, and she didn't tell us about the cakes *or* Lord Boislegrand, or—what about that other fellow upstairs?" Suddenly remembering *that* gentleman, Rose said with some uncertainty, "I think it's just the shock?"

Brice looked down at Rose's serious little face, pointed at his shoulder. "Never let it be said your lives are simple, Miss Bickering. But I'd like to hear more about this water bill. Do you know more about it?"

"I was right here when the gentleman came!"

"Tell me everything you remember, if you please, every word."

ANNA DIDN'T TURN ROUND WHEN SHE HEARD A DOOR OPEN into the mews. Shoe leather *sshed* on the cobblestones; then she could see Jane's skirt out of the corner of her eye.

"If you plan to marry, will you tell me?" Jane murmured.

"I am not going to marry! I am a *baker*!" She had never felt it quite this way before. It went down to her bones. She was never going to be a fine lady in a carriage. She was a shopkeeper. It was like a brand that went straight through her.

"Then why have you been sneaking upstairs to see that fellow in the garret? Because I know you, Anna, and I don't believe you'd encourage him if you didn't intend to marry."

Anna's mouth gaped open as she looked up to see Jane's sad, serious face.

"I have *not* been sneaking upstairs!"

"I know you have, Anna. The tailor across the way saw you."

"Never say so!"

"Why do you think I'm so careful to pull the curtains every evening?"

Anna's shoulders slumped. "Everyone hates me and you think I'm a lightskirt."

"I know you're *not*. Which is why I am asking what's going on."

"Nothing. Not one thing that you think. Everything that is going on, every *humiliating* thing, you've seen."

Jane came around to face her. "The man upstairs?"

"I went to visit him once. He didn't even see I was *there*, Jane. I went in and went out. He no more would notice me than you'd notice a blade of grass upon your shoe."

"I'm really surprised that you did it at all."

"I have surprised myself lately."

Jane sighed. "No one hates you."

"Everyone hates me." Anna considered. "Emery *really* hates me."

"Emery doesn't hate you. It's only that it's hard, you know, when you keep insisting we follow society's rules. Emery and Rose never were *in* society. And we definitely are not now."

"I know that now. Oh Jane. That pound. He paid a *pound*."

"And I say we take it."

"We must pay him back the excess, someday. I can't bear it. It's like Widow Hampton's gift. It's too much. I feel it now. We have plenty to bear without the weight of charity."

Jane just shrugged. "We can keep an account. We will be lucky, one day, if we have the money to pay it back." She reached out to touch Anna's hand. "It will pay for a few more cakes."

"Yes, it will. Did it work, do you think?" Anna looked up.

"People don't always pay for what they say they will pay for, and free cake differs from cake that costs money. But I think we could sell cake." Jane had the look she had when she was calculating something, and Anna had never been so glad to see it. "That Lady Arnold might be an important patron."

"I hope so." The sigh seemed to let free all the air in Anna's body.

"You must tell me everything you used, and the price. I must understand what the costs and possible profits may be, and we must find the best sources."

Anna still looked miserable. "Are you sure you don't hate me?"

"How could I ever hate you?"

It was true. They all had their spats, but Jane had been staunchly by Anna's side ever since that day of the evil governess.

"I hope that's true. Because I've written a letter. To Aunt Eden."

Episode 10: An even closer man

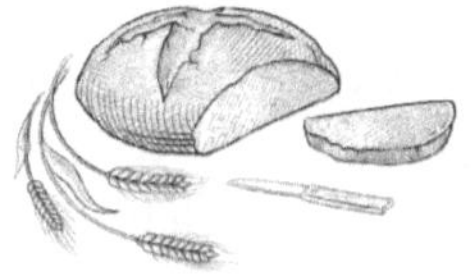

"Emery says to say when there's an egg for her."

Jane looked down at Sal's uncompromising little face. "Tell her do come up."

"Is there an egg?"

Jane bent down and looked seriously at the little girl who was looking so seriously at her. "I admire your ability to follow instructions, Sally, but you see, I am Emery's older sister. I give instructions to *her*. Mine are to come up for her breakfast."

"I'll tell her," said Sal with the open doubt of a messenger who knows they won't be blamed for the message, "but I don't think she wants to."

"Emery hasn't come up?" Rose emerged from their bedroom, her fingers twisting her hair ribbon into the end of her braid. Her sister usually came back to their rooms to break fast of a morning, then bake a second round of bread. During the mid-day rush, she napped.

"I cannot take tension. I'm simply not built for it. Mother wasn't built for it, don't you agree?" Anna was turning in a circle before their tiny stove, four eggs nestled together in a pan sizzling away on top.

It was only a few minutes before Emery came in, wiping her hands on her apron. "Eggs are ready?"

"Yes. No. Sit down for a moment." Jane gestured at the empty room. "No, sorry, you can't. Come, stand for a moment."

"We shall never have chairs," Rose sighed, pulling the bow tight at the end of her braid.

Anna's circle was spinning tighter and tighter. "Emery, I cannot work through the day knowing that you are angry with me."

"Oh, it's not just Emery," Jane put in. "I think we're all a little discouraged by your high-handedness, Anna."

"Jane! You said you'd help me!"

Jane shrugged. "I didn't say I'd *lie*."

"Anna, you are a woman fully grown. It's not my place to tell *you* what to do." Emery's nose was high in the air, with the clear implication that she didn't care for older sisters telling *her* what to do.

"Emery, you must let go of this idea that I am double-dealing with you. Why should you be *so* convinced that I intend to marry and leave?" Anna folded her hands under her apron again, coming to a stop before her tallest sister.

Emery met her eyes. "Tell me you wouldn't rather live in a fine house full of servants and never come back here again."

Anna blinked.

When her gaze dropped to the floor, Emery just shrugged.

"I think I'm being remarkably understanding, Anna," Emery said. "Simply tell me the truth."

There was a long, uncomfortable silence until Anna finally answered, "I can tell you one truth. I think I kept Lord Zachary's presence a secret both so I could pretend we were still living as ladies ought, and... and because I enjoyed daydreaming about what might be... "

When her voice trailed away, Rose prompted her. "What?"

"If only he noticed me," Anna almost whispered.

Now the uncomfortable silence was shared all round. Till finally Emery said, "I wish you would put yourself in my shoes for a moment. For as distressing as it must be to hope that a man might see you and fancy you and make your whole life different, you don't seem to grasp that I have never hoped that, not for one moment. That door will never open for me; that door doesn't *exist* for me."

Something in Anna fired up at Emery's words, words she'd heard in some version from Emery ever since she was tiny. "But it exists for *me*! Or at least it did! Let me mourn the life I thought I'd have. That I *wish* I had! I can be your sister and *not be you*!"

"And is it so bad, Anna? Is it the worst thing, to wind up living as I live? As I will always live?" Emery's face hadn't been red from the ovens, but it was red now.

Rose broke in. "I don't know why you are sniping at each other when keeping a *man* in the *garret secret* is a far greater blow to all our reputations even than Anna fleecing viscounts for cake money!"

"Oh stars above," said Anna, hiding her face in her apron.

Rose went on. "You do realize that the rest of the entire *square* no doubt knew he lived up there. I mean, *really*, Anna. The nerve of asking us to keep up the appearance of being ladylike while you did *that*."

Anna's face in the apron just shook back and forth.

Suddenly, Jane slapped a hand against the wall and stomped her foot. Her shoe heel was loud on the floorboards. "I will burn this place *down* before I let every word among us be something about blame!"

"No offense meant, Jane," said Emery with a cool shrug, "but your coming to Anna's defense is hardly new."

"Mr. Russell says communities must share until they find a consensus, which includes everyone's point of view," Rose said, twisting the end of her braid in her fingers. "I don't think we're doing it."

"When have you discussed this with Mr. Russell?" Anna immediately came out from under her apron to ask.

And then there was a *bang* at the door.

It wasn't a knock. It was a *bang*. Like someone slapping the wooden panels with an open hand.

Rose turned toward the noise and Anna, Jane, and Emery all looked at each other.

Anna spoke first. "Do we open it?"

Jane shrugged a shoulder. "Was that an *open me* noise?"

"It was some person," Rose said in her reasonable way. "We ought to see what they want."

"Ought we?" muttered Emery, but Jane was already opening the door.

Three sisters froze right where they were, and Rose stood waiting for someone to say something.

The man at the door had slick, unwashed locks of hair curling over his eyes, which were bloodshot. Obvious dark stubble shadowed his face and all down his neck; a shocking amount of skin showed at his open collar. He wore no neck-cloth, his stained green waistcoat holding in the limp folds of his shirt. He also wore trousers that were a wrinkled mess. He wore no coat.

This apparition peered around the room as if trying to focus, then gave it up as a bad job. "As drunk as I am, I can't believe I have to say this to a bunch of lacy schoolroom girls. But you lot need to *put a cork in it!*"

He stood there a moment longer, his bone-knuckled hand braced on the doorjamb. When no one said anything, he nodded, curls bobbing, apparently happy with the lowered volume.

Then he looked at Emery and tossed off some sort of salute with the hand that wasn't holding him upright. "Awright there, sailor? Guess you got in safe the other night after all."

Following this astonishing greeting, the man turned and threw his other hand out to brace himself against the opposite wall. He half-fell out the doorway, just catching himself enough to remain upright.

Anna slowly moved to the door and watched him go.

Bracing himself back and forth between two sides of the hallway, the man lurched to the tiny door at the end just before the stairs, opened it, and disappeared inside.

Just as slowly, Anna walked back to the middle of the room where all her sisters stood watching the open door.

Her jaw hung open, and her hand pointed at the wall. "What was that?"

"What do you mean?" said Emery, too quickly.

"*What* was *that*?"

"*Who* was that?" added Rose.

"Do we need to change the topic?" Emery had suddenly started fluttering her hands and looking very not like herself. She shifted her weight from foot to foot.

"Do we need to... do we *need* to change the *topic?*" Anna just came and stood in front of Emery.

"Well. Is breakfast ready? I suspect it's time to eat?" Emery went to the little table by the stove where they kept plates warm. Since they'd handed one of their plates to Lord Boislegrand, she and Rose were splitting a plate. "I'll finish my egg and leave yours, Rose, does that suit you?"

Anna just looked at Jane.

Jane turned to Rose. "I don't even... "

And Rose threw her hands in the air. "*Emery*. Was that a

man and was he talking to you?"

"I suppose." Emery was now shoveling her egg into her mouth faster than was polite in any social situation. "I need to get the bread in for the next bake, Jordan can't do it all by himself. Sal says she doesn't want arithmetic today but I'll leave that to you, Jane, shall I? I don't want to get in the way of the children's education. Jordan read to me for half an hour this morning, by the way. We really ought to get over there and speak to the children's father, shouldn't we? My, look how high the sun is already. The shop needs to open soon. Is anyone coming down to move the fresh baked bread to the shelves? I'll just go down and wait for someone to come help me move the fresh bread to the shelves. I need to shape loaves. I think I said that, didn't I?"

She set her plate down next to the candlesticks, on the crate that held their little store of crockery, and her voice grew fainter and fainter, garbled by the way she was still chewing her egg, as Emery sidled out the still-open door and disappeared down the stairs.

Jane, who was never befuddled, just leaned her back against the wall, utterly befuddled. "I really don't understand what just happened. I mean, I *really* don't understand."

"We're not getting any closer to consensus," Rose mused, adding, "Where did Emery leave our plate?"

Anna handed it to her mechanically, her mind clearly far away, even though her hands also added a clean fork and took Emery's away. "I don't know what to think."

"Mr. Russell says—"

"*Rose.*" Then Anna interrupted herself interrupting Rose. "I suppose you don't want any scolding from me *today*."

"Or ever," Rose said cheerfully after swallowing a bite of egg. "Scolding or not, Mr. Russell says that the more people speak from the heart, the closer they come to a sense of the whole."

"I don't wish to offend, Rose, but I'd put this family up against Mr. Russell any day of the week," Jane said feelingly.

IN A COMPLETE REVERSAL FROM THEIR EARLY DAYS AT THE bakery, Rose went down before either Anna or Jane. "I'll help get the bread ready to open," she called back over her shoulder as she went down.

Anna's expression verged on panic. "I ought not to have written to Aunt Eden. We cannot have her here. Not amongst... all this."

"Perhaps she won't come."

"You know as well as I do that if it would make things worse, she'll come."

"It will make things worse," said Jane with certainty.

"She'll come," said Anna with the fatalism of the ancients.

AS SOON AS THEY REACHED THE SHOP, BEFORE EITHER could say anything, there was a pounding at the door.

And through the Leicester Square window, Anna recognized the tousled black head of Captain Brice immediately. "Why must men be so *loud*?"

She pulled the door open with one yank. "And why must you always be underfoot, Captain Brice? *Why?*"

For once, the Captain walked in sedately rather than leaping. "I must speak to you, Miss Bickering, before you open the shop. All of you."

Wearily, Anna just nodded. She'd used up the fight in her for the day. "Rose, will you ask Emery to come?"

Noting that all three sisters looked as if they'd reached the end of their rope, and the shop hadn't even opened yet,

Captain Brice took it upon himself to cross the shop to the bakery door. "No need, Miss Rose," he said almost soothingly before he pushed it open and shouted, "Miss Emery, if I might have a word."

Rose's suspiciously cheerful mien had already faded. "I want to lie down."

"I want to go *home*," Anna half-whispered, half-cried into her hands, and Rose went to pat her back as Jane usually did. Emery appeared in the door.

"I've got bread to bake," Emery said to the Captain, waving back towards her ovens, before catching sight of Anna. "What's wrong?"

"What's wrong? What's *wrong?*" Anna managed to find an ability to be incensed in the middle of her despair.

"Ladies. Please. I've taken the liberty of examining your water bill situation a little more closely."

"Who told you?"

"Anna, honestly. Couldn't we use a little help?" Rose stood up straight.

And at that, Jane couldn't keep her thoughts to herself any longer. "That's not what strangers give, Rose. Especially men. You must stop being so trusting. Surely we've all been here long enough to understand that."

The truth of that settled like a pall over the room; Captain Brice opened his mouth and closed it again.

He looked closely at Jane's face, seeing the lines bitterness had planted on both sides of her mouth, and the suspicion in her eyes that was just heap after heap of humiliating remark from some man in the street.

"I can't argue, Miss Jane," the Captain said quietly, evenly, softly, "but I do want to offer some help."

He met her gaze levelly, with nothing to hide.

She'd forgotten what that looked like, a man's face with no judgement in it. He wasn't looking at her like an object, or like prey. He just looked into her eyes with the sincerity of a man who was making a kind offer.

It was the first time Jane had looked at a man as a person in a long, long time.

For the first time, she noticed the bump where his regal nose had likely been broken, the sharp tilt of his cheekbones under his sun-browned skin. He had square eyes, the kind that looked straight into you, she realized.

And he could say beautiful things without sounding parlor-polite at all.

"Ladies, I took the liberty of speaking to your water company agent, since he has the contract to supply my hotel as well. You must fight the charge for the months you were not here. Your landlords, the Scropes, must handle that, or else the water company must pursue the tenants who *were* here; your names are not on that contract. In fact, your names are not on *any* contract, though you *have* used the water in recent months. I believe you can mollify the agent by offering to pay for that, though no contract says you must, and in return he can considerably reduce your price."

"Really?" Jane had been wrong. Captain Brice wasn't merely a man. He was covered in roses and spoke the notes of music.

"Two other things you ought to know. One is that lessors are in arrears *often*. Of course, the agent wishes to collect, but many of his lessors make him wait months. He ought to give you more time to pay. And two, the reason he lets lessors go into arrears is that he does not wish to lose them to his competition. There are other water companies, ladies. You can change your agent—you *have* no agent, because you have not agreed on your water rents. You can engage another company. And negotiate a better rate."

Something let go around Jane's heart, and the sudden lightness made her dizzy. Her back thumped against the wall.

And incredibly, Anna moved closer to the Captain.

"You're sure?" she whispered.

"Yes, ma'am," he said, nodding his bare head.

And Anna threw her arms around him and hugged him.

His face was confused about how to look. Astonished eyebrows flew up and his mouth fought itself, deciding between a smile and gape-jawed surprise.

One of his hands wandered about in the air as if he considered patting her back but thought better of it. She had his other arm pinned to his side.

"Oh Jane," Anna said as she turned away from him, already forgotten.

But Jane saw the way his eyes lingered on the back of her head, and one more stone of disappointment settled in her gut. The pile there had been growing and growing since their mother's death. It would, she assumed, eventually crush her.

"Good news," Jane tried to make her nod to Anna brisk. "My lesson is learned, Captain," she said, and made sure the eyes she turned to him were as calm as ever. "I should have asked more questions before I despaired. There are always new traps, I find. It's a wonder anyone manages any business at all."

"Grown men have foundered on all the same traps," Brice said, soberly meeting her gaze over Anna's head.

Jane smiled a tight little smile. And she couldn't help answering him in that way she had, as if they knew each other well, even though she had just realized that it wasn't true and never would be. "Is that supposed to make me feel better?"

"Good news," said Anna, whose jaw was firm, "but we still must pay the charges."

"Fair charges, but charges nonetheless," Jane agreed.

"At least the Captain has given us some help!" Rose seemed annoyed that no one recognized the value of her recruitment of the Captain to their cause.

Anna turned back to look at him again. She was still close enough that she could look up into his eyes. "For months, I have been dreaming that some gentleman, *any* gentleman, might at least offer us some *help*. Thank you, Captain. You have restored some of my faith in humanity."

"Have I?" He looked surprised by that.

No one brought up Lord Boislegrand, who had helped them just as much or more by buying outrageously priced cake. That was a tender subject, while this felt cleaner. More honest.

Emery, who had been leaning against the bakery door with her arms folded across her middle, spoke out. "I suppose we still need cake to pay the water charges."

Jane turned back to her sister. How had she forgotten, even for a second, that her sister was more important than even a helpful man with piercing eyes? "Let me do more calculations. I think... I think we will still need... cake."

Emery just nodded and left.

Captain Brice looked about the shop. "I don't wish to always be the one bringing discomfort into the bakery, ladies."

"Not at all, Captain," and Anna inclined her head like a Her Majesty dismissing him, but kindly. "You've done us a great service. A *great* service. We will all eventually understand how great."

"We're getting closer to consensus, but we aren't there yet," Rose added, in a philosophical way.

NOW THAT SHE KNEW THE WAY TO THE KITCHEN SALON, AS the women called it, Emery didn't wait for Miss Hayes. She'd *like* to wait for Miss Hayes, but there was no need.

Upon admittance to the kitchen, after Emery ducked her

head under the old door frame and came down the stairs, she could see smiles as everyone watched her glance from face to face until she found Miss Hayes.

She was a bright spot among them, so cheery and pretty, and deeply engrossed in conversation with Edwina, the cook whose kitchen this was.

Emery found an empty stool at the kitchen table, and someone passed her a cup of tea. It was easy to sip and memorize Miss Hayes' smile, the way it tilted down at the corners and made Emery wish she could touch it.

This was a kind of sisterhood too, she mused as she drank the astringent, bracing cup. There was no milk or sugar in it —Edwina's wages didn't go that far, and the collection of women who gathered there didn't have the wherewithal for luxurious touches—but it was welcome, and it was kind.

Mollie, the laundress, leaned in beside her. She wore a little white cap so soft it seemed to float, with lace that contrasted sharply and beautifully with the warm dark color of her skin.

"Are you going to talk tonight, or just sit and stare at her?"

Emery rolled her eyes. In truth, she did not feel like talking. "How many women come here just to loll about and stare at Miss Hayes?"

"A few," Mollie admitted. "Enough to make it funny."

"And they all disappear after a while?"

"Oh no, not all. Most. There's a difference between being starry-eyed over a pretty woman and wanting to join the exclusive club, if you follow what I mean."

"I think so." Emery put down the teacup. "I'm not going anywhere, even if Miss Hayes never visits again. I've waited my whole life to find a group of women like this."

"Like what, if you don't mind my asking?"

"Women who stand together. Stand up for each other."

Mollie just laughed. Laughed so hard tears came to her

eyes.

"What?" Emery was in no mood today to be laughed at.

"Oh sorry, truly, I don't know you that well, Miss Bicker-ing, not to laugh at you—"

"Emery," Emery said with irritation.

"Emery." Mollie nodded in acknowledgement. "You can't count on these women to stand up for you. There's plenty of women here wouldn't talk to Miss Hayes in the daylight. Edwina won't speak to me on the street."

"Why not?"

Mollie waved her hand to show the color of it. "Why do you *think*?" She looked out over the little group, just as Emery had. "We had that Mrs. Damer, the sculpting woman, you know, the papers write about her. Stopped in for a few days, she did. I think Sophia caught her eye. She never once said a word to the rest of us; just sailed on by. I doubt she'll ever be back. And I can tell you she wouldn't cross the street to help you if you were on fire."

"But... " Emery just waved a hand toward what seemed like a convivial little group. Someone across the room was laughing at something Miss Hayes had said. Of course.

"We hang together because we have to, Emery. Because it's a way to find at least a little of what we're looking for. But it's not family." Her eyes were pitying. "You don't have a family to look after you anymore?"

"I have a family." Emery felt the odd twin sensation of losing something and gaining something at the same time. She had always wanted to be part of a circle like this. But she always *had* been part of the Bickering sisters, and she always would be. Even if Anna married. Her life was her own, not Anna's, and the reverse must obtain as well.

"Then you're well off." Mollie sipped her own sugarless tea. "Your family calls you Emery?"

Emery nodded. "My given name is Emily. My littlest sister,

Rose, when she was very tiny, she couldn't say it. She's a bit insistent about being right, even when she was two. She insisted my name was Emery, and I answered to it well enough and my sisters all called me that."

"Your mother didn't put a stop to it?"

"No." For the first time, Emery wondered at that. "No, she didn't. She wasn't forceful, in any event."

"Well, you're lucky she wasn't forceful about that, if you got a name you like."

"I am, yes." Emery felt different pieces of calmness slotting together inside her in a new way. "I am lucky."

THE AIR WAS CLOYINGLY WARM. ROSE COULDN'T HAVE LIED convincingly that she wanted to go out for fresh air, had anyone asked her. But no one asked.

So far from their first few days, it felt entirely reasonable to stand outside her own shop. There were pedestrians passing on the pavement, and carriages in the road, but it seemed normal now, not just a rush of people and noise.

Though she was now mindful that the tailor across the way was spying on her and her sisters.

"Miss Bickering."

And Mr. Russell's voice had become the happiest sound in the world. She loved the particular way he made every sound in her name. She loved how he might have meant any of her sisters, but he only meant her.

"Mr. Russell." Her grin was not ladylike, she knew it was not. But she couldn't stop it.

How was it that each time they spoke, Rose felt as though there were a million things she could say to him, yet it was also such a pleasure to be near and not talk at all?

Did he feel the same way? Because there was a long

silence between them before he said anything else, and it was the happiest silence Rose had ever heard.

"I wish I could simply take you for a walk around the square."

And how was it that his desire to walk with her was almost as lovely as actually doing it?

Rose felt very forward, but she must say it. "I would like to speak with you even more than I would like to walk with you."

She heard his feet shuffle a little; she wondered if his ears were turning hot. She knew hers were.

"I want to talk with you more than anything," he said, his voice a little lower now, at a pitch that made her very bones vibrate in sympathy. "I don't think we ought to meet in the mews again."

He'd *suggested* it. And they'd done it, not once, not twice, but many times. It was quiet there, and Rose could reach out for his hand and explore it all she liked. And she did like.

Her heart pounded, not just at the thought of Mr. Russell's big square hand, not just at the thought of meeting him secretly in the mews, but at the idea that it wasn't so bad, not at all. She wasn't *hiding* him, not like Anna and Emery had hid the fact of men in the building. Their very own building.

A month ago, Rose would have been genuinely frightened at the thought of sleeping under the same roof as strange men. Now she was only interested in this one.

Did he really not want to meet in the mews again, or was he playing the part she ought to play, of the coy one? "Ought not, or will not?"

Mr. Russell—dear Mr. Russell, as Rose now thought of him—made a noise in the back of his throat that Rose had never heard before, but her hopes swooped low when he said, "It is not like the values of the friends, to sneak into quiet places together when we know your sisters won't approve."

And that was what Rose adored most about him. He seldom spoke of himself, or of her; that *we* came naturally to him and every time he said it, it felt like a present.

"Not even if we do it so that we may talk about values?"

"Are you doing it *only* to talk about values?"

She loved his version of his voice best, when it grew low and teasing, only for her. It made her brave. She smiled as she said, "No. Are you?"

He made that noise again. "No. Miss Rose, if you wish to speak of personal things—"

"I'd prefer not to discuss personal things in the street," she said with an excess of prim propriety that made him laugh. She loved that, too. Would he keep producing new noises she would love? "But if you wish to meet in the mews, in five minutes, perhaps, we could discuss whatever you like there."

"Personal things?"

"Likely not." Rose couldn't stop her smile from coming and going. It was so thrilling, his palpable emotion and all about *her*. She wanted it to last. And he sounded so serious. As she'd never expected a man to compare personal values with her, Rose was still getting used to the shape of it. She wasn't sure it fit her.

But she'd like to talk much, much more.

"Meet me in the mews?"

"Miss Bickering."

Rose had time to wonder what excuse he was about to give. He sounded impatient; or was that worried?

She heard him *huff* out a breath. "I'll gladly meet you in the mews in five minutes."

She laughed.

"Am I funny?"

"I'll tell you exactly why I laughed, in the mews."

He stepped away. It was only a foot, but it felt like a mile.

"Miss Bickering," he said in the way that meant he was taking his leave.

She heard him go.

Rose knew this game. They had only played it a very few times, but it was a good game.

She needed to make her way through the shop, through the bakery, and out into the cramped cobbled spaces behind the building by the time Mr. Russell walked around Bear Street to the first drive that opened for him and let him back there as well.

Fortunately, by now she knew when her sisters were otherwise occupied.

"I'm going to sweep the bakery," she told Jane, grasping the broom on her way to the bakery door.

She was helped in her escape by the customer who scraped open the door just as she passed through.

"Fine," said Jane. "Penny loaf, Mrs. Ahearn?"

"The husband says I should try a reducing diet. I suppose that means for both of us. Penny loaf, Miss Bickering, it's dry toast at my house tonight."

Rose kept tight hold of the broom as she moved from table to table in the bakery proper, keeping her distance from the radiating source of heat that was the oven. "Everything all right, Emery? Jordan?"

"Yes," was all Emery said before going back to discussing whether or not they could thicken the outer surface of a ball of dough without preventing it from rising.

Rose smiled a little—Emery and Jordan together talked about bread like equals. But she kept walking. If they were busy, they wouldn't ask her why she was going out the back.

They didn't.

She'd barely closed the door when she heard that happiest of all voices murmur, "May I surprise you?"

"You must have run!"

"Not quite."

"You've already surprised me!"

"Not like this."

And with that, Mr. Russell's arms, startlingly hard and yet soft at the same time, came round her middle and she was pulled against him.

"Mr. Russell!" Rose sounded shocked as a matter of procedure, but she melted comfortably against him.

They had only done this twice before. Rose still couldn't figure out why her body felt so *new* when he held her tightly against him this way.

"Personal things?"

Rose's heart thumped. Was he going to ask her to marry him? Did she *want* him to ask? "Later."

"Then," and the brush of his breath on the tip of her nose started a shiver in her belly, "may I have a kiss?"

It was the best question Rose had ever heard.

She had so longed for him to ask, she'd thought of almost nothing else for days. It was odd, how much time she had spent imagining it, when the answer was so easy. Rose threw her arms around his neck. "I'm so glad you are not taller."

He laughed at that, a half-choked, half-burbling laugh that he clearly couldn't hold back. "I'm glad that your arms are just the right length!"

And before Rose could answer his impertinence, he kissed her.

It scattered all her thoughts, the feel of his lips on hers. They were soft and surprisingly warm, a little rough too, and made her feel soft and wobbly and very awake all at the same time.

But the best part was that Mr. Russell did not pull away when the kiss was over. He nestled her even closer in his arms, and his lips brushed her temple, too. "My apologies. You never did say I could have a kiss."

"You may have as many kisses as you like, sir, but only on loan. You must pay every one of them back."

And with that, she stood on her toes, held his face in both her hands, and kissed him in return.

When she let him go this time, she was grateful that his hands at the small of her back held her upright.

"These are the only personal things I'm prepared to discuss," she told him from inches away, and spread her fingers over the lapels of his coat. He was so *solid*.

"Tired? Or... more failure to reach consensus?"

"That is my house," Rose admitted.

"Well, it can't be blamed on you. I honestly find you very easy indeed to speak with, Miss Bickering."

"Speak to me again," she said, sliding her hands up the sides of his neck to hide her fingers behind his earlobes. He had *earlobes*.

"I wasn't making a joke, we really ought to speak of—"

"I wasn't joking either," said Rose and leaned in to kiss her Mr. Russell again.

"How long can we do this?" Rose said against his lips when they parted again. She had never drunk liquor, but feeling drunk must feel like this.

"I feel guilty doing it at all," Mr. Russell admitted.

"Remind me of your age?"

"I am an advanced twenty-two years of age, Miss Bickering."

"Then let me advise you, Mr. Russell, even though I am only twenty, that you ought not to feel guilty. First and foremost, because we have reached consensus."

"Your sisters would—"

"Mr. Russell," said Rose firmly, and accenting her words with squeezes of her arms around his neck, "my sisters get up to things with men that you cannot even imagine. Let us enjoy the moment."

Episode 11: Suspicious Frenchmen

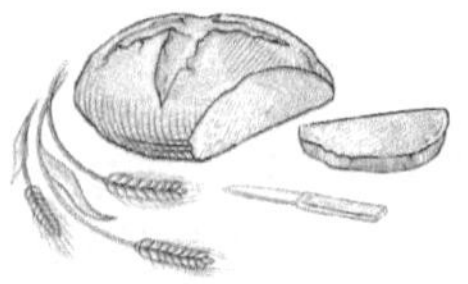

"Mrs. Coxson. Thank you." Rose still thought of her as Mrs. Bunions, but when waiting on her, was careful not to say it.

Tonight over supper she'd report that Mrs. Bunions hadn't asked once about buns, but *had* bought two pounds of the maslin. If all her sisters were there to hear it.

No one wanted to talk to anyone, and seldom were any two Bickering sisters in the same room. It had been days since the revelations about *men* in the building, and Rose would have been far more interested in interrogating her sisters about those men if she hadn't been so pleased with her own.

"You be well, girl."

It was the first time Mrs. Bunions had said anything that wasn't a demand, or a complaint about bunions. Rose smiled. This was going to be a good day.

"Thank you, Mrs. Coxson! I wish the same to you!"

She heard the door scrape open and Mrs. Bunions say, "Pardon, sir. Bunions, you know," as she clearly walked past someone coming in.

"How may I serve you today?" Rose put on her best business smile. One never knew when someone else's day wasn't going so well as hers.

"Mm hmm, mm hmm." It was a man's voice, and that wasn't an answer.

Well, that posed a problem.

Rose tried again. "Is there something you'd like? The morning quartern loaves are sold, but you might be interested in a pound of the maslin?"

"I am *definitely* not interested in *any* amount of the maslin."

He had a French accent. And from the sound of his shoes against the floorboards, he was walking around the room. Well, that was rude. Rose was right here.

Silently, she decided to offer him one more chance. She did not want to let go of her cheerful mood. Even Mrs. Bunions had been very congenial. "Then how may I serve you today?"

Rose thought he was going to ignore her again. She heard him shaking the far shelves, which were empty; in the morning there were loaves piled on the far side waiting for customers, but by this time of day they were gone.

He finally spoke. "I see you have no cake."

Rose felt the skin of her arms tighten, and on the back of her neck. She almost never felt that way. And it wasn't just the word *cake*. He'd said *I see you have no cake* the way she imagined a swordsman would unsheathe a weapon.

"No, sir, we do not." Deep down inside, she had an urge to tell him a long, long story about cake. But she was no longer new to shopkeeping; she didn't know him; and part of her knew Jane was right. She mustn't trust every stranger.

Only Mr. Russell. Who was no longer a stranger.

"I heard," the man went on, "that you sold cake."

"We have actually never sold a cake." If he didn't say

something useful in another minute, Rose was going to go knock on the bakery door and see if someone would join her here. He made her uneasy.

Then it occurred to her to ask another question. "Do you *want* a cake?"

His steps stopped in front of her. "Young woman, I provide confectionery that melts in the mouths of London's finest ladies and gentlemen. I do not *want* cake. I *create* cake."

"Then may I ask what you do want?" *Because you've got five more seconds before I get my tallest sister in here with a wooden bread peel,* Rose thought to herself.

"A wise man of business knows his competition. I heard there might be cake. I see I was misinformed." And with that, he started for the door.

Rose felt her heart pound; her fingers actually tingled. He was a *competitor*. "I am sorry you had to travel so far for no cake," she called as she heard him wrestle the door open.

"Only a few steps. A wasted trip at that," she heard him mutter under his breath as he left. He didn't bother to pull the door entirely closed.

A few steps?

He was from the hotel.

"*Emery!*" yelled Rose, too urgent even to walk to the door and bang on it.

"*What?*" Emery burst through the bakery door almost instantly.

"Did you bring a bread peel?" Rose couldn't keep from smiling.

"There's no one here."

Jane and Anna pushed in right behind Emery. "Are you all right, dear?" "Did someone frighten you?" "Is the till box safe?"

"Jane!" Anna sounded disapproving at that one.

"There was a man here from the hotel."

"Oh!" Anna rushed over to put her arm around Rose's shoulders. "Did he say something awful? Why on earth did he come *in?*"

"Not one of the street men. At least, he didn't come in to shout nasty things at me. Or those things I'm assuming are nasty. Won't you tell me what they mean?"

"No." Anna was short. "But what happened? What did he say?"

"He just roamed around the shop looking at things, and he asked about cake. And he seemed happy that there was no cake, and he said he was our competition!"

"*What?*"

"Never say so!"

"It's those hod-carriers from the hotel." Emery sounded certain.

"No one in the square is carrying hods, Emery, though there are pavers working on the south end." Jane sounded confused. Hod-carrying happened during building, and Leicester Square was full.

"I like how it sounds. I know what I meant."

Sal squeezed in between Anna and Rose, for some reason. "Jordan wants to know if he should keep making loaves by himself."

"I'll check on him," and Emery went back into the bakery.

"Would he have bought cake, do you think, if cake were displayed?" Anna had turned her attention back to Rose.

"Were you scared?" Sal's voice was closer to the floor.

Rose wanted to answer Sal first. And she wanted to lie.

It was her first experience with the desire to keep a younger, smaller person in the dark about life's more difficult moments. "Not at all," she said as she put an arm around Sal's shoulders just as Anna had around hers. "He was only a bit odd."

"She was scared," Sal said confidently to Anna.

And that was Rose's first experience that smaller, younger people were extremely good at detecting lies.

"I'm not scared now," said Rose, rubbing a hand on Sal's back. Sal seemed very interested in being scared.

"But would he have bought?" Anna reminded Rose of her question.

"I couldn't say. Anyway, it doesn't matter, as we have no cake."

"Oh, yes, we do. I have a cake in the back."

"No one's in danger of buying it in the back," said Rose in confusion. "You didn't tell me to sell cake."

Jane spoke up. "We're still trying to decide what to do with it."

"I think sell it or eat it are your options."

"We're trying to figure out *how* to sell it," Jane explained. "Should we sell the whole cake? Should we sell only slices of cake? And how do we price it?"

Anna added, "I think our customers won't want a whole cake. And we can charge more if the prices are small because we divided the price into slices, too."

"But who wants one piece of cake?" Rose heard the door open and close and assumed Emery was back with them as she spoke. "Lonely bachelors? They go to the coffeehouses to eat, don't they? Unless they are wealthy enough to take meals at the hotel."

"Exactly," said Anna. "But then how do we divide it? A quarter of a cake? And then how can we raise the price a little on the portions? Should we just sell a quarter of a two shilling cake? Or can we get—what would it be if the cake is two and six? It always takes me a moment."

"Seven and a half pence," said Sal.

Silence settled in the shop.

"That's very good," Rose told her as Anna asked Jane

under her breath, "I thought you said she wasn't—I thought you said arithmetic wasn't her finest subject."

"No, I said I can't bl—I can't *catch* her half the time to make her do any arithmetic lessons."

"It's stupid because the numbers are wrong." Sal had a grip around Rose's skirts that told Rose something was frightening Sal now.

"The numbers aren't wrong, little one, you got them right," she said soothingly.

"I know I got the answer you *want*. But it's not how numbers should work. It shouldn't be counting twelves in one place and counting twenties in another place. That's not how to sort out numbers."

"But that's how money works, darling," said Anna.

"It's *stupid*. Why not twelves in all the places?"

ANNA DIDN'T WANT TO ARGUE WITH SAL. BONY AND cranky on the best of days, the little girl now seemed genuinely shaken, and was clinging to Rose's skirts as if she expected something bad to happen.

Anna just looked at Jane. "Why *not* twelves in all the places, Jane?" Jane hadn't just been good at arithmetic, she had a genuine feel for numbers that Anna would never have.

And Sal's question seemed to have struck her. "Yes, why not?" She was muttering almost to herself. "Why *not* indeed?"

Jordan seldom said anything at all, preferring to follow his sister in and out and spend his time with the bread dough. But now he spoke. "Sal's always right about numbers, even when people don't listen."

That startled Jane out of her musings. "I listened!"

"Not much," mumbled Jordan, who clearly didn't want to fuss with Miss Jane but also clearly disagreed.

Jane, to her credit, immediately offered as graceful an apology as could be desired. "I'm so sorry. I thought I was listening, but perhaps I was only talking. I'm not a governess by trade. I should have listened."

But Jordan just cocked a thumb toward his sister, hiding in between Anna's and Rose's skirts.

Jane bent over the pitted counter toward the little girl behind it, drawing skirts around her like curtains. "I'm so sorry, Sally. I shouldn't have talked so much and not listened more. You're perfectly right, you know. It *would* be more sensible with twelves in all the places. Or even twenties."

Sal said nothing, just nodded. It was Jordan, again, who spoke for his sister in her time of need. "She's always *right;* I just said it. People don't like being right any more than they like being wrong."

Jane looked from him to Sal again. And she smiled. "I *love* when people are right with numbers, Sal, never you fear."

Sal nodded again, but her grip on Rose's skirts loosened a little.

Anna looked down at Sal's dark hair. How was it she headed a family of four sisters, but was responsible for six people, at least? Things never got easier, she thought grimly.

"Well, among other things, we must sort out some discussion of education for Sal."

"And Jordan!" Emery reached out to squeeze the boy's shoulder.

Jordan just shook his head. His short dark hair was dusted with flour. "I like bread," he said firmly.

Anna's grip on giving orders had been significantly loosened by the episode of the man upstairs. Even Jordan was defying her now.

Well, he would clearly make a happy baker, at least judging by what she saw now; but she felt the weight of responsibility that he be equipped to do other things in future should he wish.

And be able to calculate his own money.

"I like bread too, my friend, but I can still read and do sums and tell you about the Carthaginians," Emery assured him. Which made Anna feel a little better, as Emery still wasn't in charity with her oldest sister.

"Everyone ought to know something about the world." Anna addressed Jordan, but her mind was ticking over all the new things to worry about. "You are earning your bread now, but how much more may you earn with more knowledge?"

"Or just live a more interesting life?" Jane still looked very not-Jane, lost, apparently, in a world where all of the places counted twelves.

"We're responsible for your education," finished Anna.

"You're not esposible for anything about us," Jordan said, just as firmly as he had insisted he liked bread.

Wonderful. Two more young people who didn't want to be told what to do.

And it was at this auspicious moment that the sticky door unstuck, and Lord Zachary walked in.

He wore his stunning blue coat, his hair was smoothed perfectly under his gray beaver hat, and he still had that lovely face. Such fine, regular features oughtn't go with such broad shoulders.

"Oh, go *away*," Anna said without thinking. She had enough problems right now.

He spread his gloved hands. "Is this not a shop?"

"We don't want your custom." There were occasional men in the shop, but Anna definitely felt they could do without this one.

"See here, you can't refuse my money simply because you don't like me."

Anna remembered it wasn't just her and Lord Zachary in the shop. She looked around at her sisters.

Jane was the one who said, "It's true, we *cannot* stop doing business with people just because we don't like them."

"Thank you." Lord Zachary inclined his head in a regal way, and then looked more closely at Jane. "I say. Didn't I ask to paint you once?" He looked searchingly at her ears. Yes, it was most obvious that he was very closely studying her ears. "I don't suppose you'd change your mind, would you?"

Jane had become her frostiest self. "Yes, I *have* changed my mind. I've changed my mind about selling you bread."

"You've never explained what you are doing in our garret," Emery put in before the man could make himself sufficiently unpleasant that Jane took up a sausage.

He shrugged those damned broad shoulders under that damned blue coat. "I didn't know I needed to explain myself. I paint."

Emery put her hands over Jordan's ears, looked at Anna to do the same with Sal. "Paint being another word for..."

"Honestly, miss, I paint. In oils."

Emery let Jordan's head go; the boy shot her a dirty look, which she ignored. "Paint what? Women?"

"Honestly, no. I sometimes paint landscapes, but it isn't my strength. I have been practicing with still life. I would like to improve painting figures."

"What for?"

For some reason, the man seemed willing to be questioned by Emery for however long it took to buy some bread. "People pay better for portraits than for landscapes and certainly far better than they pay for vases of flowers."

Anna felt the tide shift in the room, felt opinion moving over to sympathizing with Lord Zachary. Lord Zachary, who had embarrassed her the first day they met and didn't do her the simple courtesy of noticing. Lord Zachary, who darted about with his drunken friends and didn't have a care in the world except a sister who felt this neighborhood beneath her.

Lord Zachary, of whom Anna had noted every inch of his long legs, his square-tipped fingers, and his absurdly full lower lip. Lord Zachary, who had never once looked her in the eye as a lady.

Lord Zachary who forced her to remember that she wasn't, not anymore.

"You paint for your living?" The direct question was from Rose.

"I am trying."

Anna couldn't take it. She couldn't take Rose spending sympathy on this wastrel when no one had any for her. "Does your work pay for your late evenings? And your claret? Or is it gin?"

"I beg your pardon?" Startled, Lord Zachary was looking at her *now*.

"If we are conversing, it is a reasonable topic of conversation. As we are ladies of business ourselves. So I wondered. Does your painting earn you enough to pay for your nights and your gin?"

He turned and looked behind him, as if just realizing that it was easy to see things through windows. Things like his comings and goings.

He had a frown pulling together his fine eyebrows. "If it does, will you sell me some bread?"

"I think it doesn't. I think it's just a lark to you, having a room where you come to paint and annoy your family and sleep when it doesn't suit you to go home. I think you cannot possibly make money from pallid paintings of half-dead flowers with nothing to say."

"Flowers don't speak, miss."

"Not yours, no." Anna remembered paintings she'd seen in the fine houses she had visited in her little bits of a social season, bolstered by Aunt Eden's money to buy gowns and beg invitations.

She remembered how she stood for a long time in front of a brilliantly colored, darkly shadowed painting of horses under a tree. She could almost hear them breathing and smell the fog in the early morning air. "Your painting was afraid to be colorful yet did nothing with delicacy either." The memory of watching him paint, his shirtsleeves rolled up, didn't make her blush now. What she remembered even better than the line of his figure was the smell of the lilacs that had opened in the vase of flowers he used as his model. "Lilacs are delicate, cool, and fleeting. You put them in a painting full of red and brown like a hot piece of meat, for no reason. *You* can't decide what to paint, sir."

When she came back from her memory and looked at him again, he was gaping at her. His jaw literally hung open.

He looked at her *now*, looked at her as though she had three heads, one covered in snakes.

"How did you know that?"

No one else spoke.

Anna lifted her chin. "I simply think it's true."

"Have you..." His brow still furrowed. "Have you gone up to my room while I was out?"

"No, I have *not*." Which was entirely true. "And you needn't come in here making accusations. We are the primary tenants of the building, not you."

"I know." Amazingly, he did not argue with that. "My servants use the back staircase so as not to disturb you. Mrs. Scrope said I mustn't."

"Your *servants*?" Anna couldn't help saying, just as Emery said, "Back staircase?"

"Yes." He at least had the grace to look abashed. "Some of the servants from my father's house, who tidy up the place because..." Had he really not realized this? The admission caused him some distress, "my art garret is really just an occasional room I use to annoy my family and sleep off gin." Then something else occurred to him. "Best, really, since I don't want to disturb that chap in the closet. Only just met him when—" His eyes moved to Emery and his jaw snapped shut. "If we're neighbors, you ought to sell me bread."

Rose decided the issue. "We have maslin left this time of day. How much would you like?"

"I don't suppose you have cake?" He looked about as if wishing would make it appear. "I heard some ladies outside discussing—"

"No cake," Anna bit out.

Lord Zachary looked around the room and correctly judged his chances were as good as they were going to get. "A pound of maslin, please," he said quite humbly.

Rose cut it for him. "Thruppence halfpenny, sir."

He laid his coins on the counter, and Rose gave him back a halfpenny.

"I don't suppose you sell butter?"

"Butter, in a hot bakery? No," Anna said curtly.

"Of course." It humbled him further, clearly, that despite his art garret in Leicester Square, he did not know how to buy butter. "Ladies," he said, bobbing his head to the room in general, and left.

When the door had scraped shut behind him, a cacophony of voices sounded all at once.

"*No.*" Anna's voice rose an uncharacteristic amount. "We are not discussing this now."

"Oh please!" Sal bounced on her toes. "Listening to you all argue is the *most* fun."

Anna closed her eyes. Would the new requirements of responsibility never stop? "We don't wish to be models of quarreling," she said, opening her eyes and shooting a look at

Emery, then Jane, and of course Rose even though Rose didn't see it.

"Jordan, you may mix up another half-barrel of the maslin dough if you want," Emery said, knowing the result she'd get.

"*May* I?" He raced through the door.

"Go help him, would you, Sal? It's thick to stir."

"I know you want me out." Slowly, Sal's steps moved toward the door, then again. She looked around. "You're putting me out of the room, aren't you?"

"Just for now," Emery assured her.

Emery was a reliable source of good information and no math lessons. Sal nodded and followed her brother.

The instant the door closed Anna said swiftly and softly, "If you all start in on me they'll hear it."

"You have to discuss this man *some*time," Jane shot back, though quietly.

"Yes, why not give us what you know of him?" asked Rose.

"Rose, we need to know a great deal more about Mr. Russell, whom you seem to know far better than I know Lord Zachary."

"He's a *lord*?" said Emery just as Rose said, "Never mind, then."

Anna narrowed her eyes at Emery. "And what about the chap in the closet?"

"I have to look in on the maslin—" Emery made to reach for the door.

"You do *not*! You're going to have to tell us about the chap in the closet, you know!"

"Why?" Emery shrugged. "You all know there's a chap in the closet *now*."

Anna was sorry she'd started the use of the word chap. "How on earth did you meet him? Why didn't you mention him? And *what* did he mean when he called you a sailor?"

Anna had been storing these questions and could fire them quickly.

Jane just folded her arms and leaned a hip against the counter the way Emery usually did. Her grin was rude. "Yes, Emery, do tell us *all* about him. Whatever has possessed you to keep him secret?"

Emery cut her with a glare. "Shush."

"No, really, *what?*" Jane waved a hand at Anna behind the counter. "I know why Anna didn't tell anyone about Lord Zachary."

"Do you?" Anna didn't think Jane understood everything that had been in her mind; she didn't understand it all herself.

"Yes, I think I do," Jane said, looking her in the eye and nodding. Then back to Emery. "But I can't fathom why you were keeping the closet man a secret."

"Aren't we going to hear more about Mr. Russell?" Emery looked desperate for a lifeline to pull her out of this conversational quicksand.

"No," said Rose quite firmly.

Still casting about for help, Emery landed on Jane. "What of you, Jane? You have always been not the least shy with men; why aren't we hearing about some man *you've* kept hidden?"

That made Rose perk up. "Yes, Jane, why is that? You've been so determined in the past. I thought you would be first to be married."

"What do you mean *first?*" said Emery with suspicion.

Rose ignored her. "And here we've seen nothing of your famous marriage attempts. Why?" She frowned. "Are the men here all bad-looking?"

"Why don't I have any *men* hidden in the house?!" Jane's laugh was choking and false. "Why don't I have any rats? Or beetles under my apron? Who do you think is shouting all those vile things at us when we walk down the street?"

"Are you going to tell me what they mean?" Rose cut in.

"No. Who do you think is leering at us from carriages or atop their fine horses while they watch us walk on the hard stone or dirt and never once offer us assistance? Who do you think is waiting for us to *fail?*"

That thought cooled the room considerably.

"I don't have any hidden men," Jane said bitterly, "the obvious ones are trouble enough."

"Mr. Russell doesn't want us to fail," Rose said, as if loyalty compelled her, in the face of Jane's unassailable truth, to mention the one good man that came first to her mind.

"Rose, why do you mention him so quickly?" Anna wasn't letting that pass. "You often do, you know."

Rose pressed her lips tight, then raised her chin. "I've a right to wish to know him better if I like."

"You haven't. You're not old enough."

"Anna, don't even try it. You met eligible men at nineteen."

"Who considers Mr. Russell *eligible?*"

Jane was still looking at Emery. "Meanwhile, the man in the closet..."

"What *is* his name?" Anna looked at Emery too.

"I don't know his name."

"We can't still keep calling him the man in the closet." Anna seemed quite put out by not having the closet chap's name. "At least I knew Lord Zachary's name."

"Is *that* the measure of—"

But the door opened again, reminding them that they were in the shop, with the purpose of selling bread, and it was open.

It was a man who opened the door, but a young man, in a coat of bright green. "The Right Honorable Lady Arnold," he announced, followed by a lady in a soft pink walking dress entirely embroidered with vining leaves.

She had thick, glossy brown hair twisted back from her face and pinned with a gold hair-stick. It was just visible under her tiny bonnet topped with a sweeping feather.

Her gloved hands were tiny too, and she touched nothing. But she did nod. "Ladies," she said with some grave inaccuracy.

Her very presence made Anna pull herself up. There was a *lady* in the shop, and they were arguing like little children at marbles. "Madam."

THE LADY'S EYES TOOK IN ALL OF EMERY'S FLOUR-COVERED apron and the dough drying under her fingernails. Emery thought it likely that the lady even saw the wisps of hair escaping from the braids crossed over her head.

Emery had never expected to be a fine lady the way Anna and Jane had hoped to be, because she'd always been told that came with marriage, and she wanted nothing to do with that.

But this lady was so delicate in every respect, and so clearly looking at Emery, that it made Emery wish she was at least tidier.

"How may we serve you today?" asked Anna, her back straightened, too, by Lady Arnold's look.

"You may recall that my children and I were fortunate enough to enjoy the prizes of your little cake lottery," the lady said.

"Oh yes! You must be a near neighbor to visit us again so soon."

"Not far," she said carelessly, "the southern end of the square. But the previous visit caused this one. I liked the cake and wondered if you had some for sale?" She smiled, and her face went from unremarkable to sweetly girlish. "Unless it is always a lottery? Chances at cake but no true cake?"

And drawing no one else aside for a consultation, Anna simply said, "Yes. We would delight to sell you a cake, Lady Arnold."

"Oh, very good."

Lady Arnold did not ask what type of cake, but when Anna re-emerged from the bakery door holding the plate she said, "We have a very nice *gâteau Breton* today, madam." And she set it down on the pitted counter.

The sweet, golden smell of the cake traveled through the room and had a magical effect; almost everyone's tight posture eased.

"I'll have it, thank you." Lady Arnold looked shyly down, then back at Anna, as if overwhelmed at making a purchase.

"Two and six," said Anna.

Lady Arnold just waited while the footman produced the coins and laid them on the counter.

It was only when he took up the cake that Anna cleared her throat, just a little.

"Yes?" Lady Arnold seemed eager to talk more.

"I don't want to keep you, madam, only to say...Our patrons bring a dish with which to shop, I must ask you, I'm afraid... to return the plate."

"Oh, of course!" Despite her shyness, her laugh wasn't girlish at all, but very warm and a little sultry, like the honey in the cake. "I seldom visit shops. I'll see to it. Of course."

Anna curtsied. "If you seldom shop, you do us even more of a courtesy to visit the Ladies' Own Bakery."

"Is that what it is?" She looked around again, taking in all of them, and the windows, the scuffed wooden floors, the huge half-peck loaves, and even the shelves that were bare. "I like the name. A ladies' bakery ought to have flowers in it, ought it not?"

Anna seemed stumped for a moment as to how she might point out that it was a bakery, not a drawing room. "The warmth of the bakery might cause them to wilt, madam, though I am sure you are right."

"Yes, I see what you mean." Lady Arnold seemed particularly interested in the door to the bakery proper, and kept looking from it to Emery standing next to it in flour-bedaubed clothing. "One ought never to make assumptions, of course. But I find that ladies like flowers."

She seemed to say that last to Emery, so Emery responded. "We all do like flowers, madam."

"Oh, good." And her eyes, a warm golden brown like her laugh, met Emery's. "Good," she said again with a smile, and then moved to the door.

The footman went to open it and found it stuck. He put the plate down on the counter, wrestled the door open, and held it for the lady; then picked up the plate again and went out. The door only mostly pulled closed behind him.

"Two and *six*!" Jane said immediately, though quietly.

"I just named the figure that was in my head," admitted Anna.

"What was she looking at me like that for?" Emery wondered out loud.

But her sisters weren't paying attention. Jane was shaking her head. "I don't think the partial cakes will do. We need to sell more cake, not more expensive pieces of cake."

"We just made more than a shilling on one cake." Anna slid the coins around on the counter with her fingertips. "We need at least seven shillings more a week to pay the water charges."

Rose took the coins away from her and stowed them in the till before Jane could do it. "We need more than that, if we're to eat better."

"And someday have fresh dresses. Yes," sighed Jane.

"Ten cakes a week or more." Anna stared at the counter

where the coins had just been. "Do you know, my darlings, I don't know if the local shop will *have* that much honey."

"Plus butter and eggs to match," Jane mused.

"We might need better ways to acquire them."

Anna was tapping the counter with her fingernail now. "What if we went into the country to find farmers who might sell quantities to us?"

"How would we—Oh no." Emery forgot all about the pretty lady and her flowers. "We're not going to the country. We only know one person in the country and we are not visiting *her*."

"One day at a time," Anna said with that maddeningly vague wave of her hand that she did when she didn't want to acknowledge a truth. "Today, we sold a cake."

"No, Anna, I mean it. We're not running to Aunt Eden. I have an interest in this business too, and I won't..."

Jane let her sisters follow one another into the bakery proper. She was done listening to them squabble for the day.

It bothered her a little that her sisters still thought of her as indiscriminate with her affections. She thought she had explained what happened with the gentlemen in their old neighborhood quite well. She hadn't had *affection*. She'd had a sincere desire to establish mutual financial concerns. The gentlemen hadn't.

She didn't know why Anna hadn't attracted a husband in their few social affairs, back when Aunt Eden had sponsored them a little, back before their mother had died. Anna was pretty and sweet and looked inoffensive enough... at least until conversation. Anna ought to have caught a husband.

She'd asked her mother why Anna hadn't found a

husband, and her mother had just said, "Anna has romantic ideas, my love."

And then she'd asked her mother why she herself hadn't found a husband, and her mother had said "Because you have no romantic ideas at all, my beautiful girl."

Jane still didn't know what that meant. She felt likely she could have a romantic idea, but they were less urgent than surviving. Money made a stable future, not romantic ideas.

And she didn't think the men who approached her had any romantic ideas, either. The leering looks they gave her, on the dance floor or on the street, didn't speak to any romantic thoughts.

She was still lost in thought when the door scraped open.

"How may I serve—" she reflexively responded to the noise, then stopped when she caught sight of the person.

The woman had rouge on her face, clearly visible rouge, in the middle of the afternoon. Her skirts were a bright collection of blue and yellow, with a laced bodice that reminded Jane of old-fashioned clothes Aunt Eden used to wear, but showing a good deal more bust than Aunt Eden had ever seen fit to show. Topped off with hair that seemed somehow too black, she was a study in colorful contrasts.

She stopped with one foot in the door. "I heard—it's a bakery, isn't it?"

"Yes, of course."

Had she expected to be turned away? Clearly she had, because even with Jane's clarification, she came in slowly, waiting to be rebuffed. "I heard—I heard outside that it was women in here, er, women like me doing a business, you understand."

Yes, Jane did understand. She'd studied French; she knew a few of the rude words the hotel men shouted when she walked by. In fact, she didn't know what most of them meant; but she knew a few.

"It's a bakery, just a bakery," she said, not wanting to acknowledge the rude shouts or offend her customer, but also unwilling to perpetuate the idea that their shop was a front for loose women.

"Right." The woman looked around. "Not too busy this time of day, is it?"

"No, we do most of our custom first thing in the morning, then just before noon, and about two hours after noon when the last quartern loaves come out for the day. The big ones," she added, in case this woman might be a person who had never bought an entire four-pound loaf of bread in her life.

"But there's still bread out," the woman said, nodding toward the half-peck maslin in the basket behind Jane.

"Yes, we have the big baker's loaves, and especially the brown bread, most of the day," Jane assured her.

The woman seemed to think this over for a long while.

There were no other buyers; Jane didn't want to rush her.

The woman finally said, "We've got a cook, but one of my friends needs a bit more than we get for the day and I just thought I'd bring her some bread."

That picture gave Jane the woman's entire situation.

Jane wasn't the failed social climber that she had once been. There were all kinds of women out here in the world being subjected to all the degradation she'd endured these last few months, and far worse.

"Honestly," she told her would-be patron, "I think the maslin, the brown bread, is more nourishing. And it's good even without butter."

The woman considered. "The white is kinder to the stomach, innit?" Her accent thickened as she talked.

"The maslin has a sweetness to it; it stays in the stomach."

"Like a stone. It's horse bread." The woman clearly knew all about maslin, and like most Londoners, thought little of it.

"It's cheaper," Jane said, giving her the most persuasive argument she had at her disposal, "and I eat it."

At that, the woman looked her in the eye.

Jane nodded, acknowledging their equality in the face of bread.

"Awright, give me tuppence," the woman said with a vanishing attempt at good grace.

But when she left, her shoulders were higher, and their shy slump was gone. Or perhaps it had been shame.

Jane hoped she'd come back. Ladies' Own Bakery was no place for shame.

Now that she'd left, other questions came to Jane's mind. Ones she wouldn't ask, but wondered about all the same. As far as Jane knew—and she didn't know much—men and their money hadn't made a stable future for their patron, either.

How was anyone to work out a comfortable life between all these options, all of them bad?

Emery came out of the bakery just as the woman disappeared past the edge of the Bear Street window.

To Jane's shock, Emery tore across the floor to rip open the door and race after the woman.

In moments, she was back, though. She clearly had not stopped to chat.

She greeted Jane's open-mouthed stare with a sheepish shrug. "I thought it was a friend of mine."

A friend of Emery's? In those clothes?

When had Emery become friends with such a person?

More importantly, *why?*

Then, like Sal's vision of a world with twelves in all the places, a clearer explanation for how things were in the world slid into place in Jane's mind.

Emery had always said she would never marry. Always, since she was small. But she'd never said she wanted to be alone. Only that she didn't wish to marry.

Not wanting to presume too much, Jane tried to give her little sister all the calm, loving understanding their mother had had, everything Jane had too little of. She would gladly spend it all on Emery if she could. "I would love to meet any friend of yours, Emery."

Emery was too deep in all their recent squabbling. "I don't want to discuss—"

"Emery." Jane's tone pulled Emery's attention back to the present. This present. "Any friend of yours, little sister."

There, she'd gotten through. Emery's shoulders sank, as though backing down from a fight. And as her mouth dropped open in surprise, her eyes grew soft, and sad, and a little lost. Jane hadn't seen her look that way since she was little.

She waited for whatever Emery wanted to tell her.

But all Emery said was, "Thanks," before she walked out. Not through to the bakery, but out the shop door, with no bonnet, no gloves, and no other words.

Episode 12: Hot rain

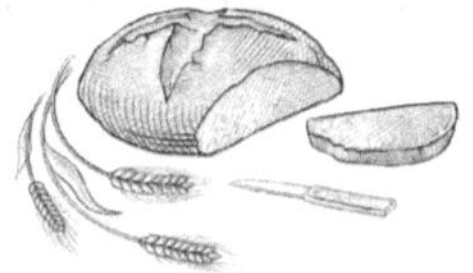

Hot rain had to be the most miserable thing about summer. When the air clung to everything and it all felt damp and sticky, rain just made it all that much worse.

The door disdained to close at all, and Jane glared at it with every ounce of her deep loathing. She was distracted from her door hatred only when an unfamiliar carriage stopped at the pavement outside.

Then she heard a voice drift all the way in from the carriage door.

"Johnson, the pavement must be slippery. Ought we put down a rug?"

"No need, madam, I believe it will be safe if you watch your footing." The footman had an oiled umbrella waiting.

A whisper escaped Jane. "Oh no."

She was by nature quick to action. She seldom questioned what had to be done in an emergency.

Faced with this emergency now, she was motionless, powerless.

Ought she call her sisters? But they'd be subjected to the disaster soon enough.

The footman pushed the door open, and in swept Aunt Eden.

"Jane. Yes. Good. At least you have a strong constitution. If someone must serve people, it ought to be you."

As always when faced with her Aunt Eden, Jane had trouble locating the exact nature of the insult. Likely, there was more than one.

Aunt Eden, with her thin face and fat curls the color of the grim sky outside. Deep grooves of constant disappointment carved down both sides of her mouth; her walking dress had buttoned stripes all across the front like military epaulets, which seemed appropriate, and a bonnet crowned with fluffy ostrich feathers, which did not.

"Aunt Eden." Jane ought to say something untrue about how good it was to see her. She ought at least to come from behind the counter. She couldn't do either.

"Yes, Jane, it is clearly me. I'm the one who has just addressed you."

"Yes. Aunt Eden."

Her great-aunt paused in organizing her skirts and peered at Jane. "Poverty hasn't made you stupid, has it?"

"No, Aunt Eden." And finally Jane decided the question in a way she never did: based on her feelings. She simply didn't want to be alone. "Let me fetch my sisters."

"Yes, I'd like to see Anna. Presumably by now she has consumption."

Jane kept her back to the wall, with the counter between them. "I'll just be a moment."

"I know," Aunt Eden nodded once, fast, like a striking bird, "why would you keep me waiting?"

Jane felt the need not just to pull the bakery door tight shut, but to keep hold of it.

"Aunt Eden."

"What?" Rose was kneading the maselin, which they still made the old way, on one of the large tables. "I can't hear you."

Likely she couldn't; Emery was thumping half-barrels on to another table where Jordan and Sal waited to shape loaves. Anna was at the dish trough with water pouring in.

For days, it had been like this. They all worked together like the meshed gears of a clock, but people didn't speak to each other. And it was easiest not to speak to each other when they couldn't hear each other.

Jane couldn't how to imagine how to cut through the barrel-thumping, dough-slapping, and dish-scrubbing. But she knew she wasn't going back out there alone.

"Aunt Eden." Jane could only say it louder. "Anna!"

"I'm busy, can't you see?" Anna called back, pushing her sleeves up to keep them out of the water. It didn't work.

"*AUNT EDEN!*"

The echo of Jane's shout brought everything in the hot, busy bakery to a standstill.

"*Yes, I'm waiting!*" came an answering shout through the bakery door.

Anna visibly slumped.

Rose muttered at the bread. "It's a bad dream, it's just a middle-of-the-day bad dream…"

Emery thumped the tub down. "Oh she can go to—"

"Emery." Anna's shoulders straightened. "Our great-aunt has no doubt traveled here at some expense, and is asking for us. We should greet her."

"You said we ought to just *consider* asking for her help." Emery raised the half-barrel in her hands again as if to slam it down with great force, then looked at the children, both watching her with big eyes. She put it down. But this was another brick in the pile of coals heaped on

Anna's head, to Emery. "You already wrote to her, didn't you?"

"I'm not going out there alone," Jane shout-whispered from the door.

"We're not at all dressed!" Rose, flour up to her forearms, didn't dare touch her hair to check if her curls were in place.

Anna's back slowly straightened. "Rose. We are in the middle of our work. If Aunt Eden wished to see us dressed for company, she would have come at a different time. Emery. Jane. Let us all say hello to Aunt Eden. Sal, Jordan. Do stay in here, won't you?"

Jordan started shaping a loaf, stretching the ball so it formed a smooth sphere; his was an unconcerned and unconcerning little soul.

But Sal looked like she wanted to see. Emery just shook her head. "Later. If ever. It isn't a pleasant experience."

So it was that all four of the Misses Bickering, Jane at the front, Emery at the rear, marched back into their own bakery shop with all the enthusiasm of soldiers armed only with knives facing a horse-mounted cavalry attack.

The effect was partly accomplished by the way they lined up just as they'd always been nudged to line up when Aunt Eden approached. Perhaps it was just to make it easier for the old woman to see whatever she wanted to see, but it made them feel like sheep lining up to be selected for dinner.

Anna did not look at her sisters as they formed their line. She knew what they looked like. If she hadn't been ready to face Aunt Eden, she wouldn't have written the letter. She wished all her sisters understood what she had to do, but even if they didn't, she was ready to do it.

Still, determination didn't make it easy.

"Aunt Eden," she said, just like Jane, unable to add anything, and curtsied.

"Your hems are all ragged. If poverty makes you wear your

dresses out, you ought at least to hem them. Though I suppose your hems would soon be up to your knees. That cotton lawn is hardly practical for constant washing."

Anna felt all the air leave her. There was no use thinking of all the greetings she'd rather have had, especially *how are you*.

Rose's hand slipped into her hand, and on her other side, Jane's shoulder was a warm pressure, too.

She was ready. She could do this. She was head of the family now. Aunt Eden never had been and never would be. Not *their* family.

"You bought me this cotton lawn, Aunt Eden," Anna reminded her.

"For other places. For other purposes." The old woman was still as upright as an army colonel. She looked just as she always had.

And that made Anna angry. If she was perfectly well and still able to travel, why hadn't she come when their mother was ill?

Then she remembered they hadn't wanted her. They had all been together, all four sisters and their mother, and they knew the loss that was coming; having Aunt Eden there would *not* have made it better.

"Yes, and here we all are now," said Anna with a faint echo of her cheerful drawing-room voice. "Clearly, you got my letter."

"Yes, though I couldn't quite follow whatever foolishness you thought you were proposing. I know you are ruined for good marriage prospects. But you're obviously not going to *stay* here." Her eyes ran over the counters and Anna could practically hear them find every pit.

"Yes, we are." Breathe and stay calm. That was the way to deal with Aunt Eden. Anna had faced leaping, hatless men, miserly landlords, and a horrifying bill for water. She wasn't the same as she had been in younger years.

And she knew now for certain no one was coming to save them. It was up to her.

"Might I be so bold as to ask if you are willing to take us on a jaunt to your neighborhood?" Anna kept her tone light, as if she were suggesting a picnic, not a desperate attempt at survival.

"A jaunt? I know what you mean, you mean to stay with me. Yes, you may. My girls are too busy with their own families to see much of me, and Sir Warren is away. I don't have the pin money for three wardrobes, but we should see to a few appropriate dresses." She stayed right where she was, but clearly peered at Emery. "We'll have to sew some ruffles inside *your* dress front, of course, but—"

"No, Aunt Eden." It came out of Anna's mouth easily after all. And it wasn't just because Emery's face was reddening. It was just... easy.

Did fighting for survival get easier with time?

"No, we don't need dresses for social calls, though if you wished to gift us with some sturdier fabric, we would gratefully accept. And Emery's figure is fine. So is her hair. All of our figures are fine, and all of our hair."

"That's not a matter of opinion, that's just demonstrably wrong." Aunt Eden never fidgeted, but Anna thought she saw one hand twitch. "Emery's hair would likely have a nice wave if we cut it. Jane's did. Why aren't you curling yours now, Jane? A woman with looks like yours needs a husband; everyone will take you for something inappropriate if you don't find one *very* soon. Of course, you know I mean that you should have had one long since. And Emery—"

"No, Aunt Eden. No husband seeking for Emery. Not for *any* of us. And everyone's hair is fine just as it is, including Rose's hair."

"Rose." As if she'd forgotten her youngest grandniece existed.

"Yes. *Rose.*" Anna took in a deep breath. This was really going very well. "We would be so glad if you would call this evening and discuss the details. It's very kind of you to take us."

"How do you expect to find husbands in this state?" Aunt Eden was clearly flabbergasted, and did not care for the state. "I can take you out of *here*," she waved a hand as if the Ladies' Own Bakery were a smoking volcano, "but you're going to have to make *efforts*."

"We are not looking for husbands, Aunt Eden. As I wrote to you, we need to purchase honey."

"Honey."

Anna nodded. "Large quantities of honey."

"You need *husbands*, not honey!"

"We are fully grown women now, Aunt Eden, and I'm sure you understand when I say that it is for us to decide what we need. As any grown person must. I'm sure you understand that."

Anna couldn't be sure, but she thought she saw Aunt Eden's storm-colored curls actually quivering in indignation.

It was a tense moment. Rose squeezed her hand again. Anna concentrated on that. She *would* wait for Aunt Eden to speak first.

"I *don't* understand that, and I won't! You've always been full of odd notions, Anna, but this is the end. You need a *hus*band! *Look* at you! So pretty and now you're all ragged and covered with flour. Your mother was a woman of odd notions too, but I know she raised you to be better than this! All of you!"

"Apparently not." It made Anna's heart light to think that she was like her mother. Even light enough to smile with Aunt Eden in the room. She did smile. "Apparently, I'm more like her than you thought! How nice. So tell us, Aunt Eden, will you call this evening?"

She shouldn't feel so light when Aunt Eden stood planted in the middle of their shop like a tree about to fall on them. Emery still wasn't speaking with her, Jane teetered on the edge of despair, and Rose was gallivanting about the square with a politician. They needed to make the cake plan work. They needed to pay the bills, to get dresses and maybe even chairs, to *eat*. They needed help to find a honey supply other than the local shops, and there was nowhere else to turn.

But she wouldn't let Aunt Eden treat her sisters badly. Nothing was worth that.

And after everything she'd been through, all the dreams she'd thrown away, it felt good to hold on to something she wouldn't let go. And that was her sisters.

At that tight moment, the door to the bakery proper poked open and Jordan's head peeked in. "I know I'm not supposed to come in, but should I get the cooling loaves out of the pans before the bottoms get wet?"

Aunt Eden's ramrod figure softened. The grooves of disappointment in her face loosened. One of her hands even opened, and she looked as though she were about to give it. To *Jordan*.

"A little boy?"

Anna watched, disbelieving her eyes, as Aunt Eden walked across the bakery and *knelt* in front of the cracked open door and looked at Jordan as if he were the last sunrise.

"A handsome little *boy*. Where did you come from, child?"

"Next street," said Jordan suspiciously, watching his limited view fill up with old lady.

Anna shot Jane a look. Jane just looked back, her own mouth open, and shrugged.

Aunt Eden's husband was a baronet who came home two or three times a year and then left. Somehow in this situation she had managed to have two daughters, and both of them married and moved far enough from their mother that visits weren't frequent. And both of them had children. All girls.

Apparently, Aunt Eden had once wanted something from life other than telling young ladies what to do.

"I don't suppose this fellow will come with you to the country, hmm?" Aunt Eden sounded lost in contemplation of Jordan.

"*Am* I?" This was the first Jordan had heard of it.

Anna seized the moment. "We can discuss it. This evening, Aunt Eden, if you would be willing to come."

"Of course," said Aunt Eden. "Yes, of course."

Breathe, Anna told herself, and squeezed Rose's hand back.

"So I'm a grown woman who can decide her life for herself?" Rose whispered.

"Don't be absurd," Anna whispered back. They really must have a serious conversation about Mr. Russell. Contrary to Aunt Eden's unwanted opinion, Rose was perfectly capable of being married. But not yet.

EMERY HADN'T SAID A WORD DURING THE ENTIRE VISIT. Once Aunt Eden had gone, she kept her mouth shut.

She wouldn't have bet on Anna to stand up to the old bat. That she had... felt good.

But Emery had no reason to trust it to last. Aunt Eden had clearly wanted to see the shop, and now she'd seen it. Who knew what she would say or do when she returned this evening? If she did come to their rooms, she would *not* be easier to handle.

Unless they kept Jordan about as a sort of soporific defense. Aunt Eden had certainly melted at the sight of him. Emery had never seen anything like it.

Their aunt had certainly never been that well inclined toward *Emery*, not even when Emery had been ten and climbed the trees on her estate.

Emery slid the last of the ready pans of bread into the oven and straightened. Surely the heat made her face red, but she'd rather be herself, red-faced and plain, than a doll dressed up to entice some man to pick her up and play with her.

She wiped sweat off her forehead with her sleeve before it could trickle into her eyes.

And there, staring into the coals, she realized that instead, she dressed up every chance she could and waited for Miss Hayes to pick her up and play with her.

She had made herself into someone else's plaything after all.

The thought made her shove the bread peel across a table, wood scraping on wood. She backed away from the heat.

"Anna, will you turn these loaves for me?"

Anna, lost in her own thoughts, nodded. "Of course."

Well, she'd have to trust Anna to remember to do it. Anna could judge when the bread was done.

Emery needed to make a call of her own.

WHEN JASMINE HAYES CLOSED THE LITTLE DOOR BEHIND her and turned to walk across the cobblestones of the mews, she saw Emery standing there, with the strings of her bonnet looped over her arm. Emery, lean and tall, her cheekbones flushed with color that might have come from the heat of the day, or an oven. Or something inside, perhaps.

It made Jasmine catch her breath. That strength, and that softness, all in the same person. It was her weakness. She was proud she had kept her distance so far. "What are you doing here?"

Emery clasped her bare hands together. "I came to find you."

Jasmine looked about as she took the few steps to where Emery stood. Emery's eyes had a kind of fire in them, though her expression was stone.

"What are you doing?"

"I came to find you," Emery said again. "I went to Edwina's kitchen and asked if someone knew where to find you, and they sent me to your house."

"Oh no!" Jasmine's hands flew to her cheeks. She didn't want others to see the plain, petty little room. She didn't want *Emery Bickering* to see.

"Never fear." Emery didn't explain that she had wanted to see, that she had spent some minutes staring about the room with its shadowy plaster, with bright dresses draped over a chair and over the bed she could not look at. "I asked about, and one lady told me you ought to be on this street." Emery drank in every detail of Miss Hayes, openly staring in a way she was usually too discreet to do. "I knew you would use the door to the mews."

"Emery, what's wrong?" Jasmine moved closer.

"You've never cared about me, have you?"

Casting worried glances about, Jasmine retreated to a spot behind one of the stable doors where moss had taken hold of the cobblestones and something nameless and green was climbing the wall. It was a quiet little spot where there was at least slightly less chance that a random stableboy would see them.

"Emery, you ought to know me a little by now," Jasmine murmured. "I flirt with everyone good-looking. You're good-looking."

"Please, I have to mean something to someone today."

"Emery, what's happened?"

"My sisters—" Something seemed to choke her; she stopped.

"Are they all right? No one is *hurt*, are they?" Jasmine gathered up her skirts in one hand as if to rush to the bakery, but Emery shook her head.

"No, no. Nothing is wrong, actually. I just feel..." When she bent her head to study the toes of her shoes, Jasmine could see the ends of the cord Emery used to tie up her braids across the top of her head. Sunshine and honey hair, held up by a drab little string. She and Emery had that in common, lives of sunshine and honey and string.

And Emery laughed, a bitter little laugh, before she went on. "You'd think it would be because my aunt can't imagine that I don't want a husband, or to dress for one, either."

"*Is* that it? You're lovely, you must know that. I wouldn't mind if you brushed out your hair and put in a new ribbon, or I..." Jasmine also seemed to have something in her throat. "I'd even do that for you."

She shouldn't say that. Emery had something more honest and strong in her than Jasmine had ever seen before. Jasmine couldn't, *wouldn't* muddle up the younger woman's life with her own. Yet she'd said that. Why had she said that?

Because she would. She would love to brush Emery's beautiful hair.

"Would you?" Emery's eyes came back again to burn into hers. "I'd do anything for that. I *want* that. But I wanted even more to be... worth something. Needed. Wanted. I knew my sisters needed me to bake their bread, and I felt like this was *it*. I was important for the first time in my life. Not to strangers and *definitely* not to Aunt Eden—" She laughed, still with a bitter note, as she shook her head, "—but to people who mattered. And now they have a new plan and they don't need me."

"What new plan?"

"Cake."

Jasmine laid a palm against Emery's cheek. "They need you, Miss Bickering, not because of cake or bread, but because they are your family."

"I liked being needed for something more than just that." Emery raised her own hand and held the little gloved hand against her cheek. "You don't need me, Jasmine, do you?"

"Oh, Emery."

Emery's eyes took in every detail of her face. "You don't want me either, do you." There was no question in her voice.

"I like attention from everyone; I always have." Jasmine Hayes struggled to find the right words for what felt like an important moment—not for her, but for this lovely young woman she'd found and lured along and liked very much. It made her dig down deep inside for something she felt but preferred not to say. She said it anyway. "You can do far better than me."

"Please." Emery didn't say what she wanted, but it was clear she hoped Jasmine would know.

It was just the way of these things. Jasmine realized in the same moment how much she ought to protect Emery from the sordid details of her life, and also how much she did like Emery. It was all equally true.

Ignoring the one realization in favor of the other, Jasmine reached up and kissed Emery's lips, soft, unbearably sweet, and just as flushed with heat.

Emery's eyes closed, and she was clearly lost in the sensation of Jasmine's lips on hers. It was a heady feeling for Jasmine, to know that someone so strong and so sweet wanted her like this.

So heady that it reminded Jasmine of the other realization. And just how she ought to protect the innocent Miss

Bickering from even more unpleasant truths than the one she was about to say.

"I would kiss anyone that way, you know," Jasmine whispered.

It opened Emery's eyes. She leaned away, half-stepped back. "I don't believe you," she said, but Jasmine could tell she was just trying out the words.

"Yes, you do." Jasmine thought she felt something break inside, but that wasn't possible. She was numb to so much.

"I'm never going to want anyone else the way I want you," Emery answered instantly, her voice low, but insistent. She had the presence of a lion, not a gaunt young woman in a worn dotted dress.

"I don't think that's true. I *hope* that's not true. You can do far better than me, I mean that."

"I can adore you and still know you're wrong," Emery said, stepping back to make more room for Miss Hayes to leave.

If Emery had just walked away, Jasmine could have made the exit Emery clearly expected. But no, the steadfast Miss Bickering pulled her bonnet off her arm, swung it by its strings, then put it on, all while her eyes stayed on Jasmine.

She forced Jasmine to look careless and smile.

"Have a good evening, Miss Bickering," Jasmine tossed back as she walked away, able to keep her voice tuned to carelessness as long as Emery couldn't see her face.

ANNA HAD LEARNED THAT THE THRESHOLD OF THE SHOP was a dangerous place. She looked carefully out all the windows, down one street and the other, before stepping up to sweep the last crumbs over the sill.

Still, just as she did, a carriage pulled alongside the pavement in front. Was there some sign that flashed by the door, that carriages arrived just at sweeping time?

She recognized that barouche. She wasn't ready for Lord Boislegrand today. Her mind spun in a circle. She'd used up all of her decisiveness on Aunt Eden that morning.

But ready or not, here he was today in a neckcloth with ruffles and trousers that were not just striped, but also tight.

That was unfortunate. She wished she knew him well enough to give him advice upon his fashions, but was also glad that she did not.

"Miss Bickering," he said as he approached. Her spinning mind couldn't decide whether it would be more appropriate to speak to him here, in the door, or inside the shop. Anyone might come into a shop. But even if they didn't, people could see them alone together through the windows, if they looked. Did she care if anyone looked?

Anna decided she could not face doing this on a public pavement. She backed inside the shop and held the door.

As soon as he was inside, he bobbed his head. "You seem in good health, Miss Bickering. I'm glad to see it."

She curtsied. "I am quite well. Thank you, Lord Boislegrand. I trust you enjoyed your cake."

"Yes, Yes I did." Somehow he managed to make clear that he was pleased by her attention, not just with the cake. Yet there was no leering in it, no innuendo. He was openly glad to see her. "I have the dish. It's in the carriage. Should I have the footman bring it in?"

"No, no," said Anna hurriedly. "Surely by the time you leave—I mean, in a few moments when you leave."

He looked a little crestfallen at that. "I brought you a small gift. It might take a few more moments to discuss."

"Oh, surely not. I mean, no, there's no need to discuss it. Of course. What I mean is, you need not give me a gift. You ought not to give me a gift."

Puffy knew that little women, perfect women like this, didn't welcome his attentions. Not because he was rude or crude, but simply because he was old, rather plump, and boring. He couldn't do anything about being older or plumper. But he could address whether or not he bored a lady. And today he would. "I've brought you a rather interesting gift, Miss Bickering. You see my chef, of course, my chef comes from Lyon, in France you know. And I have asked him if he has any recipes for cake."

"Have you?" The young lady's eyes grew softer, and Puffy could swear he saw genuine gratitude in them. "Have you really? What an incredibly sweet gesture."

"I am paying very close attention, Miss Bickering. I know that your business is struggling, and that you are extremely interested in cake. You didn't make that cake just for my benefit, did you?"

"No," she admitted. "I very much hope to make cake a profitable concern."

"And there you are," Puffy's excitement was evident now, and he didn't try to hide it. "You are interested in cake. And I am interested in you. Therefore, I have brought you knowledge about cake."

She didn't seem to know what to do with her hands. They were a little worn. They shouldn't be. Such tiny sweet little hands were meant for a life of ease. One such as he could give her. She seemed to have flour under her fingernails. Puffy noticed it as her hands fluttered about.

"Really, Lord Boislegrand. You are too kind. Truly too kind when I cannot repay you in any meaningful way."

"I specifically wish to be repaid in a meaningful way." And Puffy tried his best smile. It was not about his teeth or anything humorous. It was about letting his genuine, gentle greed for her company show in his face. It had attracted his first wife, and he had faith in it still.

It didn't seem to be working. She didn't look upset, but she didn't smile back. "But I can't, sir. And that is what I am trying to say, before you even know me. Before we spend any more time together. As I've tried to explain. We cannot spend time together. I am not of your kind, sir."

Puffy's best qualities bubbled to the surface when faced with a pretty girl that he knew could not look down on him.

"You are a fine young lady, Miss Bickering. And I am old enough to know that ladies of your caliber are difficult to find, and willing to go to some effort to get to know you better. I don't wish to be a burden, but I am not inclined to entirely quit the field when there is such a glorious prize to be won."

Oh, that had been good. He could see that the line about the prize was particularly inspired; some color came into her cheeks. She couldn't meet his eyes. Was that a good sign? "Well, thank you, sir."

He put his folded sheet of foolscap on the counter so she could not refuse to take it from his hands. "And now when we see each other again, we can discuss whether these recipes have been of any use to you. I shall be particularly interested to hear," he smiled, "and perhaps you will be kind enough to tell me."

"Thank you, sir. All I can say is thank you."

He looked happy as he left, and Anna was glad for it. He seemed like a sweet fellow. She'd thought seeing him again would be more mortification, and here he repaid her ridiculous overcharging with a gift. She could almost forget she had thrown her pride away and spoken to him in the street just to sell him an expensive cake.

He was so unfailingly kind that she couldn't feel embarrassed about it. At least, not until she remembered how many people had seen it.

No, she wouldn't be embarrassed. She had put all of this

in motion and she would see it through. It was her job. She was the head of the family.

After a few moments, she put her hand softly down on the sheet of foolscap.

THE SUN HAD NOT YET GONE DOWN WHEN JANE AND ANNA crept into their younger sister's bedroom. Emery had fallen asleep in her shift on top of the coverlet. It was only reasonable given the hot bakery, the wet July air, and the strain of a visit from Aunt Eden.

She looked younger with her face on the pillow, her straw-colored braid flowing behind her. Anna knelt at the side of the bed and brushed wisps of her hair away from her face.

Jane leaned over her shoulder, where she could breathe so quietly into Anna's ear that their sister could not possibly wake. "I think it worked. Aunt Eden will take us and Emery will go. I wouldn't have bet any amount of money on it a day ago, and yet you have made it work."

Anna wished she could feel as confident as Jane sounded. "It means closing the bakery for a few days, and losing all the income. Plus we may anger some of our customers, closing on short notice. But we must take her with us. It is almost as important that Emery have a chance to sleep and eat all she likes, as it is for us to find a reliable provider for honey."

She didn't need to turn to see Jane's agreement. She knew that both of them were of the same mind on this. Quietly, she stood, and they both went out.

Once the door was closed behind them. Jane said in a slightly more normal volume, "And where is Rose?"

Anna shook her head. "I don't know what to do about Rose. We must have a conversation with her. Of course some day she should marry if she likes, and of course Aunt Eden should buy her some new hair ribbons. But not to be on display. And certainly not for Mr. Russell."

Jane nodded, a curt nod, but her eyes were looking far away at something not there. Presumably, irresponsible men. "We really ought to have a talk with Mr. Russell."

Anna met her sister's eyes. "I only have so much in me, and I cannot do that today, nor tomorrow, either. Why, we still need to speak to Sal and Jordan's father, if we are to take them out of the city!"

"No," Jane agreed quickly. "There is only so much a person can do in one day. I only mean that sometime soon we must have a talk with Mr. Russell. I have no idea what he is saying to Rose, and possibly more alarmingly, I have no idea when and where he is saying it."

Anna shrugged one shoulder. She was too tired to shrug two. "She's right, you know, we can't keep claiming that she is a grown woman, and then keep her on short apron strings."

"But she is so innocent. She trusts everyone. And she does not know what kinds of things men want from her."

"Do *we*?" Anna's eyes grew big. "I'm not even entirely clear what kinds of things the hod carriers at the Hotel Jacques are shouting at us when we walk by."

"Well..." Jane's voice trailed it out. "I'm not entirely sure either. But it's not good. It's not for our benefit. And it's not for Rose's, either."

"She must have a good instinct about whether Mr. Russell is a trustworthy man."

"Rose thinks everyone is trustworthy."

"No, you're quite right. You're quite right," said Anna, sounding more defeated than she should have given the triumphs of the day. "Perhaps on our trip we can find a way of convincing Rose not to think the best of everyone."

"That's a depressing task," Jane said, even though she didn't argue. And the two sisters sat down beside one another, two precious needles and thread in their hands, to shorten their hems so the ragged bits would not show on the journey with Aunt Eden. "Do we want Rose to return before Aunt Eden comes to discuss the terms of our travel?"

"Don't ask. I wish Rose were here right now." Anna took out their pincushion with a set jaw that was not about the needles. "Never fear, Aunt Eden must accept that we will not accept haranguing even though we want help. She will be kinder."

Jane didn't say what she thought of the likelihood of *that*. Instead, she threaded her needle into the fabric of the dress and set it down. "We ought to go and speak to Mr. Collier before Aunt Eden comes. He cannot possibly be out so late."

"I suppose. Yes. If we are to take the children with us, I must agree." Anna's hand slowly left the fabric of her damaged dress. Her own reddened fingers against the worn fabric for some reason made her think of Lord Boislegrand and his smile. She decided to think about Aunt Eden instead, which was odd; no one ever chose to think of Aunt Eden. "I haven't ever seen Aunt Eden like she was with Jordan, have you?"

"No. And I am not above using Aunt Eden's sudden infatuation, in much the same way as the earth is not above the sky."

"How much she must have wanted a boy!"

"Well, how glad I am that we have one," Jane said. "Let me fetch gloves for both of us, and you get the bonnets."

"I have my own gloves." There weren't many places to put them, but she kept them hidden from Jane. And therefore clean.

EVEN THE HORSES GOING ROUND THE SQUARE SEEMED LIMP and tired in the heat. Knowing that Anna was mustering her strength for Aunt Eden's visit that evening, Jane had just resigned herself to a silent walk when they stepped onto Leicester Place and found in their path... their sister.

"Miss Rose," said Anna as Mr. Russell stopped in astonishment directly before them. His broad shoulders filled much of the pavement, but neither Anna nor Jane ever considered trying to go round. Both of them stopped still in their tracks and examined Rose and her escort closely.

Rose's head was nodding slowly, as she did when she was thinking, all the way up and back down again, and her cheeks were flushed.

"Miss Rose," Jane said too, so Rose would know she was there. "I had thought you wished to rest before supper?"

"Did you?" Despite the flush, Rose did not drop her hand from Mr. Russell's elbow.

Jane caught Anna's eye. Anna didn't look in the mood to let this pass.

"I'm surprised at such a public promenade unescorted," said Anna, stating as baldly as she could that an escort from an unmarried man was the same as no escort at all.

"I'm surprised you sound so much like our Aunt Eden," Rose returned swiftly. "Surely you haven't aged that much during the afternoon?"

"Aunt Eden is only one person I would not like to see you taking such liberties in public."

"I am strolling down the street with a respectable citizen, *Miss* Anna, you can hardly object to that."

Mr. Russell began to twitch, Jane noticed, which didn't suit a man with a figure like a sturdy wall.

"Where might you have strolled, Miss Rose?" Anna said just as swiftly.

Rose had a ready answer. "There are elephants in the

Queen's Mews; we went to see if I might pet them. Mr. Russell was kind enough to escort me so that I wouldn't be trampled. Elephants being so careless, you know."

Mr. Russell was looking back and forth from Jane to Anna when he quietly informed Rose, "The Queen's Mews is on the far side of the square."

"Is it? How can I keep directions straight in my tiny little head? Thank goodness Mr. Russell has been here to protect me from the elephants. And the horses in the street. And nosy tailors."

Jane had a feeling Rose knew perfectly well that they were but five steps from the front door of the nosy tailor.

"And cows," said Rose, leaning her head toward Mr. Russell for a moment and smiling a smile Rose didn't understand. Cows weren't that funny.

But Mr. Russell smiled too, and it was the way they smiled, as over a shared secret, that set real alarm bells ringing in Jane's head.

Anna did not relent. "I'm surprised at you—"

"It's not as though he were in a *carriage* in the *street*," said Rose most inadvisedly, and Jane decided to interject.

"Mr. Russell," she said as loudly as she could, yanking on Anna's elbow to keep her from answering. "If you would be so good as to show our sister home, we would appreciate it if you accompanied us on an errand. I believe we ought to have a gentleman with us. We have no idea what we'll find."

"Of course, Miss Jane," came the fast agreement, as Mr. Russell was obviously eager to leave and didn't seem to realize that he'd agreed to come back.

Both Anna and Jane watched him take every step as he escorted Rose across the street and into the bakery.

"If he doesn't come out in two minutes, I'm going in after him," seethed Anna. "What on earth does he mean, parading around on our street in broad daylight?"

"Better than in the dark," muttered Jane, watching him turn back their way. "Look here, ordering Rose won't get you anywhere. If he's up to something, we must know it and deal with it."

"Deal with it *how*?"

But Mr. Russell had already crossed wide Bear Street again, and rejoined them. "I'd be pleased to accompany you both on any errand you need," he said very properly as he settled his jacket over his shoulders and his round beaver hat upon his stocky head.

Why had his hat been *off*, Jane wondered to herself.

"Tell us about your family, Mr. Russell. We know nothing of them."

"Where were you educated?" Anna added, taking his far arm and beginning to walk him along the Place.

"Do you have siblings?" Jane possessed herself of his other arm. "And how are they employed?"

"Do they live in the city?"

"You don't keep a carriage of your own, surely?" By the time they reached the Collier residence, Jane intended to know how much Mr. Russell was worth, his family prospects, and possibly the number of his teeth.

"I think this is your destination?" Mr. Russell greeted the green door with palpable relief.

Once again, the iron grate was open; Jane left off her questions long enough to use the doorknocker.

She was just wondering if she should resume her questions when the door swung silently inward.

Whatever she was expecting, it wasn't the man who stood there.

"Mr. Collier?" His appearance startled the name out of

her, though later she couldn't remember why; they'd come to speak with him, after all.

He had extraordinarily long hair, long enough to brush his collar on both sides of his head and in the back. It was as black as Jordan's. While older men wore their hair tied back long in queues, or neatly shaved to fit under a wig, and younger men wore their hair tousled over their ears, Mr. Collier's hair looked unfinished. His expression looked the same.

But he was shaved. He wore neither collar nor cuffs, nor a coat; his shirt hung askew or was buttoned that way, she could not tell which. His black trousers had at one point been pressed.

"Mr. Collier?" Jane asked again.

"I am, yes," and it ought to have sounded just like what anyone would have said, but from him it sounded like an answer to a different question.

"Mr. Collier, we've come to discuss the children," Anna added, changing quickly from dragging Mr. Russell along by his arm to hiding a bit behind it. Nothing about Mr. Collier was menacing, yet Jane found herself quite glad to be accompanied by a man built like a mastiff dog.

"Yes?"

"Ah... may we step inside?"

Mr. Collier simply backed up without inviting them in.

Inside, the room was just as Jane remembered, the furnishings sparse. Mr. Collier's presence didn't enrich the place much. He stood staring at them, his hands dangling by his sides, and Jane found that more unnerving than if they had been in his pockets.

"Aren't the children here?" Anna asked. Sal and Jordan had left the bakery hours ago, as they usually did of a midafternoon.

Mr. Collier simply looked about to check. "Doesn't look it," he said with no consternation about it.

It was slightly cooler inside the Collier room, befitting its position just below the pavement; but Jane still felt sweat trickle down her spine.

"Mr. Collier, we'd like to take the children with us on a brief trip out of the city," said Anna, a bit loudly, Jane thought. Though he could have trouble hearing, how would she know?

"That's nice," the man said. He turned and began to move around the edge of the room. Jane thought he might be packing things for the children, but no, he was only walking about.

"You don't mind?"

He shrugged. "Why would I?"

Mr. Russell, who had let the Misses Bickering do the talking till now, stepped forward. "Have you water, sir? I've become so thirsty in the heat today."

"There's a pump out back," and Mr. Collier led his visitor away quite calmly, and not as though he were half-dressed and half-shorn.

Jane immediately began fiercely whispering to Anna. "What is wrong with him?"

"I've never *met* him before!" Anna reminded her. "Perhaps he is simply... like this?"

"But is he ill? Has he been injured?"

"Does it matter?" Anna looked at the door through which the men had left. "Whatever *this* is, he is like *this*."

"How long do you suppose he's been this way? And where is his wife?"

"I've never heard the children say a word about her. She's clearly gone."

"Ought we simply *to keep* the children?" Jane didn't like the idea, but she couldn't think of anything else. The idea of the children coming back to that blank face day after day. Of course, if they were used to it...

"Let's just begin with this journey, shall we? And school. Once we can do it. At least tutoring." Anna took in the bare table. "It's more than we have now, you know."

"No, this will take more than schooling." Jane didn't wish to disturb anything, but she also didn't anything to rub against her. The miasma of wrongness was fading, as it always did when meeting someone new. Mr. Collier had done nothing wrong. The men who shouted at her in the street were more objectionable. Still, his blankness unsettled her. "We're going to have to come back to this question, you know. If the children should live here."

"It never ends," muttered Anna, which made no sense to Jane, but then the men reappeared, stocky Mr. Russell followed by the silent drift of Mr. Collier.

"I've quite refreshed myself. Thank you, Mr. Collier. Ladies, if you are ready to leave?"

With little more conversation than quick leave-takings, none of which seemed to make much difference to Mr. Collier either, soon all three stood outside on the pavement again.

"What do you mean by it, Mr. Russell?" Anna's chin puffed out, indignant as an inflated frog. "We have so much more to discuss, especially concerning this journey!"

"The answer to everything you ask Mr. Collier will be 'fine,' I assure you." Mr. Russell looked grave, graver than he ever had while standing with Rose. "I must speak to his pastor. But I doubt he'll recognize that the children are gone. He does not know where they are now, and it isn't bothering him at all."

"Thank you, Mr. Russell." Anna deflated.

Jane agreed. That he might take on the question of what to do about the mysterious Mr. Collier felt exactly as though a heavy stone had been lifted from her shoulders. "I'm genuinely grateful to you, sir. We all are."

"Yes." Anna seemed to mean it as well. "It is lucky you could accompany us, after all."

"You are welcome," said the young man, beaming a wide grin that split his face like a happy puppy's.

They were all so in charity for a moment that Jane almost regretted gesturing them back to the middle of the pavement, and once Mr. Russell was beside her, saying, "Have you any experience in investments?"

EMERY WAS STILL ASLEEP WHEN THEY RETURNED, AND ROSE too had gone into the room they shared, and shut the door. On such a stifling day, that was no trivial thing.

Anna understood it meant that Rose was not interested in discussing Mr. Russell further. She sighed. Mr. Russell seemed a nice enough man. But he was not wealthy, had only a small income from family sources, and seemed entirely too cheerful about ruining Rose's reputation. She *must* speak to Rose.

But it was Aunt Eden who appeared first.

"You knock, Johnson; I'm sure that door would give me splinters," they heard her voice on the stair before someone, presumably Johnson, knocked.

Anna only had time to exchange a look with Jane before she opened the door and Aunt Eden swept in.

She wore a red and silver turban with a large *turquoise* stone pinned to its front. Her evening gown was undyed silk with diamond and window patterns picked out all along the hem up to the knees, outlined with red and silver thread.

She clutched a bright blue shawl that matched the stone. "As you can see, I've only a moment before I am expected. Lady Woolacre is having a small affair."

The contrast between her great-aunt's opulent robe and Anna's shabby, much-washed dressed was so acute that it cut. And then the pain gave way to a softer understanding. Aunt Eden had no reason to arrive dressed in such finery when a society ball would not begin for another hour at least, likely two. She had dressed this way to display the difference between her means and theirs. But that was no news to Anna. And Anna had nothing to prove to someone who had not one speck of happiness to show for all her silk and silver thread.

It gave Anna the balance she needed between humble and confident.

"Thank you for visiting, Aunt Eden. I'm so glad you haven't solely come to the city for our benefit. Has it been long since you've seen Lady Woolacre? You must be looking forward to it."

Aunt Eden's eyes narrowed as if she expected a trick. "She hasn't room for more guests, if you are planning to stay with her. Or me."

"Not at all. We are quite comfortable here."

Aunt Eden looked around. There were no chairs and no table. The pan and pot, clean, sat next to the stove. Their crates still stood in the corner, serving as makeshift cupboards for their crockery, their mother's silver candlesticks the only fine comforts in the room. Their dresses, with their ragged hems, still sat on the floor waiting to be patched. "You haven't come down Catholic, have you?"

Anna had no idea how to address an accusation of Catholicism that sounded like an attack of the measles. "We are just as you have always known us, Aunt Eden."

"That's an audacious lie. And I always thought you were the timid one. Still, if you meant me to see this and come round to inviting you again, so be it. The chambers my girls left will be more than enough for you."

Anna didn't even rise to the bait of whether two young

ladies' chambers would be enough for all four of them. It didn't matter. It just didn't matter.

She looked at Aunt Eden now and she saw an aging woman with no joy in her life. Someone who made an effort to come to their little rooms in jewels, someone desperate to make some sort of point. Whatever the point was, what Anna understood was that Aunt Eden was sad.

"I'm sorry I can't offer you a chair," and she meant it. "I hope those slippers are comfortable. Shall we discuss when we shall leave?"

"I've got a carriage hired day after tomorrow that will take us all the way home, but you'll have to have this stuff all follow us later." Wandering about the edge of the room, much like Mr. Collier had, she started to poke a crate with her toe, then thought better of it.

"We won't put you out more than a few days, Aunt Eden, I promise. If you have some idea where we might find a seller for the quantity of honey we need, we could even leave you in peace sooner than that."

"You really mean that." Aunt Eden was peering at Anna now as she had peered at the walls.

"I do." Anna smiled over at Jane. Beautiful Jane, who deserved so much more than Aunt Eden had ever given them. And yet she and Jane would never have known any luxuries at all if it hadn't been for Aunt Eden. Aunt Eden had never given Emery or Rose even a taste of that life; but then, Emery hadn't wanted them and Rose had been too young.

Yes, Aunt Eden was a mixed blessing. She was a nightmare, but she was family, and she was here.

Anna really wished she could offer Aunt Eden a chair. "You must have come to help, and we're grateful."

"You are?" The older woman's ears practically perked and Anna imagined her imagining some very fine groveling.

"Grateful, Aunt Eden, not desperate."

"Hmmph." Aunt Eden looked out the window over Leicester Square. "Don't have the sense to beg when begging is called for, that's what you mean. Fine. Johnson will call for you. Don't make him wait. You—" She turned and pinned Anna with a pointed look. "That young man is coming with you?"

"Jordan?" Anna *was* pretending now, pretending to the carelessness in her tone. "If you wish it. He may eat half a year's food stores in a few days, you know. He is that age. You know how boys are."

It was a masterful thing to say, as Aunt Eden would never admit that she had no idea how boys were. "He can come along," she said as if granting a favor, and Anna cast a glance over at Jane, who nodded. Anna tried not to look too triumphant.

Time, kindness, and practice. That's what it took to handle Aunt Eden a little better than she ever had before. Time, patience, and practice.

"Why do I feel like things are going well when all Aunt Eden has promised is to give us a ride?" Jane wondered after their great-aunt had gone, Johnson closing the door behind her.

"Because you expected it to be awful, and it wasn't. We just let Aunt Eden be Aunt Eden, and all will be well."

"Will it?"

He stumbled around the Bear Street corner, careful enough not to put his arm through the glass of the bakery windows.

It wasn't easy, getting this drunk; but he managed it.

In fact, in recent days he'd been a lot drunker. Maybe he was getting old, but he couldn't take many more days curled up on his pallet with a bottle of gin and staring at the ceiling. It was beyond his capability to be jolly, but even in his withered state he felt more comfort drinking some place where he wasn't entirely alone.

At the top of the stairs, he checked his feet. Checked that both of his boots were still on, but also that he wasn't treading so heavily that the young ladies would hear him. There was no light showing under their door, nor voices coming through it, but at this time of night, that was only to be expected.

He'd shuffled as silently as he could all the way to his own corner door before he realized that there was no smell of bread, either.

No smell of bread anywhere.

Had they gone?

The question hit him, hit his head and spun it round; hit him in the gut, too. Thinking about it made him queasy.

What did he care if there were ladies living next door? He never spoke to them. They looked precious and lost, in their too-washed dresses and tidy hair, and he was through with things that were precious and lost.

But some part of him must still hunger for company, because he realized in that queasy moment that it mattered to him, to know they were there.

The house felt empty.

He pushed his own door open, which was never locked, both to make it easier to open when he was drunk, and because he had nothing of value to secure. He was drunk enough to sleep, that he knew. He hoped he was drunk enough to sleep without dreaming of the emptiness, or wondering if they were coming back.

Episode 13: The open country

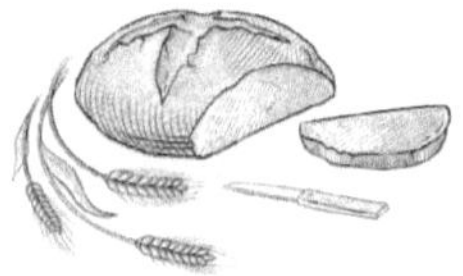

The world was bursting with greenery. Everywhere Anna looked outside the carriage windows, grass was lush and long. Trees were heavy with fat leaves and fruit. And every hedgerow they passed had exceeded its bounds to shoot runners in all directions.

Anna suspected from her childhood adventures that those hedgerows were also full of tiny creatures who had found mates and made families over the spring and summer. "Isn't it the most beautiful time of year to travel?"

"It's been cold," said Aunt Eden.

All seven of them were packed into the old carriage Aunt Eden had engaged for the trip. It creaked and swayed on wobbling wheels, and was quite close inside; even without the summer heat, the silence among the sisters made the trip somber.

Anna couldn't help enjoying herself, but she could tell she was nearly alone in that.

Aunt Eden had placed Jordan next to her. "I've always wondered how little boys maneuver a slingshot."

Jordan just stared up at her steel gray curls and grooved

face. His mouth fell open. Everything she said astonished him and seemed to raise promises of a more exciting life. "I've never had a slingshot."

"Well," said Aunt Eden. "Perhaps we will address that shortcoming when we arrive at Walbey Hall."

Aunt Eden's astonishing good temper didn't extend to entertaining Sal. But Sal's rapt attention was on the countryside, just like Anna's. "Is that a deer? Did we just see a deer? Was that a deer? Is it a baby deer, or was it a mama deer? How do you tell the difference between a baby deer and a mama deer?"

This was the longest speech that Anna had ever heard from Sal. The flood of words bewildered Anna even more than her not knowing how to answer it.

Emery seemed to be set free from the somber quiet by Sal's question. "We are quite as much children of London as you are, Sally. A few summers in the country haven't made experts of us."

This roused Jane enough to question the premise. "Oughtn't we know what a mama deer looks like? It was *several* summers."

The rueful twist to Emery's lips acknowledged the point. "We ought to at least know that, oughtn't we? Well, perhaps on this trip we will learn what we haven't before."

Rose, wedged in between Jane and Anna, wondered aloud, "Will we? I thought we must focus upon bees to the exclusion of everything else?"

"Bees most certainly," said Anna, "Bees above all, but that doesn't mean that there may not be a moment for other types of natural science."

"I wouldn't like to shoot anything with a slingshot," Jordan informed Aunt Eden in his serious way.

"I'm quite relieved to find out that there is a little boy in the world who wouldn't. However, there are several trees on my property that won't be hurt by a tossed rock."

Jane smiled. That was too rare these days, Anna thought. "Do you no longer have the targets we used to practice archery on the lawns?"

Aunt Eden's curls trembled with the rattling of the carriage. "They were straw and eaten away a long time ago, I believe," she said in a tone that brooked no further discussion of their childhood pastimes. But her armor had been pierced, and all of them saw that when it came to Jordan, she was simply a melting pile of ice.

It softened Anna's heart towards her, though Anna suspected she dropped her guard entirely at her own peril.

Perhaps suspecting their thoughts, and wishing to forgo any great-niece sort of softness, Aunt Eden quickly added, "We should arrive at Walbey Hall in time for some supper. I have sent a rider ahead to prepare everything for us. And the linens should be fresh. I hate to sleep on musty beds; I am sure you all feel the same."

Since no one else in the carriage had ever had the luxury of disdaining a place to sleep, no one answered her.

THE LONG SUMMER DAY HAD NOT YET CLOSED WHEN THEIR carriage finally rolled up the drive to the portico at Walbey Hall.

Jane hadn't expected to be so excited to see Walbey Hall again. The past was past, and she didn't dwell upon it. But it was one thing to long for what one could never have, and it was another to be dropped right into the well of memory. In the earliest summers, she and Anna had come with their father while their mother stayed at home with the younger two. Surely it had been the freedom of the countryside and a new place to play that she remembered so fondly, and not just the novelty of being one of two children instead of one of four.

Mr. Johnson, who must have been the mysterious rider sent ahead, appeared at the door. Instantly, Aunt Eden addressed him as if he had been at her elbow the entire time. "Is the ground muddy, Johnson? Should we lay down a rug?"

"Not at all, my lady," he said in a reassuring tone more suitable for children than dragons in ostrich feathers. "The weather has been quite warm and fine, as I think it was for your trip. Was the carriage everything you'd hoped, ma'am?"

"It rattles, Johnson. As one may expect for an old conveyance of this sort, but I know you engaged the best you could at such short notice. When one's family makes such quick and radical decisions, one must do the best one can."

She alighted from the carriage first and walked into the house without looking back. Sally and Jordan had doubtful looks as they climbed out after Anna and Rose, but Anna smiled at them.

"We must all go in and wash ourselves and get ready for supper; everyone is hungry, and that bread and butter dinner in the coach seems years ago. Aren't you all ready to eat?"

"Master Jordan should have the blue room," Aunt Eden called back from the shadows inside the door frame, giving away that she knew exactly that they were there and that they hadn't yet followed her.

"What about me?" Sal asked with more dismay than suspicion, making Jane look at her twice.

"You stay in the Blue Room with me," Jordan told her quite firmly.

"Not appropriate," floated out of the door from the depths of Walbey Hall.

"Never mind," Emery told the two youngest travelers. "Rose and I used to stay in the smallest room on the second floor. Let me show you where it was, Sal; perhaps you want it. Or the one next to our room now."

Jane smiled again. She couldn't seem to help herself. Was it the effect of being in familiar surroundings, or just the idea of a substantial supper? "And I have a room just down the hall, with Anna close by. Emery can show you all of them."

"But where's the Blue Room?" Jordan fixated on the room most pertinent to him according to Aunt Eden's instructions.

"I think she might mean the guest room overlooking the garden in back of the house. The one with the Chinese garden painted on the walls." Anna said this as if she couldn't believe her own perception.

"She can't mean that." Emery shook her head in disbelief. "I thought she was saving that room for some grand procession of Queen Charlotte to the sea."

"And where would the King sleep?" Anna played along.

"I never thought Aunt Eden would care." Emery was just as flabbergasted as the rest of them at Aunt Eden's open flattery of Jordan. Since none of them had ever had a brother or a boy cousin, none of them had expected such a thing. Certainly Aunt Eden's treatment of her husband, on the rare occasions that he appeared at Walbey Hall, hadn't foretold it either.

"I'll get clean," Jordan said as though he were making a great concession, "but someone is going to have to show me this room, and how to pour the water."

They had already discovered, in daily operation of the bakery, that Jordan much preferred containers that did not break. Either he preferred them, or his hands preferred them, as breakable containers tended to exit their existence quite quickly.

Sal grabbed his hand. "If we don't like the room, we'll just find the carriage and sleep in that," she told him in a loud whisper.

Jane didn't contradict them; it seemed a sound plan to her.

THEY WERE ALL CLEAN AND AS FRESHLY DRESSED AS possible when they finally arrived in the dining room for an unfashionably early supper. Jane expected little more than soup and bread, given that they had spent the entire day traveling.

The full table showed that Aunt Eden considered it a late dinner. Aunt Eden didn't lay a fancy table, but she did provide good food. Jane had fond memories of many a Walbey dinner, lavish with toasted cheese and fish and pheasant. And cakes.

Johnson must have received some orders at some point, because the entire table was groaning with food. It had been laid out in perfect parallel on all four sides, according to the rules of French service. But there were so many dishes that the platters made two squares, one inside the other. And they were so full Jane couldn't imagine the children passing them safely.

There was a full roast of mutton. Boiled turnips and carrots, sprinkled with the edible flowers that Jane now remembered Aunt Eden kept in her garden. Chicken roasted until it was golden, a terrine of clear broth, and a great mound of bright peas. It seemed they had simply placed the second course around the first: a huge trembling cream trifle, stacks of, yes, ratafia cakes, and a wedge of the local golden cheese resplendent on its platter, surrounded by currants. The cheese and currants ought to have come out between the courses.

Aunt Eden seemed to have lost her mind.

The same Aunt Eden grabbed Jordan's hand and led him

to the seat of honor, to her right. She, of course, sat at the head of the table.

"Come, my boy, you must eat your fill," said Aunt Eden as a footman pushed in her chair for her. "There's plenty more if this isn't enough to satisfy you."

Sal, left behind, just looked forlornly at Emery. Jane wished now she'd made better friends with Sal and insisted less on math lessons. She took the chance to take the little girl's hand and lead her to the seat just opposite her brother. "That includes you as well, Sal, eat your fill. If I recall correctly, the butter is particularly good."

Jane took the chair to Sal's left, and in the absence of any further instructions from Aunt Eden, Anna took the seat across from her, next to Jordan.

Rose sat next to Anna, leaving Emery to sit next to Jane.

Jane had the oddest memory of them doing this dozens of times before. Was it even hundreds? How many summers had they spent listening to Aunt Eden's lectures and stuffing their faces with food they never saw the like of in London, waiting for the next moment to get back outside and find some new adventure in a garden or under a tree?

"I thought we would speak to Mr. MacPherson first about the honey," Anna said as she sat down. One thing Jane could say for Anna, she had given herself over to this plan and clearly intended to see it through.

"That old Scot will steal you blind," their aunt said, even as she ladled peas on to Jordan's plate.

"I remember Mr. MacPherson as quite pleasant and very concerned about his bees." Since Aunt Eden was so determined to fill Jordan's plate herself, Anna turned to Rose. "Would you like pheasant, dear, and perhaps peas? No, you must start with the clear soup."

"Obviously," said Aunt Eden, even as she continued to fill

Jordan's plate with sliced meat, having moved his soup bowl aside.

Jordan, peaceful, broad-faced little Jordan, wasn't sure what to do. His expression said that he felt more attacked than served. But he was a growing boy, the day had been long, and the smells of the food eventually caused him to pick up his fork and apply it. Once he began, he picked up speed.

No one would wrestle the platters away from Aunt Eden. They awaited her pleasure, and her pleasure was to give some of everything to Jordan.

Since the table was clearly full of food, they would get some of it. Eventually. Jordan couldn't possibly eat it all. Although if he did, it was also very clear that Aunt Eden would not stop him.

"We'll go see Mr. MacPherson first thing tomorrow," Anna said as she served herself and Rose some of the soup.

And then Rose spoke up. It was clear she smelled the desserts, wanted to try out her newfound confidence, and remembered Aunt Eden's cook.

"Perhaps Mr. MacPherson will sell you some honey too, Aunt, and you can use it in your sweets. We'd be happy to consult with Mrs. Mahew."

Aunt Eden broke from staring at Jordan to stare a moment at Rose, the sister she'd never paid the least attention. "Why would I want you consulting with my cook? She's a respectable woman who makes respectable food."

Jane frowned at that. Too much of an edge to that comment, and sailing too close to said edge, at that.

She opened her mouth, but Rose was already speaking. "Because I'm a respectable baker who might be able to give her some good advice," she said, as bluntly and plainly as she did in her best moments. But then she bent her head. "Though it's really Anna who is the expert on the cakes."

"Anna!" Aunt Eden clearly wasn't sure what to say about

expertise she wished Anna didn't have, but she rallied. Any softness inspired by the presence of a real live boy hardened very quickly. "I suppose it is beneficial that Anna has detailed knowledge of the kitchen, but one oughtn't speak of it at supper. Or any meal, for that matter. I suppose it might be appealing to a certain sort of possible suitor, but certainly not any suitor Anna would wish to entertain."

"I am not entertaining *any* suitors, Aunt Eden," Anna mumbled into her soup, her spine a bit more bent than it was a moment ago.

Jane ached for her. This sort of threat was so much more difficult to fight. The two of them had been raised their whole lives to do one thing, and had failed. It was impossible to put into words for any of the rest of them how much that hurt.

"I am," said Rose.

It took Jane a moment to realize that Rose was speaking of suitors. Suitors. At the supper table. With Aunt Eden.

"*You* are?" Now Aunt Eden put down the butter knife altogether.

"Yes." Rose's dimpled smile was there for all to see. "A gentleman of important work, who will accomplish much more than convincing your cook to give up sugar. Whether or not anything more tender grows between us, I hope to see him complete that work. I think I will. We share the same sensibilities on many issues, not just the terrible effects of the sugar trade."

Aunt Eden's face could not decide what to do. "The *sugar* trade?"

Jane realized at that moment that Anna had served Rose the soup. Rose, who always skipped the soup course at Aunt Eden's table, as soup spoons did not serve blind people well.

Rose realized the same thing. And she picked up her soup bowl and sipped from its edge.

It was a perfect shape for it, like a vast teacup; she had never done it before because her mother said it would be disrespectful to Aunt Eden.

Their mother, thought Jane for the first time in her life, who had preferred being respectful to Aunt Eden over being respectful to Rose so she could have the soup.

Rose sipped her soup before she went on. "You must take a paper or two, Aunt Eden; are you not current in the world's news? But I am teasing you, because I am sure our mother explained the sugar market to you many years ago. The sugar market and its connections to slavery here and abroad." She sipped more soup from her spoon. "Why do you think we wish to buy so much honey?"

Aunt Eden looked from Rose to Anna next to her, then back again. Then at Anna again. Then, as if drawn by a pulled rope, back at Rose. "You've become interesting."

"Have I?" Rose perked up over the edge of her soup bowl.

"Men do not marry women who are interesting. There's hardly anything worse you could be. If you *are* interested in attracting a suitor."

"It may be that there are more ways of being attractive to a man than you have yet learned, Aunt Eden." And with that impertinent speech, Rose returned to smiling to herself, and sipped her soup.

Anna did not look at Rose, or Aunt Eden, or anyone else. Jane couldn't tell if she might burst into tears, or gut-ripping laughter.

Jane was leaning toward the laughter herself.

"I know a great deal more than how to bake cakes, young lady," Aunt Eden said with dry acid in her voice. "I will say men *love* impudent women, but only because they can be led to do imprudent things. I hope that will never be said of someone in *my* family."

"Yes, that would be awful," said Rose thoughtfully.

JANE FOUND HERSELF THE LAST TO RETIRE. AUNT EDEN HAD long ago retreated to her chambers, not to re-appear till dinner the next day, and the other sisters had gone right to their rooms as if the intervening years had never existed.

No, that wasn't true. If the intervening years hadn't passed, the sisters would be together, in some distant parlor, deciding whether to put pine cones in the fire or coax a tiny tree to grow in a bowl. They had never just disappeared into their rooms of an evening; their entertainment was each other.

She stopped on the stairs. Each grooved, polished pillar in the balustrade seemed unique, and suddenly Jane was back in her childhood, wondering if they were really all different or if it was only a trick of the light. Had someone set each one a few degrees twisted from the others, so that each one would be odd in its own way?

Her memories showed her the fluttering nightdresses of little girls running up and down the stairs, then up again, delighting in the overflowing wealth of stairs.

"Anna, you can't catch me!" eight-year-old Emery had shouted, whirling barefoot down the corridor so quickly that the tapestries hung on the walls flapped in her wake.

"I'm not trying to catch you," Anna had said with as much dignity as she could muster. She had been so determined to be the young lady Aunt Eden told her to be.

But where was Jane?

Oh yes, there she was, hanging over the railing on the floor above, hooting at her sisters' games. And yes, Anna had said not to do that. "You'll fall!"

Then Rose had followed Emery, racing down the hall—oh yes, a tiny Rose with smiling eyes like Anna's but touched with a bit of green. Her feet flashed too fast to see. "I can catch you, I can catch anyone!" Rose had said, racing after her sister.

Jane was still staring down the dark corridor when a flutter of white plucked at the corner of her eye, so like the nightdresses she and her sisters had worn.

She looked down into the present. "Sally, why aren't you in bed?"

The next instant, Jane wished she'd said something else. As soon as she woke from her memories, she saw how anxious Sal looked in a nightdress that was possibly one of Jane's own.

"Never mind," she said before Sal said anything, "why *should* you be in bed? It's a strange bed in a strange place. I'd wager the walls made odd noises, too."

"How did you know?" Usually so quick to argue, Sal just wanted to know how Jane knew the quirks of this old house.

Jane's impulses had dug themselves graves in her gut time and time again. She was learning to ignore them. But this one, she obeyed. She leaned down and gave Sal a swift hug around the shoulders. "Because we were all little girls in this house too, and I remember its noises very well."

"They don't mean anything?" Sal's fingers plucked at the strings tied at her nightgown's neck.

"No more than the wind." And there was wind, Jane could hear it, now that she listened. No wonder Sal was up so late. That odd late summer light showed at the windows, as the sun hadn't yet set, and the wind's uneven and unnerving whistle would keep a grown person awake.

"I don't think I'll be able to sleep away from Jordan." Sal looked down through the staircase's center, just where Jane had been looking up. "That lady means to take him away from me."

"Aunt Eden cannot simply have whatever she wants, though she likes to think otherwise."

"But if she tries *real hard*… what will happen to me?" How could Sal's cheeks tremble that way? "My father won't notice Jordan's gone, and then what?"

A week ago, Jane might have waved Sal's concern away as some excessive story from her store of childish fears. But she'd met the children's father now, and she knew Sal spoke only the simple truth.

Just like she had about the mathematics.

Jane had heard so many insults and evasive fibs that she had stopped listening. A dozen moments from her past leaped to mind. So many people who had said one thing and meant another: the men with whom she had discussed marriage, their landlords, their customers, and most often the parents who'd told her they weren't going to leave.

How could she prepare another little girl for a long series of disappointments like that?

Jane swallowed. She felt her heart race. Who *better* than she to try to be honest with Sal about the cruelty in the world? Because cruelty was too easy a possibility.

"If Jordan were to stay, you'd stay with him. Of course you would. You and I wouldn't have it any other way, and neither would he. And he's not old enough to leave home."

"He is, Emery said he's almost old enough for a real appren-tiss-or-ship." She stumbled a little on the word, but she knew it well enough. "If he's going to do that, why can't he do it at *your* bakery?"

"Emery wants you two to have the best preparation for life that we can manage. Wouldn't you like to go to school?"

"I don't like to embroider."

Jane laughed. "An actual school, Sal, where you might study mathematics to some purpose."

"I got purpose; I'm Jordan's sister."

And there it was. So little Sal knew, yet she was so wise.

"You will always be Jordan's sister. You may wish to be

other things *as well*." Jane looked around the dark, hard shapes of the wooden panelling. "Just as I will always be Rose's sister, and Emery's, and Anna's. Nothing can change that."

"Nothing?"

"Nothing at all." Jane felt the calm in her own hands as she leaned them on her knees to get her eyes level with Sal's. "You know it's true. You feel it, don't you?"

Sal's nod stuttered, jerkily, but her eyes were certain.

"Now." Still bent down, Jane pointed to a door at the far end of the corridor. "That's the Blue Room, where Jordan is. Hadn't you better check on him?"

She thought Sal would simply march in, but Sal stopped at the door. Her braid swung against her back as she scratched almost noiselessly at the polished door.

Which was opened immediately by Jordan. "Where you been?" the boy yawned, one fist twisting against one sleepy eye. "I been waiting for you."

And as Jane watched, the two of them retired.

"No, Aunt Eden can't have everything her own way," Jane felt herself whisper.

"This is madness."

"Are we really going to Mr. MacPherson's land *today*?"

"I'm sure Aunt Eden can loan us some lanterns. You will, won't you, Aunt Eden?"

Rose shook her head slowly, shoulders tense with irritation. "Oh my heavens above, whatever will we do? There's fog!"

Her sisters' fussing subsided a bit as realization spread. Moaning about fog in front of Rose was rather stupid.

"You're quite right, muffin, but if *none* of us can see, it will be a challenge." Anna's irritation seemed aimed at the fog, not her sisters.

"I can't see two yards out there." Emery was apparently at a window in the parlour where they all stood. Rose had faint memories of those windows; they went all the way from the ceiling to the floor. She'd loved them.

Rose hadn't guessed that it would matter to her that she had memories of Walbey Hall. But she did, and it did. She couldn't quite decide *how* it mattered to her, but she felt it did. She knew exactly where she was, and she moved easily, quicker; at the same time, her feet and fingers felt swollen with annoyance, as though a needle's prick would make her bleed impatience.

More so since the fog had rolled in overnight.

It mattered to her not at all. But her sisters behaved as if some great catastrophe had befallen them all, and that irritated Rose more.

"Then I suppose I'll go alone to Mr. MacPherson's," Rose said, cutting through their flying comments.

That silenced them.

"Of course not; we're all *going*."

"Mr. MacPherson does not have a driveway on this side of his land," Rose said practically. "And his land goes on for acres. Acres, if we are to understand correctly, that he has entirely given over to bees. That's meadows and such. Without a road. And bees."

"Stop saying bees," Anna half-moaned.

"Really, one can't see a thing out there." Emery didn't sound as if she *wanted* to go. But then, that only made sense; the cake plan was not hers.

And it wasn't really Anna's, either. It was Rose's, and she would see it through.

"I suppose we are all here because of me, so it makes

perfect sense for me to go. Jane must tell me how much I am to offer for the honey, that's all."

"No." Anna's tone had changed. Rose could *hear* resolve hardening it. "This is *my* plan. I called upon Aunt Eden and I will finish this."

"No, it's mine."

"Rose, I planned it all."

"It really isn't far. Not above a mile, if I recall correctly." Did Jane sound lighter than usual? She must be enjoying the trip.

Well, so might Rose if they could engage Mr. MacPherson in business.

"I am sure Mr. Johnson can provide us with some lanterns." Anna said it the way she told people what to do.

ROSE'S CERTAINTY MELTED A LITTLE AFTER THREE QUARTERS of an hour wandering up and down Aunt Eden's countryside.

"Wasn't there a stile close by here, Mr. Johnson?" Rose searched her mind for every faint impression of the land and the fences that crossed the green meadows, keeping cows and sheep in their allotments. She'd held Emery's elbow to cross the fields, and Emery had warned her about a tree to her right; she just had a faint memory of the way the fields lay, a vast old tree, and an ancient stone fence that hemmed Aunt Eden's land.

"I do believe so, Miss Rose." Johnson had been utterly, blissfully unconcerned the entire time. They'd doubled back twice, and once found themselves pinned by a beck that they couldn't cross, it was so swollen with summer waters. Johnson hadn't been the least affected.

Well, thought Rose, he's not in the house with Aunt Eden.

"I don't suppose we *must* do this today?" The mud

squelched up over Rose's shoes, which had London streets in mind, not countryside becks. In the house she'd nearly squirmed with impatience, just wanting something to happen. Out here, the moisture from the air clung to her all over, and achieving their mission seemed ten times more unlikely.

But the determination that had seized Anna in the house had not let her go. "We can and we will. We must get back to the bakery. We dare not risk losing any more customers than necessary; we do have competitors." The name *Sennet's* hung over them all, gloomy as the fog.

"Sennet's is ten minutes away. From the bakery, of course I mean." Emery sounded muffled, as if the very mist in the air had separated them.

The idea that had been bubbling in the back of Rose's mind since supper last night—or, truth be told, for some weeks now—finally surfaced. "Wasn't our original plan that one of us would get married? And wouldn't that settle the business on a sound footing?"

"But none of us expects to marry," and Jane's voice was oddly gentle, given how sure she had been that someone would see them through the window and snap one of them up.

Hadn't that happened to Rose? Hadn't that *exact thing* happened?

Perhaps Mr. Russell hadn't spoken of marriage, but he spent *so* many of their stolen moments together holding her against him, and kissing her. He was so solid, so *sturdy*. Far more so than Walbey Hall, truth be told.

Rose had lain awake last night until she lost track of time altogether, listening to Emery sleep and wondering how it would be to have warm, solid Mr. Russell in the bed instead. She wondered what his breath would sound like if it were that close.

"But what if I marry?"

"Rose, stop. You really are too young to marry." Anna dismissed the idea immediately, and the last of Rose's peace washed away in a flood of sudden anger.

"Why do you say that? Girls in their first season are *years* younger than I am. And they get married. Mother was younger than I when she married. You might have been. *Jane* might have been, had anyone accepted her offers."

"Thanks for that," Jane said lightly, her shoes swishing through the grass.

"Why shouldn't I marry? Why shouldn't that help? Wouldn't it help as much as a new effort in producing cakes?"

"No." Anna took a deep breath, then another one again. "Marriage doesn't simply make money. Does Mr. Russell have coins dropping from his pockets that your marriage would naturally fund our living? And I still say you are too young."

"You'd better mean too young, and not too blind," said Rose, with a dark edge creeping into her voice the more Anna's nonsensical objections progressed.

"I mean too young. And it isn't by number of years."

"That makes *no* sense. I don't like to think it of you, Anna, but you do seem simply jealous that it isn't you. You thought it would be you, or Jane. Well, it isn't. It's me. You should accustom yourself to the idea. Mr. Russell intends to marry me, you know."

That made Anna stop. They all stopped. Even Mr. Johnson, carrying a lantern in front of their small party, stopped.

"Does he?" Anna's voice was quiet. "Because Jane and I walked with him to Mr. Collier's just the other night, you know, and he never mentioned any such thing."

Just the quiet observation made Rose's stomach feel hollow. She couldn't be *mistaken*, could she? Not her Mr. Russell. Mr. Russell, who agreed with her and waited to see her every moment they could have together. Mr. Russell with his big warm hands that splayed so reassuringly across her back when he pulled her close.

"Don't say that," she breathed, and it was all she could manage to say. Then her voice grew stronger. "Don't *say* that. Here we are at Aunt Eden's and you are back to thinking that no one could want to marry *me*. But someone does, and someone will; it *will* happen, and then what, Anna? Then what?"

EMERY WILLED ANNA TO SAY SOMETHING REASSURING. Something about never getting married. Something about never leaving Emery all alone.

Because Emery had never dreamed of having anything she wanted until she met Jasmine Hayes. But Jasmine Hayes didn't want her in return.

Her world was not so large as her sisters'. They could bemoan the number of suitable men all they wanted, but the truth was that thousands of men might serve as husbands, if only they agreed. Emery's world was different. The number of women in their neighborhood that could even inspire Emery's thoughts of a kiss were few, Emery had met them, and Jasmine Hayes with her bouncy gold curls and delicate wrists and ready smile was the one Emery would always want. And wouldn't get.

They had stopped, Rose dropping Emery's arm, and each of them stood separately on the everlasting grass, and Emery still didn't know where they were. No one seemed to know.

"Rose, we should talk about that later."

"I seem to be talking about it now."

"Rose, we wouldn't want to bore Mr. Johnson with family business." Anna got that firm set to her lips that meant she was digging in.

Emery didn't want that. She wanted reassurance. She wanted *comfort*.

It was lovely, having all she wanted to eat and being able to sleep through the night, though she woke at the time to make loaves anyway. She had simply gone back to sleep. She felt stronger for the food and the sleep; she knew that.

But comfort, true comfort, would be something much richer. It would be food and sleep and all she wanted of Miss Hayes' company. Her hands, her smiles. Her warmth.

And she wasn't going to get that.

Emery felt embarrassed to hold such delights back from Rose, though. Rose had always been her partner in wondering about the things their older sisters had. It was just another type of alone, for Rose to leave her staring down a dark, empty tunnel of life to be spent alone. But Emery couldn't be angry with Rose.

Easier to be angry with Anna, who wasn't denying it could change things. Who was only insisting Rose was too young to marry when that was patently absurd.

It made everything that foamed dark and bitter at the bottom of Emery's soul bubble up again.

"Why, Anna? Rose shouldn't marry, because *you* have not? Or Jane?"

Anna just made a frustrated noise, her face still turned toward the place they couldn't find.

Mr. Johnson seemed eager to reassure. "Never fear, Miss Anna, I have grown quite accustomed to keeping private matters private."

Anna's much-washed pale linen dress was a column of brightness in the spreading thick gray fog. "Even from Aunt Eden?"

"Madame is a unique employer," said Johnson, in a way that wasn't really an answer.

Perhaps Emery ought to keep this for later.

All four sisters were yards apart, separated by drifting mists, surrounded by blank gray as far as the eye could see. Emery felt lost in an ocean of fog, and alone. Alone in a way she'd never felt so keenly before, and with her sisters drifting farther and farther away.

They couldn't find the stile to climb over into Mr. MacPherson's land; they couldn't even find the wall. They couldn't find their way at all.

In the end, it would be Emery left alone and completely lost.

"You *are* thinking of marrying, aren't you?" The dark bubbling bitterness congealed into a nasty thought. "You're going to marry that fellow you overcharged for cake, aren't you? He has a title, and money. He's what you always wanted, after all."

Anna's glare was not so sharp in the clinging fog. "You have *no idea* what I always wanted, Emery."

"You're going to get married and expect us to live off your pin money, isn't that it? You'll be at a lordly manor house and we'll be baking the skin off our nose and living off the coins you toss out of the carriage. I can see how it will be."

"Emery."

When she saw Anna's hand raised, white in the mist, Emery had a wild thought that Anna would actually strike her.

But no. Of course not. This was *Anna*. Even in the depths of her occasional fits of pomposity, Anna was still Emery's sister. Had been, even years back when they had run all over this property like wild little wolves.

Anna's hand reached across the shifting gray void, and her fingers wound between Emery's fingers. She held her sister's hand, tight.

"I don't know where these thoughts come from to plague you, Emery, but you *must* put them aside. I don't know what I will do. But I am not thinking of marrying Lord Boislegrand. And if I did, I wouldn't abandon the bakery. I wouldn't abandon *you*."

"I know you wouldn't abandon me." Emery felt small now, and petty. She ought to be *more* civil with so much food in her, surely. She'd had two whole eggs that morning. "But the bakery..."

"Emery, do you not remember it was I who read the paper? Where we first saw the advertisement? I knew we could make it pay. Not you, or me. But all of us. We are going to make that bakery pay and pay enough to live. Wasn't that right, Jane?"

And Jane sounded like herself again, reassuringly hard and realistic. "Yes. That money is for us to make our lives with. That's all Mother and Father left for us. And it's our freedom. Making the bakery pay is freedom for all of us."

Anna nodded. "That's it, Emery. Freedom for *all* of us. You haven't heard any of Rose's fine speeches. But she puts into words what I can't. We all deserve some choices, some *say* in our lives. *Everyone* does. That's why we aren't going to purchase sugar, not at Ladies' Own Bakery. And that's why I'm not leaving it, or you. Not that way. Maybe never."

"Maybe." Maybe didn't feel good enough.

"Emery," Anna said again, squeezing Emery's hand, "I swear to you that if the day ever comes to end our bakery, mine will be the last hand to close that door. You'll have to pry the key from my fingers. I am *not* giving up."

Emery closed her eyes. It made little difference to what she could see. But Anna's hand in hers made things so much clearer. "All right," and she knew she sounded ungracious, but Anna squeezed again as if she understood that was the best Emery could do right now.

Anna had no idea what morose disappointments plagued Emery, but it didn't matter, either. They were in this together.

"Do you feel better now?" Jane sounded almost *playful*. It was an odd counterpoint to the intensity of the back and forth between them.

But Emery managed to match her tone, at least a little. "I do."

"Good. Then I do too." Anna's words gave Emery a glimpse of what it must be like to be the oldest sister, as if Anna's happiness depended on Emery's. That lightened her mood a little too.

"I think I found the wall *and* the stile." Rose suddenly appeared out of the mist, an apparition in flowered chintz hemmed short enough to see her shoes. Her hair curled even more in the mist and hung over one eye where it had come loose from her ribbon and braids.

She *did* look too young to be married. But Emery wouldn't pursue that now.

"Then the hard part is done!" Anna said brightly.

Anna did that, Emery realized: sounded bright until things brightened.

Jane was shaking her head at Rose. "Weren't you here when Anna was saying those nice things about you?"

"Oh! Did I miss them? Say them again. We wanted the wall and the stile, though."

"Yes." Jane went to put her hand into Rose's. "Lead on. If Mr. MacPherson has a purchaser for his harvests already, we will find someone else. There are so many farmers in this area, we must be able to find one who nurtures bees."

"I hope we don't get stung," said Rose, apparently just realizing that they were going to visit a man with bees.

"One problem at a time," Jane murmured to her, as Emery let Anna's hand go; but they followed, Mr. Johnson with his lantern hurrying to keep up.

Episode 14: Bees

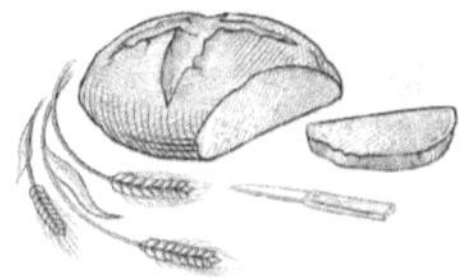

Mr MacPherson's bees didn't like the fog either. They floated, bobbing up and down over their little domed houses, and Jane preferred that to crawling. Somehow in the air they looked rather unworldly, fit to make a substance as miraculous as honey. But crawling over the surface of their home, they simply looked like bugs.

"Their house is like an egg with the bottom cut off," Jane told Rose. "There are places where they can creep inside, and some of them are moving about on the outside and some are flying in the air around."

"They're very protective of their house," Mr. MacPherson said, "so I wouldn't go any closer."

"I shan't touch their home." Though Rose's fingers were half-extended, as if she really wanted to try.

Anna, who had clearly put bees' houses at the very bottom of the list of things she would touch, said somewhat dryly, "No one will stop you if that's really what you want to do."

The question of what Rose wanted was an unwelcome

one, and everyone let it lie, untouched, much like the house of the bees.

Jane looked back at Mr MacPherson. An unprepossessing little man in wrinkled clothes, he wore a broad-brimmed hat despite the cloudy weather. Its brim flapped silently when he moved. "You have enough bees to provide us with the amount of honey we need?"

"Oh, I have bees. Bees is all I have. And I have plenty."

Behind him, still holding the dimmed lantern, Mr. Johnson visibly shuddered.

Anna's hands clasped around her waist as if holding in her breath. "You never wished to farm something like cattle or sheep, or something else more congenial?"

"Aye, I've got a few," the farmer said carelessly, and indeed he must have, or the green carpet under their feet would not be cropped so short. He didn't say if the invisible animals were cows or sheep; clearly, he didn't care. "I've got a few, but I like bees. I started liking bees a long time ago and I just like them better the more I get to know them. They don't bother you, bees."

No one asked if four sisters from London bothered him more; it was clear they did.

"How do they do it?" Faced with the actual bees, Emery was far more curious than she was about the production of cake itself. She peered very closely at one of the little hives, though she didn't go closer. "Can you see inside? Can you see how they do the thing that they are doing?"

Her question prompted the first sign of emotion that Mr MacPherson displayed. "Aye, I can see inside when I harvest the honey. It kills a lot of bees and I hate that. These ol' skep hives have run their course; I'm fed up with them, I tell you. I'm looking at a new kind a' hive that'll let me take out the honey without destroying the house."

He warmed to his topic. "It's awful cunning in there. They

make little shapes that are as perfect as any little shapes you ever saw. And they fill them up with the honey. The shapes are made of wax; have to melt it all down to get the honey out."

"And the dead bees." Emery, her hands clasped behind her and linen dress draped over her frame as she strained to see the bees without getting closer, seemed gruesomely fixated on the fate of the tiny creatures.

Mr. MacPherson didn't care for that part of his story, either. He waved the tin cone in his hand; the smoke that trickled from its tip mingled with the fog and disappeared. Apparently, it was the smoke that kept the bees so lazy. "I have to filter out the ones what die. I'm telling you, this is the last year I use these hives, I don't like them. I don't like what they do to the bees. Plus, they're expensive, getting new ones every year, even if they are made of straw. And the fellow what makes them for me, he isn't getting any cheaper either."

Jane didn't move any closer to the bees either, but her heart, which had felt bruised closed for a very long time, opened up to the little creatures. If this worked, those little bees would be their salvation. "They're giving us a chance," she said out loud to our sisters, heedless of the men listening. "These little bees, they'll be giving their lives for *us*. For the Ladies' Own Bakery."

Anna looked less than charmed by the sacrifice of the bees, but gave Jane a nod of agreement anyway. "Mr. MacPherson, it won't be any trouble, for you to sell us nearly all your harvest? And you can send it a few times a year?"

"Naw. Saves me driving around to markets, that's all. Which I don't much care for. I like bees more than markets." *And people* went unsaid and understood.

"You don't sell butter and eggs as well, Mr. MacPherson?"

"Nah, I like bees."

"Do you know of a farmer who might sell us one or both?"

"Nah." They all could have predicted what came out of Mr. MacPherson's mouth next. "I just like *bees*."

"You can stop asking me about people who sell butter, Anna. I don't *meet* people who sell butter."

Emery, bent over her sewing, wondered if Anna might take pride in being a person who actually wore out Aunt Eden. Their great-aunt was so tired of Anna's interrogations about where to find butter that she sounded almost civil.

"Your butter is always *so* good, Aunt, you must understand why I'm asking."

"Want butter? Go eat some. I don't bother my head about such things."

Emery tilted her face to catch Anna's eye. "I believe you, Aunt Eden. I'm sure you have much more important things to think about than where to buy the butter."

She saw the thought conveyed across the sitting room, saw Anna absorb it. Her sister's face lit with understanding. Aunt Eden certainly did not buy her own butter and never had.

"Excuse me a moment, would you?"

It wasn't till Anna had gone, no doubt to corner Mrs. Mahew and ask her the source of the butter, that Emery realized she was alone with Aunt Eden.

"So, what are you doing about getting married, then, Emery?" asked the old lady before Emery could lurch out of her chair and run for the door.

"Nothing," said Emery with clarity, sincerity, and relish.

"Think you're special, do you?"

That was new. So new it startled Emery into looking up from the hem she was changing; Aunt Eden had given them dresses. In typical fashion, she didn't indicate if they were hers, her daughters', or even their mother's from long ago. She'd simply pointed to the pile and said, "There."

This one was nearly long enough for Emery. Which made her wonder how tall Aunt Eden had been in her younger years; she was certainly hump-backed now.

The thing was covered with old-fashioned bows and tucks which Emery was cheerfully, ruthlessly, destroying.

Emery had never tried sparring with Aunt Eden. Her aunt was a person to endure or escape. But Anna's new approach gave Emery a new idea. Her aunt must be, above all else, bored. She *wanted* the sparring.

"It's an interesting question." Emery's heart thumped in her chest as she looked back down at her sewing. If this turned into another litany of her faults, she *would* run for the door. "For who doesn't want to believe they are special? Yet you say that as though it would be the height of pride for me to want my own future, not to hitch myself like a wagon to some ass and let him haul me along through life."

She counted seconds, feeling her palms sweat, wondering what Aunt Eden would say.

Eventually, Aunt Eden chuckled.

"It's an *interesting* question? You heard me tell your sister what a disaster it is to be interesting, and you're throwing the word back at me."

Emery tried taking another breath. "I hadn't thought to, but now that you say it, fine. Why not?"

"I'm not interesting, Emery." The older lady's face seemed to cave in on itself. She looked about the room, at the blazing little fire, the old paneled wood on the walls, the stain of centuries of smoke on the chimney stones. "Just don't know why you think you should escape a woman's lot. A woman has to marry to have a home she can keep, unless she's of a mind to be a bird of paradise. And I have never seen a woman less likely to be a bird of paradise than you."

Jasmine Hayes' rosebud lips flashed to Emery's mind. *Bird of paradise* was a pretty phrase, no matter how Aunt Eden meant it. "Thus, the bakery." It seemed safest to keep her answers short.

Aunt Eden just waved the bakery away. "They'll never let you keep it."

A chill chased down Emery's back, and she straightened in her chair. When she studied her aunt, she didn't see the usual haughty disdain on that grooved face. Bitterness, certainly, and regret.

Had her aunt once had a dream like the Ladies' Own Bakery?

"I don't know who *they* is, Aunt, but we have the bakery. It's ours."

"No, you don't." Aunt Eden looked tired; only her fingers moved this time, where her hand lay on the grooved old arm of the chair. They brushed away something invisible; perhaps her thoughts. "You don't own a blessed thing, and unless you own something, it isn't yours. And you're not allowed to own. You don't have a husband, father, or son, so you can't own. Not a home, nor, I suspect, a bakery."

An iron tang like fear tasted sharp on Emery's tongue, but it didn't seem like Aunt Eden was threatening her. More like she was sharing the bitter fruit of some tree of knowledge she wished she hadn't tasted herself.

Emery didn't trust Aunt Eden enough to tell her about their arrangements. Not the good, and certainly not the bad.

Anna had already announced that they must return home in the morning. They'd soon be free of Aunt Eden's bleak company. And Emery had the feeling that Aunt Eden's mood was even bleaker than usual because of the impending separation.

Aunt Eden had made no effort to pay for school for Emery, or for Rose. But she had given Emery this dress.

And suddenly Emery wondered why the old lady had kept it.

She turned back to the hem. Someone had stitched it incredibly carefully. There were stitches every four threads in the weave of the linen, and nothing showed on the front at all. She couldn't hem it again nearly so beautifully. But someone had put enough fabric into this hem to make it worth letting out, and Emery would do her best. That was all she had.

She could at least share some of her best with Aunt Eden in exchange for the dress.

"The night watchman pulls a string outside my window and it makes a spoon drop, and that's how I know to wake up before dawn," she began.

"Hah! Doesn't get more common than that," said Aunt Eden, but she leaned a little closer. Perhaps to make sure she didn't miss a word.

She'd likely fight every minute Emery spoke. Emery hadn't expected her to turn sweet and soft in an instant. But she wasn't stopping Emery from speaking.

Emery went on. "It's cooler in the bakery overnight than in the daytime, so the bread from the night before rises a little more slowly..."

WHEN IT CAME TIME TO CLIMB BACK IN THE HIRED carriage, full to the brim with an early breakfast and carrying, here and there, little bundles that Aunt Eden refused to acknowledge, the bakery troupe found themselves lining up before the old woman in her sitting room just as they had in their bakery when she'd come to see them.

Sal and Jordan stood next to Emery.

"I'm not going to watch the carriage go," Aunt Eden

announced from her chair. "Don't write if you only need money. Which you will."

All four Misses Bickering seemed to be nudging each other and looking about, wondering what to say as if they were little children again. Aunt Eden had shown signs of genuine kindness. They had never before entertained the idea that she had a heart inside her chest like other people, and she clearly didn't want to confirm any suspicions about it now.

It was Sal who finally stepped forward. "Aunt Eden."

Aunt Eden, who had continued to ignore her the entire trip, looked startled. "Don't address me so, child. I'm not your aunt."

"I'm sorry you're not a twin," Sal said, and stepped back into line.

That generous thought made Rose laugh, and when she laughed, her sisters nervously followed suit.

"Thank you for everything, Aunt Eden." "Thank you! It has been pleasant, to be here again." "Thank you, Aunt Eden." "Thank you, ma'am."

Even Emery bent down a little to be closer to her aunt, seated on the carved old chair like a queen's throne. "Goodbye, Aunt Eden. Thank you."

"What a disgusting show of emotion. Informality creates a chaotic society. If any of you are arrested, tell them your last name is Woodard. That was the family name of your great-grandfather's least reputable cousin. Johnson, as soon as they go, count the silver."

"Yes, madam." Johnson seemed undisturbed by this order. "This way."

As they climbed into the carriage, they shared murmurs of consternation. "Will she really have him count the silver, do you think?" Rose asked as they distributed themselves around the old mail carriage.

"Depend on it," said Emery. She tucked herself into the seat and made room for Jordan beside her.

"Will you survive, Jordan, without Aunt Eden stuffing you full of food every moment?" Rose teased. Anna checked the door was tightly latched.

"I won't like it, but I can." The cloud of minor gloom that hung over him lifted a little. "But I won't have to try to think of nice things to say back to her, will I?"

"No you will not," Anna said with crisp finality before adding out the window to the driver, "We're ready to go, sir."

"If only we had found a source of butter as good as Aunt Eden's." Jane couldn't help picking at the remaining flaw in their plan.

"The butter at her local market comes from a farmer with only a few cows." Anna drooped a little in defeat. "I suspect Aunt Eden buys half their butter."

"Well, or did for our visit."

Jane's observation wasn't lost on the people packed into the carriage: Aunt Eden had clearly shouldered the expense of feeding them a great deal. It was easier to like Aunt Eden while full of her food; even easier when she was several hours behind them.

"If only we had more time to meet more farmers!" said Rose for the dozenth time.

"We've got to get home. We've been closed this whole time. By the time we open again, it will have been a week. It will take days to get the raising going again, and that's if Mrs. Baby has kept it alive the way we asked."

The idea of entrusting Mrs. Baby with a big bowl of yeasted flour hadn't appealed to anyone. Everyone expected they would find at least one half-chewed crust of bread in it from some baby or another. But they had few friends in Leicester Square, and Mrs. Baby had seemed eager to do it.

"She wanted something to look after that wasn't a baby," Rose said what all of them thought.

"Do you realize that our side of the family will end with us? Isn't it hard to realize that we've given up on marriage and won't have any babies of our own?" Anna's eyes were misty over something.

Jane couldn't imagine what. "Not when you look at Mrs. Baby."

Rose didn't mention marriage, and Emery didn't either. That had to be a step towards better peace. Perhaps it was easier when Anna owned how *she* still thought of marriage, even though it wasn't imminent.

Jane was still contemplating Anna when the carriage lurched. Then stopped.

"Is there a problem, sir?" Anna, closest to the door, leaned out the window and called to the driver. They could see nothing but rolling green countryside.

"It's a cabbage," he called faintly back.

She sat back down, her brows drawn together in confusion. "What's a cabbage?"

Jane looked about at them all. "How would *we* know?"

"He stopped for a cabbage?" Sal hung out the window; half her little body fit right through.

"Sal, sit down."

Having successfully ordered Sal to sit down, Anna clearly hadn't any idea what to do next.

"Should I go see what it is?" Emery finally asked.

"It's apparently a cabbage," Anna answered, her hands fluttering in confusion.

"It's got to be a pretty big cabbage," Jordan said.

He clearly still had massive heaps of food on his mind, but

now the image was in all their minds and no one could escape it.

"He didn't really stop because of an enormous cabbage in the road, did he?" Rose clearly wanted there to be a huge, house-sized cabbage.

"Do you think it's dangerous?" Anna asked Jane, making her sister roll her eyes like she used to.

"Oh, for pity's sake." Emery had to sit on her knees to shuffle toward the door, unlatch it, then make some extremely inappropriate contortions to get her long legs outside.

Once standing, she disappeared from view.

"It's a regular-sized cabbage," they heard her say.

The driver responded, "No need to climb out, miss, I'm just about to press on. Startled me, that's all. Didn't expect a cabbage to come rolling along the road. Worried it would get under the horses' feet."

"Not at all, it's nice to get out, it's a fine day," they heard Emery answer. "And you don't see a cabbage in the road every day."

Anna looked at every face. "All right, everyone out to see the cabbage," she grumbled.

It *was* refreshing, to stand outside the carriage, stretch legs, and look about for the cabbage.

The road here wasn't wide, and the high-summer meadow grasses pressed against the carriage on both sides. But the ground was fairly dry, given the mists and rain of the last few days.

And yes, settled into the wheel tracks on one side of the road was a cabbage.

"Like to buy a cabbage?" The voice came from beyond the horses, where no one had looked.

Surely there was no need to stand on propriety on the side

of a road. Jane bent down and peered through the horse's legs.

There were skirts on the other side.

The driver frowned down that way and waggled his finger. "No one wants any cabbages."

"I don't know if that's true, sir. Not that I say you're lying, I just mean you might not be telling the truth. I'll hear from the ladies themselves. Sometimes ladies need cabbages."

Jane was in no mood for whatever game this was. It was a long way still to London and there were too many people in the carriage. "We're not ladies," she called through the horse's legs.

"All the more reason for cabbage," said whoever it was.

Jane finally stood and followed everyone else round the horses.

A woman like a round pile of aprons stood in the grass past the carriage. Her hair was wrapped in clean white linen; strawberry-golden curls escaped here and there. She had a soft, friendly face and wide bright eyes, and the color in her cheeks was high.

She pointed ahead of the carriage some dozen paces, and Jane saw a wheelbarrow by the side of the road.

"Filling and cheap. You can't beat cabbages."

Jane looked round. Everyone was standing there, mouths agape, just staring at the woman. Apparently, this conversation was up to Jane.

"We make *bread*."

She thought she was going to have to explain how much bread was better than cabbages, but there was clearly no need.

"*Bread!*" The woman clasped her two hands ahead of her, arms straight out with excitement. "That sounds *lovely*, surrounded by bread all day! Better than cabbages."

"It is."

"Still, you must have something to eat with your bread, eh? Why not a cabbage?" Picking up her skirts, the woman marched through the tall grass toward her wheelbarrow, and Jane had a sudden suspicion.

"Did you *put* that cabbage in the road?"

"No! I *rolled* it." She made a scooping motion of the arm as if bowling with a cabbage.

"You threw a cabbage. Into the road. In front of a horse."

"It's ever so much easier to see cabbages when they're moving. No one remarks on them when they're standing still." The woman pointed again at her cart, heaped with pearly vegetables.

"You might have hurt someone!"

"Not at all, I do it all the time." She gave the nearest horse a friendly smile. "Not bothered a bit, were you? It's a change at least, isn't it? And a nice fresh cabbage." Her smile faded a bit when she looked toward the cabbage still sitting in the road. "Well, that one's a bit worn. I've tossed it a dozen times now, it doesn't look good close up."

"You can't fling cabbages into the road with no warning!"

"Well. Does a warning matter? Suddenness always takes you aback. Though there's worse things than just being sudden."

"We don't need cabbage!"

"We don't *want* cabbage!" Anna called from her safe distance. She seemed to feel Jane needed support.

"Well, I mean," Rose said in her even-handed way. "We don't *hate* cabbage."

"Ya can't fling cabbages in road!" roared the driver.

"Of course I can; I just did. Should I show you again?"

Despite her better instincts, Jane had to ask. "How many cabbages do you sell this way?"

"*Well.*" This was some sort of sign to the woman to settle in and talk. "I sell plenty of cabbages, I must tell you, though it isn't work I like. I have a cousin what wanted some help with her cabbages last year and I thought I needed a change —like a horse plodding down the road needs a cabbage to come by. You know? But I've flung plenty of cabbages by now and the shine is off, I'll tell you."

"Did you start by flinging cabbages at passing horses, or did it just come to you in time?"

"Jane," Emery put in from beside the near horse, which was peering at the woman on the side of the road with suspicion, "I don't think we will sell more bread by flinging it at anyone."

"We're here for new ideas!" shrugged Jane.

"No, we're here for honey. And butter, and eggs; and butter isn't cabbages." Why Anna thought this obvious tidbit would improve the conversation was anyone's guess. She plucked at Rose's sleeve, clearly eager for everyone to get back in the carriage.

"Thank goodness cabbages aren't butter," agreed the woman. "If I sold butter? Or eggs? What a mess."

"Ma'am, this has been an interesting meeting, but we must get home." Emery said what they were all thinking. Well, aside from a roadway full of butter. Or eggs. "It takes half a day more to get to London—"

"More if a person's driving you lot," muttered their driver.

"We can't stay," Emery concluded, piercing him with a look.

"Well, take a cabbage or two with you! You'll be hungry once you get there."

Jane definitely admired the woman's persistence. "We're going to London. There are cabbages in London."

"Pah! Big houses and rivers and horses that shy if you so much as toss a cabbage their way. You want *these* cabbages, I tell you."

"We live in Leicester Square," added Rose. "We do get good cabbages."

"Wait." The woman paused, skirts held high. "You said you wanted butter and eggs?"

"A large quantity. Not any amount you might have under your cabbages." Anna wanted that clear.

The woman drew herself up to her full height. It wasn't much, but along with the width of her skirts and aprons, she cut a figure. "Ma'am, I hope you're not thinking cruel things about my cabbages. You haven't even looked at them. They're full grown summer cabbage, and they make a nourishing meal for anyone. Now while you think about what I said, let me think about butter for a minute." True to her word, she did, with a faraway look on her face. "Now there's a fellow not half a mile from here who's young and just got his father's dairy. Don't know that he could help with eggs, but he might, and he'd be grateful for a butter buyer."

"Really?" Anna cocked her head forward.

"We must be going, miss," the driver said.

"Sir, we have come a very long way on these errands. We won't pass this way twice. If this person has a possible solution, we must pursue it." Turning back to the woman in aprons, with all the dignity she had, Anna said, "Which way to the butter, please?"

"Now." The woman pointed a finger straight at Anna. "If I show you, you'll buy some cabbages?"

"How many cabbages?" Anna asked with pardonable suspicion.

"At least three."

"What about your cart?"

"Oh, I'll push it along and you can follow."

The driver could just imagine plodding his horses after her. "Miss!"

The woman just glared at him. "My name's Tilly, really, you ought to know it by now!"

Jane just looked at Anna. "She's not afraid of hard work, is she?"

Anna had learned a little about negotiating. "We'll buy two cabbages now. You ride by the driver and show him where to go. We'll return you to your cart when our errand is done and buy two cabbages more. Will that do?"

"What if someone takes my cabbages while I'm gone?"

"Then at least you've sold two cabbages!"

This was a complicated arrangement, and Tilly took a moment to think it over. "Promise to pay for the last two cabbages even if they're missing when we get back, and it's done."

"Yes."

"There you go!" Immediately, the woman started plodding through the tall grass toward her handcart of cabbages. "Come pick the ones you like."

"She's committed to a happy customer, isn't she?" Rose said as Anna offered her arm and they followed.

THE YOUNG MAN WAS CHARMINGLY EARNEST AND HAD inherited a cart. He'd gladly drive the butter in to them regularly, packed in straw till the weather cooled. "I'll bring the missus," and the glint in his eye was clearly for the prospect of showing the city to his little wife, who was as delighted as he was.

It was a reassuring way to start a business relationship.

But he couldn't promise them as much as they'd hoped. The "dairy" was a handful of cows as earnest-looking as their owner, and they ate almost as much butter as they sold; he had four children.

As they settled themselves back into the carriage, four cabbages now tumbling about among their feet, the sisters' mood was sober.

"It's better this way," Jane said. "If we don't sell many cakes to start, we won't need that much butter. Didn't we plan to start slowly?"

"I don't know why I thought we could achieve everything we set out to achieve in one trip. I feel I must apologize." Anna looked close to tears, and her hands gripped her skirt so tightly it looked in danger of ripping.

"You can apologize for not telling us of the plan," Emery said in her practical way. "But not for trying."

"I suppose we ought to have discussed it more," admitted Jane.

"Wait. You knew about this letter to Aunt Eden?" Having achieved a calm not seen since the cake plan was proposed, Emery clouded up like the sky above them.

"Only after I wrote it!" Anna waved downward, squashing further complaints.

"But before we knew about it. Because we didn't know, did we, Rose?"

"No we did *not*," and sweet little Rose looked ready to pinch someone.

"You two must stop doing this. Stop being the two of you against Rose and me. This won't work if you do."

"This won't work if we don't find a place for more butter," Anna said.

Emery leaned forward in the crush of bodies and skirts. "This business of business won't work if you insist on treating us younger two as if we were children."

"No, I—" Anna looked at the actual children, and subsided.

"I mean it, Anna. Rose and I are grown women, too. Didn't you say something of that sort to Aunt Eden? You can't just tell us what you please and leave out all the rest. We are all working our hearts out for this bakery."

"You mean, I shouldn't decide I alone know how to save our business, and take on the risk all by myself? Without telling anyone what I was doing?" Anna was usually up or down, but right now she met Emery's eyes perfectly evenly across the carriage.

Emery sat back. It made Rose and Jordan wiggle and rearrange themselves.

"Well, we've learned a thing or two in the last few weeks, haven't we?" said Emery, not taking her eyes from Anna's.

"Don't try to stare each other down." Jane's peculiar burst of positivity made her sisters break eye contact and look at her. "We've learned *many* things over the last few weeks. You both came up with clever plans; they simply might have been more clever had you discussed them."

"I don't think I would have forced myself to do everything I did if I hadn't seen Emery wear so thin making more bread," admitted Anna.

"I didn't try the new way of making bread till Jane made me understand how dire the water bill was," added Emery.

"How clever I was to tell the Captain all about it," put in Rose, and everyone laughed.

"He didn't make it go away, but he made it better," said Jane. "We've made our situation better and better piece by piece. I will admit I thought at the beginning it was all or nothing, but there have been little hills all along the way, and little valleys of success."

"We still must make more money than we could with the bread alone. We still must try to make these honey cakes and make them sell. If not, we will be on the street in winter, and the Scropes will take every last thing we have." Anna's tight blunt tone pushed out the little wave of good feeling.

"We needn't be on the street, I suppose. We could ask for Aunt Eden's charity."

Everyone looked aghast at Emery saying such a thing.

"If anyone in the world would ever *suggest* living with Aunt Eden, I would never have ascribed it to you." Anna couldn't look more shocked if Emery had kicked her.

"I think she's lonely."

"That's because she's not very nice," Sal put in from her corner of the carriage, and there were amused little *huffs* all around at that.

"I'm not suggesting it. I can all too easily imagine all four of us moldering away in Walbey Hall, listening to Aunt Eden's corrections all day year after year." Emery seemed struck by a thought. "Until one of us goes mad and kills her!"

"*Emery!*" Anna put her hands over Sal's ears. "What a thing to even say!"

"I can still hear, you know," Sal said.

"Rather a stirring novel it would make, though, wouldn't it?" Emery looked unrepentant. "I'm not *suggesting* it. We have a chance at something more than the bakery in Leicester Square. We have a chance at a place in the larger world. Eating our own food from our own table."

"Perhaps even to get married," added Rose, who wasn't letting anyone forget how it was on her mind.

"Perhaps," Anna agreed faintly.

"Don't you think so, Jane? Tell the truth. You didn't like the idea of a bakery, or even Leicester Square. What do you think now? You usually think clearly, without a huge fog of feeling."

"Do I?" When Jane looked at Emery, she wondered what appealed to Emery about Leicester Square. She and Anna had spent so much time worrying about Rose, they hadn't watched Emery nearly as closely. And Emery wouldn't like to be watched.

But Emery had some sort of spark about the idea of Leicester Square that wasn't just bread. She wanted the life she was finding there, that was clear enough. Perhaps they all did.

Or at least her sisters did.

"It isn't quite home, is it? But neither is Walbey Hall. No, the bakery is closer to home than Walbey Hall. And after all, we're just getting started, aren't we?" Jane had to dig deep within herself to bring out thoughts she hadn't even realized she had. "Look how far we've come. We're all a bit different from when we began this, aren't we? And we aren't growing different for no reason. I think we're getting better at this, honestly."

"Perhaps," said Rose, "perhaps even better at being sisters."

"Perhaps," said Jane, and reached across the space between them to take Rose's hand and squeeze it between her own.

"Well good, because what about us?" Jordan put in from his seat, and they all realized that this was perhaps not the conversation to have before the children, murder or no murder.

And, as much as they all insisted they were grown women able to live their own lives, in the moment of stress, they all waited for Anna to speak.

She fully expected it. It was her job. She was the oldest.

"You're quite right," said Anna, "and we should tell you that we want the bakery to succeed for you two as well. You are part of this, aren't you?"

"And if it doesn't work, can we molder away at Walbey Hall with Aunt Eden?" Jordan sounded like he might be fine with that.

Anna looked around her sisters' faces. They were all so young. Even she wasn't exactly old yet. And many things might happen in Leicester Square that wouldn't happen at Walbey Hall. "We won't abandon you, Jordan," was all she could promise, but that she did gladly. "We want you happy and healthy and safe and educated—"

"I don't mind missing books," he clarified.

"—just as if you were part of our family." That felt too much to say, and Anna wished she hadn't said it. But *could* they leave Sal and Jordan alone with their father if the bakery closed? It was unthinkable.

The stakes just kept getting bigger, but right at this moment, Anna felt as if she could stand up underneath them, and push.

THE LATE SUMMER EVENING WAS STILL LIGHT WHEN THEY reached number 17 in Leicester Square, but only just, and only because most of the clouds had rolled away.

The drowsy silence in the carriage lifted as the wheels rolled to a stop. There was their familiar shop window just outside the door.

"Don't forget the cabbages," said the driver as he unlatched the door and began to hand out everyone he could reach. Clearly, he'd hoped this day to be shorter.

Well, so had they all.

Emery went first to the door to the bakery shop and shoved her shoulder against it a few times. It was still good and locked.

"I'll help—" About to turn and help her sisters fetch their bundles and cabbages, Emery stopped.

The door to the rooms upstairs stood open.

Episode 15: Hard Truths and Love Tokens

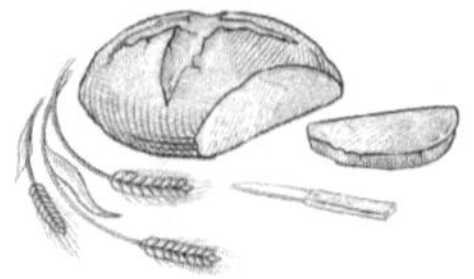

"We can't go up there!" Anna plucked at Jane's sleeve, and even Emery and Jane looked solemn.

"Someone has been there." Jane put her foot on the first step.

"Someone might still *be* there!"

"'Struth, they might." The carriage driver, who had tired of this work many, many hours before, had no enthusiasm for investigating an open door.

Rose pushed her way to the front. "Clearly, one of the building men, whom we never discuss, has left it open."

Jane turned to point a finger at the driver. "Don't say a single word. We are not what you are thinking."

The sight of Rose marching up the stairs by herself shamed her sisters into following. Jane crept up just after her, followed by Emery.

Anna turned to the carriage driver. "You will stay with the children a moment while we check, won't you?"

"Not another instant!" said he, gripping the side of the carriage as if he was about to swing himself up.

Anna grabbed the sideboard, her hand next to his, her knuckles white.

"Just...be a decent man for five more minutes."

The sound he made as he settled back on his feet was indescribable, but Anna wasted no more time on him. "Just a moment, children, I'll fetch you directly."

Then she gathered her skirts in her hand and ran up the stairs after her sisters in as ladylike a fashion as she could.

THEY WERE STANDING IN THE MIDDLE OF THE SITTING room. The room that had been their home now for months. Bare as it was, it was the room where they ate their meals, talked, patched clothes, and kept secrets.

And someone had been inside without their permission.

"Nothing is... broken, is it?" Anna turned around in the dark and tried to peer into corners. She didn't ask if anyone was still there.

"No." Rose sat in a heap of skirts by the wooden crate that held plates and linens. It was clear why no one had lit a candle.

The candlesticks, their mother's last silver, were gone.

Anna went and knelt beside her. Her hand reached out for Rose's, but Rose pulled hers away.

All the bouncy light that had grown in Rose's face these last few months had gone out. "It's like she died again," Rose said in a flat, dry voice.

"No, let's not think that."

"I *do* think that. Stop telling me what to think."

Unable to cope with a thorny Rose, Anna looked over her shoulder at Jane and Emery, side by side against the far wall. "Mother was glad to leave them to us, but the money she left meant far more. The money meant the bakery, and lives of our own. We will open the bakery again soon, and we'll keep going. That's what Mother wanted."

"It isn't about what Mother wanted. It's about what *I* want. I want my mother back. When we first came here, I could barely get out of bed every morning, I missed her so much. And it only made it worse that you didn't miss her at all."

"Why—"

Rose didn't stop. "*None* of you missed her like I did. I wasn't ready to lose her. I don't know how to be a grown lady without her. Not yet. And you all just put your shoes on and went about your business and I wanted to hear her voice just *one more time*."

From the gloom by the stove, Emery said, "So did I."

Jane put her arm around Emery's shoulders. "I did too."

Anna wiggled closer to Rose. "We all did, Rose, we all did. We just—talking about it wouldn't have changed anything."

"It would have changed things for *me*. I'm still here. I'm the one missing her. And it feels worse because I didn't die; why do I want sympathy when it's Mother had such poor luck? Mother who—" Cutting herself off, Rose leaned into Anna's arms after all.

"Mother, who never had a grandchild, because I failed to marry," Anna told her quietly.

"Nor any of us. Don't blame yourself for that, Anna, never that." Jane hadn't sounded for months as though she regretted her failed attempts at marriage, but she sounded like it now.

"It's not as though you disappointed her every day since childhood, like I did," Emery put in.

"So you were all busy feeling bad about letting Mother down? I was busy *missing* her."

Emery and Jane came close and put their arms around

their littlest sister, too, and for a moment all four of them held each other in silence.

"I can't believe someone broke in and took our things." Emery sounded angrier with every word.

"*Touched* our things," shuddered Jane.

"What good is it to have men in the house if they don't even keep away intruders?" Emery sounded as if men were the same as guarding dogs, and no one disagreed.

"Lord Zachary is all the way up in the garret, probably didn't even sleep here, and is a bit useless, besides," Anna reminded her. "And no one knows anything about the drunken fellow but you. And you haven't said."

Thrusting herself upright, Emery stalked from the room.

Jane followed her.

Emery didn't look behind her. She went to the tiny door in the corner of the hall and pounded on the door.

When no one answered her thunderous pounding, Jane whispered, "Perhaps he's out. It's the best part of the evening for drunkards, isn't it?"

"If he's out—" It wasn't clear what dire thing Emery would do. She pounded again.

Then laid her ear against the door.

"Is he in there?" Jane still whispered, though why anyone needed to keep quiet after Emery had made such a thunderous noise wasn't clear.

"Someone groaned," Emery said grimly, and pounded again. Just as loud, but slowly. Over and over and over and over and—

"What?" The tousled greasy head of their neighbor barely showed under the low door sill.

"I don't meddle in your business. I didn't even tell my sisters you lived here! I've kept secrets for you—"

"Wait, wait, wait." He raised a hand, palm out. He didn't appear to be drunk, but perhaps that was only because he had recently recovered; his red eyes had dark circles. "Were we married at some point that I forgot?"

"I kept your secrets and you can't even keep watch over this building for one rat-bitten week?" Emery, face red and eyes flashing sparks, stomped her foot. "What is *wrong* with you?"

"Many things," but he didn't elaborate on that, only rubbed a hand across his face. It looked as though he were trying to get the blood moving somewhere between his neck and his hair. "What happened to the building?" He looked up. "It hasn't burned down."

"My mother's candlesticks were stolen, that's what! Right out from under your *useless* nose! We ought to be able to leave the building for a few days without criminals rifling through our belongings and taking *our mother's candlesticks!*" Emery had converted all her frustrated sorrow to rage, and she vented it all right here, right now.

His head bent forward, too heavy to hold up, and he looked up at her through his lashes. "Are you sure she didn't come get them?"

Emery pushed her face close to his. "*She's dead.*"

"Oh, no." Muttering oaths, not in English, his ashen face turned even grayer. "Show me."

Disarmed by his actual interest, Emery's shoulders slumped a little.

But she backed away from his door and waved toward hers.

The neighbor bent down to get out his small door and approached the sisters' rooms slowly, as if fearing what he might see.

In the gloom inside it was still easy to see Rose, a pale crumpled ball of linen, leaning on Anna, who rocked her back and forth.

Next to the wooden crate that clearly held no candlesticks.

None of them understood what the man muttered under his breath, but he rubbed his face again, this time with both hands. "Silver candlesticks?" he said, and there was a thickness to his voice that made Anna and Jane at least wonder for the first time if he were English. "What did they look like? Describe them to me?"

Jane seemed the only one able to speak. "Ah—not tall. Like a Greek column, you know, scrolled at the top and bottom? Does that make sense?"

"Yes." He shook himself and turned away from the empty spot on the crate, looked at Jane for the first time. "No one is hurt?"

"No."

Anna interrupted. "We must bring up our baggage. And the children!"

"You have children?" This alarmed him somehow.

"No. We must see them home, and it is so late. Will the nightwatchman be—"

"Give me their direction; I will see them home." He looked at Emery then, and his dark, bloodshot eyes looked so full of regret it might spill over. "You are right. I am sorry."

Then he thudded down the stairs.

Anna just looked at Emery, who shrugged.

"I'll get the things," Jane put in.

The idea that the apartment wasn't safe floated in the air but couldn't be settled, as it was the only place to sleep; so they ignored it, as they had all the inconveniences and discomforts of brand-new poverty.

"HOW DID YOU MEET THE GENTLEMAN?" ANNA ASKED quietly as she and Emery helped Rose, worn out, into a nightshirt.

"Another night," Emery told her brusquely, unbuttoning Anna's buttons for her, and Anna could tell it was because they were all tired, not because Emery wished to hide anything for him anymore.

THE RATTLE OF THE WAGON WHEELS AND THE CLOPPING OF horses' hooves seemed familiar now in a way they hadn't just three months before. The countryside now seemed very quiet and far away, now that they were back on Leicester Square.

That first short night's sleep had not put everything to rights, but a few more nights helped. They were young and agile; without discussing it, they agreed to climb back to a normal pattern of life as best they could.

If Rose jumped a bit when a wagon went by, they all hoped that her last few months of confidence would return.

Anna ignored the noise of the street outside as if she had been born in just such a neighborhood. "We must get patrons who wish to purchase cakes; they may not be the same as those who buy bread. I don't know how to reach them, but we must; we must have some way of telling them we will have cakes for sale." She didn't have to say what they all knew, even Jordan and Sal: they had spent the money they had, nearly all of it, to lay in a stock of Mr. MacPherson's pure, rich honey, as well as other ingredients for cake. Lots of cake.

Her fingers trembled, but her voice was steady. "As soon as the day's bread is done on Thursday, I'll begin baking cakes. I'll be ready." Part of the precious money had gone for more pans in which to bake the cakes, and that was a sore spot for all of them. If this didn't work, if no one bought the cakes, they could at least live on honey for quite some time; but they couldn't eat those pans.

Anna went on. "I don't think it's wise to be up all night. I must see how the customers take the cakes the next morning. I will make a few before I must sleep."

It would be better to bake the cakes fresh in the morning, but Anna simply couldn't be awake before Emery started stoking the fire in the small hours.

During the entire carriage ride home, courtesy, if that's what it could be called, of Aunt Eden, all four of them had turned over every possible question regarding how many cakes to make on their first day. Jane and Anna wanted to make their invested money back as quickly as possible, while everything was fresh; Rose and Emery counseled a slower start. After all, honey did not age.

They'd agreed, all four of them, on six cakes to begin with, especially since Anna had spent a night making four, and had a better idea now how long that would take.

"It's easier than you think," Emery encouraged her, "to sleep a bit during the day. You'll be surprised." Emery looked better off for the food and sleep at Walbey Hall, but she'd fallen back into her routine easily, and the bakery was once again full of bread with crumbs scattered on the floor.

Anna's smile for her sister was quick and grateful, a small flag of peace in their fragile truce. "You've given us all a wonderful example."

Sal stared thoughtfully at the counter. "We got to tell everyone. That speech Mr. Russell is giving, in a few days? There's a paper up about that."

"Is there?" No one had mentioned the paper to Rose. No one had felt the need, since Rose had informed them of Mr. Russell's speech long before the paper appeared.

"Yeah," Sal warmed to her subject, "there's a paper up outside the meeting hall. I couldn't read all of it, but I know it said meeting." She flushed a little. She hadn't fought the reading lessons as hard as she had fought the mathematics, but she hadn't cooperated, either. She seemed embarrassed that her reading had not progressed farther. "I'm pretty sure part of it may have said something about Mr. Russell."

"That's very good," Emery said encouragingly, apparently full of the milk of human kindness from her days of rest, and that *was* courtesy of Aunt Eden.

To whom Jane sent some grateful thoughts, though she wouldn't have liked to try to explain them in person. "What brings it to mind, Sal?"

"Well, the cakes. Can't we put up a paper about cakes?"

Anna's color got even higher as she clapped her hands together. "Sally, you are clever. I have a sheet of foolscap and I know just how to use it. You are so bright."

For once, it was Sal who flushed and dropped her eyes; the praise seemed to put her off balance. "I just saw it and thought of it, that's all."

"I believe I can draw the letters very large. Yes, I know I can. I'm good at lettering." Looking at her assembled little family, Anna's eyes sparkled. The food and the sleep during their brief holiday had done them all a great deal of good. "Yes, that is the right answer. We shall tack a paper outside. Someone must be able to loan us some nails. Our tailor neighbor, Mr. Morley, may loan us some heavy pins. We tack the paper outside and people will know that on the appointed day, they may come and buy cakes."

"They will." Rose sounded just as certain, clearly because she wanted to sound certain.

"They have to do it," said Emery.

"Yes," Jane said, "they do."

"Just a minute while I talk to Jane in the bakery." Jane found Anna pulling her in even as Jordan asked, "What's Anna have to talk to Jane in the bakery for?"

Anna lowered her voice to a hiss. "Did you tell her to mention the handbill?"

"Of course I didn't tell her to mention the handbill. I told you *I* was going to mention the handbill. In fact, I didn't say I was going to mention the handbill. I told you I was going to *do* the handbill. And what do you mean, you can draw better than me?"

Anna's lips pressed tight before she spoke again. "Now I feel awkward asking the children to go around shouting about the sale of cake, because they know there's a handbill."

"There can be a handbill and children shouting at the same time."

"But *they* have had the clever idea for the handbill, so now putting them to work shouting seems excessive."

"No." Jane felt definitive in this. "They're children. They like to shout. Sal especially likes to shout. I suspect Jordan will enjoy shouting once his sister sets him an example. Trust me, they can shout, and you will have shouting, and that will be in addition to the handbill."

Anna turned back towards the shop, giving Jane one last narrow-eyed look. "You'd better not have told Sal to mention the handbill."

Jane gave her back the same narrow-eyed look. Both of them must have learned it somewhere; Jane desperately hoped it wasn't from Aunt Eden. "You'd better not lose your courage, just because Sal thought of a handbill."

"I won't. I'm planning to nail it to the wall outside, aren't I? Without a care whether Mrs. Scrope will object to the nail holes in the wall."

"Mrs. Scrope. She hasn't been in for ages. They don't care as long as we pay our lease."

"They haven't forgot us. Just like I haven't forgot them." Anna rubbed her fingers together. "Or that carpenter who was supposed to smooth the counters. What I wouldn't like to do to him, if we ever see him again."

"HEY, LITTLE LADY, I HEAR YOU HAVE SOMETHING SWEET for me."

Jane disliked walking past the paving men in the middle of what had been a good day. She had been toying with the idea of feeling hopeful.

The paver was broad in the shoulders and then the same all the way down, with no thought of a waist interrupting. "Saw the sign by your door, said you've got sweet things for all of us." He looked around at his colleagues and laughed. "It's enough for all of us, right?"

Between picking her way through the street mud to pass by where they were paving, and losing her good temper, Jane snapped. She *felt* something snap. It was just in the middle of her chest, and it stung.

"What makes you think you can talk that way to me? You can't. You think you can talk that way to me because we don't know each other, because I don't know your name? I don't want to know your name. Who would want to know the name of a man like you? Do you say those things to women because you can get away with it, or is it that the existence of women is a shock to you? Is that why you are so brutal, because you have no women in your life? I see how it is. No one has ever been kind to you. No one has ever done anything pleasant for you. And now you justify everyone's opinion of you." At the end of the speech she was breathing so hard, she forgot to wonder what he might do.

One of the other men stood up, his paving hoe in one hand and reached his other towards her.

She drew back as if he might strike her, but he just

wiggled his fingers. His eyes were nearly black under the brim of his cap, and he was laughing. Yes, those eyes snapped with some sort of twinkle, and he was laughing, but not at her. "Well, you've pegged him right. Don't even say anything about it, Bill, she's got you right. And everybody knows it. You'll only make yourself look dumber if you try." He wiggled his fingers again. "Here, miss, can I help you across? You can get back on the pavement this side if you like."

She knew him; she recognized him. The narrow sun-browned face with surprisingly full lips. Underneath that cap, she'd seen it before. It was only because she'd seen it before that she took his hand.

She was still surprised when, as claimed, he simply helped her pass the mud and back up onto the pavement. When he held her hand in his bigger one a second longer, it frightened her, enough that she had to lie. "I'm not afraid of you."

He laughed some more. He had a good laugh. It was a nice sound. And it came from deep inside him like he meant it.

"Bill's afraid of you, miss. You've got him dead right on that." Still holding on to her fingers, he drew her a few inches closer. "But me? I'm not afraid of you, either."

Unlike her, he seemed to be telling the truth.

Jane finally remembered to pull her fingers back. It wasn't as though she wanted him to keep them.

"I'd be obliged," she said if speaking only to him, "if all of you would remember that my sisters and I don't wish to be treated the way you've been treating us."

"The way we've been treating you?" the fellow with the dancing eyes and big hand said, "or the way those slop-jar carriers down at the hotel have been treating you?"

The very fact that he knew the hotel men had been harassing them for weeks revived a spark of Jane's anger. "If you know how badly they treat us, why don't you do something about it?"

His eyes never stopped dancing, and the corners of his lips turned up in a way that was distracting. "Because I'm not a gentleman," he said.

ROSE FELT BETTER, SNUGGLING INTO MR. RUSSELL'S ARMS. But not all the way better, and now she felt bad keeping secrets when her sisters were telling theirs. "Talking in the back of the mews doesn't seem as comfortable as it did before I went away."

Rose expected Mr. Russell to say something comforting. Something about how he had missed her. Or how glad he was that she had returned.

Instead, he said something she hadn't expected at all. "That's a good reason women ought to stay home, isn't it? You can't miss what you've never had."

It was a speech that threw a cold blanket of snow all over their cozy little corner of the mews, even though it was almost August.

She stepped away. "You can't miss what you've never had? What kind of thing is that to say to a person?"

"I don't know," Mr. Russell clearly hadn't expected his words to be controversial. "Doesn't everyone say that?"

"*Do* they? Please excuse me, Mr. Russell, I must go in. I have work to do." Shaking out her skirts, Rose made it clear that she wanted no more of the delicious feel of Mr. Russell's strong arms around her. She'd rather make bread.

"See, now you're angry. You were never angry before you went away." Helplessly, Mr. Russell watched as Rose stepped carefully over the mews cobblestones to the bakery's back door.

"Well, you're right about one thing. I'm angry now!" said Rose, before disappearing inside.

BY MUTUAL AGREEMENT, THE SISTERS LET SAL AND JORDAN watch the shop proper so they could have some good, serious time to to complain.

Rose could remember when Jane and Anna had arrived home from balls and musicales, brought to the door by Aunt Eden's carriage, and had run upstairs on slippered feet to tell their mother all about their evening. Every touch, every look, every young man they'd met, it all had to be described in detail.

It had all seemed the height of sophistication to Rose. She'd longed for a man to discuss.

Now she had one, and she was ready to throw him back.

"Women don't miss what they've never *had?* What kind of remark is that? I suppose that means that I'll be happy with Mr. Russell's company as long as I try no one *else's?* How is that flattering to Mr. Russell?"

"It's not." Anna was stirring a vast vat of the new wet dough. "Men have no confidence. If they did, they would trust women more."

"It's *appalling.* Father never spoke to Mother that way, did he?"

"No," Jane answered slowly. "He didn't. They didn't discuss things much between them, not where we could hear. But didn't Mother always do what Father wanted?" She was shaping loaves, and so used to it now she barely needed to watch her hands. "Wasn't that partly why Mother kept making cake?"

The thought settled over them like a chilled fog, but Emery shook it off first. "Perhaps. But Father wasn't simple. He didn't think of women as poorly trained *dogs.*"

"Mr. Russell isn't simple." For someone irritated with him,

Rose was quick to defend him. "He doesn't think of me like a dog. Just—well…"

"Just rather foolish. Like a dog." Emery could afford to be dry; she had spent very little time with Mr. Russell and had no great need to think highly of him. Today aside, Rose had expressed a sincere interest in him, and anyone luring her little sister away was due short shrift from Emery.

"I honestly think they're just lazy. The simpler we are, the simpler they can afford to be." Anna put the energy of her irritation with the entire category of men into stirring. "If we're simple, then they needn't expend the effort to amuse us or charm us. They needn't take the time to discern what sort of presents we might like, or how to court us."

"Presents?" Rose was surprised that presents and courting came in the same sentence.

Emery raised her head, too. "Presents? That makes us sound like birds of paradise."

Anna was already flushed with effort and too matter-of-fact today to blush. "It does *not*. A gift can express how a man feels. What sort of life he wants to offer his lady love. How he treasures her."

Rose plopped a ball of dough down into the pan with rather more force than necessary. "I don't feel treasured," she muttered.

"I honestly think love tokens come from men who think they are buying our time, rather *like* birds of paradise," Jane added.

"Oh, surely not!" From her slight bout of bitterness, Anna suddenly was awash with romanticism. "A gentleman, a *real* gentleman, puts great thought into gifts to make his lady feel special. Honored. You can't say you didn't feel special, Jane, when that young man with the *tendresse* for you sent you that lovely little gold chain."

"The one who ran once I took him seriously? I felt special when I sold it."

Emery was thinking hard. "I never heard anything about these presents."

"Did you not?"

"You just weren't paying attention, Emery," Rose reminded her. "I hung on every word."

Anna went on, "Just little things, you know. Or at least, little things *we* got. Aside from that gold chain. They needn't be ancient Roman sapphires, you know. Any little gift, right down to sugared almonds or some such—"

"*No,*" Jane and Emery said together, and Rose laughed.

"No, not for *us*, not *now*, obviously," Anna sniffed at being put off her stride. "Dried flowers to put in the hearth in the summer, or lovely smelling herbs; just anything. Anything little and thoughtful and pretty."

"But not paying for your time?"

"No, Emery! Honestly. I think..." Anna had run out of steam, pretending she knew how love affairs were conducted. "I think a man shouldn't simply march up to a woman and demand her heart, much less her hand. Some consideration should be shown, some *effort* made."

"I can tell you they're not a bit grateful if you try to save them the effort," Jane added, but Emery was clearly lost in thought.

"My *point*," Rose said loudly, "was that Mr. Russell behaved like an absolute clod, and I am not best pleased with him."

"Quite right," Jane was quick to say, and Anna added, "Oh yes. I always said you need someone with just a *little* more refinement, muffin. Someone gentler."

"Mr. Russell is perfectly gentle!" retorted Rose, leaving Jane and Anna wondering what they were supposed to say while Emery mused to herself.

"CAKES FOR SALE! CAKES TODAY AT LADIES' OWN BAKERY! Cakes for sale!"

The horrifying shame of paying someone to shout about them *in the street* was weighing on Anna, but not as heavily as the fact that she had six cakes to sell and hadn't sold one.

Even Emery had come out from the bakery proper to pace and peer out the window. At Sal and Jordan, who marched hand in hand along the north side of the Square and shouted.

Emery smiled at every woman who came in and bought her daily twopenny or quartern loaf, but fell to pacing again once they left.

A man pushed his way past the front door, his stovepipe hat nearly knocked askew with the effort. As he righted himself, Anna saw he was not young; the gray at his temples disappeared under that hat.

And as he approached the counter, she could see sagging wrinkles under his eyes. The rest of his face was barely lined; the sagging seemed evidence of exhaustion.

He looked about the shop, shelves full of bread behind the counter, empty ones opposite, Emery pacing by the Bear Street window. His gaze fell on Anna and the cake in prideful glamor before her.

"That is the cake for sale?" he said briefly, causing Mrs. Bunions, whose turn was next, to huff.

"Yes, sir." Anna didn't wish to annoy Mrs. Bunions, but she suspected Mrs. Bunions would be there daily whether or not some new buyer made her wait.

"I'll have it," he said simply, one hand already reaching into his waistcoat pocket for coins. "What is the cost?"

"Two shillings, sir," said Anna, coming down considerably

from their highest price to the one Jane had said was the best middle between profit and greed.

Without hesitation, he laid two shillings on the counter, and with his other hand scooped up the cake.

"Ah—"

"Yes?" He raised an imperious eyebrow as Anna's hesitant voice made him pause, and she almost lost the nerve to finish speaking. But she had to do it.

"Our shoppers carry plates for—"

He didn't even let her finish. "Yes, I see." And when he looked down at the cake in his hands, she saw the droop on the side of his mouth. He must truly be exhausted. Was it his cook's day off? Why was he so ready with money, yet so hungry for this particular cake?

His answer surprised her. "I am your neighbor, miss, Dr. Shelton, at number thirty. I shall return the plate forthwith." And with that, he was gone. He clearly felt no further need to justify carrying off the cake plate.

Very well, at least that was one cake sold! Anna wouldn't worry that the plate would be lost. He had seemed a trustworthy person, albeit one in a hurry.

Mrs. Bunions approached the counter, but Anna was focused on cake. "I'll just step out, Miss Rose," she managed to say, to let Rose know she should take over. And she hurried to the back to fetch another cake.

"I have been waiting, you know. And I have *bunions*."

There was no need to identify the customer to Rose.

"Did you want cake today, Mrs. B—Mrs. Coxson?" Rose asked as brightly as she could from behind the counter.

"How would I carry it home? On my head? My basket's no' big enough for a great cake." Mrs. Bunions did look longingly at the golden disk as Anna set it down right where the other had been. "I don't want to load myself up with such things, anyway. It's not a short walk home, and I have bunions."

"But Mrs. Coxson," Anna put in, "you've been asking for sugar buns for so long."

Mrs. Bunions gaped at Anna. "You can't tell the difference between cake and buns? You're a baker!"

"Yes ma'am, I am," said Anna, subsiding in defeat. Only one cake sold, then.

Mrs. Bunions left, pulling the shop door mostly shut just as the Bickerings' closest neighbor stumbled from the residence door into the street.

HE'D WASHED HIMSELF A BIT, THOUGH THERE WAS STILL dark stubble all along his jaw, and he suspected his eyes looked as fiery red as they felt.

He saw the sheet of foolscap tacked to the wall that read *CAKES TODAY.*

He saw Emery pacing inside the bakery.

He strongly considered buying a cake.

Before he could move, he heard a clump of Frenchmen passing from the hotel down the street. It was a matter of habit not to reveal that he understood their language. But he fell into step behind them, as they were going his way.

Buying a cake would not be a sufficient act of attrition.

Before the cluster of men crossed Leicester Street to the west side of the square, before they cut through Sidney's Alley as he'd been about to do, he pulled back on the elbow of one of them. They all stopped.

In his finest cut-glass British accent, he said, "I say, you're not making fun of those young ladies in the bakery, are you?"

"What d'you have to do with it?" The man he'd stopped shrugged off the grip on his coat.

The vagabond neighbor looked as wide-eyed and innocent as he could. "They're nothing to me. But I thought you worked at Jacquier's hotel? If I tell Lord Farlingbrook of this, I daresay it will do Monsieur Jacquier no good!"

And with that, he walked on, down the wider street. He'd no more go down an alley with those dirt-swallowers than he would cut his own throat.

But he hoped they might be interested enough in their employment to keep their mouths shut. There was no Lord Farlingbrook, and he didn't know if Monsieur Jacquier cared. But he wanted those men wary. Positions were hard to find in London right now for Frenchmen.

BY THE TIME HE MADE HIS WAY PAST THE DARKENED threshold of the Bitter Rose, his head was pounding.

The cool, dark interior of the inn triggered his thirst.

But he wasn't here today to drink. There had to be one day a year without drinking, surely? This might as well be it.

"Owen," he said without preamble to the thick-armed man rolling barrels inside, "where do the thieves sell these days?"

"Good day to you too, R—"

"No names; you would use a man's name in public after a question like that?"

"Gonna steal something?" the innkeeper asked practically as he straightened.

"No."

"Then what do you care if I say your name?"

"Habit," his visitor finally said. "Come, where am I going?"

"To hell, looks like," the innkeeper said, though in rather a friendly way.

"Owen, give me a hint. I know you know."

"Now how—or why—would *I* know?"

"Want me to answer that?"

"No," the innkeeper finally answered, with a bit of the friendliness rubbed away from his tone.

"Give me a hint."

The innkeeper rested burly hands on the rough-hewn table before him and gave the visitor a serious look. "You workin' for anyone anymore?"

"No."

Neither one of them said anything about what he used to do.

"You done altogether, then? You're out of the war?"

"Out," bit the man.

"Then what does it matter if anyone hears your name?" the innkeeper asked him softly.

"You're right," the visitor said after a long while and a few long ragged breaths. "No one remembers it, anyway."

The empty finality with which his guest said this seemed to soften the innkeeper a little. Owen had, no doubt, seen his share of men back from the war, and he'd grown tired of reassuring them. But this man's blank rejection of his own name made the innkeeper a little sorry for him. "There's a man who buys trinkets—"

"Precious metal. Heavy."

The innkeeper revised his sentence without pausing for an instant. "There's a fellow buys silver, if that's your thought, by a stair south of the Strand, carries it off in his boat. Nasty job following him, that's why he stays on the river." He named the stair.

"Marvelous. Owen," the visitor added, just before he went out, as abruptly as he came in, "Have you visited the bakery at the northeast on Leicester Square? This place needs cake."

LADY ARNOLD TOOK A DEEP BREATH, THEN ANOTHER, before she nodded to her footman to open the door.

Yes, there was the tall, strong woman she'd seen before, pacing a ditch into the floor. Lady Arnold was determined to pretend that she had come here only for cake, not to see that woman.

She stole glances every step of the way across the floor, though. Were the woman's eyes a little less tired? Had she eaten more lately? Her throat, still long and lovely, didn't look quite as hollow as it used to.

Not that she was looking.

"I understand that there is more cake today," she said softly as the little crowd parted for her.

All the surrounding women clutched their loaves of bread and stared. At her hair, perhaps, in its spun gold netting; or her day dress, embroidered again, with flowers like fireworks all around the hem. Lady Arnold wished for a moment that she had not worked so hard to look lovely.

But that was over in an instant. It would only take her a few moments to purchase the cake. What would she say then? Could she be blunt? Would it be *dangerous* to be blunt?

She couldn't wait.

The young lady behind the counter curtsied there, and after a second, her blind sister curtsied, too. "It is an honor to have you at the Ladies' Own Bakery, my lady," the curly-haired Miss Bickering said.

There. There was her opening. Lady Arnold turned and waved toward the door.

The footman came in, carrying a wooden crate wider than he was.

"I so admired the name," Lady Arnold said with a gentle smile, "and I thought, as we are neighbors, I ought to recognize your establishment, oughtn't I? As I said on my last visit, a ladies' bakery should have some finery in it. We need more than bread to live, don't we? We need a little beauty, and a little love."

Her voice had become so quiet that the last few words were almost lost. But they would have been drowned out in the next moment by the collective gasp as the footman lifted out the crate's contents.

It was an enormous vase in the Japanese lacquerware style, its glossy clear surface so full of pressed and paper flowers that the black background could barely be seen. Where many vases pulled inward at the top, this one did so at the foot, then swelled out into a graceful shape, a bowl-like chalice. It was wide enough to hold many apples, or oranges —or a twopenny loaf of bread. Perhaps two.

Encased in the shining lacquer were graceful draping petals of yellow flags, petite cowslip blossoms, primrose petals, whole periwinkles of deep blue, even delicate traceries of lavender. The paper cutouts behind them—of roses, white apple blossoms, bright pink clusters of foxgloves, and the waving yellow centers of honeysuckle—contrasted with the colors and textures of the whole flowers above and around them.

In the faint spaces between petals, tiny flakes of gold caught the light and sparkled like drops of dew.

Lady Arnold moved to stand next to the tallest Miss Bickering—the interesting one—while the footman proudly displayed the piece to the gawking little crowd.

"I saw Mrs. Delany's paper flower mosaics when I was young, and they had a great effect on me." As everyone now gave her rapt attention, her voice carried easily through the shop. "I cannot come close to her delicacy, but she inspired me to try to catch the real look of flowers. My mother made many lacquerware pieces, as was the fashion then, and taught me how; I have a shop that finishes them for me," she said, almost apologetically, as if it were a discredit to her that she did not hand-paint every layer of *shel lac* upon its surface. "I thought—" and here she turned to the woman beside her. "I thought perhaps it might look nice... there?"

She pointed to one of the empty shelves high up on the wall with the door to the bakery proper. It would be visible to everyone as soon as they entered, but a little protected from the direct sunlight of the Bear Street windows.

Higher than Lady Arnold could reach, but within reach for *her*.

"It would be *beautiful* there." The woman's stunned look made Lady Arnold smile a little, and she nodded to the footman, who handed the tall baker the vase.

She stretched high and put the vase in its nook.

"It should be quite sturdy," Lady Arnold said as she studied it in its new place, "but one never knows how such pieces will last until they are tried."

The older sister came out from behind the counter. "Lady Arnold, we cannot repay this tremendous honor—"

"No payment." Lady Arnold found it easy to smile now. The beautiful bakery woman liked the vase, she did! "We ought to be friends, after all."

The idea of *friendship* seemed to make the oldest Miss Bickering a bit uncomfortable. But Lady Arnold did not retract it. She was widowed, she was still young, she was bored; but most of all, she was lonely. Mixing back into London society, to be besieged with offers of marriage from do-nothing men eager for a comfortable bed, held no appeal for her at all.

Whereas the young woman beside her held very great appeal.

She had to ask one more time. "Miss Bickering," she said in her quiet way, "you *do* like it?"

"Lady Arnold, it is the most beautiful thing I have ever seen." Her eyes, Lady Arnold noticed, were the color of emeralds under water, a subdued green shot with the remnants of sunbeams. Open wide as she stared at Lady Arnold's handiwork. They shone with deep-seated calm and excitement at the same time. "I have never seen the work of this Mrs. Delany you mentioned, but I cannot imagine it outshines yours for sheer splendor."

Lady Arnold smiled so hard her nose wrinkled with delight.

"Well!" She was suddenly so hungry she could eat one of those cakes by herself! "I must purchase my cake and be on my way. You can spare me a cake, can you not, Miss Bickering?"

The oldest one bustled toward the kitchen. "We can spare you *two*, if you'd like, my lady."

"How lovely! Do you have the *gâteau Breton* again? Or is there something new?"

"We have both the *gâteau Breton* and a *galette des Rois*, if madame would like to try something different."

JANE, WHO HAD STAYED IN THE QUIET SPOT NEAR THE basement door during this whole affair, silently applauded Anna's clever phrasing, which introduced their wealthy patron to the new cake and to the idea of buying two.

As hoped, Lady Arnold expansively nodded. "I would be happy to try them both! François, you have the vessels, do you not?" The footman nodded and took the vase's crate out, to return in seconds with a platter. There must be other footmen waiting outside.

"Only one plate, my lady," he said apologetically, but placed it on the counter where Anna deftly used the large bread knife to transfer first one, then the other, delicate cake.

"You are welcome to subscribe to our cakes, Lady Arnold, and we will deliver them to you freshly made."

Jane held her breath. She and Anna had discussed the subscription idea, as it worked for books and theater tickets, and wondered if wealthy patrons might not pay for a steady production of cake, as well. But they had not planned to try it yet.

Anna was pushing this to the limit.

Lady Arnold's face fell a little, and though her smile stayed in place, she shook her head. "I prefer to visit sometimes. Whenever the need for cake strikes me." Her voice, which had been loud enough to carry for a moment, grew soft again; Jane almost lost the last words.

"I quite understand. We welcome your patronage in any form," and Anna's warm smile, Jane knew, was very real. Jane herself felt inclined to kiss Lady Arnold right at that moment.

As Lady Arnold, after a few more words with Emery, finally withdrew, and the noise of chatter in the bakery went up.

"That's three cakes sold," Rose said, sticking her head around the corner to where she knew Jane was hiding.

"And plenty of bread," Jane added.

"Quite," and Rose was pulled away by a customer who wanted to hear all about the cake Lady Arnold had just purchased.

Anna would have been better at describing the differences between the buttery, fruit-filled *gâteau Breton* and the cream-filled, flaky *galette des Rois*. But she left Rose to handle the request and came to put her head together with Jane's. "She did not wish to subscribe."

"But she bought *two cakes*."

"She wants to come buy them herself? Whatever for? Why would such a grand lady wish to visit *our* shop?"

Emery had stopped pacing and gone to help Rose cut and sell bread. From time to time, her eyes slid over to the spectacular vase in its new home.

Thinking of their conversation about love tokens, Jane had an idea or two, but didn't want to cause any trouble, least of all for Emery.

"I don't know, but let's hope she does, because she will gain attention every time," said Jane, just as the door opened again and they could faintly hear Sal and Jordan's united "*Cake today!*" shout in the street.

EMERY COULDN'T STOP WATCHING THE CUSTOMERS. SHE had bread to set and bake, but she couldn't stop darting out to the shop every few minutes to see whether the cake had sold.

So she was there when a barrel of a man under an oil-stained cap came in and made his way through the last lingering customers gossiping by the window.

"Got any cake?" he said roughly to Rose.

And formerly shy Rose said right back, "We do. Would you like to purchase it, sir?"

"Aye," Emery heard from her place by the bakery door, "I'll have two, I guess."

"Four shillings, sir," and Emery saw him wince.

"I'll have one," he mumbled a bit sullenly.

"I'll fetch it," she called to Rose, as only the cream-filled cake stood on the counter and Emery just had the feeling this fellow wanted something sturdier.

When she returned, he was shifting from foot to foot, his

torn coat pocket practically shouting that he spent little time in feminine company. This bakery must tax him.

"What brought you in today, sir?" asked Emery as she put down the cake. If Sal and Jordan shouting in the street were effective, then they were effective; but Emery doubted anyone on or around the square was unaware of the attempts to sell cake at the Ladies' Own Bakery.

"Friend o' mine," the fellow said brusquely, sweeping up the plate in a meaty hand.

"We need the plate, sir," said Rose immediately, laying her hand where the plate had just been.

"Didn't bring no plate."

And Rose had an answer for that, too. "You're welcome to leave a shilling and collect it when you return the plate."

"A shilling!" The burly man pulled a sour face. "This ain't that grand a plate!"

"And yet it's ours," said Rose with an implacability that truly impressed Emery.

"Awright," the man grumbled, surprising Emery, who expected him to walk out.

"It must be a good friend who suggested our bakery, sir," she prompted him as he grudgingly laid down another shilling.

"He's a good 'un t'owe you a favor," the fellow muttered. "I won't be long back. I keep the Bitter Rose, ain't far away."

And with that, he was gone.

"Just when I think we've met everyone," Rose said after she heard the door scrape nearly closed.

"It's not on the square." Emery frowned. "How far away must it be?"

As they didn't frequent inns, neither of them had run across or remembered the Bitter Rose.

"But it's all to the good," Rose said, her solid new confidence unshaken. "That only means our reputation is spreading!"

One lady in the cluster by the window broke away to approach the counter diffidently. "I do have a plate," she said in a tiny voice, "but I can't buy a whole cake. It's too dear. I don't suppose you will sell me just a piece?"

Rose didn't even consult Emery, much less wait for Anna or Jane. "We can sell you a piece, ma'am, but it'll be thruppence."

"Oh, *would* you? *Thank* you!"

Emery sliced and served as best she could, hoping the almond cream would stay at least partly in the cake before the woman got it home. Judging from her dress, Emery had no doubt that the cake would be shared between at least two people, possibly more if she had children.

"You didn't hesitate," she murmured under her breath to Rose.

"Closing time can't be far off," Rose murmured back. "Better to sell even a partial cake than no cake, and the almond cream won't keep."

"Yes ma'am, Baker Bickering," Emery said, not really making fun.

It was the same confidence that steeled Rose's spine when she heard Mr. Russell's familiar footstep.

"Might you have one more fresh twopenny loaf for me?" he said as he approached the counter in the empty shop.

It was their code for a kiss, and had he said anything else, Rose might have wavered. But those words transformed her spine from steel to stone.

"Mr. Russell, I'm afraid I have given you the wrong

impression. I am not a lightskirt. I am a woman of business, and this is my shop."

"I know!"

"I'm afraid I have let so many new experiences make me a bit giddy. Like bubbling wine. I'm sure you will understand if I ask you to leave me to regain my soberness."

"Miss Rose, I had no desire to offend you." His voice was so familiar now, and Rose could hear the remorse in it. It almost made her relent. Truth was, she wanted his kiss, too. His kisses were the sweetness in her day, every day, with no sugar or honey needed.

And then the bucket-headed man went and put his foot in his mouth again.

"I'm not sure why I should be blamed for repeating common sayings. If something is commonly known, why should I be punished for saying what everyone knows?"

"Things everyone knows? Such as the futility of fighting slavery? After all, it is legal. Why raise a fuss?" Her indignation drove her out from behind the counter, and she leaned close—not to kiss him, but to poke his broad chest with her finger. "Such as the oddity of the Quakers?"

"Here now, there are rumors and then there's common knowledge—"

She poked him again; she heard him step back. "Common knowledge? So *you* are the bank of common knowledge regarding women, whereas I am not even though I am one? I have felt a partnership with you, Mr. Russell, a meeting of the minds. Your remark made me out to be only a woman who allows you far too many liberties. If you knew me at all, if you were truly pleased by the open and public support I have given you, you would not have suggested that *one* uneasy feeling resulted from a few days' travel. To visit a *relative*, no less."

He didn't know about the loss of the candlesticks, and she

didn't care to tell him. If he couldn't be trusted with her feelings, she wouldn't share them.

"I do, I do feel that way about you! I don't know why I said what I did, I couldn't think of anything else *to* say."

She poked him again, and he stepped back again. The door must be at his back. "You're a clever man and good with words, Mr. Russell. So good that I have let myself be persuaded into situations I ought not to have done. But we are at cross-purposes, sir. I thought you special, but now I see you are only full of *common knowledge*. I thought your conversation was a love token. I..." Here she drew one wavering breath and changed her mind about sharing her feelings. "I miss my mother. And I think you've taken advantage of my loneliness, and my better nature, to compromise me until I risk the reputation of this very establishment. No more, sir. I have been something easy for you till now. But that's done with. Good day."

And turning her back on him, she marched back to the counter.

She heard the door scrape open again, and he stepped out and pulled it shut.

Anna stepped behind the counter and put her arm around Rose's waist.

"Did you hear?" Rose's face dropped forward.

"I'm sorry, muffin. I was behind the bakery door, about to come in. I didn't want to interrupt."

"Was I too harsh with him?"

Anna said the thing that was hardest for her to say. "I don't know, dear. It sounds as though he hurt your feelings terribly. Only you know if you needed to say what you said. But I do know this. There's no drawing room in the United

Kingdom in which you couldn't hold your own. I think you *should* say what you think. I'm proud of you when you do."

"Thank you," and Rose put her arms around Anna and squeezed. "I feel a little hollow. But I don't trust him anymore. It was as though, coming back to him, I had escaped the glamor; do you know what I mean?"

Anna thought of the way she'd trailed after Lord Zachary when they first arrived, and how little by little his polish had worn away until she saw exactly who he was. "I think so. We're a little wiser every day, aren't we?"

Rose squeezed again, then turned her face into Anna's shoulder. "And yet I hope he comes back."

Anna laughed at that, and Rose laughed a little too.

"Well," said Anna, "one day at a time is plenty. Perhaps Mr. Russell has learned something. There's no *rush*, Rose."

"He doesn't understand me, that's all. Though I don't think he understands *women* as well as I thought," Rose said, backing up a little. "Not that I understand men. I can never guess what any particular man may do."

THE VAGABOND HAD FOUND THE STAIRS BY THE THAMES, and hid behind them.

The silver dealer came down one step, two; on the third, his foot was caught in a hidden loop of rope that pulled tight. Off-balance, the dealer fell, awkwardly at first against the rail to keep himself upright, then flipping himself over the rail to try to roll away.

Instead, the rope round his feet drew tighter, and became attached to something he couldn't see. As he thrashed about, trying to reach his feet, hanging from his arms off the railing, the vagabond revealed himself from the shadows.

"Just a moment of your time," he said, turning to rifle

through the sack of pillaged goods while his captive thrashed and swore.

"What in the name of hell's crawling arse-bumper are you doing?" The dealer's voice was hoarse with fury, but quiet; he did not want to draw attention to his temporary inability to defend his property.

"As I said. Won't be a moment." From the depths of the stained, rough sack made from the rags of ships' sails, the vagabond pulled one squat silver candlestick in the shape of a Greek column.

He went to the sweating head of the stolen goods dealer and waved the candlestick in his face. "Where's the other one?"

Episode 16: You Can't Live on Cake

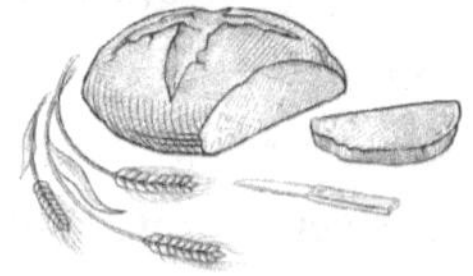

"We can't live eating our own cake."

"I am prepared to die trying," Rose told Jane with great certainty.

Summer warmth forced them to open the window over the square, but they kept in mind their spying neighbor. He would see nothing looking in the window tonight... because they all sat on the floor. But had he seen in, all there was to see was four sisters sitting on the floor eating cake with their fingers.

Jane's chuckle kept them all in good humor. The cake sales were slow. Twice, they'd had to suffer through eating half a *galette des Rois* at the end of the day.

"Perhaps we should make only *gâteau Breton*," Anna said, unconsciously tapping her finger to her lower lip, as Rose did sometimes. "It keeps better."

"We need to *sell more cake*," Jane contradicted. They had also invested in a slate for Jane, so she could be more sure of her numbers. She pulled it back onto her lap. "Lady Arnold buys a cake a week, and so does Dr. Shelton. That innkeeper hasn't been back. Lord Boislegrand purchases a cake—"

"Please don't speak of it," said Anna, waving her hands.

Jane only shrugged. "I'm totalling the sales. Random customers buy a cake or two, but we always wind up with cake we have to sell by the slice."

"And some very loyal customers for that, too!" Emery put in, proud of the fact that patrons came back often.

"My point is that we barely sell seven cakes a week, when we had hoped to sell four a day."

"We do have the ability to do far more." Anna was torn between the desire to sleep occasionally, and the desire to have enough money for the water charges and something, anything, frivolous.

"Our cakes simply aren't grand enough." Jane and Emery had ventured to St. James' Park, where the lords of Parliament and their ladies promenaded in clothing the like of which they only faintly remembered. They found its nearby bakeries. "We saw cakes of two and three tiers, with glazed fruit, and with pastry shapes all round."

"That requires height. From the cake. And frosting. With sugar," said Anna, a little fretted. She had done everything she could to give the cakes more height and make them look fashionable, including baking them topped with meringue, but the fluffy egg-white mixture stayed untenably thick and sticky in the summer weather.

"It is the honey that makes them unique. We must find a way to sell the *honey*." Jane regarded her slate.

"Aside from Lady Arnold, the wealthy residents on the square have their own cooks." Anna couldn't stand being right back to where they were when they began. "It's precisely why they don't buy their bread from us, either."

"We have enough buyers of all sorts for bread." They still sold more bread every day, thanks to Emery's new way of making it, and between that and the cake, none of them looked as tired and underfed as they had before the visit to

Aunt Eden's. Emery still had every reason to stand tall, and she did. But she grasped now the financial benefit of cake, which brought in a whole shilling at every sale.

"But we need a different type of custom for the cakes," sighed Rose.

"We must attach our cake to the reputation of good society. We need a particular kind of purchaser. Someone of fame and fortune. Someone of *note*," said Jane, still not looking up.

"Lady Arnold buys the cakes," Emery repeated. "There is no one more well-known on Leicester Square."

"Then by definition, it must be someone *off* Leicester Square," Rose said with certainty.

"Please, we *cannot* put up a handbill advertising that Lord Boislegrand buys cake here," moaned Anna.

Jane looked up, and her gaze was hard, but she nodded. "You're safe. I don't think Lord Boislegrand is that popular. Did you ever see him at a social affair during your Aunt Eden-funded season?"

Anna looked mollified, but Emery just slumped against the wall. "Ugh. We must have someone well-known and *popular* buy our cake?"

"Someone who will allow us to make it known, too," added Jane, seemingly struck by the magnitude of her own request.

"If our cake were well-known, people of good repute would buy it." Rose criss-crossed her legs under her skirt as she had as a child. "But to get them well-known, we must have a person of good repute buy one? That is a circle of logic."

"I hate repeating myself," Jane could only agree.

TAP.

Not much woke Emery once she fell asleep, but that was the natural effect of her broken sleep habits. Rose slept like a stone because she always had.

Tap, tap.

Emery had to struggle up through layers of sleep. What was that sound?

Tap. Had something hit the window?

Tangled in her nightgown, she jerked its folds free and stumbled to the window, barely remembering to grab the suspended spoon before she opened it.

And looked out below to see Mr. Russell standing on the pavement.

"What are you doing?" Emery was glad he was so far below because if she could have reached him, she'd have hit him. If only with the spoon.

"Ah... I..." He seemed to struggle to find an excuse. Even blinking madly in the summer evening shadows, Emery saw him give up the struggle. "I hoped to wake Miss Rose."

He was an honest fellow, she had to give him that.

"She's asleep!"

"That's not right," said Rose, and turned over, startling Emery into looking at her. But it had been just another speech in her sleep, apparently; she didn't move again.

"Ah... And you shouldn't wake her."

He obviously wanted Emery to wake her. "I won't wake her."

"Right. Right."

He clearly couldn't think of anything to say next; why didn't he simply walk away?

Emery peered up and down the fortunately empty street. "What made you pick this window?"

"Mr., ah..." He was *really* unused to subterfuge, realizing a moment too late he was about to give up the name of a co-conspirator. "The night watchman mentioned he earned something for waking you, and I saw the string."

Emery didn't care for feminine airs, but neither did she care for masculine ones. Swearing aloud, however, did seem appealing right now.

At the end of Bear Street she thought she saw a window lit, but in the warm August night, this street was quiet. She quieted her voice, hoping none of the neighbors would notice. That tailor likely slept above his shop, right? She leaned her forearms on the windowsill to get a little closer to her annoyance. "Have you lost your mind?"

He followed suit. "I suppose?" he said quietly, and with his hat off, head tilted upwards, she could just see his drooping face. "I miss her."

Emery didn't want to lose any sisters. But the feeling of sitting so many nights in the kitchen salon, watching Miss Hayes with longing eyes, rushed back to her, and introduced sympathy to her feelings for Mr. Russell.

"If I woke her right now, and she was awake, and I was awake, and you had woken us both, do you think she would be inclined to listen to whatever you wish to say?"

"...No," said Mr. Russell like a little boy.

"Then hadn't you better say it during the day?"

"I don't wish to say it in the shop, and she won't come out to visit with me," he expressed his frustrations all in a rush.

"Then you have a problem, don't you?" And, sympathy over, Emery closed the window.

ON THE NEXT CAKE DAY, AS THE BICKERING SISTERS HAD come to think of it, by late afternoon they still had an entire *gâteau Breton*.

Jane and Sal stood behind the counter.

"Why does multiplication work on the slate but not in the shop?" asked Sal, and by now Jane was a little more used to her thinking and could formulate an answer.

"You are asking me why the abstract world does not apply in the material world, and I am not philosopher enough to know the answer," she said.

Sal opened her mouth to question the intricacies of that statement, but the door scrape-squeaked open.

The man who came in had his whole head tilted backward with haughtiness. His head looked like it had wished to be left behind. Sal slid her slate under the counter where he couldn't see.

His eyes immediately lit upon the *gâteau Breton*.

"Selling cake, I see," and the way he said it implied that they were ladies of the evening plying their wares in the street.

"Yes." Jane didn't owe him any more of an answer. His accent was French, and she strongly suspected this was the fellow who had come in asking Rose about cake.

He circled the shop, taking in the empty shelves on the far side and turning slowly round till his eyes lit on Lady Arnold's spectacular flowered chalice.

That bothered him.

Jane couldn't imagine why, but she knew it did. He took in its every detail, the yellow and the dainty lavender flowers, the gold flecks in between. The sisters turned it every day to see a new angle. Well, Emery turned it; the rest of them were too short.

The vase seemed to stay with him as he approached the counter.

Jane had learned the repetitive speeches as well as any of them. "May I serve you, sir?"

He looked down at the little golden cake on its plate, then back at her. "No," he sniffed.

Jane knew the results of bluntness. She had failed to marry, several times, due to her bluntness; but that had been for the best, as she couldn't have been anyone but herself during a whole long marriage.

Customers necessarily had shorter relationships with her; non-customers, even shorter.

So she could have gone either way in responding to this one, and considered it a victory for her better nature when all she said in return was, "Very well."

He glared at her. She looked calmly back.

"Hmph," he sniffed and drew up his chest; then, instead of saying anything else, he left.

Jane looked down at Sal. "There's no good abstract explanation for that, for instance."

"DAMN."

There was the candlestick in the center of the mantlepiece he could just see through the window.

He was far east of Leicester Square now, and the once-grand house was filled with small families, or couples, or elderly ladies.

This wasn't the rooms of elderly ladies, thank God, but it was a young buck and his wife in there, and the wife was expecting a baby, and the whole thought of simply stealing the candlestick back (which had been his plan) sickened him.

They'd polished the bright metal till it shone, too. Probably had some sugary sentiment already attached to the thing, such as they would buy a candlestick a year for the new baby. Or a candlestick each time she had a child, more likely. That would at least be slightly less often.

No, he couldn't simply steal it. He'd have to buy it back, and that was a problem because he had no money.

Well, the simplest solution still applied.

He turned a few corners, walked down a few alleys till he came to one that met a busy enough street. And he waited.

He'd waited in barns and ditches to steal a meal, whether it was milk from a cow or buried pickles in a crock. He'd waited on roofs for days in the rain, and he'd waited behind trees to kill a man.

This was, by comparison, easy.

When the right one came along, a fine-coated fellow with a proud tilt to his hat, it was easy to catch his arm, swing him into the alley (carefully chosen for the hiding capacity of its stone buttress—ah, it was a church), and show him the knife.

"Give me your money," was all he said.

It was a smooth enough bit of business; the man was astonished and unable to imagine mussing his coat.

Released, his quarry returned to the stream of pedestrians as smoothly as a caught fish returning to the water.

And out the alley's other end went a man with a pouch full of coins and a mission to buy a candlestick.

THE BAKERY'S VISITOR WAS MUCH DISCUSSED OVER SUPPER.

"We don't *know* that he is from M. Jacquier's hotel." Anna didn't wish to attribute any suspicions to him without proof.

"No. But he is from some hotel. They are all on this side of the square, and they are all French." Jane had no such compunction.

"Why come back?" Emery asked through the last bite of cake. It was lovely, but familiar now, and they were all tired of the taste of failure.

"Keeping watch." Rose shivered theatrically. "How sinister."

"He was perfectly pleased to see that we had unsold cake. But Lady Arnold's vase gave him pause for some reason."

"It's a mark of favor." On that, Anna was quite sure. "A patron. Not just one of the plain women who come to buy our bread. A patron, and one who buys our expensive wares. Cakes."

"I hadn't thought of that. It's practically a handbill, isn't it?" mused Jane.

"Can we simply ask Lady Arnold to recommend us to her friends?" Not in charity with Mr. Russell, Rose was still inclined to be in charity with everyone else; and she'd absorbed a great many Quaker ideas about the equality of everyone.

"If she hasn't already done so, I wouldn't presume to ask. No, it's not that I am a reluctant baker," Anna added before anyone objected. "I'm simply saying what is true. She has already given us her public favor, and asking for more is greedy and apt to lose it."

"But it hasn't brought in more custom." Jane's concern was, as always, the practical.

"It may have brought in all the custom she can provide right now."

"We need—" Emery fell still, interrupted by a knock.

The knock on the door came again.

They all rose to their feet.

By silent accord, they let Emery open it by virtue of suspicion about who it must be.

And it was. "Ladies," said their neighbor, still unwashed, but sober, and with a fresh scrape on his cheek.

He held out their mother's silver candlesticks.

The collective gasp drew Rose forward. "What is it?"

Stepping into the room, he laid the candlesticks in her hands, slipping one in her palm and, when she raised both hands to take it, then the other.

"Not really," she breathed, and hugged them to her breast.

"With my apologies," was all he said, and turned to go.

"Wait!"

Anna's voice stopped him.

"We—you will give us a moment to thank you, will you not?"

He shook his head, and his chin drooped for a moment before he recovered. He looked over Anna's head, met Emery's eye. "A real man would not have let them be stolen to begin with. Perhaps I am no man, but I have only repaired what I let be broken."

"Oh," Rose kept rocking the candlesticks like a doll. "Mother would be so pleased."

No one argued with her.

But Anna couldn't just let him walk out. He looked worse than any cabbage repeatedly rolled into the road under horses' hooves. But he had done them such a good deed, it could not go unthanked. And it was her job. She was the oldest. "Please, sir," she said. "We must thank you. You have done *such* a kindness. For all of us."

"Have I?" His eyes were less bloodshot, but under the lank hair no one could see their color. "I saved my self-respect, madame. If anything, I did it for me."

Before he could move away, Anna stepped closer again and said swiftly, "Did it feel selfish?"

"A little." She'd surprised the answer from him.

And surprised him again when she went on. "And is that so wrong?"

He did not move, his eyes on her, but he stayed silent.

It was Anna who spoke. "At my first party, I had a nice white dress my great-aunt had ordered for me, and orange blossoms in my hair. The world was beautiful and I was so happy. After only my third dance ever, the gentleman walked me back to my great-aunt, a mark of favor. I thought I had already found a husband. I thought he liked me. He asked me what I hoped for in a marriage, right there in front of my great-aunt, and I told him. I hope for love, of course, I said. And he said—"

Anna had to pause for a breath, either because she'd talked so fast, or because all the air had left her. But no one moved, not even their neighbor.

"—he said a girl like me shouldn't hope for love. And he left. Just like that."

"And?" His voice was hoarse, as if it were unused, or used too much.

"Yes." Having started this story, she didn't seem to want to finish it. But she did. "I asked my great-aunt what he'd meant. Why shouldn't a girl like me hope for love? And she told me that marriage was a practical matter, that a husband wanted a pretty wife to manage his home and make his life easy, but that hoping for love made me sound like a lightskirt." Anna laughed a fake little laugh. "She said I was too pretty to tell people I hoped for love, and too poor to be anything but practical about marriage. But I didn't think so, sir. It felt selfish, to want love, but I still wanted it. I think it was self-respect. And I don't think that's worthless. Perhaps selfish, as I think every day now watching my sisters work so hard. But not worthless."

And shocking them all, perhaps even herself, Anna curtsied.

"Here's to what remains of self-respect, sir."

An odd expression twisted his mouth. "And doing what must be done. You are right, madame." And he bowed, his body bending toward her, just a little, an arm sweeping before him.

With one long arm, Emery scooped up the plate with the last piece of cake.

She held it out. "Our thanks."

"No need." He didn't look around to emphasize how little they had to give; that was apparent enough.

"We haven't much," said Emery with a wry smile, "but we do have cake."

The tension eased, and all the Bickering sisters made their own noises of amusement over the word *cake*. Their neighbor couldn't have understood what it meant, but he took the plate.

"Cake is a difficult issue?" he asked with delicacy.

"Only funding and making it," Anna admitted with good grace.

"And selling it," added Rose with a laugh.

"Well. Thank you," he said, nodding to them all.

And, holding their plate, he went out and pulled the door closed behind him.

They heard his boots on the floorboards, and it was odd, hearing his door open and close, faintly, but so nearby.

It was a moment before anyone spoke.

"You never told me that story," Jane said softly.

"Didn't I?" Pretending to sound careless, Anna bent to pick up their dishes.

"I *wouldn't* want you married to a man you didn't love, and I'd much rather worry about cake than worry if you were happy." Rose was as certain as the solid silver candlesticks she returned to their place on their little shelf.

"Would you?" Anna's eyes looked suspiciously bright. "I'd much rather worry about being happy than see you hungry, little muffin."

"We're going to sell cake, I just know it. We had all given up these candlesticks, hadn't we? And here they are again, through the grace of a stranger."

"Sort of a stranger," mumbled Emery.

"Don't you know what this is? It's *luck*. We've already gathered enough money for the water rents, haven't we?

We've earned three shillings a week from cake so far. We are halfway there."

"Three shillings is not half of seven," said Jane, but her heart wasn't in it. Her eyes followed Anna, circling before the little dish tub.

"Luck, sisters. We're going to find a patron so famous that all of London will want our cakes. Our luck has turned."

"That wasn't luck," Emery objected. "That was determination. Our neighbor's."

"*Who* is he, Emery?" Jane hadn't wanted to know before tonight.

Emery only shrugged. "A man who does what must be done, I suppose."

ALL FOUR SISTERS BRUSHED THEIR HAIR AND WENT TO BED that night fairly silent.

Rendering quite useless that it was the first night their neighbor spent listening to see what he could hear.

THE NEXT MORNING, AFTER HER SISTERS HAD GONE DOWN to the bakery, Jane brought out the little bottle of ink, and the leftover paper, and wrote Aunt Eden a note.

EMERY, THOUGH, STOPPED AT THE LITTLE DOOR OF THEIR neighbor and knocked, more softly than she had ever done.

And he answered.

When he looked surprised to see her at his door, before

he could say anything, Emery said, "I need to earn some money."

When Puffy came in to the bakery that morning, finally bearing their borrowed plate, Anna came round the counter to curtsey to him.

"Sal, will you weigh some bread for Mrs. Smith? And there's Mrs. Wallace coming down the street, get a nice tuppence loaf for her. Lord Boislegrand, if you please?"

And she led him out to the street.

"Miss Bickering." Puffy followed her without question, like a faithful dog.

He wasn't handsome, but he was kind, and his regard seemed genuine.

Perhaps the selfish part of Anna's girlhood dreams had been that she had wanted to fall in love herself. Perhaps being loved, after a fashion, was good enough.

Perhaps that was all a *girl like her* could hope for.

She stood close enough not to be overheard, not that any of the morning pedestrians paid any mind to a viscount and a baker talking on the pavement.

"Lord Boislegrand, it is a pleasure to see you again." Her hands folded together at her waist as if this were a drawing-room.

"And for me to see you too, Miss Bickering." There was no condescension in his voice, and he bowed as if this were indeed a fine drawing room, and he were addressing her among silver and polished wood and hand-painted wallpaper.

"I hope you recognize how grateful we are for your custom." Anna had planned another speech, a much more Jane speech, but in the end, this was all she could bring herself to say.

But Puffy rescued the situation beautifully. "Your gratitude is kind, but unnecessary. I am happy to do it. If it is the only glimpse of you I get in a week, Miss Bickering, it is a slender thread of happiness to which I will cling."

Clasping her hands tight, Anna began her second planned speech. "It is ungrateful of me to turn down all your kind invitations. My sisters and I would be glad to drive with you this Sunday afternoon, if you wish."

"Miss Bickering, it is *all* that I wish." And the beaming smile on his face showed he meant it.

LEAVING HIS HOTEL, CAPTAIN BRICE WENT NORTH AS HE usually did these days to look in to the window at the Ladies' Own Bakery before proceeding on his business for the day. If his ship spent much more time at dock, it would forget how to sail; but politicians being who they were, he had not finished securing support for his mission.

And he needed it, for it wouldn't suit him to be a pirate. Again.

But before he got close, he saw that viscount, the one with the expensive carriage, bowing over Her Majesty's hand. Not the Queen, Miss Anna Bickering.

And she let him. Right there on the pavement.

Well, no need to check in on the young ladies today.

AND WHEN A FAMILIAR STEP SOUNDED ON THE floorboards of the shop, Rose made up her mind.

"There you are, Miss Weatherby, a very soft loaf for your master and mistress." Miss Weatherby was very proud of being their maid, and Rose never crushed that pride by pointing out that she worked for a tiny family who could only afford a maid and a cook, and purchased ready food on the cook's night off.

Serving customers all day behind a pitted counter, Rose had a great deal to think about regarding pride.

"A pound of the maslin, please," said Mr. Russell's dear, familiar voice.

Rose didn't answer, just cut the piece, till it was in the scale and the door had closed behind their customer.

Her finger touched the scale's needle. "It's a bit over, but not enough to mean a farthing between friends."

"Are we friends?"

He sounded so forlorn.

And she missed him *so* much.

"I miss thinking well of you," she said softly. "I thought highly of you, you know."

The words came out of him in a rush. "I valued your opinion, Miss Rose. You know I did. I value it still. May I not earn your regard again? I would if I could."

"Was that what you wanted to tell me when you threw rocks at my window in the middle of the night?"

He was silent a moment. "Your sister told you?"

"Of course she told me." In fact, she hadn't *told*, she had complained of it, rather bitterly, and said some sarcastic things about suitors who threw pebbles in the night.

But Rose hadn't found it awful, and in fact she was sorry she'd missed it.

"I don't know if you can," she told him, because she was a frank person even before keeping company with a member of the Society of Friends, "but I would like it if you tried."

And that restored his good spirits again. "Challenge accepted!" he whooped. "And you've been more than fair."

"It isn't a game, Mr. Russell," Rose warned, but he swept

his chunk of bread off the counter and reached out and took her hand.

"No, it isn't," said the man as he stroked a thumb across her small palm, just once, before dropping his payment in her palm. "I never said it was."

Episode 17: What One Must Do

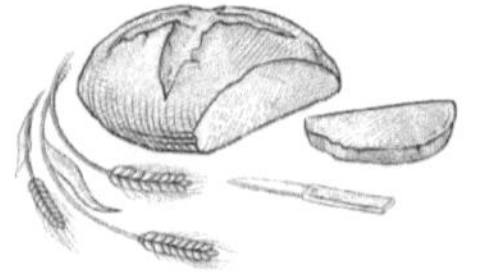

"Lady Tratterton? Everyone knows she is mad for her food. Never travels without her cook."

"She doesn't care for sweets!" Anna said this as if it were criminal.

"No? Has she joined the sugar boycotts?" Jane shifted her grocery basket to her other arm.

"No idea, that's all I know. Lady Sherrin?"

"No, Lady Sherrin has something of an air of desperation about her."

Anna's laugh was short and bitter. "Don't we all. Lady Villeneuve?"

"Never say so!" Jane picked her way around a smudge on the pavement. Who chewed tobacco and then spat it out in public? "The things I've heard about Lady Villeneuve and her coterie of virgins would make your hair stand on end."

"My stars."

"What about Lady Ayles?"

"No," and Anna shook her head so quickly the curls bounced over her shoulders, "She's got a terribly attractive son, and I stepped on his foot once during a quadrille. I couldn't possibly."

"Anna, we need a sponsor for our cakes who is known throughout the *ton*. We are not looking for social engagements for ourselves."

"Well it's not as if we plan to simply toss a cake at them and leave." Anna's tone had turned more acidic, thought Jane, since her admission to their neighbor. Or at least, since they had decided to plunge back into London society, not to find husbands, but to find a partner in selling cake. "We might have a conversation or two, you know, during the whole affair."

"We cannot sell cake all over London, but we must find a person with a broad enough circle to make it worthwhile."

As they approached the bakery, Anna peered toward the tailor's window. "I know it's wrong of me, but I feel like I must constantly check now to see if the poisonous man is staring at us."

"Perhaps he's developed new interests. It isn't as though he can watch you sneaking up to the garret every night."

Anna paused and looked up at their building. And up.

Jane paused too. "It *isn't*, is it?"

"Don't be absurd. I haven't given Lord Zachary a second thought since he showed himself in the bakery and decided to be human. But Jane." Anna was looking at the top of number seventeen, where the pointed roof made sharp gables, each with a glass window that let in the light. "Perhaps this is the perfect time to see if the useless Lord Zachary could be of any use."

"I BEG YOUR PARDON, *WHAT*?"

The sisters had bounded straight up to the garret. What was the point of knocking? It had no real door.

"Please don't touch that," Lord Zachary added as Jane bent over a pile of mixing vessels stained with paint.

Anna ignored everything about Lord Zachary—his stained shirt, his nimble fingers, the way his hair shone when he was hatless, and his extremely puzzled face. This was business.

She refused to check to see if her hair ribbon was straight.

"I think we were clear. We need the name of a lady who can help bring our cakes to the attention of London. Someone titled."

"Not you," Jane put in helpfully, in case that wasn't clear.

"Thank goodness for that. You think I can tell you what lady could help you? And willing, I suppose. Or do you intend to bounce right into others' houses as well?"

Anna's fingers fluttered in a circle, indicating all the surrounding clutter: the pencils and paper showing half-completed studies, the brushes, vessels of noisome liquids, pigment-stained palettes. "This isn't a house." One finger lingered towards the palette he still held. "What a predictable shade of blue."

Jane continued walking around the edge of the garret, exploring the space between gapping floorboards and the beams of the roof. "We've already eliminated Lady Ayles, Lady Sherrin, Lady Villeneuve—"

"Lady Winpole!" Anna snapped her fingers.

"Who is Lady Winpole?" Jane looked at her sister as if she'd lost the thread of conversation entirely. "If I don't even remember her, how influential can she be?"

Lord Zachary was clearly torn between his work, reining in the invasion of his garret, and the flood of names. "You *know* all these people?"

"Well, I had a season, and during Jane's I did sometimes

attend..." Anna was not about to explain the penny-pinching that went with trying to impress the *ton* while being poor.

Jane called from the far end, "I found that mysterious back staircase! We must try it."

"Who *are* you two?"

"Never mind, Jane; I don't think he knows anyone."

"Wait, wait." Lord Zachary put down his brush and palette, picked up a rag and wiped color off his hand. He braced his feet wide to think. "You are not being systematic. Start at the top and work your way down."

"We don't want the *King*." Jane was aghast. "People haven't stopped making fun since he ate brown bread. Besides, he isn't well!"

"No," Anna snapped her fingers again. "I see what you mean, Lord Zachary; you're quite right. We must have a method. The Prince won't do either, he destroys ladies' nerves, but why not a duke?"

"Ah." Jane wandered back across the empty floorboards to her sister. "I do see. But the Duke of Oakland is eighty if he's a day—is his wife even alive?" Jane didn't recall all the shiny people of society like Anna did; she never had. The name of the eldest duke in London only came to mind because she'd met him once, and in her mind he was the example of a duke.

"Yes, I believe she is. But doesn't often entertain." Anna's eyes were sparkling with excitement. "The Duke of Gravenshire isn't married, and he's a bit gruff as well. His daughter hosts their parties, but she's flighty. What about—"

"Talbourne, that's who you want." Lord Zachary rolled down one sleeve, then the other. He appeared to have let himself be well and truly interrupted.

"Talbourne!" Anna was shocked. "He entertains, but never leaves home. And his wife is dead."

"No, he's remarried. Just recently. Pretty young wife. You

are out of society, aren't you? She's a prime target of gossip all over London."

"We can't all be as enamored of gossip as you."

The young man took this barb in good enough humor, though he blinked a bit. "I don't care much for gossip, but I do have a sister."

"Does she know this Duchess of Talbourne?" Anna looked ready to be a little gentler to Lord Zachary if this were the case. "Do *you?*"

"Do *we?*" Jane put in. "How young? Might we know her?"

"I do think she's about your age, but dropped out of society for some time. Not sure what happened. Because I *don't follow gossip*, Miss Bickering," Lord Zachary said slowly and with more than a touch of sarcasm.

Jane admired him for finally showing some starch. But Anna brushed right past it. "But do you know her?"

"No. I do not pay court to duchesses, more's the pity. I didn't know it would one day be required to get two young ladies out of my art studio so I could work."

"We should have a few more names!" Anna clearly didn't want to depend on one name from Lord Zachary when he was such a weak reed.

Jane, closer to the stairs, started down. "One is plenty. Let the man get back to his drawing."

"It's a painting," the young man said haplessly, watching Jane's dark head disappear.

"It is a painting, and serviceable, too." Anna was clearly trying not to sound condescending. "Though really, Lord Zachary. Sweet peas and love-in-a-mist? Don't they make rather delicate subjects?"

Zachary looked at his painting, some tall flowers with marching little cups, some feathery blue. He hadn't been thrilled with it before, and he was definitely thinking less of it now. "I wanted to practice capturing detail," he said, a little lost. Two young women had just swept into his studio, derailed his work, and swept out, leaving him with the odd sensation that if he didn't know the new duchess, he was of no clear use. Nor could he paint sweet peas.

"They're too close in size," Anna said sweetly before she, too, started down the stairs. "Do come tell us, Lord Zachary, if you think of anyone else!"

IT WAS ASTONISHING HOW MUCH TIME ONE COULD SPEND kissing.

The spot behind the ivy had become like a second home to Rose. Mr. Russell swore no one could see them back there.

It was cool and smelled fresh, and the sensation of fitting herself against Mr. Russell's powerful body was intoxicating.

"I missed this." She'd missed *him*. But it seemed easier to admit she'd missed the indulgence of these long, slow kisses that made time stop.

They seemed to have the same effect on him. "I must accomplish more with my day than kissing you," he murmured against her lips and then, thrillingly, against the spot just below her left ear. "Though I forget what."

"Surely this is life's greatest accomplishment," sighed Rose. He had pulled her close with a big, warm hand against the small of her back, and it was just about her favorite thing in life.

He paused, and Rose swam back to awareness, wondering what she'd said.

"It may be life's greatest accomplishment," he said, his voice low in her ear.

She shivered.

"Miss Bickering," he said, and he didn't sound as though

he were teasing, "would you attend meeting with me this evening?"

"Is there a meeting? Of course!" Why did he sound so serious? She'd attended meetings of his before.

"The Society meeting. The friends who are here in Leicester Square."

Rose's heart thumped. She hoped he couldn't feel it. She was a woman full grown; her thrills shouldn't give themselves away like that.

The community of the Society of Friends was Mr. Russell's closest circle in London. His parents lived in the country, and he had not seen them in some time. The Friends gathered round him and supported his work.

It would be like meeting his family.

Yet it would also be like going to church. "May I attend, if I am not one of the Society?"

"Of course. You'd be welcome. You've met some of them in passing." His arms tightened around her, and Rose's head fell against his shoulder. "I think you should come with me."

Should she? His kisses were like wine, luxurious, intoxicating. But like wine, she doubted she could afford them. Rose shivered again, as if cold air swept over her from a sudden chasm at her feet.

This was what she wanted. She wanted to think of marrying Mr. Russell. She *did*, several times a day.

But she had just let him close again. He'd disappointed her so. And she'd never spent a day apart from her sisters in her life.

Something tickled in the back of her mind, some little worry that they had only just reconciled, and spent more time kissing than talking. She squashed it.

Being in his arms again felt right. As if he had not caused the chasm before her, but was ready to help her over it.

It felt huge and mysterious and frightening and grand to

say, "Yes, Mr. Russell. I would be happy to accompany you."

Then it was simply frightening. "Oh no. But what shall I wear? How shall we leave the house? What shall I *wear*?"

EMERY EXPECTED THE INSIDE OF A TAILOR SHOP TO LOOK mysterious and manly somehow. She'd never even been inside a dressmaker's, and this was a place where men came and took their clothes off and dressed themselves in new ones among other men.

Actually, she felt an odd sort of kinship for it.

Mr. Morley bustled up to her from behind his sewing table the second she walked in. "What are you doing in here? You *hoyden*!"

She didn't know what that was. "Looking for work."

Their neighbor had suggested this. Why she'd asked him, Emery didn't know; he was no source of reputable information. And why she'd come, she *really* didn't know. There was nothing outside the tailor's shop to make one think that a woman would be welcome.

Nor inside, either.

"You can't steal anything in here!" The fellow tried to cover up his entire shop by spreading his arms. "I won't let you!"

Emery looked around the bolts of wool leaning against the wall, which was also hung with coats of various drab colors meant, apparently, to entice the current London man. The tailor shifted from side to side, trying to block her from everything he owned.

"You can't come in here and help yourself to..." He looked around as if noticing his shop contained mostly bolts of wool and men's coats. It seemed difficult to imagine her wrestling him to the ground to steal either.

"See here," said Emery, a saying of her mother's coming back to her in the face of his fear and anger. "Stop expecting the worst of people, and you'll stop getting the worst of people."

Slowly, his arms dropped.

Emery folded hers and just waited.

He settled back on his heels. "Really? Looking for work? You work at the bakery. I've seen you. You're the only one of your sisters who isn't a slattern."

Emery felt her face warm. It was odd how even when she didn't know the words, she recognized an insult. "Not true, but not the point. I want to know if you have any work."

"Why? You aren't running around on the streets like your flash sisters. You bake. I know baking. That takes work. All day. Why would you want more work?" His face squashed in on itself like a hunting dog's, and his nose quivered. He seemed ready to sniff out lies.

"I want some money of my own. The bakery is a family business; I want money I don't need to take from my sisters."

"And why would you need money of your own, eh?"

When she stretched, she could be even taller. Her very bonnet seemed to loom over him as she looked down at the little man. "That is my own affair."

In fact, she needed it because it had been borne in on her that love required more than her heart. Love required money.

If love tokens were the path to persuasion, she needed a love token for Jasmine. But she couldn't make anything besides bread. And Jasmine would want something fine.

She wasn't really sure how to make this work. She baked all day and most of the night.

But she had a fairly fine hand with a needle, and even though her stitches weren't as even as Aunt Eden's, she might be able to earn some money of her own.

"I might have some work if your sewing is fine." He sniffed. "But your sisters are not entering my establishment."

"Sir, let's keep to business and not discuss my sisters."

"We must leave directly after dinner." The dinner they'd just eaten, consisting of exactly five minutes of bread and butter. But Anna had asked Rose and Emery to stay a moment and let her explain her plan.

"Oh no!" Rose couldn't stifle the exclamation. Fortunately, her sisters would take it for reluctance to spend the afternoon alone in the shop rather than a wish to spend the afternoon preparing for an important visit from Mr. Russell.

As much as she wanted some time to brush her hair, Rose immediately saw the benefit. Her sisters would be gone into the evening. She didn't have to find a way to sneak out. She could just leave.

She'd simply have to resign herself that Anna would have already taken the nicest hair ribbon.

Anna was already brushing her hair and demanding it. "I must wear the flowered dress, too, it will look presentable."

"It will look as if you've come to wash the floors." The shabbiness of their surroundings bore down on Emery, suddenly attuned to the finer things in life. What could she ever afford that would be worth the color of Jasmine's eyes?

Jane was far more reluctant for this adventure than Anna. "It is an enormous sum, the money it will take to hire a carriage. What if it does not work?"

"We have the money for the past water bill now, and we cannot move forward unless we take some risks." Anna whirled about the room, looking for a rag to polish the flour off her slippers.

"This will take all *day*."

"Rose will mind the counter, Emery has the afternoon loaves rising, and Sal and Jordan will help them both. I believe Sal has a history lesson to read today."

"Romans?" asked Emery, who would likely have to hear the lesson. Sal liked things a bit bloodthirsty.

"Battle of Hastings. She'll love it."

"I don't mind," Rose put in, making Anna answer, "No one asked if you did."

Emery had planned to sew, and her secret plan made her guilty and cranky. "Anna, you needn't rub our noses in the fact that only you and Jane are presentable enough for a duke's house."

Anna paused in her whirl to look at Emery, really look. She laid her hand against Emery's cheek. "You must eat more, little sister," she said with a gentle pat. Her hand dropped. "We won't look presentable enough. We will be dressed more poorly than the maids. But we know what to *say*, and if there's any chance of seeing the Duchess we must give the impression that we were once ladies of quality."

"Well, we aren't now." Jane bent her head as if already hiding her face.

"No, we're not!" Anna's gay little laugh surprised them all. "We're simply *not*, my little titmice! So much freer to know what we are and what we are not. And what we are is women who *must* make our cake more fashionable if we are to succeed."

"I hate the idea of fawning over a duke, but I must say, I'd like to eat beef again some day." Rose was decisive on this.

For months, they'd eaten such thin fare it had come to seem normal. But after the riches of Aunt Eden's table, it was easier to remember what they missed.

"We must do what we must do. And in this case, we must try." Anna tied her last nice bonnet on her head, letting the hair ribbons flutter below it. From under the crate, she pulled the unstained gloves, which meant she also lost her last good hiding place for them. "Off we go!"

Rose felt guilty that she planned to take complete advantage of the situation.

She and Emery both stewed in their guilt alone.

"HOW CAN SOMEBODY FAIL AT WASHING BOWLS?" SAL HAD grown strong these last months, heaving the half-barrels up to the dishtub. The dark sheen of her braid swung across her back as she hauled up another and opened the ballcock to let the water flow.

Both twins had been carefully instructed regarding washing. It was their largest task. Their hands were growing stronger, too, with scrubbing, and Sal felt that their expertise at this point was beyond question.

Emery seemed to agree. "You won't fail. I'm just asking you to pay attention. I won't be here to point out if you miss a spot."

Had Sal stopped for even a moment to look uncertain, or wonder where Emery was going, Emery might have stayed. But the young girl just looked delighted to be left in charge. For in charge she would be; Jordan was playing with a new dough and lost to the rest of the world.

"I'll be back before it's time to bake, and Rose is in front," said Emery, slipping out and trying to decide how many different types of guilt she felt.

FABRIC WAS ROLLED AND FOLDED INTO EVERY INCH OF THE closet where Emery found herself.

It was well lit, with a high clear window that let in the summer light. But it was a closet.

"I see it in your face. Don't ask again. I won't have you sewing with the men. Too much trouble."

"Let me take the pieces home and I'll bring them back tomorrow."

Mr. Morley's squat head shook with outrage at the very thought. "You'll make off with them, and then what will I do?"

Emery waved the cut pieces of a waistcoat right under his nose. "I *live* across the *street*. I expect you'd come *get* them."

"I'd swear out a complaint, that's what I'd do!"

If she'd gone to school, Emery mused, she might have learned if there was a book that described how to measure love. Was her wish to impress dazzling Miss Hayes of greater weight than this constant harangue? "Mr. Morley, I have no doubt you would. Therefore, I wouldn't steal anything. If you don't wish me to work, why give me the pieces?"

A grudging, muttered answer. "I need someone who can do nice buttonholes."

Emery had shown him the stitches in the hem of her skirt. It had been awkward enough, watching him bend nearly double while she lifted her hem. It had felt more indecorous than anything Mr. Morley complained about her sisters doing.

But he had shown no interest in anything but the size of her stitches.

Thinking of the time, Emery judged how soon she'd have to return. "I can finish these buttonholes if you pay me today."

"I pay my tailors once a week."

"But *me* you'll pay *today*. Why, how do I know you won't take the waistcoat and claim I never did the work?"

"I live across the—no, never mind, fine, I'll pay you today. I'll pay you."

And so it was that Emery sat, in a chair, and learned the peculiar luxury of earning some coins for herself, for a little dream of her own, rather than only to survive.

It was a good little dream, and sustained her through all the vest's buttonholes.

"What if I say the wrong things? They could think me improper. I do speak up at the wrong times." Rose couldn't help but fidget. Mr. Russell would tell her if her hair was bunched up, or if there were stairs. But would he tell her when not to speak? She hated the idea, but couldn't bear the thought of repulsing his friends.

Mr. Russell pulled the door closed to the sisters' apartments. "I love the way you speak up."

It was the first time he'd used the word. Rose's very heart fluttered.

It did not make her calmer. Indeed, she felt she might accidentally hop out of her shoes.

"But what if it *is* wrong?" The memory now of speaking up in front of Mr. Russell's entire political meeting, *twice*, stunned Rose. What had she been thinking? "These people are close to you. Their opinion of you matters. Their opinion of *me* will matter."

"My opinion isn't likely to change." The warm comfort of that voice was so good, even more so close to her ear as they paused at the bottom of the stairs.

"What if I say the exact wrong thing at the moment we meet and they think poorly of me forever?" Rose half-turned, as if to go right back up the stairs.

"You needn't say anything at all. Or you can say what you

are moved to say. Indeed, that is the very nature of the meeting, as I've explained. To me, it sounds like a perfect place for you to be."

Sighing, reconciling herself to the horror of the unknown, Rose slipped her hand back along his arm and took his hand.

She was more comfortable in the shop because she always knew what to say. It was her shop, and there were few sentences one really needed with most customers. She'd learned that the women who bought things in the middle of the day wanted company as much as bread, and if she simply asked about their day, she'd get more conversation than she wanted. It wasn't difficult.

When she was with Mr. Russell, he talked of important things, and she wanted to support those things.

Or he didn't talk at all, and she was comfortable that way now, too.

But people who didn't know her and didn't buy bread? "I don't wish to embarrass you."

"I will be the gentleman there with the prettiest young lady beside him. Nothing will detract from that."

Rose settled against him. It was a little skill she had recently learned. "Really?"

"Miss Bickering, you look lovely."

Mr. Russell's voice could be teasing or low with honest pleasure, but this was something deeper. Rose felt warm. "Do I? I'm so glad. I do want to be a credit to you."

"You will be."

When they stepped out the door to the street, Rose made sure it closed tightly. Emery had promised to close the shop, but Rose would have to leave the door to the residence unlocked. She didn't have the key, as she didn't know where it was kept in their rooms and couldn't ask; everyone thought she'd be there all evening.

She worried a bit for the candlesticks, and that was a

mark of how momentous this felt. She'd even risk losing them to do this.

When she stepped out on Mr. Russell's arm, for all of Leicester Square to see, she felt, as she often did with him, that *this* was what being a grown woman was like.

The adventures of being a grown woman were rather wonderful.

"Miss Rose Bickering, may I introduce Mrs. Jonah Swofford?"

"Do come in," said a woman's voice, soft like risen bread; it would be easy to sink into it. "Please."

Mrs. Swofford's parlor provided space for the meeting, and Rose had learned all the names. It was an effort to keep them straight and learn their voices: the gentleman who had originally invited Mr. Russell to come to London; the lady who knew his parents; Mr. Swofford whose house this was. The group wasn't large, but she didn't want to make one mistake.

"I'm glad you were led to join us," Mrs. Swofford told her softly and patted her hand as the group rustled their way into chairs in her parlor, and Rose had the sense that her hostess meant more than that Mr. Russell had brought her here.

That was almost all she said. The murmured greetings spoke of long acquaintance, but also of a shared purpose. Rose liked the feeling. It reminded her of her parents. They hadn't had an easy road to walk, but they walked it together.

When the silence came, Rose wasn't startled; Mr. Russell had explained how the service would go.

She *was* startled that she found the quiet peaceful. There was no time to be anxious while listening to her own thoughts and the breathing of the surrounding people. She felt as though she could see the soft colors of their thoughts swirling all around her.

Clarity, Mr. Russell had said. Being together would help them arrive at clarity.

She suspected she'd brought her little nugget of clarity with her, but in the peaceful quiet, Rose felt it take root and grow. It was real, and it was alive. Mr. Russell was her friend. They could love one another. Perhaps they already did. It would be clearer with time.

And Rose wasn't frightened of that.

"We've traveled for *so* long. You must tell us if Her Grace will speak with us."

"Her Grace does not receive unexpected callers. With Her Grace's regrets." The butler was so starched that his back must creak, Jane thought. She had a tired impulse to poke him and see what sort of sound he made.

The trip had been long and quite warm in the carriage, a tiny brougham barely big enough for two. Their driver was a square-faced fellow, with a slightly crushed hat, who was very, very drunk. He'd arrived that way and had been that way for the entire drive. Jane suspected he had a bottle in his pocket.

She and Anna had alighted through the brougham's rocking wheels thanks to the quick movements of Talbourne footmen, who had also seen them into the receiving hall.

Its giant staircase swooping above them, its marble floors, its delicate medallions carved into the walls, all created a majestic space. In other circumstances, both sisters would be pointing and whispering at all the beautiful little touches that made Talbourne House the rival of royal palaces.

Instead, they stood, limp and tired, in the hallway, asking to see a duchess and carrying a cake.

"I don't suppose Lady Ayles has recommended me to Her Grace," Anna said with fake brightness, shamelessly using the name of the lady she didn't want to see because she'd trod on her son's toes.

"I couldn't say, Miss Bickering."

"Lady Villeneuve must still be in residence?"

Jane held her breath on that one. Lady Villeneuve traveled all over London with her coterie of husband-seeking young ladies. It was plausible to ask for her, but Lady Villeneuve would know perfectly well that she didn't know the Bickering sisters.

"Lady Villeneuve, I regret to inform you, has retired to her house in town." His perfectly stiff collar never moved. None of these various regrets showed on his face.

Before Anna recited the name of everyone they had ever met in a desperate attempt to get one right, Jane thought she had better try something else. "We wished to bring a cake to celebrate the Duchess' recent wedding."

"An appreciated gesture." The way he looked down at the simple golden cake made Jane wish it had been more heavily decorated; it ought to have flowers. "Her Grace is accepting gifts and I will inform her of this one."

Anna didn't wish to turn over the cake; for one thing, she now realized she must get the plate back. Caught between the price of another plate and the price of another trip out here to fetch it, she burst out, "It's only the cake, you see. Not the plate."

The butler behaved as though he had heard odder things.

"This way, please."

LADY ARNOLD LIKED TO PRETEND THAT SHE DID NOT sometimes walk past the Ladies' Own Bakery and look in the windows just to see if the tall sister was alone in the shop.

She liked to pretend. Her life was just as she had expected it to be, and always had been. At her ripe old age, past thirty, there was nothing left to do but pretend. Oh, she would watch her children grow up and have children of their own, perhaps. She would like to help James do a good job of replacing his father. But in general, anything adventurous would happen only in daydreams.

So adventurous, she thought, with a little self-recrimination, as she turned the corner from Bear Street and glanced in the window.

There *was* a figure inside; clearly a woman. Slumped over the counter, next to that wicked-looking knife!

She rushed inside without a care for how it would look for her to run without a word to the maid walking with her, leaving her to follow.

The moment she stood by the body and saw that river of dark golden hair, her blood froze. No. It couldn't be.

The horror of possibly touching someone already gone seized her even as she was doing it.

"Miss Bickering. Miss Bickering!" She shook the slender shoulders as hard as she dared.

"What? *What?*" The tallest Miss Bickering leaped away from the counter as if burnt.

She was alive. *She was fine.* There were marks on her face from the pits in the counter, and breadcrumbs stuck to her cheek. And her *décolleté*, Lady Arnold noticed, and tried not to stare. The galloping of her heart from fright turned into a slower, steadier pounding that was hard to ignore. Surely it wouldn't show.

The young woman was such a combination of smooth skin and strength, Lady Arnold thought, watching her brush away breadcrumbs.

Then finally notice her visitor.

"Lady Arnold!" She dropped a wavering curtsey. Unpracticed more than unbalanced, though the young woman seemed barely awake.

"No need. Marie, I'll be right out." Her maid looked puzzled, but left.

Lady Arnold would never have a chance like this again.

Moving behind the wide counter, she reached up to the startled Miss Bickering and brushed breadcrumbs from her cheek.

The young woman startled backwards again, like a deer.

She was being shameless, but she would enjoy every instant of her little adventure. She reached all the way up to flick a speck of crust from a lock of golden hair, and then brushed away the ones clinging to Miss Bickering's palm.

She couldn't bring herself to be so bold as to brush anything from the baker's *décolleté*, but those Miss Bickering had brushed away herself.

Lady Arnold steadied herself. "What a fright you gave me! You were slumped across the counter. Did someone attack you? Or did you fall ill?"

An extraordinary array of expressions crossed the fine features. There was a strong line to her cheekbone. It was determined, yet still soft as flower petals.

"I fell asleep," she admitted.

"Fell asleep!"

"Yes, I—" Clearly she couldn't think of any explanation beyond her next words: "I must sleep more."

"I should say so! There is nothing so restoring as good sleep, Miss—" Oh, she would take advantage of her little adventure. The scare it had given her to think that this Miss Bickering, *her* Miss Bickering, might have never woken up! "Miss Bickering, will you tell me your given name?"

"Emery. Ah, that is, Emily, but everyone calls me Emery. They always have."

Her eyes were still a little foggy from the sleep. She pushed a loose hair behind her ear and peered about, as if looking for one of her sisters.

"My sisters all do, I mean," she clarified, "but, uh, they're out."

She really must not be quite awake.

"Emery." Yes, that was a very pleasing name. "Why aren't you sleeping?"

The green eyes cleared. "There's always so much to do," she simply said.

What would that be like? Lady Arnold struggled to fill her days, and this young woman had so much to do that she used her nights as well.

Well. She'd taken about as many liberties as she could for one day. She backed up a step.

It wasn't only the broad windows. She just wasn't brave enough to live the life she wanted to live.

But these little memories would be treasured for a long, long time.

"Emery," she said again, and put on the face she used with the children. Perhaps maternal behavior could excuse being so close. "People *need* sleep to live. You cannot simply do without, no more than you can do without water or food."

Emery looked down with equal parts chagrin and bitterness. "Both food and water are surprisingly expensive."

"But sleep is free." Lady Arnold wouldn't get lost in that look, she wouldn't. "Do promise me you'll sleep tonight."

Emery looked away as if calculating how many minutes of sleep she planned to get.

Lady Arnold stomped her foot.

That surprised Emery. Fair enough; it had surprised *her*.

Lady Arnold clung to her adamance. "Sleep for a night, please? You will feel so much better tomorrow."

"I'm very strong, Lady Arnold."

"I know." She must draw away, she must. This was too much adventure for one day.

Tearing herself away from Emery's puzzled eyes, Lady Arnold thought it wisest to leave before she settled in for the rest of day.

Then she remembered: why not? The children were engaged with other things, and she was so desperately bored.

She wished there were somewhere to sit. But for this, she could spend a little more time on her feet.

"I don't suppose you'll tell me what is so dire you cannot even sleep?"

A slow smile that almost stopped her heart. "I don't suppose I will."

"Well, then. Tell me about baking. I know nothing about it."

That made Emery's eyes widen, and Lady Arnold just barely recalled herself to tell Marie to finish any errands she had and return later. Lady Arnold might be engaged in learning about baking for some time.

THE POLISHED SIDEBOARD GROANED UNDER ALL SORTS OF platters and tureens. There was one tiny opening left, near a silver tray of ratafia cakes.

The butler beckoned a footman with a tiny crook of his finger, who leaped away, and returned instantly with a porcelain plate so fine they could almost see through it.

"Her Grace will be most pleased with your gift." The butler recited it as if he said it many times a day.

The cake would wind up on to that table. The guests laughing and shouting all around would eat it. The Duchess would never even see the cake.

"We must give it only to *her*."

The butler raised an eyebrow and glanced toward the plate in the footman's hands. Perhaps he could only encourage them with his eyes to deposit their cake and leave.

"It is for Her Grace, you see." Anna fiercely tried to keep the desperation out of her voice. "We baked it specially for her."

"I see."

"I'll just... hold on to it in case she arrives."

The eyebrow again. "She will not."

Anna made a show of looking around. "With so many guests?"

"The Duke and Duchess are pleased to entertain. They themselves only rarely attend."

"Perhaps this is one of those evenings when they do!"

"No," he said, with the bluntness of a man losing his patience.

Jane, envisioning Anna and the butler standing there facing each other for the rest of the night, broke in with the phrase that brought most conversations to a halt. "Thank you," she said in that way that indicated the person was no longer needed.

The butler was quite accustomed to *thank you* delivered in that way, even from shabbily dressed young ladies. His face said that he recognized the dismissal; he gestured to the footman. The footman placed his empty plate on the table with delicate finality, thereby locking their hopes away more effectively than iron bars.

"As you wish," the butler said in return, in that way that meant they would get nothing they wished, nothing at all. "You are welcome to join the play at the tables, of course."

"MISS ROSE. MR. RUSSELL."

The quiet of the service had clung to Rose all through the walk home. She'd been so lost in it, and in the feeling of her hand in the crook of Mr. Russell's thickly muscled arm, that Captain Brice's voice startled her; she'd forgotten they were walking down the street. "Captain."

He paused, and she realized he was trying to decide what to say. "I haven't seen Miss Bickering or Miss Jane for weeks," he said, in a sort of coded flag. He hadn't seen them; he wouldn't tell them.

Full of light, Rose just smiled. "No fear, Captain, there is no secret."

"Did you tell them you would attend services with me this evening?" Mr. Russell, startled, blurted out the question.

"No, but nothing can be secret forever."

"I don't know." The Captain sounded as though he took Rose's comment more seriously than a chance meeting might cause. "I think evil secrets can be hidden all too well. But this is no evil secret, is it?"

"No indeed!" Almost giddy with possibility, Rose laughed aloud, clutching Mr. Russell's arm with both hands. "Here we are. There is no secret."

"Is there, Mr. Russell?" He said it in an easy way, but something male bristled in the air.

Rose thought well of the way Mr. Russell answered. He wouldn't justify himself, or her. "Miss Rose can speak for herself, as you know, Captain."

"Indeed. Forgive the occasional burst of gallantry, Russell. I feel some interest in the Bickering sisters' welfare."

The male bristling feeling didn't go away. Rose knew the Captain was far taller, and given the way he'd alarmed Anna at first meeting, he must look fierce. But Mr. Russell was strongly built, and not easily swayed.

"Captain Brice," said Rose, "you ought to have come to the meeting with us. You can leave suspicion at the door and simply be with other people. And if you feel moved to speak, you speak."

After a pause, the Captain said in a different voice, "I don't think that would suit me. But thank you. I can certainly understand the appeal, if all the people there are like you."

"I think at least a little like me," Rose faltered. She had felt so welcome.

"Very much like you," said Mr. Russell immediately, and squeezed the hand she had tucked in his elbow.

"I ought to call," mused the Captain. "Just to see how everyone fares."

"Well enough. Jane and Anna have gone to Talbourne House to gift Her Grace with a cake."

"Really?" Now the Captain sounded a bit worried. "That doesn't sound terribly good. All the way to Talbourne House? That's hours there and back. Just to give Her Grace a cake?"

"Yes, I'm sure she will like it," said Rose in the perfect confidence of someone who had never met anyone whose life held more than enough cake.

The Captain, who well knew how little a cake would mean to a duchess, was not so sure. "I hope it makes a pleasant trip, and I'll have to call if only to hear how it went."

"I'm not getting back in that carriage with this cake."

"We look so foolish carrying a cake through a palace like this!" Anna sounded distraught, but she marched alongside her sister and carried the actual cake.

The palace was a nightmare. Room after room of people chatting, playing cards, drinking; but no way to find Her Grace, and no one they knew.

"If we put down the cake, it will be eaten in seconds." Jane grimly measured the people in front of her, who carelessly dripped claret down their embroidery. Some of them literally glittered with spilled sugar from devoured desserts.

"Do you play cards at all?" Anna wasn't ready to give up. She'd come this far, as mortifying as it was to walk through these silk- and pearl-draped fashion drawings carrying a cake.

"They're not playing. They're *betting*."

So they were. There was the dull gleam of coins, and their little clinks carried from table to table.

"We could sit anywhere." Anna refused to believe they'd hit a wall. They were here. They were right here in the splendid house of a duke and duchess, and they had cake.

"Yes. We could. I think they would let anyone walk in here." Jane could see ladies with lace fans coming and going to the sounds of tinkling laughter, as well as gentlemen with disreputable hair. They prevented no one from coming in to *these* rooms.

But there were footmen at the far doors, and both sisters knew they were not allowed any further.

They couldn't get the Duchess to come out, and they couldn't get in. And there were plates of little foods everywhere, dried apricots, cheese, sausages—even, on a platter going by, astonishingly, tiny saucers of cut pineapple.

They knew of ladies who'd had pineapples on their tables, long ago. They'd never met anyone who actually *ate* one.

The smell was mouth-watering.

"You don't suppose we could try a bite of that pineapple?" Anna whispered.

Swooping upon the slow-moving footman, Jane relieved him of a dish he'd been about to serve.

"Thank you," she said solemnly, backing away to where Anna stood still holding their plate, leaving him to solve the problem of serving pineapple when he was a saucer short.

She felt a little guilty, but only a little.

"Just hold still," she said and popped a golden triangle into Anna's mouth.

Anna's whole face dissolved in hedonistic delight. "Oh, Jane."

Quickly, Jane captured a piece for herself.

The sweetness, the tart golden flavor of it spreading across her tongue, was *heavenly*. It was as if all the crisp sour fruits she knew had melted into a bed of flowers; it was the concentrated taste of heavenly sunlight.

"Oh my," Jane murmured back.

There were only a few tiny bites of the fruit in the dish; silently they stood and nibbled, one then the other, both silently grateful that there had been an even number of morsels, so they needn't even question how to split the last.

"If we could bake something that tasted like that. Jane, don't." Anna scolded a little as Jane tipped the last of the juice from the saucer onto her tongue, but her heart wasn't in it. She'd have done the same if she hadn't been holding the cake.

Jane looked around the room. No one had spoken to them but the butler; likely, no one would. She regarded their *galette des Rois*, a little ragged from shifting on the plate during the long carriage ride on their knees in the cramped brougham. "Should we leave them the cake?"

"No! If the Duchess won't accept it, we'll sell it."

"We just stole some countess' pineapple, Anna; we could leave something to eat in return."

"No." Anna's fingers gripped the plate edge. "We are here on business, not pleasure." Though the pineapple had been nothing but.

Talbourne House offered its pleasures freely enough. But it didn't offer the one thing they wanted: an audience with the Duchess.

The frustration of being so close and unable to reach their

goal was going to eat at them both all the way home. "I could run at the footman," murmured Jane.

"We are ladies. At least, we were." Anna's back straightened in her much-washed gown. "We can go home knowing we conducted ourselves as such, even on a business errand. If we behave."

Jane didn't want to behave. She was ready to throw that cake through a window if it would get where she wanted it to be. "This can't possibly be where we stop."

"We haven't stopped yet."

They both felt, however, the many indignities of turning around to go home.

THE WHEELS ON THE PAVEMENT RATTLED AND STOPPED AT number 17, drawing Zachary's attention away from his painting.

In truth, it easily distracted him, because he'd spent several hours chasing the thought round his head that Miss Bickering had been right. His painting was boring, it was predictable, and above all, it wasn't lovely.

No one bought unlovely paintings.

So he was ready for the wheels to distract him, ready to gallop down the stairs to see what was going on.

He was shocked, though, to see Miss Bickering and her sister alighting, warm and rumpled, from a brougham. Their walking dresses might have been fine for afternoon, but it was early evening now, even if the sun had not set.

"Ladies."

He put out his hand to take a plate with a cake on it from Miss Anna so she could climb out. She gripped it more tightly.

Then, "Sorry," she said, and let him have it.

He held it as both sisters shook out their skirts on the pavement, and Miss Anna took some coins from a purse.

"Allow me," he said, long training intervening before a lady handed common money to a servant.

"Thanks." The driver's *ks* was a long-drawn out, mushy sound. Zachary looked again. The fellow was very drunk. "Ladieszh."

Zachary watched as the brougham pulled away, the horse far steadier than its driver. "He didn't take you all the way to Talbourne House?"

"He did," said Miss Jane, tiredness almost running from her fingers.

"Ladies." This time it held true concern. "You mustn't take such risks. Anything could have happened with such a fellow driving you for so long! What if he had simply driven you somewhere you wouldn't have been safe?" What if he'd left them there? What if he *hadn't*?

Gently shaking her head, Miss Bickering, she of the far too accurate cutting remarks about painting, reached out to grasp one of his hands.

Hers was small, but full of surprising strength.

"We're quite accustomed now to the odd little danger," she said, showing gratitude for his concern and dismissing it at the same time. "Thank you, Lord Zachary."

She could have meant for his worry or for holding the cake, which she now took back.

He did not relent. "This is madness, you two darting off to spend the day in such a wild errand. You could have waited till we found a way to get you an introduction, at least."

Shaking off her burst of informality, Miss Bickering's smile had a touch of bitterness to it. He could never capture that in a painting. "*We?* That's a kind way of answering our intrusion into your garret, sir. But we didn't expect further help from you." And true to her words, she moved to open the door to their staircase herself. "Nor will we in future."

He stretched, reached the door first by virtue of longer arms and legs.

Pulling it open for her, he looked from her to Miss Jane. Exhausted, dispirited, neither shied away from him, but neither did they confide.

"We have had a bad start to being neighbors," Zachary said, choosing his words as carefully as he ever had in any drawing room. "I *am* your neighbor, you know."

Above them, a dark hairy head showed over the edge of the balustrade. A strained voice echoed down the stairwell. "Is everything all right?"

Zachary felt a moment's annoyance; then, surprised by it, he let it pass. It wasn't as if he'd been having a moment alone with the Bickering sisters.

He jerked his chin upward. "You see? Neighbors look out for one another, do they not?"

Jane started upwards. He might have heard her mutter something about too many names for some neighbors and not enough for others.

But Anna smiled at him again, and this one had no bitterness in it. It was the first time he saw a little of her soul, perhaps, in her smile. There was a sunniness in it even as the sun went down behind them.

"That is kind, Lord Zachary, thank you. If you would be willing to bring up that cake..." She looked at the plate in his hand with resigned loathing. "You've no idea how long I've been carrying that plate."

"I'd be happy to." Something easier between him and his neighbors could only be good, he thought.

"We're quite well," Anna called up to the fellow from the closet on the floor above, and the dark head just nodded and disappeared.

He would have thought it burdensome had someone described it a moment before, but it was pleasant, knowing he was part of the little group looking out for the Misses Bickering.

EMERY AND ROSE WERE ALREADY ASLEEP WHEN JANE AND Anna came in; their bedroom door was closed.

Quietly, Jane and Anna went to theirs.

They'd had the whole trip back to talk, but it wasn't till they were in their room, unbuttoning each other's gowns and washing their hands and faces with the clean water in the wash bucket, that Anna said, "Wasn't it beyond peculiar, being in a place like that again as we are now?"

"We have never before been in a place like *that*." Jane's fingers undid the bow that held back her hair, its dark waves falling about her face as she laid the hair ribbon carefully along a windowsill.

"No, but very fine places. We *have* been among them, you know. It seems so long ago now. And tonight felt so very different."

A few strokes of the comb and Jane's hair had been tamed; she handed it to Anna to sort out her much more difficult mass of brown curls. "We were neither wanted nor needed. That felt very familiar to *me*."

"I'm so sorry, Jane." Anna let the curls cling to her fingers, twisted one thoughtfully. "We never did do well at it, I'm afraid. But I was so convinced we would, all those years ago, when it began."

"If only conviction were success."

"Perhaps we must change our convictions."

Jane looked up from where she sat on the edge of the bed, her mouth falling open. "Never say so! Was my sister switched for someone else during that long carriage ride home? Have I been drugged?"

Anna laughed a little. "That butler likely thought we poisoned the cake."

"I had the same thought. One reason I agreed we might as well bring it home."

"Cake won't keep forever." It had gotten even more ragged on the return ride. The swerving of the carriage as the drunken driver occasionally took up the reins then seemed to forget them didn't help. "Nothing keeps forever."

"Except the convictions of a Bickering sister," sighed Jane, half-chuckling, as she pulled back the sheets before sliding off one stocking and then the other.

That stocking snagged Anna's eyes. It was no longer pristine, and a hole had appeared in the toe; they must mend it.

But it was a white stocking. A lady's stocking.

Their clothes were literally turning to rags with every passing moment. And they didn't have money for more.

"We must do what we must do," said Anna, almost to herself; Jane was already half-asleep.

THE NEXT DAY, WHEN LORD BOISLEGRAND ARRIVED TO pick up his cake, Anna gave him a fresh one.

And a smile.

It animated him; he almost hopped from one foot to the other, he was so eager for more of the same. "I await the realization of your promise to drive, Miss Bickering. Your promise itself is a great pleasure, but the drive itself will be far more."

So quickly, before any other customers came in, before she lost hold of her courage and gave in to her pride, Anna answered. "You're quite right, Lord Boislegrand. I am enjoying the anticipation myself. It was very kind of you to offer both the anticipation and the drive."

He was still bursting with eager questions when she finally urged him out of the door a few moments later. "Just tell me what time to call. I have the drive all planned. You will want to breathe some cleaner air, won't you, Miss Bickering? And your sisters will enjoy themselves, I promise. So kind of you. I will be counting the moments. Very good of you to accompany me!"

She stayed in the shop's door, but did curtsey.

"Counting the moments!" he called most indecorously out of his carriage window as he pulled away.

She smiled a little as she went back to the counter. He'd been transported. He'd have forgotten his cake had she not put it into his hands herself.

There were a gentleman's hands, unscarred, uncalloused. He had oddly nimble fingers.

It was peculiar to think about Lord Boislegrand's fingers.

"What was all that about?" Lord Zachary stood in the door that led to their rooms upstairs, in a billowing shirt stained with blue and ochre.

"What was what about?"

"I heard some fellow calling *Counting the moments!* like a little girl who'd snuck into a ball."

"Lord Boislegrand. He's a viscount. Fully grown."

Zachary craned his head around the corner to look out the shop window, but Lord Boislegrand's lacquered carriage was long gone.

"He's not a neighbor." He frowned, and that made Anna want to laugh too. It was such an unaccustomed expression for his smooth-shaven, worryless face.

"No, he isn't." She felt giddy with her new convictions. One must do what one must do. And she'd come as far as she could with her old convictions. It was long past time for something new.

She'd opened a shop. She'd worked with her hands for long days. She'd stood up to Aunt Eden, she'd talked to men in the street. She'd done many things she would have sworn a year ago she would never do.

Seven years before, she'd begun her season with the conviction that she would find a true, perfect love, and that she could not settle for anything less.

Much older now, she thought it time to renovate a few convictions. Much the way she would turn a dress, putting the inside out in order to be a little fresher to the world.

Lord Zachary, however, didn't look pleased. Well, her aim wasn't to please him.

He said, "I mean, neighbors are reasonable acquaintances on whom to rely. Customers in carriages, not as much."

"Why not, sir?" Yes, the viscount had many fine features. He was kind, and generous, and clearly interested. Anna could do with a little of that. "Without a carriage, he could not take me and my sisters for a drive. And we will do just that."

No, Lord Boislegrand didn't make her stomach flutter. But Anna didn't want that any more.

Why, she'd felt that way about Lord Zachary at first meeting, and for what? His blue eyes and broad shoulders? She knew him better now, and he didn't make her stomach flutter at all.

Perhaps she'd stop needling him. She would like to be as kind as Lord Boislegrand.

"You can't go riding with him in public." Lord Zachary still had that frown. It looked as out of place on him as on a puppy. "You will be seen."

"And what of it?" Anna shooed him back into the stairwell with her hands. She must get back to work. "He isn't drunk."

Episode 18: The Risks of Pleasure

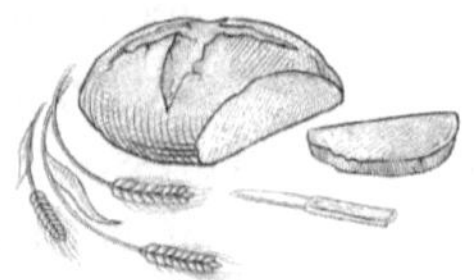

Jane had no misgivings about their Sunday drive till she spotted her paving-man on the corner of Leicester Square.

Lord Boislegrand was a man of soft demeanor, but also of his word. He arrived exactly on time in an open carriage beautifully suited to a summer drive.

All the square must have seen the procession of Bickering sisters, again in the last of their fading finery, parading out the humble door from the rooms above their shop and climbing one by one into Lord Boislegrand's vast carriage.

They couldn't all be taken for strumpets, surely, was Jane's thought as she settled herself against the feather-filled cushions.

They were in public view. Ladies did go riding. Though not without chaperones, and not with men, unless they had an understanding.

Well. Four sisters would have to equal one chaperone.

It was so delightful to be in a properly-sprung carriage that Jane felt herself melt into the cushions.

That was when she caught sight of him, that chiseled lean

face under his cap watching her. Just her. She knew his eyes were on her as surely as she'd known when he'd taken her hand to help her across the street.

He wasn't working; he wore his Sunday coat. He had just happened to catch sight of her passing by.

And he watched her, openly, for all the time it took the carriage to navigate the sharp corner and start away from Leicester Square.

And it was only that which made her feel uncomfortable. Not to be out in the open, and not just to be so obviously stared at, as she had been stared at before. It was the way he made new decisions about her, silently. She could see it in his face.

ANNA'S PLAN LACKED SUBTLETY. THAT, AT LEAST, KEPT IT moral.

Her enthusiasm bubbled out in the open air carriage, now that Lord Boislegrand's time was finally social. Or rather, social, except that she wanted to make use of it.

"You see, we think the cakes will do well if Her Grace likes them. But we haven't a way to reach her with one to try it!"

Her sisters sat rocking in the carriage in various stages of shock. She hadn't told them she planned to enlist Lord Boislegrand's help, but surely that had been obvious?

Why else would they be riding in an open carriage where anyone could see?

The blush on Anna's cheeks would be permanent.

Nonetheless, she kept on.

"You have *met* Her Grace, haven't you, sir?"

"Met her? Can't say I have, not socially. I don't venture all the way out to Talbourne House; no taste for games, I admit.

I saw her at a ball at the Duke of Gravenshire's house; do you know it? The big one on Claremont Square?"

"No. You did meet her, then?"

"Greeted her. And the Duke, he's a cold sort of fellow. Odd match. I think she left drunk."

Anna had no interest in the Talbourne marriage; only the social standing of the Duchess. "They entertain so often; they must be well-known in London. Apart from their positions, I mean."

Lord Boislegrand rubbed his chin—not across bristles, there were none, but moving the lump of his chin all around in a circle. It was not attractive. "I suppose so. They have a set, of course. Her Grace keeps to some young ladies-in-waiting, as it were, friends of hers."

"No, that won't do at all."

"Anna," whispered Rose with some urgency. Anna patted her quiet. This was no place to have an argument. It must be obvious what she was trying to do.

"She's young, she's apparently pretty, and she married a duke. She *must* be wanted all over town."

"I suppose. She's a flirty little thing, I've heard; charming. But she's blind, and talks mostly to men, and that doesn't appeal to many ladies in London."

"She's *blind?*" That made Rose raise her voice.

The energy of this traveled through the carriage occupants as they rolled past fine stone houses that had once housed earls and ambassadors. "She's blind?" "Why did no one tell us that?" "Does it make a difference?" "It's interesting, you must admit!" "Surely that must help!"

At that last comment from Jane, Rose leaned forward a little so everyone would be sure to hear her. "London is full of blind people, you know. It isn't a *club.*"

That settled them a little.

"Wouldn't it help, though? If Rose went to take a cake to Talbourne House?" Jane wasn't ready to abandon the idea.

"You were there, Jane. Do you think those servants would simply admit her because she was blind?"

Jane slumped a little in her seat. "No."

That made their host clear his throat, reminding them he was there. "I had thought we would drive north," he said mildly, "where you can see the kind of green place Leicester Square was a hundred years ago. But if you care for London society, we can drive along the Strand."

"No! I mean…" What *did* Anna mean? She was over her horror at being compromised in public places. She'd committed them to this drive, after all!

"Fresh air sounds lovely, my lord." Emery was peering out over the people walking along the pavements and letting the breeze under her bonnet. She clearly wanted to see sights more than be seen.

Well, she'd never been committed to the cake plan, Anna thought a little sourly.

But if Anna were truly committed, oughtn't they drive right down to the Strand and see if they could cross paths with the Duchess of Talbourne? Or some friend of hers?

No. Brazenness wouldn't sell cakes. Anna wanted Her Grace to be enamored of their business and their cake, not repulsed. And if the duchess had a reputation for flirting, she might not be the right choice anyway.

"Let's enjoy the drive," Jane said, reaching across their sisters to put a hand on Anna's hand.

"Quite," but Anna only pretended to surrender to the allure of fresh air.

By the time they had taken a turn or two more, Anna could rouse her thoughts from cakes and duchesses to look about. "We aren't driving all the way to the countryside, surely?"

Puffy hadn't expected the drive to go like this. But life often surprised him, and he was just glad the shining star, as he now sometimes thought of Miss Bickering, had agreed to come. Carting along three sisters was a small price to pay.

"I had thought the Park," which always meant Hyde Park, "but perhaps you ladies would prefer Marylebone? It is being rebuilt, and very fine."

"How does one build a park?" The dark-haired sister, Miss Jane, had arresting looks, and that made Puffy uncomfortable. Sultry women were a mystery he didn't care to unravel, and with her dark, flashing eyes, Miss Jane didn't look like she cared to be unraveled, either.

But now she simply lay against the carriage cushions, taking the view, as if leaving Leicester Square had unstarched her. That made it possible for Puffy to answer.

"It's a greenery thing, I suppose." In truth, he had no idea how one built a park, and thought it an odd question.

"I wish someone would build *our* park," said Miss Emery. "Everything is so overgrown in our square you can't even see inside it."

A patently true observation, but Puffy wanted to impress all Miss Bickering's sisters. "You can see the statue of the King, and that's enough."

"It's not as if we could walk inside it," said the youngest sister, baldly stating what no one else would say. Only house-holders on the Square would have a key to it, and their bakery wouldn't qualify them.

"But it would be more pleasant to look over. You can see it from our windows."

Puffy desperately wanted to shower Miss Bickering with

gifts. Had it been in his power to get her a key to Leicester Square, he would gladly have done it.

And watching her sit quietly in the corner of the carriage opposite him, her pink cheeks hardened as she clenched her jaw, her soft curls playing in the breeze, he realized that the best gifts, the ones that truly caught a woman's attention, were the ones they wanted.

Puffy wasn't stupid.

"I think you will not enjoy our drive, Miss Bickering, unless you can put your worries aside."

She flashed him a short smile, but the little pucker in her brow came back. "Only thinking, my lord, as we go. It is very pleasant, I assure you."

"Perhaps you would enjoy it more if I offered to take one of your cakes to Talbourne House myself, and present it to Her Grace?"

"Would you?" Startled out of her frown, her bright smile came back. And it held everything about her he found most appealing. Her brown eyes had a soft sweetness to them that brightened with laughing sparkle when she smiled like that.

He'd had plenty of time to think. Especially during all those weeks of traipsing to Leicester Square for cake with nary an encouragement from the hope of his heart.

He had simply never seen another young lady in London with that particular look in her eye. She was pretty, but so were many London ladies. She was more. And the intelligence in her face appealed to Puffy as much as the sweetness that no amount of hard work could hide.

Ladies did not take well to compliments about their intelligence. And her sweetness was so obvious it bore no remark.

"I would be happy to do it," he said, the truth of it on his face, he knew, because hiding things was not his strength.

"Oh *thank* you, Lord Boislegrand!" She clapped her hands

with delight, the sound muffled by her gloves, but the excitement obvious nonetheless.

Feeling he'd already done a good day's work, Puffy nodded happily to himself. Yes, the task was already done, in his mind. "Think nothing of it, Miss Bickering."

He wanted to add that she should feel free to call him Puffy. His mother had, and some close friends from school still did. He wanted her to feel familiar with him. He already felt familiar with her, he'd spent so much time thinking about her charms.

But for now, surrounded by all manner of sisters, disquieting as they were, that would be too much.

Perhaps for another day.

MARYLEBONE PARK WAS LOVELY, AND IT WAS AS interesting to see the men digging trenches and laying new stone as it was to see the flowers blooming and see the trees all a-rustle.

People spoke of fresh air, thought Emery, but didn't really convey how bracing it was to just see something new. Her daily rounds of washing, mixing, shaping, and baking were beginning to run together into a river of memories that were all the same. Her forays to Mr. Morley's tailor shop to sew a few pieces here and there had come to mean a change as much as more coins. But that was the opposite of fresh air, closed up in a tiny room of wool.

She'd stopped asking him to take the pieces home, because where would she put them? The bakery was full of flour, and flour and wool wouldn't mix.

As they rolled back toward the square and the sights became familiar again, Emery found herself wondering which of the fine houses nearby belonged to Lady Arnold. The lady hadn't returned to buy her own cake, at least not that Emery saw; but perhaps she'd missed it.

Emery must work more at the counter.

Being the tallest, she was the first to spot the broad shoulders of a man waiting by the bakery door as they passed Jacquier's Hotel. "Is that Mr. Russell by our bakery door?"

"Is he?" Rose's spine straightened instantly and one hand moved to smooth her hair.

Everything about the Russell man made Emery contradict herself. She was suspicious of marriage, but loved the idea of a happy Rose. She supported Rose against Anna's insistence that Rose wasn't old enough to marry, but secretly agreed with it.

Above all, she had yet to determine if this fellow was good enough for her little sister.

"I think that's him," she teased. "Reddish hair and a look like a boxer?"

"He has reddish hair?" Rose was taken aback.

Jane examined all the faces on the sidewalk as well. "Miss Emery. Don't tease. Mr. Russell's hair could be said to have a slight tint of red. He's perfectly respectable."

"Not *perfectly* respectable," muttered Anna, as their carriage rolled up beside the gentleman in question.

Emery wanted to warn Rose that the perfectly respectable Mr. Russell looked rather thunderous. But there wasn't time, as he announced his temper himself.

"Miss Rose." He bit out the words. "What a surprise this is."

"Is it?"

Lord Boislegrand had alighted first and leaned in to hand Rose out of the carriage. Whether to get this encounter out of the way first, or only to be gallant to the youngest sister, wasn't clear.

"I wasn't aware I'd be seeing you today, Mr. Russell." One of Rose's gloved hands crept up to check her hair again.

"Yes, I can see that. Do you mind, sir?" Mr. Russell didn't exactly elbow the viscount out of the way, but he did push himself into the space where he could hand Rose out himself.

Rose took his hand, but frowned. "Why have you bothered to call, then, if you're in a bad temper?" She released his hand the moment she was on her feet.

"I wasn't planning to *call*. I heard that a fellow in a grand carriage took you for a drive and I didn't credit the rumor at all. Yet here you are." He turned and gave the barest inclination of his head to Lord Boislegrand. "Your pardon, sir."

"No offense taken," said Lord Boislegrand, with a shrug. He wasn't the sort of man to take offense.

Emery put out her hand to alight next; she wanted to go stand by Rose.

Who was still looking puzzled. "Yes, as you can see, that's exactly what we did."

Mr. Russell stepped closer. "Hardly proper, Miss Rose."

Rose's mouth dropped open. "Nothing *im*proper, Mr. Russell, as you can clearly see!"

"I see you out riding with a man who could be your father in front of all Leicester Square and everybody!"

Reaching the pavement, Anna shooed her hands around the pair. "Perhaps we should go inside. Let me open the bakery door."

"It should be obvious that I was accompanying my sister, who was actually Lord Boislegrand's guest!"

Anna closed her eyes. Perhaps she was just hoping if she couldn't see this, it wasn't happening. "Why don't we *all* go inside?"

Jane was on the pavement now, and stood on Rose's other side. "Miss Rose is free to do as she likes, Mr. Russell, especially when she likes to accompany her sisters on a Sunday drive."

"It was rather a good one, wasn't it?" Lord Boislegrand stuck his thumbs in his pockets and puffed out his chest. He was clearly pleased with his entertainment.

"It really was," said Anna, with a gentle smile that Emery thought wasn't appropriate to the moment, not at all.

"Are you coming in, or aren't you?" Rose had the clipped tones of someone on the other side of their patience.

And Mr. Russell seemed to have used his up before they even arrived. "It's one thing to walk out with me. Everyone knows we've been keeping company. Everyone in Leicester Square, anyway!"

Anna made a little moaning noise. "We could do this inside," she half-whispered.

"We could do it right here! I don't keep company with you, whatever that means! What a thing to say! Right in the street!" Rose's tone grew louder and louder, as if she didn't realize that she too was in the street.

"No? Then what do you call it? What *do* you call it, Miss Rose?" Mr. Russell's face had gotten red, though whether it was anger or some kind of tears, Emery couldn't tell. He was clearly as full of emotion as a rising loaf was full of air, and looked like he might burst.

"I don't know what to call it! What do *you* call it, Mr. Russell? You're so wise and all, you tell me!"

"I can't be associated with a woman who can't behave in public!" Mr. Russell was nearly shouting now, completely unaware of the existence of irony.

"That's easy to arrange! I'm not associated with you in the least. Does that satisfy you, sir?"

"Any idea what's happening?" Emery heard Lord Boislegrand ask Anna, to which Anna only made another little moaning noise.

People were gathering.

Emery thought she saw a shadow, a crack in the door that led up to their rooms. Someone standing there.

She left Rose's side to go look.

Their closet neighbor had washed his hair at some point. Emery was surprised that it was brown, not black. He had on a jacquard waistcoat that had once been fine, but his hair was still mad and he had not shaved.

His eyes flicked toward her as she approached.

"Does anyone need to be silenced, Miss Bickering?" she heard his voice float out of the doorway.

"No!" Emery turned to look over her shoulder. Rose was red now too, and some of their customers were in the gathering crowd. "Or rather, if they do, I'll let you know."

MRS. PARKER FOUND IT EASY TO KEEP CAPTAIN BRICE'S rooms at the hotel in order. He had the neatness of a man who kept things in their place on a ship. His razor and soap were always in the same place and spotless before she arrived; his bathing sheets and stockings, the same.

His sitting room looked out over the square, and when home, he spent much of his time there, often at the finely carved desk.

He was at the desk now, when she ventured in from his bedchamber. His dark head was bent over a letter, one hand scratching the paper with a pen, the other hand tugging at his hair with frustration.

"Do you hear anything, sir?"

"No, Mrs. Parker; what do *you* hear?" He looked grateful for a reason to raise his head.

"Nothing untoward in the square?"

Captain Brice looked up and squinted into the sun. It was

the wrong angle for afternoon; he must move soon, but he'd wanted to finish this letter first. "I don't see anyone, not that anyone could see anything in that overgrown wilderness in the middle of the square. Why do you ask?"

"I could swear I heard something." Mrs. Parker had lived through quite a bit in London, and she knew restless people when she heard them. "You don't suppose there's going to be a riot?"

The word *riot* made Captain Brice throw down his pen and throw open a window.

The park was quiet, but he immediately looked to his right, toward the Ladies' Own Bakery.

"I think I see it, Mrs. Parker. Hand me my hat, please."

"I WOULDN'T TALK TO YOU IF YOU WERE THE LAST MAN IN London!" Rose was really in full voice now. Jane had never seen her do anything like it.

"Keep a list, then; even if I'm at the bottom, I'm sure you'll make your way there eventually!"

Her littlest sister, the one too shy to talk to customers, gave Mr. Russell's shout right back to him. "*If* I were working my way down such a list, I'd stop before I had to crawl *under a rock* to find the end of it!"

This was too much. Anna looked like she might faint.

Lord Boislegrand didn't seem disturbed, but Jane was beginning to realize that Lord Boislegrand never *was* disturbed.

Ought she lead Rose inside? Somehow, this seemed up to Rose. She was perfectly capable of turning on her heel and walking away. She could even call upon any of her sisters to send this appalling man away, and they'd make short work of him.

But Rose wasn't walking away. She had planted her feet and seemed determined to have this out, even as her face told Jane that she was near tears.

Oddly, so was Mr. Russell.

The neighbors had begun to chime in.

"She's breaking his heart, she is. Just look at 'im," said one of their usual ladies, who often bought the littlest tuppence loaves.

"And what call does he have, throwin' his weight around like that? They're not married, y'know. He 'as no right."

"I see 'em walking, you know!"

"A walk ain't a ring," said another, quite wisely.

Indeed, Mr. Russell had an odd set to his chin, as if he were holding in quite a lot. "I had no idea you felt this way," he said, stiffly.

"Oh, I'm telling you how I feel right now!"

The crowd parted and Captain Brice cut through, head above everyone else's. Jane could see his frown even under the hat he'd remembered to put on.

"Afternoon. Russell." The murmurs died down as soon as the Captain reached the center of the *fracas*. "Miss Rose." He took in Emery and Jane, and his eyes lingered on Anna, leaning on Lord Boislegrand's arm. "Ladies."

He gave the viscount a little bow. "Lord Boislegrand, isn't it?"

His lordship looked delighted. He didn't look at all like a man watching a street fight. "Quite! Have we met?"

"In passing. Joshua Brice, captain of the *Halia*."

"You don't say. Sound colonial. Aren't we still at war?"

This sounded like small talk about a tiny thing compared to the conflagration happening right in front of them. The Captain ignored it.

"I'm sure you've reminded our young friend Mr. Russell

that a gentleman doesn't conduct his personal business in public."

"Haven't told him a thing," his lordship said cheerfully. "He seems to be holding his own, wouldn't you say?"

Jane took a hard look at his lordship. He wasn't half as flighty as Jane had thought. He knew exactly what was going on, and simply wanted to see it play out.

This had all gone far enough.

"Surely Rose should go in," Jane murmured, just loudly enough for the Captain to hear. He usually listened to her.

Indeed, his eyes flicked her way now, and he nodded.

"Do see the Misses Bickering inside, would you, my lord? I would be in your debt."

"Certainly." Finally activated, Lord Boislegrand brought Anna on his arm up to Rose.

Whether Rose was shaking with anger or exhaustion wasn't clear. But his lordship simply offered her his arm, raising it right under her hand so she couldn't miss it. "Let's do go in. I think it might be about to rain."

"I agree," said Rose, ignoring the fact that it was a clear dry day, just as Lord Boislegrand had when he made the suggestion.

Captain Brice stalked by to stand over Mr. Russell, and Jane couldn't hear what he said.

"THESE WOMEN ARE UNDER MY PROTECTION. DO YOU understand what that means?"

The half-growl seemed to wake Mr. Russell from his despairing rage. He had so little to give Rose, and he'd thought she'd wanted it. Wanted him. He couldn't blame her for wanting a fine carriage ride on a fine day; who wouldn't? But she'd done it right out in the open where everyone could see. Everyone who'd seen them walking arm in arm all round the square. Likely everyone who had seen them sneaking into the mews, too.

She hadn't a care for her reputation or his. And he felt like a fool.

He had come to London with one purpose: to make it better. People were fundamentally good inside; sometimes they just had to be prompted to do the right thing.

But they wouldn't listen to his prompts if they thought he was lascivious, or foolish, or both. And now everyone in Leicester Square probably thought exactly that.

And below all that, he was just hurt. She was *his* open secret, the sweetness in *his* day. He'd thought she was willing to walk with him in public because he was special to her, too. But now he felt he'd been stupid all along. She didn't think that much of him. If she did, she wouldn't have stood there yelling at him in the street like a fishwife.

Even if he had started it.

If he let a tear fall in public, he'd have to leave London.

"I don't know what that means," he responded to Brice's sally hoarsely, though pitched just for the Captain's ears. "You're not saying one of them is your mistress, surely?"

"I'm saying no harm will come to them, not while I can stop it. Do you hear?"

Mr. Russell blinked hard. "I'm doing no harm."

"Aren't you?"

The Captain's eyes just flicked to the side, and Mr. Russell became aware of the men and women, disappointed, perhaps, that the fight hadn't been more exciting, murmuring to themselves and trailing away.

"Now what do they think of Miss Rose?"

"Miss Rose has been walking all over the square with me," Mr. Russell said with tight bitterness. "As you know perfectly well."

"And you did that. You've responsibility, man. If you aren't going to offer for her, you're harming her already. And then this." Disgust was written all over the older man's face. "Are you a man or a baby?"

He wanted to tell the Captain that he *had* been planning to offer for Miss Rose.

He'd thought they had an understanding. That was what hurt.

The hell was, he *still* wanted to offer for Miss Rose.

She had the spine of a public speaker and a kiss like honey and he wanted nothing more than to offer for Miss Rose.

But he had exactly one leased room, a tiny income, and no prospects unless he could win a ministry seat in the next election.

Which he likely wouldn't win after today.

He found the loss didn't hurt as much as thinking he might never see Rose again. She wouldn't have turned to look at him, of course; but he'd thought she might turn back to say *some*thing.

She didn't.

She marched inside with that lord and two of her sisters and never came back to him at all.

He didn't understand what was between them the way he thought he had.

"I'd die before I hurt her," the words ripped out of him before he could stop them.

They'd have to do. He wasn't about to tell someone else he wanted to marry Rose Bickering before he told her.

And right now, it looked like that would happen... never.

"Pull yourself together. Look lively. Take a deep breath. Walk away as though you had a pair and see what you can do with yourself tomorrow." The frown the Captain gave him was menacing. "Without bothering Miss Rose."

"You're right." Mr. Russell couldn't say anything else.

He left.

WHATEVER THE CAPTAIN HAD SAID TO MR. RUSSELL, THE younger, burlier man walked away.

That ability to look frightening must come in handy on a ship, Jane mused.

The Captain took the few steps back to her and nodded, looking over her shoulder to where her sisters had disappeared inside. "Miss Rose will be well?"

"Oh yes. I think this might have been good for her."

That startled him. "How?"

Jane couldn't explain how sometimes she just wanted to scream with the pressure of it all. She suspected her littlest sister sometimes felt the same way; today she'd just... let it out. "Rose isn't that delicate," was all she could think to tell him.

He nodded as if this made sense. "Miss Anna is, though. Will she be well? I thought she might faint, she looked so pale."

"She'll be fine." Anna wasn't that delicate either, but this sort of thing definitely mattered to her.

Jane was surprised to realize that she herself hadn't been bothered at all.

"This Boislegrand fellow." The Captain jerked his chin towards the shop. "He is trustworthy?"

"I barely know him. He seems a decent man."

"Is he? Be careful. He seems quite happy to over-pay for cakes, and I can only hope he doesn't think that entitles him to anything."

Usually Jane would merely have agreed. Today, she thought Anna might have made better choices than she realized. "I don't know. If there's a kind man in London, it might be him."

He just made a noise of disapproval deep in his throat. "I ought to have someone follow him, find out what he's like. I'll admit, I cannot spare the money; but if she's in danger, I'll have to find a way."

His words caused a swirling, dizzy pit in Jane's stomach. What would it be like to have a man worry about her like that? What would it be like to be the target of that fierce, dark gaze and have someone who would make anything happen if it meant she would be safe?

It would be heavenly, she thought.

But if there were one Bickering sister who deserved that, who *needed* it, it was Anna.

So Jane was glad the Captain's glare was following where her sister had gone. Truly, glad.

"Don't trouble yourself, Captain. You have already been as good a friend to my family as ever there has been."

He allowed himself half a rueful smile. "Kind of you. I've done nothing, and likely I should. Miss Emery clearly loves the bakery, and you and Miss Rose should be able to do as you like." The carelessness with which he tossed out that thought made Jane feel as light as a feather, and as inconsequential. She wasn't worth worrying about. "Miss Anna seems concerned for her reputation still. She may have left society, but it will never leave her. There's no way to save her reputation even if I offered for her myself." His eyes went back to the bakery, over Jane's shoulder. "Do you think I should?"

She'd made a mistake; the pit wasn't in her stomach. It was under her feet, and opening wide; she just hadn't noticed that she'd already fallen in.

The very idea of the Captain offering for Anna's hand made her feel sick, and indescribably sad, and eternally lonely.

But if he did, she would attend their wedding and smile.

"Are you likely to?" was all she could say. She tried to lie and make it sound light.

He shook his head, a sad, slow shake. "My life has no steady moments. Indeed, I must soon leave on a voyage, if I'm lucky, with no guarantee when I return. Or if." This news hit Jane somewhere below the rib cage as well, a different kind of blow, one with ice in it. He went on. "I wouldn't wish a life with me on my worst enemy. But if it could help—"

"Nothing dire has occurred, Captain." Jane made herself smile. "A little display of temper in the street. It will be forgotten tomorrow."

"I don't mean that. What's she doing with that viscount? What does she mean by it?"

"I'm not sure," and now Jane was telling the truth, "but I *do* intend to find out."

AND INDEED, IT WAS EXACTLY WHAT SHE ASKED ANNA when they finally had a moment alone.

Anna was sitting on the floor fanning herself, and Jane made her some of their precious supply of tea.

"Thank you. I do need this," her sister admitted faintly, cradling the cup in both hands. "My stars. What a day."

Rose had shut herself up in her room and would not come out. Jane hoped she brushed her hair till it went straight.

Emery had disappeared somewhere, but that was fine. Jane wanted a moment alone with Anna.

"While the tea is bracing you, then, let me ask. What are you doing with Lord Boislegrand?"

Anna's big brown eyes looked up. "Nothing you haven't seen!"

"I don't mean that. I mean what are you *planning*?"

"I have no plans." But her eyes dropped to her cup.

"You've made a great many plans in recent weeks and shared none of them. I'm on your side, remember. Tell me. What is it you hope of Lord Boislegrand?"

"He offered to take a cake to the Duchess of Talbourne! Isn't that grand?"

"It's lovely." Jane's voice brushed that away. "What about *you*? And *him*?"

The teacup shook a little in Anna's hands. She watched its golden-brown wavelets come and go. "Would it be so bad? If he wished to marry me?"

"No, it wouldn't be bad." Jane bent over and sat facing her sister. "Not if you love him. Do you love him?"

Anna didn't answer that. "But what if he loves *me*, Jane?"

"What if he does?"

Anna spun the teacup now, one way, and then the other. To Jane, the liquid inside it looked the same either way. Anna seemed rapt watching it move. "If he loves me, and offers me a life, would that be so bad?"

"I can think of only two concerns. One, you swore you would be the last person to leave this bakery. Swore it to Emery. And two, do you love him?"

"I *will* be the last person to leave this bakery." Even as Anna stared into a teacup, Jane could see her muscles locking with determination. Her jaw set. "A little money would mean we need bake only bread, just like Emery wishes."

"And you would be back in comfort."

"I would be in comfort for the first time. Not borrowed finery from a grudging relative."

"And you love him?"

Anna met her eyes.

"What if love is something you learn how to do?" she asked.

Jane didn't know how to answer that. She had a suspicion she was learning what love felt like.

And it was awful.

"I don't know. We weren't there when our parents met. I don't know that I've ever seen anyone else in love. But my older sister said we must make this bakery pay so that we needn't marry *except* for love. I do remember her saying that."

"Did she? That's sweet." Anna's grip on the cup loosened a little. "What kind of love, though?"

"What do you mean?"

"Would it be so bad to marry a pleasant man who loves me, if it meant my sisters could have whatever they wanted to eat?"

Jane reached over Anna's lap, and Anna let her take her hand. Their clasped hands held on to each other, tightly, tightly.

"What if he just takes a cake to the Duchess? Wouldn't that be enough?" whispered Jane. Her voice seemed to have gone away somewhere.

Anna laughed, a choked, desperate little laugh. But it was a laugh. "That would be a start, wouldn't it?"

"Perhaps that would be enough."

"Perhaps," said Anna, and didn't let go.

ROSE SAT WITH HER BACK TO THE DOOR AND LISTENED TO her sisters talk.

No one had been more adamant than Anna that they should only marry for love.

She'd been saying it for half Rose's life. She'd said it even when Father died; and when Mother died, it had shaped everything the sisters decided to do.

London was full of ladies marrying for all kinds of reasons, but the Bickering sisters had decided on love because Anna had decided on love.

And if Anna had changed her mind, what were they to do?

There was a cold emptiness inside her where it felt like everything she cared about had been ripped away. How could Mr. Russell have behaved so? In front of everyone they knew!

Rose wasn't mortified; she was *furious*.

He knew perfectly well how she felt about him. Hadn't she thrown caution to the wind to sneak out into the mews and let him kiss her silly? Hadn't she publicly supported him? Hadn't she been proud to walk beside him?

Hadn't he taken her to the meeting that meant the most to him?

Clearly, he couldn't be trusted not to say appalling things. And she had a feeling, deep down inside, that he didn't know her. Oh, he knew perfectly well she had no designs on Lord Boislegrand; he would come to his senses about that once he calmed down. But she had the sinking, sick feeling that he didn't really know her, not down to her bones.

And that was a problem.

Because she suspected she was in love with an idiot.

And Rose didn't know much about marriage, but her limited exposure to it through her parents led her to think that this would be a bad way to start.

JANE THOUGHT ANNA WOULD BE TOO ENERGIZED BY THE tea to rest, but it had the opposite effect. As soon as the cup was empty, Anna nearly staggered to their bedroom and lay down.

Jane just pulled the door gently closed. She herself was too ragged to rest. She wanted some more fresh air.

Her one remaining shawl was light. When the cold

weather came, it would not be enough. They had lost their mother in the spring, and had made do with everything since, losing one little thing after another till they had reached the bottom.

She draped it over her shoulders and went out, quietly closing the door behind her.

The Square was too overgrown to even see into, as well as being behind a locked fence. But if she walked along the pavement she could look over there to where there was green life, a life for the gentry, the people with keys.

All down the eastern side of the square she walked, then around to the south and kept going.

When she passed Mr. Morley's tailor shop and had rounded the entire square, she still wasn't ready to go in.

Instead, she turned, and when she reached Castle Street, she joined the flood of Sunday walkers and gawkers taking the air and enjoying the public bustle.

No one shouted at her, no one whistled. It would have been peaceful, but for the hollowness inside.

If Anna broke, Jane would break.

Jane had always wanted a practical security. Marriage ought to be practical. It meant houses and food and perhaps children; all that should be organized, and she could organize things.

Men wanted other things. To stare at her, or worse. She never understood what was in *their* minds when marriage came up, but it wasn't organization. If they hadn't looked at her with those belittling looks that felt sticky, she'd have wanted to know more.

She only knew one man whose look didn't feel sticky, and who wouldn't be better suited for her sister.

When she spotted him, he was outside a public inn. The kind of place she'd never even been near in her life.

He leaned against the wall, cap pulled down over his eyes.

There were boys playing marbles on the packed-earth drive next to the inn, but he wasn't watching them, either.

She had the feeling he was watching her. That he'd seen her before she'd seen him.

She walked straight up to him, the way a person who went unnoticed by everyone else could be brave.

When she reached him, he pushed up his cap, and she saw his dark eyes looking straight at her.

He wasn't afraid of her, and he wasn't like the other men, either. Not any of them.

His invitation was in his eyes, and he meant it. Not to humiliate her, but out of service to plain, simple truth.

"What's your name?" he said, low, so the marble-boys wouldn't hear.

"Kiss me," she said in the same quiet voice.

"Odd name, but all right," he said without a moment's hesitation, and she liked that so much she could barely stand it.

He led her round the side of the inn, where the carriages would drive into its mews, if there were any carriages.

Behind a chimney, there was a little space into which both of them could tuck.

He didn't hesitate. He didn't swoop, either. His arms braced on either side of her, and Jane liked the feeling he was keeping her hidden, a little safe.

His eyes dipped to her lips, and she opened them. Then his mouth was soft against hers.

Soft, and suddenly hot, tasting, tasted, and everything in Jane pulled together from where she had been scattered. She felt only whole, and the longer he kissed her, the more she wanted more.

He was *good* at this. She didn't know how she knew. But those men who whistled at her in the street wouldn't have kissed like this. He knew nothing about her; but he knew more than every other man.

Her plain truth was that she wanted this.

"What's your name?" he said, letting her go but only an inch away. His breath tickled along her cheek.

"Thank you, I needed that," she murmured back, and laughed, a breathy little sound she'd never made before. Kisses were powerful things.

"Odd name, but if it keeps you talking," and when his mouth came over hers, he let go, his body pressing her into the wall even as his arms stayed locked in place.

"That's not talking," she said, finally, when her lips were free to move without his against them.

"You're not answering," he pointed out.

"Fair enough," she said, and let go her shawl with one hand so she could slide it around his neck and pull him down again.

Eventually, finally, it was him who pulled back. "My name's Hughes, not that you asked."

"Fine," said Jane, and pulled him down for another kiss.

Episode 19: Reaching Decisions

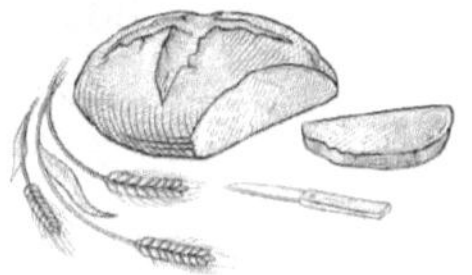

The knock on the door to their rooms startled all of them out of what had been a blessedly routine morning.

"Who could that be?"

"We haven't any appointment!"

"It wouldn't be the fellow in the closet?"

"More likely that stuffed shirt upstairs."

"My hair isn't done!"

"Button the side of this for me, would you?"

"Don't let the toast burn!"

There was more shuffling, exclaiming, and questioning, so much so that by the time they were all ready to open the door, they weren't sure if anyone was still out there.

"Should I check?" Emery, who hadn't fussed at all with her hair or clothes, stood closest.

"Oh, for pity's sake." Jane went and threw the door open.

It was Mr. Russell, his hat in his hand.

"You have gall, sir!" Jane drew herself up to her full height.

"Now, Miss Jane." He sounded contrite, and his eyes were

red-rimmed, and Jane looked as if she could kill him with her bare hands.

Emery went immediately and stood by Jane, and Anna, amazingly, took her other side.

"You aren't welcome." Here was one person Emery could treat as brusquely as she liked.

"Good day, sir." Anna made shoo-ing motions with her hand, and her *good day* was as brusque as she got.

"I'd like to see—"

"If you say *Miss Rose*," and Jane's tone was as poisonously cold as anyone had ever heard her be, "I swear to you your body will wind up in a place no one will ever find it."

The chill settled over the room.

"Well, I mean, Jane," said Anna quietly. "Is it a bit much?"

"I think it is *exactly right*."

"Really, Anna. Make up your mind whether public humiliation matters to you or not," said Emery reasonably, from Jane's other side.

"You're quite right. You're all quite right." The young man juggled his hat for a second, as if trying to think of what else to say, and clearly couldn't. "You're quite right," he said, his face crumpling—a terrible thing to see on a strong young man —and he turned away.

"Stop."

Rose shoved herself between Jane and Anna. Stood in the door facing him.

"What could you possibly have to say," her voice was calm but had a quaver in it, "that you didn't shout at me yesterday in the street, Mr. Russell?"

He looked at the faces of her sisters, all different but the same now in the way they glared at him. His hat changed hands again. "I, uh..." He looked at Emery again. Then back at Rose. Jane was clearly too much. "If we could have a *quiet* moment alone?"

"Oh, you did not just ask—" Jane's hand groped backwards as if looking for a fire iron. Anna grabbed and squeezed it.

"There is *nothing* I wish to hear you say," Rose said, a little quake in her voice but standing up every one of her few inches. "Nothing, therefore, you cannot say in front of my sisters."

He was clearly struggling. Unwilling to walk away, and finding it nearly impossible to stay. All four sisters stood in a line just inside the door, and a more forbidding crew he had never faced in his life.

"Miss Rose." From somewhere deep inside him, he found his core, that of a man who could stand up in public and say what had to be said. "It offends my deepest sensibilities that you and I, who had been in such charity with one another, have such a gulf between us now. I cannot reconcile myself to the idea that my worst moments will be our last moments in conversation."

"Since you caused *my* worst moments, I'm fine with it," Rose said shortly.

"I see." For a broad-shouldered fellow, he collapsed rather small. "My sincerest apologies, then, for yesterday and—everything else. Anything else. I was—at my worst. I don't know what came over me, but it was nothing of the best nature. Nothing of the good nature of any man. We speak in the meeting of being led to what is true and right, and nothing led me to behave that way yesterday except something inside me I never suspected was there."

"True," said Rose, but the quaver was gone from her voice.

"So that's—that's all," he looked round her sisters' faces again. "My deepest apologies to you all. Hopefully, the contemplation and discussion of my meeting will lead me to a better place. A better version of myself. I will only—" here he looked at Rose's shoes, "miss you there."

When his heel scraped against the floor again, as he once more turned to go, Rose stepped forward. "Wait."

He stopped.

All her sisters turned to look at her.

"Since I am the offended party, Mr. Russell, I believe there is still reconciliation needed." Rose tapped a finger against her lip, and her head bent forward as it was when she thought hard. "You had better try harder to explain yourself."

"Oh, *no!*" Anna's shout rang up and down the staircase.

Mr. Russell, Emery, and Jane turned to look at *her*.

"This is enough. Enough! You are dragging us all into affairs we will *not* recover from, Rose. This isn't a society game. That display in the street won't affect just our social standing. It will affect our *livelihood*. No more games! No more flirting with light-skirted behavior! We have to stand downstairs in that bakery and face our customers and none of us deserve to have to explain what you did, not yesterday or any time before."

"Well." Jane shuffled a little at *that*. "A person may take a false step, you know, Anna."

"A false step? Or long strolls at night with an unmarried man? Rose, I know it's hard to put this all aside. I know Mr. Russell's feelings matter to you. I know."

"No, Anna, I don't think you do." Rose was still standing all her tiny inches, straight and tall. "Unless you have bound up many hopes and dreams in the hands of someone else, and he let them fall, I don't think you do understand."

There was a dreadful silence.

"Miss Rose. *Rose*." Mr. Russell sounded shattered. "I am so sorry."

"As you should be. I'm wronged." Rose made it sound very simple and utterly devastating. "What could you do to heal the breach between us? What can you say to make it right?"

"Nothing." His answer was immediate. "I cannot make it

right. It was wrong. I was wrong. I only wish to come to agreement with you again."

"We agree you were wrong," said Rose.

"And that's enough," put in Anna. "You needn't get close enough to hurt her again, Mr. Russell."

And that argument from Anna was strong enough that the sisters closed their ranks again.

"I'm not sure." Oddy, Rose sounded *more* sure, but kept talking. "I think Mr. Russell does need to explain himself. Perhaps I need that as well."

"He doesn't. You don't. End of story." Emery was quite willing to put herself in between the two of them; that was clear.

"*No*, I think we do."

"I'm not having this. Not any of it." Jane put her arms on either side of the door's frame, and leaned into it; Mr. Russell, more than twice her size, backed up. "We don't need any more shouting, because Anna is right. We have to face our customers today. We've all had enough."

"I won't raise my voice." Mr. Russell now gripped the brim of his hat with the determination caused by hope. "I do wish to repair things between us, Miss Rose."

"You can talk," said Rose, stepping back as though to let him in.

"No, he *can't*." Jane didn't move.

"Jane, it's just talk. Believe me." And reaching out to take her sister's arm, Rose found it locked to the door frame. Tugged on the sleeve till Jane had to step back with her a few steps, or let the fabric rip.

Rose leaned up to reach the ear of her taller sister and spoke so quietly no one else could hear.

"Jane," Rose murmured, "I know your refusals hurt, but they didn't *matter*, if you see the distinction. This matters. To me."

There was a long, silent pause while Jane looked at her sister.

"All right." She whirled back to the door and folded her arms over her chest, then pointed an accusatory finger at Mr. Russell. "I am staying *right* here. Anna and Emery should go down and open the bakery; the twins will be here soon. We cannot be late opening. Not today."

Anna leaned closer. "Do you really think we should?"

"Yes." Jane never stopped looking forbiddingly at the interloping gentleman, but her voice was soft. "It's fine. Rose can do anything, you know. If she wants this..." Jane just shrugged.

"If you say so."

"Oh! Lord Boislegrand! You startled me." Anna nearly dropped her tray of bread.

The viscount took it from her, set it on the counter.

That just made Anna look sadly at the counter's pitted surface. "That carpenter will never come back."

"Miss Bickering. I came to see if you were quite well this morning."

The morning, as it were, was gone. They'd sold the first batch of bread, and the second was cooling on the counter.

But Anna knew what he meant. Normally, a titled gentleman wouldn't be out and about before mid-afternoon. He must be concerned.

"I do apologize, Lord Boislegrand, and I quite understand if you no longer wish your—"

"Cake?" He smiled and took both her hands in his.

Anna was so startled she didn't even squeak. It was an unexpected gesture, but not unpleasant. His hands were so much larger than hers.

"Miss Bickering," he said, and his smile was so kind, so gentle. "I asked if *you* were well."

"I'm well enough." Anna knew she mustn't stand in the shop with her hands in his hands, but it was just... peaceful, for a moment.

His smile went all the way to the corners of his eyes, she noticed. Which were brown.

Like hers.

"I don't wish to put you in a compromising position, Miss Bickering; I only wished to say that I hope you've recovered from your upset yesterday and ask if there was anything I could do to help."

The feeling that swept over Anna was indescribable. How many months had she longed for some man, for anyone really, to offer her some help? And now here he was with those kind brown eyes, holding her hands and asking what she needed.

It was such a relief that she completely forgot that he had done absolutely nothing the day before while the tempest had raged on the pavement.

"Thank you, Lord Boislegrand; you have done quite enough. And I appreciate your gift and that you entertained me and all my sisters yesterday. It was so kind of you to take us for a drive and all of us enjoyed it, truly."

"It was my pleasure, Miss Bickering, as it afforded me the pleasure of your company, as well as that of your sisters."

He patted her hands. It was an extremely odd sensation. It had nothing to do with the gropings of young boys who haunted corners when she was dancing her way through society balls. But neither was it fatherly or avuncular. "I like to spend time with you, Miss Bickering," he said, and the very simplicity of his speech made it not just believable, but a compliment. "If there is anything I can do to make your life easier, I hope you will tell me."

"Lord Boislegrand," Anna said, almost overcome with the

sensations flooding through her, all peculiar, all unfamiliar, some of them guilt-inducing. "You don't know what you have already done to help. Suffice it to say that I have not been as good a friend to you as you have been to me. Though I would do it all again and more if it meant that my sisters might have food to eat and a roof over their heads." There. That was as honest as she could possibly be.

If he ran away now, it would only be reasonable. She had as much as said that her reason for spending time with him was financial.

But he didn't run away. He patted her hands once more, and let them drop. But he didn't run screaming. He didn't even leave.

"Miss Bickering," he said, "I am sure to a clever young woman like you, I appear foolish. Perhaps even doddering. But I assure you I am familiar with the ways of the world. I see nothing wrong with a lovely young woman like you building a friendship with a lonely gentleman like me, knowing that it can only benefit both of us. There are things you need, of course, which you know far better than I; perhaps you do not know what *I* need. I need company, Miss Bickering. I need friendship. I am not old, not yet, no matter how it may seem from my hair."

Here he put up a hand self-consciously, and Anna thought it reminded her of herself.

"I have many years left to my life," he went on, "and few ways to fill them. I have never engaged in politics, trade, or any of the things that my compatriots enjoy. At my age, I expect little. But surely I should be allowed some company, if I may be so bold." He paused and seemed to sincerely want encouragement.

"Yes, please, sir, do go on," Anna said, flapping her hands to embolden him.

"I miss my wife, Miss Bickering. She died young and I—

wish she hadn't." Anna made a sympathetic noise, encouraging him to go on. "I have grieved her loss, and it no longer hurts in quite the same way. But I do miss her." His gentle smile had faded. "I'm sad to say that it was she who was closer to my children. She paid attention to their lives, while I paid attention to hers. Perhaps that would have been an excellent bargain had she not had to leave us all so soon. At it is, my children are distant." He had been looking at something far away; now his eyes returned to her. "I am lonely, Miss Bickering. But also honorable. I assure you, I mean no disrespect to you or your sisters. You are an exquisite diamond that London has cast in the gutter."

Anna blinked. "Not exactly a gutter, sir." She waved weakly around the bakery shop.

"Cast away when you should have been held to its very bosom and cherished as the rare jewel that you are," the gentleman insisted. "I know I appear foolish. But one benefit of being no longer in my first youth is that I know what is valuable and what is not. You are a diamond, Miss Bickering, and you deserve to be set in gold. And if I may be so bold, you deserve to be cherished."

Those words pulled at a place underneath Anna's ribs.

The warm ocean of comfort she felt at the idea that he valued her ebbed and pulled sand from under her feet. She rocked a little. She would love to be cherished. But she wasn't yet sure that she could manage being cherished by Lord Boislegrand.

Yet who was she to say that any intention of such a gentle, generous man wasn't appealing?

"Sir, you are extremely kind." She hoped he could see in her face how much she meant it. "You have never been anything but kind to me and my sisters, and I know you will continue to be. I hope you forgive me for not being as sure of my feelings as you are."

"Quite," he said with a truly good-natured grin. "In the meantime—is there nothing I can do to make your life a little easier?"

"Truly, sir. We are doing well. The business has done better than we expected."

That was true in the sense that they weren't yet out on the street. But a few more weeks of baking cakes and they could be. They still had plenty of Mr. McPherson's honey in the cellar, which had cost a great deal. And they were contracted to receive more soon.

While Anna had found a great deal of self-determination in the most recent weeks, she was not yet ready for the shame of breaking a contract with a family neighbor.

"We still wish to reach the Duchess of Talbourne with one of our cakes," she reminded him. "I do hope that if such a gracious sponsor were to make known in London society that she enjoys cakes baked with honey instead of sugar, we might do more business with the gentry near us, as well as perhaps a little farther abroad."

"So you did say!" Lord Boislegrand seemed genuinely animated by the reminder. "My carriage is here; I shall take one of your cakes to Talbourne House today."

"We have been to Talbourne House, sir," Anna warned him, "and the question was not simply one of transporting the cake. There was no guarantee that it would reach her unless we had an audience with her, and no way of gaining that audience."

"Well," said his lordship with the confidence of an aristocratic man, "perhaps the errand will go better for me."

Whether or not his confidence was misplaced, Anna didn't know; but she was definitely willing to let him try. It would cost, at most, one cake; and the benefit could be immeasurable. "Sir, I would be eternally grateful if you wish to wait while I fetch a cake from the back. Perhaps you can return in time to tell us how your errand went today."

"Oh, undoubtedly!"

Anna still couldn't tell if it was his simple enthusiasm, or if he intuitively understood the urgency of the errand.

Either way, he needed a cake.

"THIS IS INTOLERABLE." JANE COULD PRETEND THAT HER muttering pertained only to attempting to darn a stocking for the twelfth time. She leaned her back against the wall and turned her knees toward the window, but no amount of light would create thread where there was none. No one in the room where she felt trapped seemed to be fooled.

But if Mr. Russell was too polite to say so, Rose was not. "If our conversation bores you, feel free to retire," she said in her calm way.

That sounded very grown up, and yet somehow reminded Jane of when Rose had been very little and demanded oranges.

The truth was that Jane had been wondering how she could reasonably withdraw for an hour at least. Their conversation was so tepid and unspecific. And yet neither of them wished to quit the field. Their frank conversation about *pleasant times together* made her itch.

Had this man been kissing her sister? Had he treated her the way her paving man had treated her, pressing her body into the wall and knowing lips against her mouth? The very idea made Jane feel ill. Rose was her baby sister, her very smallest sister in every sense of the word, except maybe regarding the size of her heart. The idea of a man handling her that way was appalling.

But Rose didn't seem to be appalled by Mr. Russell. Only cautious.

"I believe I may go to my room and see if there are other items that need mending," Jane said in a completely transparent attempt to leave. Neither Mr. Russell nor Rose objected.

From the safety of her bedroom, behind the closed door, she sighed.

Mr. Russell and Rose, during a months-long friendship, already had a great deal of history between them. They shared political beliefs and determinations.

Jane couldn't stop feeling guilty about the fellow who had pressed her up against the stone wall in such a delightful way. She had no idea what his convictions were or his politics. She barely remembered his name. She had just wanted to feel something, sure that he could accomplish that. And he had, and she had. But now she felt terribly guilty.

It occurred to her—as she sat on the corner of the bed, reveling in the sensation of having somewhere to sit—that despite her reckless indulgence, she still lacked something that Rose and Mr. Russell perhaps had. Something so hard to find that she couldn't fault their desire to rescue it, if it were possible at all.

THEIR CLOSET NEIGHBOR HAD SNEAKED INSIDE THE BACK door of the bakery.

"Good Lord," Emery swore and jumped as he gently touched her elbow.

"My apologies, miss," he said in his slow voice. "I just wanted to make sure that you and your sisters were all right."

"Yes, why shouldn't we be?" Emery's eyes narrowed. "Is there shouting upstairs? Is Mr. Russell shouting again?" Her look made clear that if that were the case, his help wouldn't be needed but that Mr. Russell would be leaving immediately, possibly by the window.

"No, but there are voices during the day when there usually isn't, and earlier, a carriage outside. Lord Boislegrand spent more time than usual fetching his cake. It seemed there might be trouble."

Emery's shoulders relaxed, but she took in the tension of his fingers and the bridge of his nose. He seemed ready for action based solely on the information gathered from upper windows. "How did you see a carriage in the street?" she wondered. His closet faced the back.

"I go up to the garret to see out," he said simply. "Down the back stairs if must see anything in the mews."

"Does everyone know about that staircase but us?"

"You should know where you are," he said with a seriousness that impressed her more than the simple words.

She knew where she was, but then again, she hadn't known about that staircase, nor had she known about Lord Zachary in the garret. Maybe she only thought she knew where she was.

"I didn't see Lord Boislegrand, but Anna came for a cake and said he was going to try and give it to the Duchess."

"Which duchess?" asked their neighbor, which was odd. As if their unwashed ale-swilling friend spent a lot of time with duchesses and needed to keep them straight.

"The Duchess of Talbourne," Emery said. "We have some hope that she will be our cake's social champion."

"Why do you want a champion for your cake?"

His directness unnerved her. He took the whole affair so seriously, and she was used to people brushing off her needs and her concerns. He had already saved their candlesticks and taken a great interest in their safety.

"Bills, sir, it is always bills," Emery said, trying to make it sound light.

Surely in the man who lived in the closet down the hall was also light in the pocket. Speaking to him of money seemed tasteless.

"I thought you paid your bills with bread." He was even an inch or two shorter than she, but had square shoulders and a muscle-corded neck. That made him look, in the intensity of his interest, powerful. It was disconcerting and persuading at the same time.

"It is a long, long story," Emery said on a sigh, "and I don't even know your name to tell it to you."

"Why would you need to know my name to tell me a story?"

"You ask a lot of questions, don't you?"

"What made you choose the Duchess of Talbourne specifically?"

If he would not answer her questions, she thought she might not answer his. But she wanted to. It was such a relief to have someone besides a sister interested in her problems.

Suddenly she felt a wave of homesickness for the kitchen salon. Why had she not talked more? She might have had friends there, had she spent those precious moments less intent on staring at Jasmine.

She wanted to answer his questions, but... "By nature," she told him, "I don't care for a flood of questions. And I'm not sure if I wish to answer your good will, or because I have no other friend."

He nodded a little, his chin dropping toward his chest. "I do pursue only the moment's critical questions. I could have asked, for instance, why you sneak out now, not to see friends, but for more work."

The chill that stopped Emery's breath was animal, and came from her bones. *He knew.*

The animal fear extended to the children. Where had they gone? At least they weren't here. But he knew them. He knew their faces, probably where they lived. And she knew nothing of him, not really.

"No need to look so. I *am* a friend. I have no ill motives. I only wish to know where I am, so to speak. A habit."

Dinner. That was where the children had gone. They must have taken a loaf of bread to the cellar to devour honey with their bread. They were virtuously restrained about all the honey, and Sal and Jordan deserved all the honey they wanted.

"Miss Emery." He spread his empty hands, hinting that he was harmless. "I am not much of a man, but thanks to you, and your sisters, I have regained a little... self-respect, as Miss Anna called it." The tension was gone from his face; he looked open, honest.

But then he would, if he were trying to trick her...

He seemed to read her thoughts in her tiniest, unavoidable movements. In her breath, and the motion of her eyelashes.

He said, "When one keeps important secrets, especially for a long, long time, there is a danger that one will lose the ability to trust. That silence becomes a habit. Also, I shouldn't have mentioned your evenings. It was only curiosity. Perhaps a selfish one. I have no work and you have nothing but. I wondered at the contrast. Forgive me."

Of course he was interested. He had *told* her to visit the tailor to look for work.

Of course he didn't wish her ill.

And what he said was true.

She was suspicious, that was all, suspicious and tired and... tired.

Emery wondered if fatigue could send her to an early grave. The same determination that made her strong could also kill her. No one could stop her from working more but herself.

Hadn't Lady Arnold said something like that?

"If my sister doesn't mind telling Lord Boislegrand her hopes, I don't know she would mind telling you." Emery put aside any more personal discussion of the kitchen salon. "The Duchess is new to her position, and we heard she was pretty. Charming."

"I like your hopefulness," their neighbor said. "I admire it. It makes you strong."

"Does it?" Emery's voice betrayed her surprise. "I'm not sure that I am strong, apart from my ability to lift things." She looked around at the deep glowing oven, rising pans of dough, and the half-barrels waiting to be washed. Work was also simple. Unlike people, it made sense.

"You have a great deal that makes you strong." Then, without another word, he slipped out the back door.

Emery thought that an awkward goodbye.

"MISS BICKERING, AS I LIVE AND BREATHE!"

The sudden bellow made the windows ring. Anna jumped a mile.

"I'm sorry!" A bundle of skirts and aprons followed the bellow, rushing to the counter, extending both hands in supplication. "I am sorry. Just excited, you know. I get so excited that it's very hard to be calm."

"Tilly?" Anna felt the odd sensation of seeing someone in the wrong place; she looked around for cabbages.

"Now you do remember! I'm that pleased. Kind of you! I doubt half the people I met selling cabbages would remember me, and most of them not by name. At least, not *my* name."

Anna didn't have time to untangle this, as the door

opened again, and Mrs. Mornay came in, followed by Mrs. Baby and her three children.

This was a disastrous combination. Mrs. Baby—Mrs. Wallace—seldom had complete control of her young ones, and Mrs. Mornay was a starched lady with a husband who worked for a ministry of the government and leased an entire house on the west side of the square.

Her hope was to get Mrs. Mornay out the quickest. "Tuppence loaf today, Mrs. Mornay?"

"No," that lady said with a frosty look, a look she then turned on the Wallace child tugging his mother's skirts and asking for toast.

"Toast, Ma. Toast. Toast."

"I wish to inquire about the maslin."

"Toast."

Into this spin of conversation, Tilly inserted herself. "Never you mind, Miss Anna, I'll attend to this lady."

"Tilly, no, I—"

"Never you fear. It's as easy as rolling a cabbage on the ground." She drew near Mrs. Mornay. "Now you tell me what interests you about the maslin. Because I wouldn't want to guess when there are so many possibilities."

Anna, who couldn't think of two things that would interest anyone about the maslin, gave up. Well, there went one of their richest customers.

She went over to the window, where the tallest baby of Mrs. Baby still tugged at his mother's skirt. "Toast, Ma."

Anna bent over and swept him up in her arms. He was always a little grubby, but she could wash her hands afterwards; and maybe a light dusting of flour would hide any marks he made on her apron. "Jimmy, let your mother rest."

"Oh, I'm *sorry*, Miss Bickering." Mrs. Wallace's worn, pretty face seemed more faded every time Anna saw her, as if she were slowly being rubbed off a sheet of paper.

"Never mind it! We're a shop, and glad to make Jimmy's bread." Anna poked said Jimmy in the tummy, and he giggled.

The weight of it all nearly knocked her off her feet. If this shop closed, she would have nothing. But there was also Mrs. Wallace. She would have to walk another quarter hour for bread. And she looked so tired.

It was too much, the responsibility for all of it.

The door scraped open again.

"Now the health of this bread is in how much you need to chew it," Tilly was telling the government minister's wife, when a brawny man wrestled through the door. He had a wooden stool in each hand.

It was Mr. Harding, the long-lost carpenter.

He wasted not a moment on greetings, only walked right to her. "Miss."

He bent to put down both stools, but Anna reached out for one.

It was beautiful. When he'd said he would make it of spare wood, Anna had pictured something rough and uneven. This stool was perfect, smooth as velvet and smelling of beeswax.

Anna set it down. It glowed in the light, the same color as her hair.

"It is perfect, Mr. Harding."

"Good. Can't stay; Lady DeMings has a crisis with her dishtub. I'll be back."

With that he was gone, all muscle and silent hurry.

"Well!" Mrs. Wallace just stared after him, along with Anna.

Tilly and Mrs. Mornay, deep in consideration of health-giving bread, had ignored the whole thing.

"Mine," said little Jimmy, reaching for the stool.

"No it isn't, Jimmy. It's mine."

Anna gestured to it, just as if she had been in a fine

drawing room. The light from Bear Street through the window glass made striped warm shapes on the wood. "Mrs. Wallace. Won't you please sit?"

And once her customer sank gratefully down and rested the two little children in her arms upon her knees, Anna joined her.

She felt part of her own shop for the first time. She could sit, and provide rest for others.

When Tilly sidled over to whisper, "How much is the maslin, anyway?" Anna told her without a qualm.

It wasn't hard for Jane to listen at the door; the people she was listening to could not see her.

"Was I unreasonable to think we had an understanding?" Rose had finally gotten down to the meat of the discussion now that she was free of her sister's presence, and perhaps now that simple time had worn away some of the awkwardness of having Mr. Russell sitting on the floor of their parlor.

"No," he said immediately and warmly, making Jane think a little better of him. She had given up on the stocking as a lost cause, but had moved on to mending a hole in the finger of one of their gloves. Anna couldn't hide gloves any more, and they were all now jointly owned. It was only fair for Jane to fix them; she did seem to get the most tears.

"I trusted you," Rose was saying in her soft steady way, her voice carrying just as clearly as it had in the middle of the hall when speaking about a horrific miscarriage of justice. "I thought you better than other men, and I trusted you with my reputation as well as my heart."

Jane put down the glove.

"I have never had a more important gift," Mr. Russell said, all his feeling in his voice.

"Hadn't you? Because now I feel as though it was all luck, as though you simply came upon a girl wandering into the street, about to be run over by cows, and felt obliged to keep her company because you saved her."

"It was luck, but not like that. I had the luck of meeting a pretty girl with a quick wit taking the air one day, and I have been grateful every day since. I think we were meant to meet."

Jane had always thought the declarations of love would be flowery and profuse and perhaps make a mess all over the floor, like flower petals did. But these words were simple. It was just that they were so terribly important.

"I trusted you so completely that all of my trust was yours. And when you destroyed it yesterday... I think you've used it all up."

Again, Rose was simply stating the truth. All the more devastating because she refused to whine or berate.

"Perhaps," said Mr. Russell, "my job is to have so much trust that you can borrow some of me. Or simply take what you need without needing to give it back."

Jane's heart went out to him. This man wasn't good enough for Rose, but he was making such an effort. He understood how truly wonderful Rose was.

She would always be on her sister's side, but she was no longer entirely against Mr. Russell.

Puffy had never been inside Talbourne House before. But its grandeur didn't intimidate him; the absence of its owners did.

The butler looked at him with a sort of pity.

"His Grace is engaged, as is Her Grace, I am sorry to say; would the gentleman care to leave either a message?"

Puffy had the sick sensation that the Duke and Duchess would heed a message from him shortly after hell froze over.

Talbourne spent his time on politics, which Puffy cared nothing about, and so their paths seldom crossed. But Puffy did occasionally go to the House of Lords, and voted how his friends told him to vote. He'd seen Talbourne from a distance, had thought it wouldn't be so difficult to see him up close. Certainly not in the gentleman's own house.

"I don't suppose you can tell him I'm here." As soon as the words were out of his mouth, Puffy knew he ought to have made it more of an order than a request.

But the butler had the sort of air that permitted one and not the other. "I certainly will, sir. I inform you only for your convenience that I do believe he is unavoidably occupied elsewhere."

Puffy had heard that there was a broad reception hall frequently full of gaming tables just past the sweeping Talbourne staircase. He could probably find his way there. But at this time of day, in the middle of the afternoon, he suspected the only people there would be drunkards and dangerously good card players. Nor did he want them to eat the cake.

"This gift is for the Duchess," he tried again. "You do understand that I must ensure it reaches her. Personally."

"I understand that is your goal, sir," said the butler with the sort of bureaucratic ability to slice words that Puffy despised.

"If I leave it with you, can I be sure that Her Grace will eat it?"

The fellow looked sadly at the cake on a plate in Puffy's hands. Perhaps he grasped Puffy's doggedness, or perhaps he felt he simply needed to explain the world slowly to him. "The Duke and Duchess of Talbourne have already enjoyed their dinner. Regarding supper, the courses on the table are determined by the *chef*, in consultation with the housekeeper, according to wishes expressed by Her Grace. They may or may not permit of the addition of another course. And in addition, as I'm sure you know, Her Grace may or may not eat of any particular course on the table."

Puffy was willing to go a long way to do what Miss Bickering wanted. Indeed, he would, in his own mind, do absolutely anything for her. It was simply that *absolutely anything* didn't include anything as aggressive and socially damaging as barging in to supper at a duke's table.

"I'm trusting you, sir," he said with a sort of honest look into the eyes that sometimes worked on other people and sometimes did not, "to please place this on the table and, if at all possible, tell Her Grace that Lord Boislegrand enjoins her to try it."

"Sir, I can assure you that I will do my very best," said the butler, relieving him of the plate and leaving Puffy with no great confidence that his mission had been achieved.

"I'M JUST RUNNING DOWN TO MAKE SURE THAT ANNA IS well at the counter," said Jane, taking advantage of a moment of quiet in the conversation between Mr. Russell and Rose to slip out.

It was unbearable sitting and listening to two such earnest people with such deep feelings, expressing things to each other that they very much needed to say. Jane, who had never had any such feelings, nor anyone to tell them to, felt more and more as if she were watching, or at least listening to, something that was nearly indecent.

She found Anna elbow-deep in customers in the post-dinner hurry and realized she'd forgotten to eat.

And Tilly, cabbage-tossing Tilly, was helping.

"What are you doing down here?" Anna hissed, backing Rose out the door to the stairs again. "Is Rose all right?"

"Rose is made of iron," Jane said quite honestly, "and still holding her own with Mr. Russell, whom I fear may crumble at any second."

"You can't mean he's still up there."

"Oh, he's still up there," Jane assured her.

"What on earth do they have to talk about?"

Jane wasn't about to repeat any of the things that she had heard. "Many things," was all she said, even though Anna gave her a sharp look for her reticence. "Is that Tilly selling bread? Do you need my help?"

"Yes! Do help. Miss Weatherby is on the verge of buying some maslin; I don't know whether to celebrate or cry."

"Did you eat any dinner? Perhaps you should see Emery in back. Rest. I can cut bread for Miss Weatherby." Their first and haughtiest customer was never Jane's favorite; the maid was busy judging tuppence loaves with her eyes. But Jane could wait on her or anyone now without a qualm; she no longer expected them to treat her as a person.

"I can't rest." Anna shook her hands, as if shaking off the possibility. "Lord Boislegrand said he would take one of our cakes to Talbourne House, and I am on complete pins and needles until he returns with news."

"You mean he's already gone?"

"Yes, yes, he took a cake and went, just like that. He can be a man of action, you know."

Jane had a deep suspicion that it was less that Lord Boislegrand was a man of action, and more that Anna had simply placed the cake in his hands and made any other course of action unlikely. "Does he know them? Do you think it will reach them? Astonishing! I wasn't expecting this."

"He said he would. What were you expecting?"

Jane avoided Anna's question. "Is that Mrs. Baby? Surely

she's not ready for another quartern loaf already. And is she on a chair?"

A customer beckoned Anna away. Jane went to the window.

Mrs. Baby—Mrs. Wallace—patted the little one who was clinging to her calf. It was an amazing feat given the two smaller children in her arms, one on each knee.

"I would just love a little company," she said.

Opposite her was an empty stool. For sitting. In their shop.

Something had changed. Something good had happened.

Jane wanted to interrogate Anna about this miracle, but she felt so tender inside from listening to the lovers conversation upstairs—for lovers she now knew they definitely were—that she felt a little blossom of hope in that sore and tired place inside her. A little blossom of hope she hadn't felt during her paving-man's kiss.

"HOW LONG HAVE WE BEEN HERE? YOU MUST BE TIRED." Rose shifted a little. The floor was hard and uncomfortable. She would have ushered him out long since, except that something in her told her she wasn't finished with him yet, not yet.

The longer they sat together, the more Rose realized it did not embarrass her to tell him anything. About their bare little rooms, about how much she missed her mother, about her appalling Aunt Eden. All that remained was to twist the threads of the past together and spin out a possible future.

So why hadn't she?

In their little silence, Mr. Russell voiced the same realization. "We haven't spoken of marriage at all."

The fluttering sensation in Rose's chest made it hard to

breathe. "It would be unseemly for me to mention such a thing, especially after yesterday."

"Unseemly? Or unwanted? As I have been reluctant to speak of it unless you wish to hear it."

That made Rose huff, a half-strangled chuckle. "Someone must speak of it first!"

The truth of this seemed to pierce Mr. Russell's silence. "I want to marry you, Rose."

It was like falling into a rushing river. All the feelings threatened to drown her, and they were all different. She knew more about herself—and less about him. "What crashing confusion!"

"Is it?" If she sounded hesitant, he sounded as certain as mountains. "I think it very simple. I love you."

That was all crashing confusion in a *different* way. Rose wanted to insist they talk about those two things separately, but it was hard, because he'd said he *loved* her, and that made her feel like a banked ember two stories tall. She felt huge, like she could step on the house, and hot, and perhaps could burn down half of London.

But Mr. Russell's words poured out as though they'd been a long time apart and had just come back together.

"I love everything about you. Your beauty, your kisses, but most of all, your *opinions*. When you aren't with me, I feel half gone. Hollow. Bereft. I never dreamed I'd find a woman like you. I never dreamed there *were* women like you."

In all her imaginings, Rose hadn't imagined quite this. It was giddying... and sobering.

For she wasn't sure she felt like *that*. He wasn't her missing half; he was simply her lovely Mr. Russell.

It would be rude—no, it would be painful for her to ask him if he thought they might suit each other even if they were in different kinds of love.

But if she couldn't ask him, whom could she ask?

"You needn't answer," Mr. Russell said, even though she could hear him longing for her answer. "I know trust takes time to build; how much longer must it take to rebuild? I began yesterday's fight like a child, and did not end it. Poor of me. I was... jealous, and so... ashamed. I was ashamed that I could not take you riding in a fine carriage, and that another man had, and that you didn't mind that all the world saw. I felt like you were showing the world my shortcomings."

"But I wasn't. I was just riding in a carriage," Rose said in her most reasonable way. "No one would have thought a thing of it had you not made such a fuss."

"They would have. Some would." Mr. Russell's tone was grim.

Rose nodded, tapping her lower lip thoughtfully. "When it comes to *our* hearts, surely what matters is what *we* think."

"You are right." Shifting across the space between them to press his arm against hers, Mr. Russell murmured very close by, "You're very right. Sadly, my chosen profession does depend on what others think. Your opinion, however, is first with me. So what do *you* think?"

"I think you're very dear. So dear that I must have more time to think. For what a *horror* yesterday was. We cannot become trapped in *that*."

"I see." He paused.

She willed him, hard, to say something that still made her feel better about yesterday. For what had mainly upset her was that he had been so foolish. How could she consider marrying a man, even if she loved him, who showed such evidence of an empty head?

But he didn't say something that made her feel better; he said something that made her feel worse. "Do you think our hearts will agree? For I'll admit, Rose, after yesterday I may not win my seat. And if I have no public life here, I don't know how I'll serve. I may have to return home. And I cannot imagine asking you to leave your sisters; yet, selfishly, I would."

That wasn't a flood; that was a yawning chasm of an idea. "I can barely fathom it. Give me a little more time, please."

But Rose's hand reached over and found his, and they held each other's hand, and it was soothing at least that she knew they both would rather be in each other's arms, and both willing to wait till they resolved more of their vast, desire-eclipsing questions.

"THAT WAS FUN!" TILLY SHOOK FLOUR OFF HER APRON AND settled herself. "I'll be back tomorrow."

"Oh no, Tilly, you needn't." Anna had slumped on to one stool as if it were the largest easy chair. The delight of sitting did not erase her trepidation at the idea of Tilly coming back.

"Of course I do. I wouldn't expect you to pay me if I'm not *here*."

"Uh... why would I pay you?" A twanging little worry crawled up Anna's spine.

"That's what work means." Tilly answered slowly, as if it were Anna unable to keep up; Anna feared she was right. "I do work, and you pay me."

"I haven't offered you a position!"

"No need to embarrass yourself, miss, I can see you need my help. I like to work, and I tend to take what presents itself. How do you think I wound up selling cabbages?"

Anna didn't like to wonder. "Tilly, work is a serious business."

She intended to say more, but Tilly just threw up her hands. "So I'm always saying to my cousin! She has five children now, and she doesn't see the seriousness of anything else."

"Five children is serious enough for anyone."

"I'll tell her you said so. Tomorrow, then!"

And with that, Tilly was out the door, leaving Anna to decide how to give her the news that she was not employed.

Before she could spend any more time worrying about that, Emery emerged from the bakery proper. "Let's go up."

"He's not still up there; he can't be," Jane insisted.

And indeed he wasn't. When her three sisters arrived, Rose had chopped and cooked cabbage and potatoes. Their supper was waiting.

"Mr. Russell has gone?"

"Of course. You didn't expect him to *still* be here."

Anna wanted to launch a barrage of questions—*when did he leave? What did you two talk about for so long? What are we to say to him?*—but Rose looked peaceful, and Anna didn't wish to take that away.

Jane and Emery must have seen the same thing, because they didn't ask either. Emery just said, "I'm glad he's gone," and began to scoop dinner into a ridiculously large wooden bowl from the bakery. With one thing and another, they were down to two plates.

Rose might have answered, but outside their rooms they heard thundering footsteps on the stairs, and someone crashing open their neighbor's little door.

"*Hey!*" their neighbor yelled, and they heard Tilly say "Sorry."

Before they could move, Tilly had performed the same office again, thrusting open their door.

None of the sisters yelled "Hey!" They just looked at Tilly in their various poses, about to help themselves to the hot supper.

Tilly's big eyes took in the bare rooms with no furniture but a crate and a stove, and Emery and Jane holding massive wooden baking bowls to eat from, but she said nothing of them. "I didn't ask what time you want me in the morning."

Anna felt exposed in a fragile moment, and couldn't bring herself to say that she *didn't* want Tilly in the morning. "Come at seven, if you like, and we'll see if there's work," she said instead.

"There's always work somewhere. Say, does this house just keep going up?"

"Yes, I—"

But Tilly was off. The empty floor above them might have discouraged her, but no. They heard her heavy shoes pounding in the hall above, and the rattle of a locked door, before she *kept going*. Far above, they heard her pounding up the stairs to the garret, and distantly heard Lord Zachary yell, "*Hey!*"

"Did I mention that Tilly has come to London?" Anna sighed.

JANE'S LITTLE BLOSSOM OF HOPE STAYED WITH HER through the evening, up till the moment there came a knock on their door.

Lord Boislegrand stood there, his hat in his hand, and Anna didn't have to ask him anything. No one did. The look on his face said everything.

Anna just went to him and gave him a little curtsey. "Never mind, Lord Boislegrand," she said, as if nothing were wrong, even though she was clearly fighting back tears. "It means so much to us that you tried."

That spurred all the sisters into action, and they crowded the door.

"Oh yes, we do care so much that you tried!"

"It was very kind of you. So kind."

"Don't look sad, sir, truly, don't."

"I am sure that with each try, we get closer," said Anna, and everyone ignored how patently false that was.

"You must come in! We have—" Jane couldn't bring herself to say *cake*.

"No no, I've troubled you ladies enough today. It's home for me, and a sherry. You must—" Lord Boislegrand looked about, noticing the bare room. "I say. Are you sure you wouldn't all like to come with me?"

The laughter was forced but with a genuine edge, and all the sisters assured him they were fine just as they were.

Even Anna, when Jane thought she didn't mean it at all.

"Do go to sleep, Jane."

"Did you see that I mended the nice gloves? How do you think it looks?" Jane was clinging to wakefulness.

All Anna wanted was quiet for ten minutes to herself. Rose and Emery had gone to bed; why wouldn't Jane?

"It looks fine," Anna assured her.

"But you didn't—"

Without staying to point out that Anna hadn't even looked at the glove in Jane's hand, Jane finally retreated to her room.

Sighing, Anna turned in place, looking at the bare little room in which they'd washed and eaten and talked and planned for so many months. The room that had even given Tilly pause.

Hope *hurt*.

As quietly as she could, she slid out their door and pulled it shut behind her. The hallway gave her at least the illusion of being alone.

And quietly she sank into the farthest corner, beyond the

stairs that led up, wrapping her arms around her knees and leaning her forehead against them so she could cry out her feelings in peace.

LORD BOISLEGRAND'S AUDIBLE VISIT HAD NOT MOTIVATED their neighbor to cork his cask of ale. Rather, he'd taken another pull.

He had been too obvious with Miss Emery today. He wasn't fit company for their like. The young ladies suffered his near presence, but what choice did they have? It wasn't as though they wished for his friendship.

They had made it impossible for him to quietly drink himself to death, or whatever he had been doing here for so long he forgot all calendars. But that didn't mean they wanted his meddling.

Especially meddling that posed, for him, a danger.

The sound of muffled tears, however, finally decided him.

A small traveling trunk stood against the wall; he hadn't touched it since the day he'd arrived. From it, he pulled a short quill and a tightly sealed pot of ink. A few strokes of the pen-knife and his equipment was ready.

Scraps of cut paper from past notes also lay crumpled in the trunk; he snatched one up, smoothed it, and began to compose.

There is a cake on your table. A gift. For the sake of the past and the young ladies who sent it, I ask you the great favor of tasting that cake; and to ask your lady wife, whom I'm sure is rare and lovely, to taste it as well. It comes to you from

Here he stopped. It was too revealing to put the location. But then again, the Duke wouldn't suspect that he was literally in a room upstairs from the bakery. And since the Duke would never visit such a place, he would never find out.

The Ladies' Own Bakery at number seventeen in Leicester Square. With the entirely self-interested purpose, he went on writing, *of gaining them more customers. Should your lady enjoy it, and only if she enjoys it, you might wish to let the proprietors know.*

He folded the note with some trepidation. He'd had every intention of delivering it himself when he'd started writing. But now he realized that that, too, exposed more than he could bear.

Entrusting the note to someone else, however, went against every inch of his person.

Perhaps if he simply engaged a messenger and watched them to ensure the note was delivered. It would be sufficient. He would not see the Duke, nor would the Duke see him, he thought, engaging those parts of his mind he'd been drowning in alcohol since his return from the war.

What if he went himself to the Duke's palace and found a passer-by to give the note? There was nothing safer than an unaware courier.

NICHOLAS HAYDEN, DUKE OF TALBOURNE, HAD BEEN studying a treatise on chess for several days, based on the arrangement of the board in front of him. It had done nothing to improve his game. "Are you a natural player, my lady," he asked his wife curiously, "or did you study in order to sharpen this skill?"

She smiled that flirtatious smile he loved so well and leaned closer. "I believe I am naturally a good player, I must admit, but my father read me books on chess when I was young. I've also practiced often in my mind. Remembering a good game fortified me when I desperately wanted entertainment."

"I find it encouraging," he said. "It gives me hope I may yet improve as well."

A footman knocked, paused, then entered to announce "Lord Thomas Hayden," with all appropriate pomp for a visiting gentleman, even one only a few feet tall.

"Lord Thomas," his father greeted him just as gravely. "Is Lord Fettanby joining us this evening?"

Lord Thomas, whose older brother had just deemed him old enough to reliably convey messages, puffed up his chest with importance. "No. Lord Fettanby has decided to dine elsewhere this evening."

"Dine elsewhere this evening!" said the Duchess. "Well, that has an important ring to it while conveying nothing, doesn't it?"

Nicholas chuckled as another footman arrived with a silver tray holding a small folded letter and a letter opener.

Laughing was a skill that he had not practiced much in his life, but his wife was making it easier every day. He was determined to improve that skill as well. "I believe that Lord Fettanby may be slightly smitten with a young lady, and does not wish us to know, Selene. As then, he would be required to tell us much more than he is prepared to say."

He took the letter and the opener, with a nod; both footmen retired.

The Duchess, who took her duties as second mother to his children very seriously, dropped her smile. "If he isn't prepared to say, then he shouldn't be paying such a marked attention to the young lady, should he?"

"That is very true," said the Duke implacably, "and yet, as you have discovered, it is not easy to make my older son do things I think he should do."

Lord Thomas went and leaned against his new mother. "Who cares what he does?" he said with the simplicity of a fellow whose cares were only immediate. "Soon we shall all be in Scotland for a good long holiday, and I am going to show Atlas where are the best places to run near the lake."

"Atlas is very fond of water," Selene told him in all seriousness, "and you must give her a good example of when to be restrained."

"I'm not the best on when to be restrained," said his tiny lordship.

To which the Duchess replied, "But you're making progress."

Thomas watched his father scan the contents of the letter in his hand. "Is it bad, sir? You look unhappy."

That unfailingly drew Selene's attention as well. Nothing that made her husband unhappy could be ignored.

"I'm quite well," he assured them both, folding the paper and sliding it into his coat pocket. "Nothing of major import."

"Lord Thomas," Selene said immediately, "Since you have mentioned your father's dog, I must ask about her. Have you left her outside?"

"She didn't want to come in," Thomas said, with his tendency to justify himself.

"And yet it is very warm out, and late, so perhaps you had better see to her."

Nicholas had planned to use their time alone this evening to ask his wife some pointed and important questions about whether Thomas should have the chance to be a big brother in his own right. But that discussion would have to wait. He knew his lady had questions for him; indeed, once the child was gone, she did.

"Tell me about the letter, Nicholas. Is it about an upcoming vote?"

"Nothing so dire, madame. It appears some young ladies in the city have sent you a cake, and I am entreated to ensure that you taste it."

At that, his duchess rose and, fingers trailing around the side of the small gaming table, wound up balanced on one of his knees. She was extremely good at that. And Nicholas liked to think that he was fairly good at that as well.

"Must I be persuasive to get further information from you?" she said with her lips close to his ear. "Or perhaps you're willing to play a game with me? The winner gets to tell the truth."

"No games, madame," he said, but enjoyed the way his breath against the side of her throat made her shiver a little. "It truly is only that; nothing to worry about. Nothing more momentous than cake."

"Apparently, this cake is of great import to someone," said Selene. She was far more clever than most of the politicians in London; she was not about to think anyone bothered to send a letter about unimportant cake. But she was willing to take it upon faith for the moment, for the sake of her love for him, and he loved that. "Must I eat it all? Lady Viola and Virginia must have a taste. And Thomas, of course."

"I think," said Nicholas, settling his arms about his wife, "that you would have far more trouble preventing Thomas from eating the cake than you would have convincing him."

"But he doesn't mean the cake is upon the table at this moment, surely? We've eaten, Nicholas. The table is surely cleared."

"Let me send and see if there is any cake remaining."

"I'm not moving."

Nicholas was familiar with this game, but he had a strategy for it.

He stood, lifting her with him, then in two strides was at the door. "Shall I put you down or let the footman see you like this?"

"Put me down. Ruffian."

Trying to hide the smile that could destroy his London

reputation, Nicholas put her down and opened the door. To the footman he said, "George, see if there is any cake left over from supper. A gift was sent."

"Of course, sir."

When he closed the door, there was his pretty duchess behind it.

"Shall we return to our seat?"

"You're getting quite good at teasing, Nicholas. I think I hate it. He will return directly."

"Yes." His eyes roamed the edges of her new sarcenet gown; he intended to help her out of it. But the cake question nagged at him. The note was written by a hand he did not ignore. "The real problem is what to do about it if the cake is gone. And I suspect the cake is gone."

"Ah. As I said. Important cake. Well, we shall have to address it."

The *we* wasn't just in her words, in was in the tone of her voice, and the way she moved closer to him even as they both waited impatiently for the footman to return and be gone. "Thank you," he said as her arm came around his waist.

"I haven't done anything yet," she said with a smile.

"But I know you. You will."

Episode 20: Leicester Square Comes
to a Halt

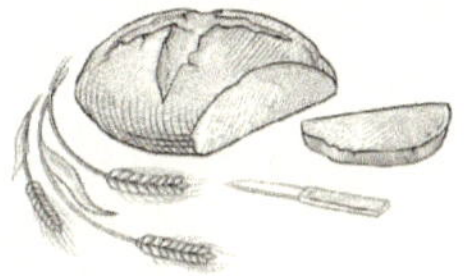

L eicester Square had many sounds to it. There were carts full of goods to sell, vegetable wagons, herds of sheep for slaughter, cows ambling towards parks to be milked. There were horses pulling little phaetons, heavy broughams, rattling hackney cabs, and people. There were all sorts of people, doing everything from running hard to standing and spitting.

The rushing, rambling, murmuring call of it all made a river of sound that ebbed and flowed in a way that the Bickering sisters had come to find familiar.

This morning, Leicester Square went silent.

In the growing silence, a town coach rolled to a stop before the Ladies' Own Bakery, just tipping the corner with Bear Street. It was highly sprung, so sprung that it bounced as four footmen climbed out and leaped to attend the coach behind.

The one behind was vast and even more handsome, covered with curlicues made of gilt and lacquer.

"It's not Aunt Eden again, is it?" Anna called to Jane at the window.

"No, she said she wouldn't come."

"What do you—"

Anna meant to ask more, but her questions and her feet stopped by Jane at the window.

The footmen placed a subtle carpet on the pavement. Then a carved oak step.

The coach door opened just as a third coach rolled up behind, but the sisters' eyes fixed on that little carpet.

The gentleman who stepped out was imposing, with a broad build and strong hands that belied a need for his silver-topped cane. In a plain dark coat and fawn breeches, he dressed like every other fine gentleman in London; but the tassels on the front of his boots had silver caps, and the hair at his temples under his stovepipe hat was silver as well. He looked like a man who would not be easily moved.

He reached back into the carriage and handed out a lady exquisite in every detail. The pale pink of her summer-silk skirts floated over embroidered slippers; her husband murmured to her, perhaps guiding her to the step, then on to the carpet. She nodded, a half-smile playing about her lips, making the Bickerings wonder what amused her so. Her gown was clearly cool for the hot summer day, cut so low it was almost daring; but a *fichu* of lace like transparent snowflakes draped over her shoulders, gathered and pinned at the front with a ruby buckle. The matching buckle was clasped in the mass of her tawny hair.

"They cannot be coming here," breathed Anna, as the gentleman's eyes scanned not only the front of the Ladies' Own Bakery, but the corner and all the pavement.

"No, of course not." Jane looked transfixed by the magnificent sight.

The footmen hadn't finished yet; from the third carriage, though it received only the step, climbed another footman. He helped out two beautiful dark ladies, one in a blue gown paler than the sky, the other in a sunny primrose yellow. Both had dark eyes and hair, but no other resemblance: the blue-gowned lady was pale, with a look that was at best grim, while the other had a deep brown complexion and a merry smile under her froth of gathered curls.

They were followed by a broad wall of a man with a scarred chin whose eyes went everywhere and expected the worst.

The ladies clustered on the carpet, laughing together, while the silver-tipped gentleman and one footman approached *their bakery*.

It wasn't possible. Anna thought her heart might stop. That was surely a duke scraping open their door.

The footman spoke first. "His Grace, the Duke of Talbourne."

"Ladies." He stopped just inside, sweeping off his hat and giving them both a small but flawless bow. "We hope you will forgive a visit without warning."

Perhaps he gave a signal, or perhaps it was by arrangement, but the footman strode straight through the bakery to the far doors. "Cellar," said the footman after opening and closing that door, then he went on to the bakery proper.

Anna heard Emery squeak.

Since even the footman was quite a sight, in his faultless white stockings and cut-front coat, the squeak seemed understandable.

The footman returned forthwith, followed by Emery and Rose drying their hands on their aprons, Sal, and Jordan.

When Tilly hadn't come that morning as expected, Anna had been peeved. Now she was deliriously grateful.

"There's one door more, leading to the mews," the footman reported to His Grace, who hadn't moved.

"Thank you, Jonathan. Stay at that rear door, would you?

I'll take a look at the cellar. And this?" He pointed the head of his cane at the closed door behind him.

"Goes…to the residences upstairs." Anna couldn't believe that had just come out of her mouth. "Your Grace. Please excuse me."

"For having a door? Not at all." He smiled a little, almost to himself, and went down to their cellar.

Anna wanted Jane's reassurance—had she said something wrong?—but all those coaches and all those people were still outside, and there was a duke in the cellar.

Who reappeared in moments, then out their scraping front door.

The door scraped one last time, and the Duke returned with the Duchess on his arm.

"Now this is charming," said the lady. "What a *heavenly* smell. Ladies, please forgive our abrupt call. I decided to do some shopping, and I'm afraid all this accompanies every such impulse. His Grace is very cautious. Please, let us meet."

"Her Grace, the Duchess of Talbourne. My apologies, ladies," said the Duke in his gravelly voice, "I did not ask your names. Perhaps you will do Her Grace the honor of introducing yourselves?"

The Duchess' companions entered, with a gasp of excitement from the one in yellow. "So novel!" she said. "And it smells so *delicious*. I thought I wasn't hungry at all, but I am quite wrong!"

"Miss Díaz. We also should introduce ourselves," said her friend, by way of quelling her. Which was impossible; Miss Díaz floated into every corner of the bakery.

The Duke, with a flick of his finger, set the wall-shaped man at the door to the residences above.

The rest of the footmen ranged themselves outside. They must have blocked the road; no other carriages rolled by.

Dimly, Anna heard the voices of pedestrians passing the

train of incredible carriages, the carpeted pavement, the rank of footmen, and wondering what on earth was happening at the Ladies' Own Bakery.

Well, so was Anna.

"Y—Your Grace." Training took over and Anna executed a deep, deep curtsey. "We are delighted to welcome you. I am Miss Anna Bickering, and if you please, these are my sisters. Jane, Emery, and Rose—and Sally and Jordan Collier, our apprentices."

"How delightful!"

"Ladies." The Duke still had his wife's hand tucked firmly into the crook of his elbow, and something about it made Anna's stomach flutter too. "We are delighted to meet you. We have brought my wife's two maids-in-waiting as well; Lady Viola Evelyn, and Miss Virginia Díaz de la Peña."

"Great friends," the Duchess corrected him.

"We are very honored." Anna's mind could not make sense of all this, and for once she was grateful for Aunt Eden drilling her in meaningless phrases; they came to mind just when they should.

Did one ask a duchess why she'd come in?

Aha. This was a shop, *not* a drawing room. And it had its own set dialogues, its own phrases.

"May I serve you, Your Grace? Or Lady Viola? Miss Díaz?"

"Yes!" Miss Díaz of the fluttering yellow gown seemed to mean her hunger. "We shall purchase one of those, and one of those—" She pointed to one of the massive half-peck loaves, and a smaller quartern of the maslin. "And is this the famous cake?"

"Is it famous?" Now that her heart was beating again, Anna noticed that some of those pedestrians she could hear outside were pressing their noses to the Bear Street windows. "I mean—you honor us by saying so. We do believe it is the only cake sold in London made with honey."

"I am curious to taste it." The serious-looking lady in blue, Lady Viola, peered at the counter, where rested both a *galette des Rois* and a *gâteau Breton*, on the Bickering sisters' last two plates.

Miss Díaz didn't hesitate. "There are two kinds! We must try both, and decide what to take."

Panic grabbed Anna by the throat. They ought to have porcelain plates and silver forks to serve pastry to a duke and duchess.

Again, she calmed. They didn't have porcelain plates or silver forks. Anna had learned to let go of what should have been. "Let me cut you a morsel, Miss Díaz."

"We must all try it!" the lady insisted.

So Anna used the bread knife to cut both cakes into bite-sized portions, just as she had when they'd originally introduced the cakes to Leicester Square.

This time, though, she did not ration the portions.

She'd never seen clothes so dainty outside a ballroom. But her season had taught her that if nothing else, society ladies had plenty of clothes; what they wanted was amusement. This was an adventure for them, no matter why they had come, and it was up to Anna to make it cheery and delightful.

Anna had never been a hostess before, but she had seen it done.

"In a bakery, one must dine without plates!" The nods and smiles from the ladies encouraged her. "Let me serve you. Taste as often as you like."

And as Jane dashed toward the back, returning with a bowl of clean water and snowy linens with which to wash their hands, Anna passed the plate among them, letting them all take cut pieces with their fingertips.

"We are flying in the face of tradition by serving the *galette des Rois* in summer," she told them, watching the ladies' faces. Each one wore its own version of surprise, delight, and surrender to the flaky pastry. "It is for the feast of the Epiphany! Though during the Revolution it became the *galette de l'Égalité*. We do not make the distinction. The prescription for this cake I learned from my mother. We make it from pure butter and our lightest flour, and sweeten the almond cream with a touch of honey. What do you think?"

The Duchess led the way in agreeing moans of ecstasy, and Anna was glad the cakes were fresh.

"Let me cut you the *gâteau Breton!*" Feeling drunk on the pleasure of having a dream come true, Anna sliced the *gâteau* into larger pieces. "This is also an experience of rich butter, with a touch of apricots. We hope to make our own apricot jam this autumn, also with honey. These are stewed very simply on our stove, apricots alone, and they keep their fresh taste."

"Oh!" The Duchess covered her mouth, unable to keep the exclamation inside while the buttery apricot tart spread on her tongue. "So luscious! It is summer in a cake. And why honey, Miss Bickering?"

All four sisters drew closer together, and the air was thick with portent. Anna knew Rose was right behind her.

She turned and drew her sister forward.

"Our mother was part of the Sugar Boycotts, Your Grace, and impressed upon us the role of sugar in slavery," Anna said, her hand sliding down to catch her sister's. "My sister Rose has led us all to support her cause, as a generation later, it is still pressing. And what is sweeter than British honey?"

And little Rose spoke up, squeezing Anna's hand back. "Pleasure should be without guilt, Your Grace, and so are our cakes."

That made the Duchess' eyebrows go up. Her eyes were a soft brown and touched by her smile.

"I'm delighted to hear it," she said, delicately brushing a

cake crumb from her lips. "Britain is what *we* make of her, in what we do about what we believe, every day. Yet we worship sugar so much, fashionable tables are decorated with sculptures made of it! My husband has never liked the fashion; we have plaster ones. Not that they make any difference to me." She smiled.

Rose piped up again. "I am also blind, and wonder if we might need more decorative art to our cakes than we have. I, of course, judge by their taste."

"It needn't be prettier when it is so delectable. I could dine on nothing but this cake." It was clearly the cake itself that had captured Miss Díaz' attention. "I find myself only more hungry. Shouldn't we slice some of this bread? A ladies' bakery must have some butter in it."

Far from the days of their threadbare opening, when the Captain had asked for butter, Anna was now delighted that their cool cellar held plenty, awaiting its fate in further cakes. "Absolutely, madame. It's just in the cellar."

"A cellar?" the Duchess said quickly, "perfect. Miss Rose, will you show it to me? I would like to fetch the butter myself."

The idea of the Duchess fetching butter in her silk and jewels was patently absurd, but no one laughed.

Unwilling to let the moment be awkward, Rose stepped forward. "I would be happy to show you the basement, Your Grace. If you will come with me."

They met in the middle of the room, Rose's arm extended and the Duke somewhat unwillingly transferring his wife's hand to Rose's arm.

"Sally, go with them," whispered Anna, waving her toward where Rose slowly led the Duchess toward their basement door. She couldn't bear the idea of a duchess carrying butter.

"How many cakes have you, Miss Bickering? As we have destroyed these," and Miss Díaz laughed as she pointed to the sampled cakes. "We must have a few more to take home. And Mr. Lyall, shouldn't the footmen taste as well?"

Mr. Lyall exchanged a glance with the silent Duke, then they traded places. The huge man took up one devasted plate of cake and carried it out the door.

"This is beautiful." Lady Viola stood below Lady Arnold's vase, eyeing it. "Is this the work of one of you?"

"A patron—a neighbor," Emery said quickly, reaching the vase down to the empty counter so that Lady Viola could examine it more closely.

Lady Viola nodded. "There is always someone who discovers new treasure first. But at least Her Grace has not been far behind."

"Take the butter upstairs, would you please, Sally?"

Rose had thought Her Grace had ignored Sally's accompaniment, but no, she had been aware of the girl the whole time.

"Yes, ma'am!" Sally may have curtseyed; there was an awkward shuffle. Rose was sure that however Her Grace looked, Sally had never been so close to one so fine.

"Thank you, Sally," the Duchess answered gravely. "I am delighted to make your acquaintance. Will you also be a baker of cakes, or will it be bread?"

"I want a work that has to do with numbers, ma'am," Sally surprised Rose by saying.

"Really." At that, the Duchess paused. Rose thought she might have made a note of the moment. "Well. I shall be interested to hear how that progresses."

"Thank you, ma'am!" And Sal, never impressed by much, almost giggled as she ran up the stairs holding, Rose hoped, the little pan of butter.

In the ensuing silence, Rose wondered how to converse when the Duchess had clearly had no intention of carrying any butter.

"This room smells lovely!" Just as enthusiastic in the cellar as she had been in the bakery, the Duchess slowly explored the shelves where they stored the crocks of honey and butter. "Do you come here often? It's so beautifully cool."

The hot summer outside did not, in fact, penetrate the stone this far. "I used to," Rose admitted, realizing how very long ago the opening of the bakery seemed. "I liked hiding down here from... well, everything."

"But you don't anymore? Because of your work? I'm curious. Or is it because of a gentleman?"

"Actually, the work came first, the gentleman second."

"Ah!" The Duchess treated this like a delightfully final piece to a puzzle. "So there *is* a gentleman. I want to know everything! Tell me, do."

As if they weren't a baker and a duchess standing in a cellar. As if they had nothing but time.

Rose tried to answer as if they were having a reasonable conversation in a drawing room. "His name is..." She stumbled a little over his first name; she never used it herself. It felt awkward to say it. "Mr. Luke Russell. He is standing for election in this next by-election."

"The date hasn't been set yet," Her Grace said swiftly.

Surprised, Rose said, "No, but it will soon will be. Mr. Wallenbush has, after all, died. We expect the writ soon."

"We? So you are quite tied to your Mr. Russell, then. Personally, I mean."

This was a difficult question, given the ups and downs of the last few days. But Rose wanted to be as honest as she could. "The gentleman is known to me, and I am known to him. More than that, we have not settled."

"I see. And he is an associate of Mr. Wallenbush's, I suppose?"

"No. He is a member of the Society of Friends, a Quaker, and they have sponsored him to come to London to try for this seat."

The crackling force of the Duchess' full attention snapped Rose's spine straight. She hadn't felt like she was slouching.

The Duchess had stepped closer. "And are you aware, Miss Bickering, that the Quakers do not serve the King in such office because they will not swear allegiance to him? What does your Mr. Russell hope to accomplish by being elected? Will he separate from the Quakers?"

Rose felt like these were much bigger questions than she had been expecting. "I... forgive me, I must compose myself. I had not expected such a deep conversation so quickly with such an august personage."

"I'd rather be abrupt than stupid, and you interest me very much. Your cakes are delicious, your bread smells like the stuff of life itself, and you are quite attached to a gentleman preparing to agitate Parliament. I'm riveted. *Is* there a deeper hope to his election?"

It felt like this moment was a test. Of her, of her Mr. Russell, of their relationship. The Duchess had opened the question like a trap, wondering, clearly, if Rose knew of this difficulty, and then beyond that what sort of man this Mr. Russell was.

And all Mr. Russell's honesty, with her and with everyone, made this moment easy.

Rose had never been prouder of him than she was as she answered, as clearly and honestly as Mr. Russell would have himself.

"Mr. Russell and his meeting wish to force the discussion, madame. If there will ever come a time when anyone may serve in public office, not just Anglicans, there must come a time when they must swear other oaths. If they are not to swear to the Crown, then perhaps to the people of Britain. If he wins, it will force the discussion to open again between the Crown and the Society of Friends, and perhaps others."

"And he is sincere in his wish to abolish slavery."

"Utterly. As is the entire meeting. Your Grace."

"A radical! This bakery surprises me more and more! Indeed, you must call your cake *galette de l'Égalité!*" If the Duchess was angry, she didn't sound it. She was, if anything, intensely interested. "You and your Mr. Russell have revolutionary plans, Miss Bickering!"

"In a quiet little way. Yes, we do." Rose felt very comfortable and settled in the idea that the plans were *theirs*, hers and Mr. Russell's.

"Tell me everything," demanded the Duchess of Talbourne.

EMERY'S HEAD DREW CLOSER TO LADY VIOLA'S AS THEY bent over Lady Arnold's lacquered gift. Miss Díaz joined them.

"So much work!" Miss Díaz could not stop tracing a finger along the edge of one paper flower's petals. "It is like love solidified for our sight."

"Surely not, Virginia." Viola sounded surprised. "It is art, not love."

"Aren't they the same?" Miss Díaz gestured. "Come get some bread, Viola. You need to eat."

"You say that every day."

"Oddly, it is true every day."

Just then, the door to the apartments upstairs opened, and Lord Zachary nearly walked straight into the back of a duke.

"I beg your pardon." He saw the ladies. "I beg your pardon." He half-stepped back, then checked overhead, to one side, then the other, to see where he was. This was indeed the bakery; it was just full of extremely fine people. "I'm sorry, is the bakery hosting a salon today?"

Lady Viola couldn't seem to take her eyes off the composition of glowing metal, flower petals, and blackness. "Just imagine pouring all that time and attention and *feeling* into paper and paint, and making something of them that contained part of you. Part of what you'd put into it."

"I beg your pardon," Lord Zachary said again. Anna swept up to him, apron in her hands as if to shoo him toward the counter; but he walked straight to the cluster of ladies on the other side of the room.

He stared at the vase just as hard.

"It's very decorative, I can't deny it; but can the merely decorative contain a part of the soul?"

Lady Viola just looked up at him. "And who are you?"

"I'm very sympathetic to your causes, and Mr. Russell's," the Duchess in the cellar was saying. "And support them openly. But there are times to ally and times to wait. Let us see what happens with the by-election. And I am interested to hear what your Quaker friends propose. Everything they propose."

"Thank you, Your Grace." It might be stupid to curtsey again to a blind woman, but Rose wanted to do it anyway, and did. "I feel awkward imposing on you, when you have already done us the great honor of visiting us here."

"Please don't feel awkward. I'd like to think this is why news reached us of your bakery and your cakes."

Rose wanted to ask *how* that news had reached them, but the Duchess didn't offer to explain.

Instead she said, "Besides, you must learn to impose. Whenever we ask for something—and politics is the art of trading what people want—others say that they needn't listen to a woman, or a duchess, or a baker for that matter, when all they really mean is *no*. And *no* must be the trumpet that draws us into the field, Miss Bickering, not the weapon that drives us from it."

Little Rose had never been invited on to a battlefield.

She loved it. "Thank you."

"In addition," and here the Duchess sounded a little mischievous, "I am now very curious both about your Mr. Russell and about your relationship to him."

"He has asked me to marry him."

"Has he? Delightful! Or rather... is it delightful?"

"I found it a welcome honor and a bit confusing. He'd just been shouting at me in the street the day before."

"My." The Duchess seemed to find this far more alarming than a political conversation in a basement. "That sounds...like you must think very hard about your attachment to him."

"My attachment to him is...permanent." It was. Rose felt so more at that moment than she ever had. "The question is, what is our future?"

"Take my hand for a moment, Miss Bickering," said the Duchess, and they found each others' hands to squeeze. "You sound wiser than most women," Her Grace almost whispered, "and it seems to me that whatever you do will be the right decision. He is not the only man in the world. Unless he is the only man for *you*."

"How did you decide to accept your husband, my lady? If you don't mind my asking."

"Oh. Well..." The Duchess of Talbourne sounded startled.

"To be honest, I thought I understood what marriage was, and I was wrong. Or rather, I was right, but it was all a much larger undertaking than I suspected. I accepted him long before I chose him. But I do choose him, every day. And I can't imagine ever choosing differently."

"How interesting! One day I hope we may sit—not in our cellar—and have a long conversation about so many things."

"I don't think that unlikely."

"I do." Rose couldn't keep *all* the ruefulness out of her voice. "I am a baker, Your Grace. I doubt our paths will cross again."

The Duchess still had hold of Rose's hand. She leaned closer and lowered her voice. "And I was once a housemaid, Miss Bickering. I wouldn't presume to guess what else may happen."

"Do *not* address His Grace." Anna hissed at her lordly neighbor when she wanted to flap her apron at him. And where had Jane gone?

"Why shouldn't I? He's standing in your shop."

"It's just—you can only make things worse."

For once, Lord Zachary didn't look confused or dismissive. His green-and-brown eyes settled on her and studied her the way she thought he must study the surface of a canvas before it bore paint.

"Is that truly what you think of me? I have been chivalrous enough, surely, since the day you met me and ordered me out of my own stairway while carrying a slop jar. What consideration have I failed to give you, Miss Bickering?"

His gentle puzzlement halted for a moment what had become Anna's habitual disdain. He was just a man, handsome, only adequate as a painter, with a haughty sister and, sometimes, flowers. He didn't deserve her worship, but neither did he deserve her constant scorn.

"I'd forgotten that," she blurted out.

"How could you?" His eyes crinkled in the corners from his smile.

Were it not for the crinkled eyes, she could have clung to her annoyance, but they made it too difficult. "Do you know him?"

"No, but I'd like to." Lord Zachary eyed the dark and forbidding figure of the Duke. "Perhaps he buys art."

It hit Anna like a bolt of lightning that Lord Zachary was a merchant, just like her. Trying to make a living from the fruit of his hands.

"You can afford to make friends with him first."

"Why is he even here?"

"I've no idea."

When the Duchess emerged from the cellar, Rose behind her, things moved at a whirlwind pace.

"Are we leaving? We must have several cakes!" Miss Díaz, her eyes sparkling, had not cooled on the idea at all.

Emery was ready to be blunt with the truth. "We can only offer two plates."

"Of course." Miss Díaz noted this information as if it happened every day. "If you don't mind, we'll employ them, and perhaps you will send a few more cakes to the house."

Jane, her cheeks pink, came in through the shop door, causing it to scrape. Everyone turned.

"Excuse me," she said, with a little curtsey, but said nothing else as she went to stand by the counter.

"We can send you as many cakes as you like," Anna

assured Miss Díaz, airily wiping away the question of *how,* when they were all eating off of bread paddles and bowls.

"Good. Send four. We'll have them next week, too. The bread we'll only take this week. It's so delicious, but—"

"But we wouldn't want to offend our cook," put in Her Grace with a smile.

Lady Viola took up the last delicately thin slice of their finest white bread, thickly buttered, and popped it into her mouth.

"It's been delightful," she said in that serious way of hers, as if they were discussing natural history, or Roman emperors.

In the flurry of people withdrawing, there were goodbyes and thanks and no one even thought to mention money.

Till their Graces had gone, their ladies and footmen with them, and only the big grizzled man remained.

"Ladies." He tipped his hat. "I believe that this will settle the account?"

And he laid two pounds sterling on their pitted bread counter.

"Thank you," Anna said stoutly, picking up one coin without the least sign of embarrassment. "This coin is more than enough."

The man looked startled. "His Grace can well afford—"

"Six cakes at two shillings apiece, then the half-peck loaf and the butter. Plus two shillings for the delivery of all. That's two and a half shillings back to you, sir."

Anna counted out the money with the sturdy assurance of someone who knew exactly how this worked.

She didn't look at her sisters. It had been her decision to overcharge Lord Boislegrand, and while he never seemed to mind it, Anna did. She wanted this business plain and honest.

And His Grace didn't look like the sort of man Anna wanted to owe a favor.

The grizzled man didn't argue, just pocketed his coin and left.

"You didn't ask if they wanted cakes on subscription," Emery said in the silence when they'd gone.

It was the only thing to say. Nothing else suited the majesty, the unexpected grandeur of what had just happened.

"Cakes on subscription? To Talbourne House?" Anna's laugh was short. "I already charged an enormous amount for their delivery. You think they wish to pay that every week?"

"They might. Miss Díaz *loved* your cake."

This, from Emery, whose mixed feelings about cake still showed, made Anna want to hug her.

"Do you know what's been happening?" Jane's cheeks were still pink, and she looked as though she were full to bursting with something.

"Yes! We had a duke and duchess in the shop!" Rose didn't know what else there was to say.

"I mean outside! Everyone saw, I mean *everyone*. Not one move has been made around this entire square that wasn't buzzing with conversation. We have been very publicly visited by Their Graces, and *everyone knows it*."

"Well, that's nice." Anna slumped down on to one of their stools. She looked worn out by the whole affair. "We wanted our cakes known."

"We wanted it known that a duchess admired our cakes, and everyone *does* know. They know the Talbourne name, and they are talking of nothing but that, along with our cakes— our bakery!"

"Do you mean we've done it?" Rose asked.

"I think we have." Jane's eyes still glittered, almost as if she had a fever. She leaned against the counter and just opened her hands as if to embrace the whole world. "I think we have!"

THE CLOSET DOOR OPENED, AND MR. MORLEY'S ARM appeared. "Buttonholes," he said briefly, dropping two pieces of gray wool on the little table, and started to withdraw.

It was too much. After all the commotion in the bakery, with duchesses and all, sitting in silence in this hot little closet was too much for Emery. "Mr. Morley!"

"What?" His head popped back in, clearly shocked that Emery had talked.

Emery didn't know what to add. The solitary silence just felt... barren. Hollow. "That is—don't you wish to... say hello? Or anything?"

An odd request, in the late summer evening, but Emery wanted to ask.

"I said *buttonholes*. You want conversation? Get married."

Wisdom imparted, he left.

Was that what Emery wanted? She conversed with her sisters all the time. About their bakery, and their lives together—wasn't that enough? What other type of conversation was there?

What else could she possibly want?

The clever conversation of the ladies-in-waiting. They were beautiful ladies, certainly, but they were also interested, and interesting.

Emery thought back to the kitchen salon. The women there had been full of talking. Insults, laughter, news, gossip, even things they had read in books. Emery had been there primarily to admire Miss Hayes.

If she went back again, wouldn't she simply prefer to listen rather than stare?

Now that she thought about it, Miss Hayes hadn't said much. She loved to talk, but Emery couldn't remember any specific thoughts of hers. She'd had new gowns and slippers to show, she liked to laugh at others' witty remarks, and she had talked of... what? Emery couldn't recall.

If love tokens were necessary to offer a particular life to the object of one's affection, and marriage meant conversation (not that Mr. Morley was a reliable source of information; Emery had not even met *Mrs.* Morley), if Emery went to all this work to impress Jasmine... what would be the end of it all?

The two of them in a room somewhere growing old together discussing hair ribbons?

Emery didn't even like hair ribbons.

Emery hadn't once in her life contemplated life in the orbit of Britain's great titles. If she had, she wouldn't have imagined it much like today. Yet those women were not so different from the women of the kitchen salon. They lacked the undercurrent of shared secret interests, and their gowns were *much* finer; but still, they were women sharing their thoughts about life. The Duke had said little.

Had she overlooked the simple pleasures of the company of like-minded people because she was so blinded by Jasmine's beauty?

She looked down at the buttonhole. The money she earned from Mr. Morley wasn't just for a gift for Jasmine. It could be for the *possibility* of a gift. It could be for any possibility. It could be freedom.

Every second of Emery's day was used for work. Yet buttonholes, like making bread, occupied the hands while leaving time for thought. Emery needed to learn to use that time more wisely.

"ARE THEY GONE?"

Jane nearly fell over, she whirled so fast. Their neighbor in the little closet room always made her draw back a bit. She wasn't *afraid* of him, not when Emery seemed so friendly with him; but his bathing habits and constantly watching eyes poked into Jane's skin the wrong way.

"Yes, they're gone," she reassured him. It must have been a huge disturbance for him. "They won't be back."

"Good," he said after a moment, and closed his narrow door.

THERE WAS NO ONE FOR ROSE TO TELL EXCEPT MR. Russell, she thought, serving the rush of customers who flooded the store once the massive carriages had rolled away.

Well, there was everyone to tell, but Rose wanted to tell Mr. Russell first.

About the whole day, all of it, unbelievable as anything could be, of course.

But first and foremost, that Rose had decided to marry him.

HE CAME IN AFTER THE FIRST FLOOD HAD RECEDED, BUT there were still people everywhere in the bakery's shop, all of them pretending to buy bread (everything for the day had nearly sold) and gossiping wildly.

He caught her at the counter, trying to split a quartern loaf so that two of their patrons would be happy. Neither wanted a piece of the remaining half-peck, and neither wanted to leave without some of the *fine ladies' bread*.

"Miss Rose."

His voice caught under her ribs and pulled her to him.

"Rose, don't you dare!" Anna hissed as she moved to take Rose's place at the bread knife.

Rose couldn't help it. "I'll only be a moment." Her words were airy, though she felt both guilty and embarrassed. Not only her sisters knew of her attachment to this man; likely everyone in the shop had heard about it.

Well.

"If you can spare a moment, Mr. Russell," and Rose tugged his sleeve, moving for the door of the bakery proper.

"Always for you, Miss Rose," but he sounded surprised, too.

It wouldn't be seemly to tow him along behind her. She must trust that he was following. Surely he was.

Once the door between the bakery proper and the shop was closed, she turned and walked into his gloriously strong arms. "First of all, *yes*."

The hard warmth of his arms tightened all around her. "Yes?"

"Yes!"

Laughter seemed to bubble out of him, way down deep in his chest. Clasping her close, he pulled her off her feet, her body tight against him. "Yes?" His voice was happiness, and rich deep hope all together.

"Yes. A thousand times yes."

"Yes what?" Jordan, no doubt bent over a vat of dough, spoke up.

Sally was probably watching too.

"Excuse us," and Rose towed him openly this time, pulling his sleeve along to the back door and out into the mews, smelling of warm stone and green ivy.

He didn't wait, just swept her up again, carrying her the few steps to their little spot where no one could see.

"Tell me yes again," Mr. Russell murmured, then his

mouth came down over hers, preventing her from doing as he asked.

When she could speak, Rose found herself melted against him. This feeling inside, this feeling of *rightness*. Rose knew when something was right, and this was right.

"I'll tell you *yes* as much as you like, whenever you aren't preventing it by kissing me," she murmured, feeling herself smile so hard it pulled her whole face tight.

"Guess I won't hear it much then," he said right back, and kissed her again.

Episode 21: Of Plates and Slates

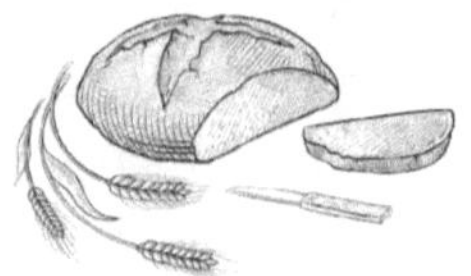

"I wish we had the money to go to Scotland." Rose had not found the evening's meeting of friends satisfying. The rest of the meeting had some odd notion that she ought to tell her family before she got married.

Rose didn't want to. She didn't want the arguments and she didn't want to wait.

Mr. Russell was not in agreement. "You don't mean it! You would be sad, I think, if your sisters were not at our wedding."

Rose had never imagined her own wedding. She had long suspected marriage was not the impossibility that Aunt Eden made it sound; but she hadn't spun any dreams about it, either. Even if Mr. Russell were right, the way he said it only proved he didn't understand Rose's position. She wanted to be married. Done. Her sisters wouldn't make it easier, she knew that.

She couldn't explain the pressure she felt inside to have it done, not to argue; but she also felt that if Mr. Russell understood her, she shouldn't have to explain.

"I'd want them if they were to come and be happy for me. But they won't."

"And if they are not, we must come to agreement with them." This was Mr. Russell at his most serious. "A marriage should be something new, not a destruction of everything old. Your sisters will always be your sisters. And I do not wish to hurt them."

"What if we got married on the pavement just in front of the store? They would know about it then."

"Marriage is more solemn than you make it sound."

"I don't feel solemn!" Rose briefly leaned her head against the strength of his shoulder; he paused in his steps to let her. "I feel happy! And ready to be married. "

"It's going to last a little longer than a bath." Did he sound a little disgruntled? "It's for life."

"Are you sure you don't wish to make the journey to Scotland?"

"I don't. The meeting's marriages are recognized by the Crown partly because they do just as the Church does by reading the banns: broadcast the news to make a marriage legal in the community, without question. Even if you were of age."

Rose bristled. "Do you wish to wait another six months until I am?"

"No!" They paused again, and Rose thought he would take her in his arms again. It was thrilling; it had become hungry, the way he clasped her close, and yet as solid and sure as the earth under her feet.

He didn't, but Rose could tell he wanted to.

"I can't wait that long," he said through his teeth, and pressed a chaste kiss to her temple when Rose knew he wanted to press them all down her throat.

"We should go to Scotland," Rose muttered again, before he just pulled away and kept walking.

"Why, Mrs. Scrope! To what do we owe the pleasure?"

Anna squashed the urge to brush at her apron. This was her place of business, and she had no need to impress Mrs. Scrope, who hadn't been seen in weeks. Not since she had unwillingly agreed to settle the water bill from the previous tenant.

The shop was bustling, with both Sally and Jane helping patrons left and right, but Mrs. Scrope was scowling.

"You are doing a great deal of business."

Anna tried to keep the confusion off her face. "Yes. It's a shop."

"A great deal more than previously."

"Yes." Anna still didn't understand this conversation. "Isn't it lucky?"

"No, it isn't." Mrs. Scrope looked as firmly ordered as always, with a cap set on like a rooftop and her shawl a prisoner in one hand. But her words were a bit ruffled. "I didn't expect your business to succeed like this, Miss Bickering."

"Like *what?*"

"Like... All this." The hand not clutching the shawl emerged to wave weakly around in the air. It looked like she had captured an arm from someone else.

"It's a *shop*," Anna said again. "I—"

Then she remembered. Captain Brice's warning that the Scropes wanted them to fail.

Did they want it badly enough to come and *insist* on it?

Anna didn't believe in assuming the worst of people, even when they displayed their worst blatantly.

Fortunately, this was a moment to adapt what she had learned from society affairs and pretend to someone else's good wishes.

"It's wonderful, isn't it? I know you and Mr. Scrope took a chance leasing the bakery to us, and you must know how grateful we are." Anna's hands clasped tightly at her waist so she wouldn't pull Mrs. Scrope's cap off. "We are seeing more custom than you even hoped, I'm sure. And we are very glad to have made good on our business arrangements, with you and all our other partners in business."

She hoped if she said *business* enough times, it would settle into Mrs. Scrope's skin.

"This is hardly seemly, though, women doing so much business and attracting all that attention."

"Attention?"

"The Duke's visit!"

Anna's jaw clenched till she wondered if she might break a tooth. "We were *so* glad to have the Duke and Duchess visit. Our cakes are something special, and they had heard of them."

"That's just what I mean! Too much attention."

"Mrs. Scrope," Anna tried to say as evenly as she could, "baking is our business. How exactly does a shop carry on *too much* business?"

"Someone will notice that we've let the place to a bunch of girls. Someone will question it."

"A great many people have noticed, and I haven't heard any questions."

"They won't question *you*," and the word dripped with disdain. "They will question Mr. Scrope! The idea of him doing business with the likes of you!"

Anna wanted to shout for Jane, or Emery. She didn't need their help. She just wanted to *shout*.

This type of attack must be repulsed by something more subtle than a sausage.

"I don't know who is even aware that Mr. Scrope is our landlord, Mrs. Scrope. As both you and he have been good enough to keep your distance and let us carry on our work, I imagine that situation will persist, don't you? Which is lucky. As I recall, this bakery had two tenants in the last year. We don't want anyone to suspect that Mr. Scrope enjoys leasing to concerns that fail, or swearing out complaints to bankrupt the owners."

Startlement shook and rattled Mrs. Scrope's features like a glass jar full of dry sticks. "No, we don't want anyone to think that."

"I thought not. So hadn't you better go, Mrs. Scropes?" Anna wanted the woman out of *her* bakery. "We'll let you know if we need anything."

Like the counters planed smooth, or the door fixed, or anything else they'd asked for the day they moved in, Anna thought bitterly.

Mrs. Scrope had done *nothing* to help them, and Anna wasn't interested in appeasing her any more.

Mrs. Scrope was still clearly deciding what to say when Anna punctuated their meeting. "Good day, madam."

And went back to her paying customers.

FROM THE BAKERY SHOP TO THE TAILOR'S ACROSS BEAR Street, it was perhaps thirty feet.

Emery always had to make the trip quite long by slipping out the back and through the mews to emerge onto Castle Street and come all the way around on Bear Street. All to slip into the tailor's unnoticed.

This summery day she stopped, just at the entrance to the mews.

There was Miss Hayes, golden curls shining below the edge of a bonnet that would be demure had it not born, sewn to its side, an enormous bouquet of silk roses.

Miss Hayes—Jasmine—was walking along the street and

seemed to be enjoying the flowers, swinging her head from side to side and laughing at the wobbling weight.

She caught sight of Emery inside the old mews gate and paused, and Emery felt sparks shooting under her skin, felt herself leaning toward those curls, that smile.

Jasmine just waved.

When she moved on, Emery felt hollow. All that prickling, hot energy under her skin simply fell into the hollow space inside her, leaving her empty.

The *idea* of seeing Jasmine again and speaking to her, perhaps over a gift, had been theoretical, abstract as Sally's numbers. Emery could debate with herself whether it meant much, as long as it was all hypothetical.

Seeing Jasmine was real, as was Jasmine simply waving and walking away.

It was brutal and cold to know that Emery had been right: she had been earning those extra coins only for herself, all along.

ANNA, PRACTICED BAKER, NO LONGER FELT AWKWARD accompanying Lord Boislegrand as he carried his cake to his carriage.

"Thank you for coming," she said as she did every time, with a for-the-customer smile.

He reached in the open door of his usual carriage and set the plate on the seat. He was so steady, Anna thought to herself. Now that he knew about the plate situation, he never forgot to bring one of his own.

Which was good, as their last two had disappeared, along with awkwardly-packed cakes in bowls, into Talbourne House.

But Anna didn't regret it. Indeed, she could hardly keep the glow off her face.

His lordship bent close as if attracted by that glow—or searching for it. "Aren't you going to tell me?"

"Tell you what?"

"About the Duke and Duchess of Talbourne visiting your bakery."

"Oh!" Anna waved a hand dismissively. "How did you hear about that?"

He stood by the open carriage door, his warm eyes searching hers until Anna's smile faded.

"Miss Bickering, it is all that you have hoped for during long weeks. How could I ignore news of it? Have I so entirely failed to convince you that your happiness is all I want?"

"Well, but..." Anna didn't know what he expected. "I *am* happy."

"And I wish to hear all about it. I wish to hear what you think, Miss Bickering, what you hope, what you like and what you love. I wish for your conversation. Your company." His own gentle face settled into an expression that was almost sad. "I wish for you."

This very forward speech shook Anna down to her shoes. "I—Lord Boislegrand, I'm so flattered."

"Only flattered?"

The rest of the street's bustle seemed to melt away as he stepped closer. He was taller than she, and his hand was gentle as he made so bold as to take hers.

"Miss Bickering. Would you marry me?"

Anna seemed to fall out of time, out of herself. When she realized what was happening, she was still standing there, staring wide-eyed at the gentleman, her hand still in his.

"Well," he said in a soft voice, "I can see that you are at least thinking seriously about my question."

"I—" A voice in the back of Anna's head screamed *Say*

anything but yes! "I am thinking seriously about it, my lord. You must—you must let me think about it for a little."

"All right." Far from vague or silly, Lord Boislegrand looked... well, proud. The set of his shoulders was a little harder, his head a little taller. "I would be honored if you would, Miss Bickering."

"I'm honored that you asked," she said softly. That was the truth.

And with that, a viscount with very kind eyes kissed her hand, right in the street, and walked her the few feet back to the bakery door.

Then he climbed in his carriage, taking his cake with him, and was gone.

ANNA WENT IN THE DOOR TO THE STAIRS INSTEAD OF THE bakery.

She wasn't shaking; she wasn't cold or hot or anything. She was just a little stunned.

He had offered for her. He had been utterly serious. He had offered. For *her*.

The pounding of boots on the stairs made her look up.

Lord Zachary, coatless, shirt arms rolled up, was pounding his way down to the entryway where she stood, or perhaps hid, from the people in the bakery.

Just behind him was their nameless neighbor, ragged hair flying.

"What was that all about?" the young Lord demanded.

"What was what about?"

"Don't act stupid. Puffy kissed your hand. In the street."

"Puffy? What an odd thing to call him."

Zachary waved that away. "It's what his friends call him. What was that about?"

"Are you all right?" the nameless neighbor asked, cutting across with his voice.

"Regarding Lord Boislegrand, or regarding him?" Anna pointed at Lord Zachary, who looked red.

"Either one." The neighbor shrugged, watching Anna's pointing finger warily. "I am not *with* him, you know. I just followed him down."

It seemed odd not to have a name for a neighbor who took so much interest in their wellbeing. "Shouldn't I know your name?"

"Why?" the neighbor asked immediately, brows lowering in suspicion. "What would you do with it?"

"The hand kissing?" Lord Zachary was waving his arms in their billowing white linen. "Get on with explaining that?"

"You have blue on your sleeve."

"Not the point."

"Lord Zachary. I can't see what the situation has to do with you."

"Neighbors." He pointed at himself, then the nameless neighbor, then himself again, and finally at her. "Looking out for each other."

"I'm fine, Lord Zachary. Go back to painting."

"You are *not* fine!" Astonishingly, he persisted. "The Miss Bickering I know doesn't just let a man kiss her hand on the street and then say she's fine!"

"He proposed, so I suppose that makes it different!"

All three of them stared at one another.

"I think it does. I think it does make it different," put in their neighbor.

"You can go back up at any time," Zachary told him with some heat.

"No, I think I am interested in this conversation," the other man said, folding his arms over his chest.

All Anna had wanted was some peace and quiet. Well,

those things were in short supply in everyone's life, she supposed.

"I'm going back to work," she announced, and slipped through the inner door to the shop before either of the men could answer.

The neighbor from the closet just shrugged, arms still folded across his chest. "What the hell is the matter with you?" he asked the painter from the garret.

NO ONE COULD TALK TO JANE; SHE SAT ON THE STOOL IN the window doing sums over and over again on her slate. Her eyes glittered as if with a fever.

It was the mid-afternoon quiet, and Rose wanted to talk about something, anything other than her decision to marry Mr. Russell.

But every conversational attempt died in the face of silence. Rose was pretty sure Jane was still there; she was just lost to the world.

"Anna said to leave the stool for customers," Rose reminded her, but that got her nothing either.

There was a knock at the shop door.

Suspecting Jane wouldn't hear that either, Rose went to open it. "Yes? We are open today; you may come right in."

"I have a few crates to bring in, miss."

That wasn't something people usually said; Rose frowned. "Crates of what?"

"I believe it's crockery, miss. From Talbourne House."

Just like that, Jane was at her elbow. "Bring it in!" She shoved the door so far open it screeched.

"Go get Anna and Emery," she whispered to Rose as the man's heavy steps crossed the floor. "By that empty counter, would you please, sir?"

Rose didn't understand her excitement. "It's surely what we sent. Those big bowls, and the two plates."

"Rose, the crates are too *big!* Go get them!"

Sure enough, the man's boots crossed the floor again, and he returned with another heavy load.

Rose slid around behind the counter to knock three times on the bakery door, hard.

That was the signal they'd all agreed meant "Come to the front," and Anna and Emery were there in seconds.

"It's all right," Emery called back to Jordan and Sal, forestalling any potential alarm, before she and Anna both went over to the far counter, no doubt to stare at the crates.

"You're sure this is all for the bakery?" Anna asked the man as he came in with a third crate; Rose heard it creak as he set it down.

"Indeed, madam."

From the window Jane called, "Anna, it's one of those coaches!"

Emery had left and come back. "To open it," she said. She must have fetched the iron bar they used to pry open crates of honey and butter.

"It isn't closed tight." Anna rustled around in dry straw, which must have been packed just under the crate's top.

The gentleman—he must be a footman—said formally, "The Duke and Duchess of Talbourne thank the Ladies' Own Bakery for their singular provisions, and make the proprietors this gift in memory of their visit."

Rose came over to stand by her sisters. She heard Anna gasp. There was a clink, a soft musical clink of a slight glancing bump between two hard and delicate things.

"Rose, it's dishes." Jane sounded in awe. She placed one in Rose's hands. It was delicately made, with a thin edge, and broad enough for an entire dinner.

"Talbourne dishes," breathed Anna.

"The blue flowers, all that paintwork—" Emery had clearly never seen their like.

"There are flowers all over them, Rose, flowers with petals that swirl open like a lady's skirt when she's dancing. And with a few buds, and what looks like pods? For seeds?"

"They look like Lady Arnold's vase," Emery said.

Once she'd said it, her sisters murmured agreement.

"They do." Anna's voice was faint. "Flowers in every stage of life. With a blue patterned border to remind one of fluted silver."

Rose didn't know what fluted silver was like, but she appreciated the knowledge. The plate in her hands was smooth and cool, and she just knew that if she struck it with a fingernail, it would make that little *tink* sound again.

The footman cleared his throat, the sort of sound a person makes to draw unobtrusive attention, not because there was anything in his throat. "Her Grace wishes to add personally that she wishes you all, Misses Bickering, good fortune as well, and that the silver pieces are a gift from her mother, Lady Redbeck, whom she hopes will be able to visit."

"*Silver* pieces?"

Jane's astonishment caused the man to rustle through the straw in the crate and pull out something else. Rose heard one of them set it on the counter with a rather different *clink*.

"She regrets to send only a small selection, but hopes you enjoy their use."

"Forks? Knives?" Emery sounded as if she couldn't overcome her shock. "Spoons?"

Jane, on the other hand, barely held back her crow of exultation. "The crockery is for the shop, don't you see? We will be able to serve our cakes on Talbourne plates. It is the mark of the ducal patronage!"

"But the silver is for us." Rose couldn't believe it. What a large gift! Why?

Then she realized. For the Duchess, and certainly for the Duke, such a gift would be no more than the last few coins found in their pocket. They might forget it tomorrow, it would be so little to them.

But to the Bickerings...

Jordan said, "That's the prettiest thing I ever touched."

"And you did it carefully too," Emery assured him.

Rose hadn't noticed the children come in, but Sal had clearly come with her brother. "Are those for us?"

And Anna, lovely Anna, said immediately, "Yes. They are. For all of us."

"Our cakes will be served on *Talbourne plates!*" Jane gloated over each *tink* as she took them out of the crates, one by one.

"Our *dinner* will be served on Talbourne plates, and yours too," Emery added.

"Does this mean you won't marry that man?" asked Sally.

Rose's heart stopped. Her mind went blank. What did plates have to do with Mr. Russell? And how did Sal know?

But before she could say anything, Anna made a *tush* sound. "What gave you the idea that I'm going to marry any man?"

"You went with him out to his carriage. And he kissed your hand."

"My stars! This building has too many windows."

Even Jane stopped unpacking plates to listen to this. "Wait. What was that?"

"Nothing. And I'm not getting married. When people plan to get married, Sally, they tell other people. It's not complicated at all. I haven't said anything about it because I'm not going to get married. All right?"

"And when you do get married, you'll tell me? And Jordan?"

"Yes, of course!"

Anna's blithe logic, that if people were betrothed they

would say so, clawed at something inside Rose. She should say something.

But she couldn't bear to imagine the fuss.

It would sully what she had, the pure sweetness of these moments with Mr. Russell where they were perfectly in charity with one another.

Well, except about whether or not to elope to Scotland's Gretna Green.

THE SUN WOULDN'T GO DOWN FOR HOURS YET, BUT THE shop had closed. Emery had disappeared, and Rose was upstairs cooking their supper. As often happened, Jordan and Sal had gone with her.

They sent the children home with boiled eggs and left-over bread as often as they could, since they knew now that Mr. Collier could do very little for himself. Anna found herself wondering if Tilly could still get them cabbage.

Perhaps all the answers to all the questions—all the questions swirling in Anna's head—could be found on Jane's little slate.

"Jane."

Her sister looked up. She might truly have a fever now, hunching over that slate for the better part of two days.

"Jane, what did you mean that Aunt Eden said she wouldn't come?"

Blinking, Jane seemed to return to the world. The world of bread, not numbers.

"I wrote to her, that's all. She said she wouldn't come, that we'd made our choice."

"But why should she come?"

Jane's eyes flickered around the room, not wanting to meet Anna's. "I thought—I thought you might do something foolish. You seemed inclined to do something foolish."

"What kind of foolish?"

Anna didn't feel foolish. She felt grown up, and a little harder than she used to be, that was all.

"Foolish enough to set your cap for that silly Lord Boislegrand. He has some money, Anna, but he's not for you. And what kind of life would he offer you?"

It was the perfect moment; Anna had to speak.

"He offered himself."

Jane's fingers, nerveless, let the slate slide.

Anna leaned forward and caught it.

"You mean...?"

"He asked me to marry him, Jane."

"He did?" The idea seemed to wash all the life out of Jane.

But then in the next moment, she snatched the slate out of Anna's hands.

"But look! See here? I have done the arithmetic any number of ways. Even if only half the new business continues, we will sell enough bread and cakes to pay the water bill every quarter! And to pay for the honey when it comes."

Water. And honey.

Anna looked at her beautiful sister, perched on a three-legged stool that was one of their proudest possessions, sitting by the window of the shop where they all worked. The floorboards were clean, but bare. The second counter they never used because they couldn't bake enough bread to use it bore the last remnant of Jane's chalk, a mere nub. The shelves all around were empty but for the remainder of the day's maslin, which would likely be their dinner and the Colliers'.

Jane's hem was so short it came nowhere near the floor, and her stockings in her shoes, Anna knew, were so frayed now that soon they could not be said to have a toe portion at all.

"Jane." Anna reached out and took the slate from her, laid it on that empty counter. "I haven't decided what to say to him yet."

"What to *say?* You'll say no! What else is there to say? You don't love him. And look—"

When she reached for her slate again, Anna caught up Jane's hands in her own.

"I'm tired," Anna said. "I'm so tired. I want to sit in a comfortable chair. I want *you* to sit in a comfortable chair. I want Emery to sleep and eat. There is nothing wrong in that."

"But—"

"He likes me, Jane. Isn't that lucky?"

Jane just shook her head. Wisps of dark hair had worked themselves free around her face, waving in the summer warmth.

Anna wanted to be able to give her, even if not sweet ices, a cool drink of water.

"I don't want the world, Jane, not anymore. I just want us to be all right."

"But—"

Before Jane could begin again, forcing Anna to ask her how many years she expected them to live this way, and whether they could look back on their lives when they were as old as Aunt Eden and feel any kind of satisfaction about scraping after every coin every single day, both of them saw movement through the panes of window-glass that drew their attention to the street.

They saw Emery casting around a glance before she slipped into the tailor's across the way.

When she'd gone inside, their eyes met.

Somehow Jane sensed that it was only more bad news, from Anna's point of view. "Emery has been living a bigger life, and that's good," Jane began hotly.

Anna didn't fight. Any questions she had about what

Emery was doing were smothered, for the moment, under the heavy blanket of care that also seemed to be smothering Anna's own self. "I won't argue that Rose and Emery have had chances here they never would have had if we had stayed in our parents' little rooms and starved to death. I'm glad we came; don't get me wrong. I'm just tired. Tell me we'll be able to buy meat. Tell me we could have tea. Just wild amounts of tea, whenever we wanted it! Go ahead, Jane. You know I trust you. Tell me so."

Flashing with desperation, Jane's eyes cast toward the slate again, then back to her sister. She must see the hollows Anna felt under her own eyes; Jane had the same ones.

"We will be *all right*, Anna."

"We will survive, Jane." Anna pressed her work-roughened hands to her cheeks, feeling every burn and every new callus. "But will that be life?"

BICKERINGS DIDN'T HAVE THE MONEY TO DRINK, EXCEPT for Aunt Eden, so Jane had not seen many people drunk in her life.

On the other hand, at society affairs, so many people were drunk that it was impossible to tell how many of them had imbibed too much and how many of them were just silly.

Jane knew some people had a deep thirst for drink they couldn't satisfy. Their next-door neighbor seemed to be of that sort. His love for drink, or his need for it, obviously overwhelmed his other good senses until he swallowed enough of that vile burning liquid to drive him completely out of his head.

Jane had never seen him drunk, but the way she always saw him—disheveled and aimless, but for the sharp spikes of attention he paid to anything that threatened the house—

looked like the aftermath of a passion for drink. Perhaps she had seen more of it in her life than she remembered.

That passion had never made sense to Jane until now.

Her head was a whirlwind of worries about how to calculate the numbers so that somehow, somehow, it would come right. Somehow, it had to produce enough coins to live. Not just sufficient food and water, but a little bit of living. Anna was right about that.

And those worries were shot through with worries about Emery's habit of keeping secrets, and Rose's inability to keep even one, and the near-panic Jane felt whenever she thought of Anna marrying Lord Boislegrand for his money, as if it were her own heart at stake.

Jane didn't want gin or sherry. But she desperately wanted to walk out into the square and find her paver-man—hadn't he told her his name? Hughes? She didn't care about his name. She just wanted the way he could make her feel, his lips on hers, his hard body next to hers. It would be the only way she could concentrate and forget about all this for a while.

It wasn't lost on her that the nearest comparison she could think of to the man was a deep glass of gin. That probably wasn't good.

And she realized, as she sat alone in the empty bakery, flour-dusted window glass separating her from the bustling sounds of the street outside, that to use him so when she didn't care a thing about him made her like those men who visited ladies of the evening, except that she didn't pay him.

Jane had walked through her life dogged by lectures on how to be good. Her mother had not been a lecturer, nor her father. But lectures were everywhere. In church, certainly, but also in every ballroom, where sharp-eyed matrons loved to hold forth on the behavior of the young ladies in view. Aunt Eden had no conversation *but* to lecture. Even those horrid hotel men shouting things at her in the street; they were a kind of lecture, trying to force her with their words to behave the way they thought she ought to behave.

Jane had always thought them all equally stupid, and ignored them all equally.

But was she the only Bickering sister who suffered from the constant *weight* of those lectures? She felt them all pushing at her, pushing till all she wanted was to escape. The constant hectoring about who to be and how to act pressured Jane far more than any lack of money.

When she had asked those men to consider marriage, she had only been sensible. They needed things, she needed things; simple fairness must be valuable enough to offer.

If she thought for a moment that they had turned her down because they had realized that she was too young to know what she was offering, that she hadn't considered the intimate nature of marriage at all in her calculations, she would have thought better of those men.

But they hadn't. She just knew that, the way she knew she was breathing air. It was almost too obvious to notice. They hadn't thought enough of her to seriously consider what she was offering. They thought her beneath them.

She'd found an escape from the furious pressure of the world's expectations in the kiss of a man she didn't know at all, and it felt very dangerous to want it more.

Jane closed her eyes and forced herself to breathe.

Emery didn't wish to marry, and Rose forged her own path. But Jane had come on this adventure following Anna. Anna who said they must marry for love.

If she married Lord Boislegrand, where did that leave Jane?

If Anna quit the field of this battle, and Jane felt herself on a battlefield, then Jane might be forced to surrender.

She felt hemmed in on all sides, death or imprisonment hanging over her. Anna's conviction had meant freedom.

She could slip out and seek her own form of intoxication. Or she could stand firm and plan counter-attacks.

Jane was a Bickering sister. She had determination even when she had nothing else.

Letting go of a breath, she let go of that nagging urge for the pleasure of momentary escape. Anna couldn't let go of her belief in love. It would be giving up herself.

Jane would have to look beyond her slate for answers.

Episode 22: Season Finale

Tilly's appearance startled Anna as it always did; today, because it was ten minutes till closing.

Anna had been sweeping. Or as she thought of it, fighting the floor. The bread crumbs of the day did not want to be brushed out; they clung to the floorboards, taunting Anna with the impossibility of forcing every one of them out of the shop.

No matter how much she bent over the broom, trying to get each straw to accomplish the most it could, unless she got down on her hands and knees and picked at each crumb, some of them took irretrievable refuge amongst the boards and would still continue to live there.

Anna worried about rats, and mice, and rats, but after a long day of serving the panoply of Ladies' Own Bakery customers, simply didn't have it in her to get down on the floor to clean it.

And into this bleak moment dashed Tilly, waving a tart.

"Here now, Miss Anna, I've got blackberry—"

Startlement made Anna drop the broom. The loud *thwack* didn't slow Tilly down one bit.

"—tart, you've got to try it. Perhaps the bakery should sell blackberry tarts? My cousin's best friend has a neighbor who—"

"Tilly. You cannot simply appear when you like. The work day is over."

"Is it?" Tilly looked around at the empty shop with its empty shelves. "Just as well; I haven't time to work today. You've got to try this blackberry—"

"Tilly." Picking up the broom gave Anna some support. "You are not an employee."

"No, of course not! I've always ordered myself about what to do. I don't mean to give you orders, Miss Bickering, really I don't. But you must try—"

The pastry in her hand did indeed look golden and luscious, with a fat blackberry poised right at the edge.

But the way she attempted to jab it toward Anna's mouth was not appealing.

Anna had never felt more like sorting this out than she did at that very moment. "We have a very busy bakery, Tilly, and we must concentrate on the work. We cannot be distracted by amusements."

"Amusements! Let me tell you, this blackberry tart was no Christmas pantomime. This was hours of work, and the fruit needed no sugar at all. That was why I thought to bring you some. If you're that busy, I'm *willing* to give you a bit of help, but that wasn't why I came."

That Tilly had put effort into baking a sugarless tart threatened to soften Anna's resolve. Anna held on to it. "Tilly—"

But Tilly decided she would do the interrupting for a bit. "Anyhow, your busiest days are Monday and Tuesday, and I reckoned I'd come in those mornings. Unless you *want* to pay me more often. Which reminds me, you haven't paid me yet."

"Because we haven't discussed wages. Because I didn't *hire* you."

"You're that ladylike, I know you don't like to talk about such things. I thought it would be easier if I didn't bring it up."

Anna took a deep breath. The waist of her dress, she noticed, did not tighten. She couldn't see herself, but she must have lost weight along with all of her sisters. "I appreciate your consideration. But we do not need you to wait on the customers."

"All right." Tilly gave in surprisingly quickly, her shoulders rising and falling in her loose country blouse. "I can learn to make bread, I s'pose. Easier'n learning how to milk a cow. I can tell you, if you do it wrong, those cows do *not* like it."

Anna shuddered at the thought of Tilly explaining the wrong way to milk a cow.

She took off her apron and laid it on the counter, preparing to walk Tilly all the way out to the mews if she had to in order to be quit of the woman. Since she'd come in the front door, it might be easiest to keep her momentum going and ease her out the back. "Tilly, we don't need you to make bread. We don't need you to wait on customers. We don't need you to do any work, all right?"

"All right, though I think you'll be sorry once the business starts a'whirling like it's going to. I've talked to a lot of women about how much time they'd save if they bought bread from you, and I think they will, too."

Against her will, Anna's heart leaped. How many women? Where? "In the square?"

"No, out by my cousin's friend's place, lots of them. You know my cousin."

"I truly do not."

"She has a whole house where people can let a room, like, and I've been staying there for no coin because she's my cousin, you see? As it should be. But her friend two streets away has more dealings with a *lot* of women, and they want to save their work for other things. You know?"

Anna had the uncomfortable feeling that Tilly was talking about a bawdy house. She didn't want to be overly prim or turn away business, but the image of a gang of lightskirts marching along Leicester Square to shop at the Ladies' Own Bakery did not thrill her.

"That would be lovely, but it really isn't necessary."

"It's my cousin's friend bakes the blackberry tart. They're barely more than a couple of bites; you have to eat them quick before they crumble. You've got to try it!"

The tart she held was indeed appealingly golden around its pinched edge, and full of glistening purple-black fruit.

So appealing it forced Tilly to take a bite, apparently.

"So good." Anna had a good view of the cavern of her mouth as Tilly opened wide and bit away a third of the tartlet at one snap. Through the mouthful of tart, Tilly said, "You have to try."

Anna, suddenly overcome with visions of lions, jerked away. Tilly only followed, her diving attempt to present the tart only stopping once she approached Anna's mouth with it...

...and a fat baked blackberry dropped out and rolled down the front of her dress.

Anna looked down at the purple stain. It was a forever mark. Even if she could acquire lemon juice to try removing it —and where would she get lemon juice?

It would always be there, trumpeting to the world that she had so few dresses that she must wear this one, even when it bore a huge, obvious, irredeemable blackberry stain. That she couldn't remove.

And right at that moment, Anna resolved to marry Lord Boislegrand.

"Oh, I'm sorry," Tilly was saying. "A waste of the blackberry, too. I suppose I should find it and—"

"Thank you, Tilly. Thank you for calling. But we don't need help, or to be leaped at with berries. Or cabbages, or anything, actually."

Distracted from her half-bitten tart and the lost berry, Tilly finally looked up, wide-set eyes blinking as she focused on Anna.

Anna pointed at the door. The blackberry stain had tightened her resolve in several ways. "Thank you, but please go. You needn't come back."

THAT NIGHT, ANNA LET HER SISTERS COOK AND EAT THEIR supper without her. She could hear them outside the bedroom, chattering and even laughing.

She didn't feel like she would ever laugh again.

She lay in bed, staring at her dress hanging on the wall peg. At the stain of that blackberry.

Tomorrow she would wear another dress, but she couldn't avoid the blackberry's shameful stain forever. They had few dresses between the four of them, and Emery and Jane's were too long for Anna.

Or at least they used to be. Now they were probably just the right length, Anna thought grimly, and soon Jane and Emery's knees would be in public view.

At least the shop apron would cover the stain.

She tried to be happy about that. *At least the apron would cover the stain*. But she couldn't manage happiness.

The years ahead were an endless parade of blackberry-stained dresses over crumb-covered floors. Nothing was clean, nothing was nice. Nothing ever would be, either.

Not till she escaped.

Anna didn't intend to go back on her promise. She didn't intend to leave the bakery. But she couldn't stop imagining how clean Lord Boislegrand's house would be, with other people to carry the chamber pots and empty rooms of their spiders.

And she couldn't stop thinking about the blackberry of doom.

She fell asleep caved in with hunger, dreaming of spotless marble floors.

WHEN ROSE WOKE, IT FELT EARLY. EMERY WAS GONE, BUT then Emery was often gone.

Listening, Rose didn't hear anyone clacking together their pots on their little stove. Now they had fine china plates, too, and those made much more refined *tink* noises. But outside her room, nothing. Bathing and breakfast didn't seem to be underway.

She stretched her arms overhead, out from under the sheet, a bit warm in the summer air even by itself. Weariness couldn't drag her back to sleep. She had to tell her sisters about her wedding.

Rose had never attended a wedding, but it sounded like a lot of spectacle for no reason. Hers felt... personal.

Her fingers spread over her belly, sliding between her thin chemise and the sheet. Her wedding wasn't *for* them. It was for her. And Mr. Russell.

She had only the vaguest idea what liberties a husband might take. But she knew there would be liberties. It was odd to think that Mr. Russell might touch her through fabric just this thin, or even none at all. He would be able to see her *navel*. No one saw her navel.

Perhaps that was why she had that wavering, wobbling sensation there.

The prospect of such nearness was unsettling, but Rose wanted no naysaying, not even from her insides. Right or wrong, she wanted to be married.

Her sisters would only pick at her and ask why she even thought the words *right or wrong*. Perhaps they would say something foolish, like she should wait until it only felt right.

But when did that ever happen?

It hadn't felt right to leave her home and come here with her sisters, but she'd done it. It hadn't felt right to talk to people in the shop she didn't know; now she did it every day.

It hadn't felt right to go back to Aunt Eden's, but now Rose knew she was a different person from the little girl she had been.

She could speak right to Aunt Eden, and the neighbors, and the men who ought to vote for Mr. Russell. And petition the government to end slavery.

She could convince her sisters to boycott sugar; she *had*. And by extension, she had made a little change in the life of everyone who now ate one of their cakes.

Including a duke and a duchess.

It was a huge leap. Of course she had doubts. What woman wouldn't?

But her sisters, who'd none of those dreams and therefore none of those doubts, were not reliable judges of what she should do.

Rolling under the sheet, Rose let herself get tangled in her linen shift, letting it wrap her up. She was going to get married. And if she was going to get married, she was going to have to tell her sisters.

THE EARLY MORNING HUBBUB CUT ITSELF SILENT WHEN someone knocked on the door.

"Shouldn't there be a lock at the bottom of the stairs?" Anna wondered, even as Jane went to see who could it could be.

"And we'd share a key with the neighbors?" Emery asked pointedly as the door swung open.

In the hall, an upright young lad hoisted a crate against his chest.

"Here's a ham," he announced to the room as if he did this every day. "Miss Emery Bickering?"

"Yes." Emery shoved into the doorframe next to Jane.

"Here's a ham," said the lad. And half-tossed her the crate.

Before anyone could conceive of paying him for his delivery, he thumped away down the stairs with half-grown feet as loud as any full-grown man's.

"Who sent us a ham?" Rose drew near.

The scent of the salted meat in its nest of clean straw was so mouthwatering that Emery nearly snatched it out to gnaw on it.

But she remained restrained and simply lifted it up.

Underneath the rough weave of its wrapping, the dry ham was positively beautiful. Thick and heavy, its skin had salt and pepper markings. Emery couldn't wait any longer.

Seizing their one knife, she shaved off a bit of the rind, and then the pink meat underneath.

"It will be too salty to eat!" Jane warned, even as put her nose as close to the plate as she could.

"Just a few bites." Filling one of their new flowered plates with clean water from their bucket, Emery dropped in the shavings of ham, willing the salt to flow out of them as quickly as possible.

Jane turned back to the open crate spilling straw. From its depths, she pulled a little paper, folded into sharp corners and sealed with wax. "Here's something. Miss Emery, it says." She waved it towards Emery.

"What does it say?"

"I don't know, it's sealed." Jane brandished it again. "It's your name on it."

Not much could have torn Emery's attention away from the meat, but the waving letter distracted her. "Well, read it."

So Jane broke the seal while Rose, who had just tidied from their breakfast, put their iron pan back on the stove.

Dear Miss Bickering, the note said,

I have heard about your visit from the Duke and Duchess. One must celebrate the happy events in life. Suspecting your happiness, I offer a celebratory ham. Do enjoy.

Sincerely,

Lady Arnold

"It's from Lady Arnold." Emery said unnecessarily, her fingers swirling the bits of ham around in the water to hasten their preparation. "She's sent us a ham."

"She's sent *you* a ham."

Something in the way Jane said it made Emery look up.

"Your name on the note," Jane simply said, but her eyes spoke of deeper questions. "And what the messenger said. She sent the ham to *you.*"

Indeed, the note didn't mention her sisters at all.

"Should I add butter?" Rose still stood by the pan, its hot iron smell creeping outward.

Their littlest sister didn't even remember how to cook ham, it seemed. "A touch, Rose." Squeezing the little fragments of meat mostly dry, Emery dropped them in the pan.

Instantly, the savory smell permeated the entire room. Emery had just finished her egg and toast, but felt her stomach gurgle. The vocal noises of the other sisters were just as evocative.

No one interfered as Emery took the pan off the heat

almost immediately, setting it on their crate—well, now she supposed they had two—and fishing out one of the crisp-edged bits with her fingernails.

"*Oh.*" There was no other word for the taste spreading over her tongue than ecstasy.

When she opened her eyes—when had she closed them?—her sisters were all staring at her, open hunger in their eyes, but standing no closer.

"What are you all staring for? Take a piece!"

"It's *your* ham, Emery," Jane just said. She still had the note in her fingers.

"It's to celebrate the bakery. And isn't that all of us?"

Emery's words flatly contradicted all available evidence, but the smell drove all the sisters forward, Emery fishing a piece of ham out for Rose.

The meat was too salty, but the flavor was heavenly. Just to chew meat was heavenly. Emery shied away from blasphemous applications of the word, but she couldn't imagine an angel's life would be much better than their first taste of fried ham in months.

"You must go thank her," Anna said decidedly, licking her fingertips and quickly hiding them in her skirts to pretend that she hadn't.

"How much does a ham cost?" Rose was tapping her lip with her finger, either for her thoughts or for the lingering taste of the precious ham.

"Much more than we have," sighed Anna, making Jane give her a sharp look.

Emery carefully wrapped the ham back up.

"Well," Rose said, "now we have this one. If Emery will share it, we can use it to celebrate both the Duchess' visit and my wedding."

The stillness that greeted this wouldn't permit even the air to move.

"Don't be silly," said Anna, "that's a long way off, and this ham won't last forever. Though we should be sparing with it."

Emery's thoughts of ham and peas, or ham and turnips, or ham and eggs, faded. "What wedding?"

"Mine. I just said."

Rose's reasonable tone wasn't winning any affection today. "You're not getting married," Anna said flatly.

"I am. Mr. Russell has asked me, and I've accepted."

"Nonsense," said Anna, making Rose flush. "You're not even of age."

"Which is why I am letting you know." Rose's temper was rising. "I didn't wish to, but Mr. Russell insisted."

"Mr. Russell insisted? *Mr. Russell* insisted? The man who made a spectacle of all of us just days ago? When I think what might have happened if word of that had kept the Duke and Duchess away."

"I think it would have made them more curious." Rose did not, however, wish to be swept into conversation about the Duchess. "Have it out, then. I'm going to be married, so get this all over with."

"Oh no, Rose, no!" Jane's horror balanced her crushing hug. "It isn't to be gotten over. It *is* to be celebrated, it is!"

"Worth a ham, I suppose," Emery said morosely. The glory of the taste of ham faded on her tongue at the idea that her little sister would leave them. Rose was *her* ally. Rose slept in the same *bed*.

It would be a cold winter, she supposed, trying not to say anything bitter aloud.

"It isn't a trade." Rose, freed from Jane's hug, looked happier. "I didn't mean to take away from your ham, Emery. I just thought we might as well celebrate both."

"If Mr. Russell wishes to marry you, he can ask when you're of age." Anna stayed on that point.

"I'm not waiting six more months, and I've already accepted."

"He can't just come in here—"

"He didn't," Rose pointed out.

The look on her face said that she knew full well her reasonable tone would drive Anna to distraction.

Which it did.

"No, he didn't. He ought to have, Rose. He can't just up and ask you to marry him on a whim."

"It isn't a whim! We've known each other for months now!"

"And *we* know nothing! We haven't met his family. We don't know his plans. What kind of life is he offering you? My stars. Mary Wittenberg knew Mr. Crafts for two years before they were even betrothed."

"I don't know either of those people, but Mr. Crafts must be lazy. Anna. If I had expected anyone to be happy for me, I would have thought it to be you."

They all knew what she meant. Anna had cuddled and spoiled Rose from the moment she was born.

"It is *because* I love you that I don't wish you to rush. You're so young, Rose, and this is for life! You cannot think only about tomorrow, and you cannot think only about what you want. You must think of what you need."

"Like you?" Jane broke in suddenly. "Are you thinking of what *you* need?"

"Why, what does Anna need?" Emery asked suspiciously, all thought of sweet, sweet ham forgotten.

"I am thinking of what we *all* need." Anna pulled herself very upright, clasping her hands at her waist. String restrained her honey-brown curls, the absence of hair ribbons more glaring than at any moment since they began this venture.

This venture which was, to Emery, life itself.

The venture crumbling before her eyes.

There was Anna, romantic, stars-in-her-eyes Anna, stoutly insisting that they be practical about things. "If I were to marry, it would mean food for all of us, hearty food. And shoes, and yes, new dresses, not because we wish to be frivolous but because otherwise we will be wearing rags."

"Who are you marrying for shoes?" But Emery already suspected.

"Lord Boislegrand has offered me marriage."

This too stunned the sisters until one could have heard a pin drop, had they a pin.

"Well, I'd rather have the ham," was Rose's tart reply.

"There's nothing wrong with Lord Boislegrand." Anna was, though not passionate, at least adamant.

"A sterling reason for marriage. There's nothing wrong with him." Rose had tipped over into open sarcasm.

"I thought neither one of you was getting married. I thought we'd agreed to stay with the bakery." Emery felt sicker and sicker every minute.

She'd told them. This bakery was her *life*. She'd *told* that to them. Were they leaving it?

Were they leaving her?

Arguing hadn't helped. They would move on—they would all move on. None of them wanted to stay with her. It wasn't enough to keep them here, keeping Emery from being alone.

"Excuse me," Emery said abruptly, and strode out the door.

"There, you've upset her," Rose said as the door closed after their sister.

"*I've* upset her? You're the one supposedly getting

married!" Anna was not ready to take on blame when she had the chance to put it elsewhere.

"I *am* getting married. Do you want to be there, or not?"

"Rose!" Even Jane was shocked by the baldness of Rose's ultimatum.

But Rose's little frame was set. "I am getting married. I suppose I want you to be there. If you want to come, I hope you come. Next week."

"Next *week?* But Rose! Be reasonable! Even if I were to marry Lord Boislegrand, I would wait a seemly amount of time before I did so!"

"Seemly? What's seemly about him kissing your hand in the street?"

"At least he didn't *shout at me* in the street!"

"Rose. Anna. This is madness. Please." Jane stood between them, arms outstretched to both, their words yanking her in both directions. This couldn't go this way, it couldn't.

Though she was more willing to see Rose married, if...

"Rose. Do you love Mr. Russell?"

"Yes. I do." Rose's answer was immediate and firm.

"Oh my *stars*," Anna rolled her eyes, "how does one love a man who made a public spectacle of you both?"

"He was startled. He is not by habit a shouter. You know that."

"I wouldn't marry even an *occasional* shouter!"

"Anna." Jane felt like, since Emery had quit the field, only she could bring these endless loops of recrimination to a halt. "Do you love Lord Boislegrand?"

"He is kind, thoughtful, and well prepared to help support not only me, but all of us!"

"Anna." Jane just shook her head at her sister sorrowfully. "I would have been more likely to support you in this had you simply said *no*."

"But she said she wouldn't marry him! You said you wouldn't marry him." Rose turned on Anna.

"I haven't agreed to marry him." Chastising Rose about Mr. Russell's unseemly lack of interaction with the family made Anna squirm a little and avoid casting Lord Boislegrand in the same light.

"But are you going to marry him?"

"I am *inclined towards it*. It involves taking some time to weigh all the positive and negative aspects of the situation. You should consider thinking about things, Rose; it would change your life."

"Anna—"

"No, Jane, stop. I am only being practical. Didn't you want one of those men you approached to look at things *practically?* Marriage must be considered if it is to happen at all. I told his lordship I would consider it. What is more practical than that?"

"Getting married next week in a dress I already own," said Rose, practically.

"That will not happen."

Rose's face flushed again, and Jane felt very much in danger of an explosion of temper the likes of which the street had not yet seen, even after her public shouting match with the problematic Mr. Russell.

But instead Rose just said, "Even if Mother were here, I would not let her order me so. And she is *not*."

And with that, Rose marched to the door of the room she shared with Emery, and once in, slammed it behind her.

Jane just stood staring at Anna with a rising horror—for Rose's words, and for Anna herself, and for Anna's whole way of thinking.

"Don't do this," she said.

But Anna's jaw clenched tight. "If anyone ought to understand a practical approach to marriage, I thought it would be you."

"That was for me. This is for you."

"Why not believe I know what is best for me? For *all* of us? I'm the oldest, Jane; that is my *job*." The set of her jaw did, in fact, make Anna look older. "We cannot keep scraping this way. Or more truthfully, we may very well keep scraping this way our whole lives. And if we are this tired and bitter after only a few months, what will the years do to us? Be sensible. You've done the arithmetic. You ought to have told Emery, too. We will be able to afford to keep working. Do you know what that means? We can *keep working* all hours of the day and night. That's *all* we will be able to afford."

Jane felt like she ought to take Anna's hand, or hug her. If she could move, if she could touch Anna in times of crisis like this, perhaps things would be different.

But she had never had to convince Anna not to abandon herself before.

Instead Jane said, "This time last year Mother was still with us. Life can change so fast. *So* fast. You don't know what will happen next week, or next year. You don't know what you might be giving up. You can't change this if you do this."

"I won't change this if I do this. I mean to be a good wife to Lord Boislegrand." She didn't sound like she was only *thinking* about marrying him.

"And do you want that? Want *him?*"

They had exchanged so many girlish little confidences about the things men tried to do while dancing, and afterward in dark corners. They hadn't talked about any of that in a long, long time.

But surely Anna knew what Jane meant. She was asking if Anna was really prepared to embrace Lord Boislegrand as a husband must be embraced.

Anna didn't share any girlish confidences. All she said was, "I don't want anything but not to feel tired."

And with that frank admission, Anna went out of the rooms herself, leaving Jane alone.

Jane looked at the iron pan, where tiny specks of cooked meat still glistened with butter in the now-cooling pan. It was lowering to realize that she would gladly lick that pan to get even a little more taste of the delicious, salty ham.

Perhaps they couldn't go on like this forever. But what could happen next month? Next year? A week ago, they hadn't even imagined a duke and duchess might visit their shop. Now they ate off the plates of near-royalty.

Jane had felt something new at Aunt Eden's, and it had stayed with her. Something soft and hopeful. Now it felt in danger of fluttering away.

Anna had lost faith, that was all. In the shop, in love. Perhaps in the future.

Heart pounding, Jane blindly grabbed a bonnet and shawl from the shelf in her room, hers and Anna's, and left their rooms altogether. In search of faith.

AT THE LAST MOMENT, EMERY COULDN'T BRING HERSELF TO knock on Lady Arnold's grand front door. It was wide and glossy and more imposing than welcoming.

Instead, she went below the front stairs to the kitchen entrance, and knocked there.

"Is Lady Arnold at home?" she asked the bewildered cook.

The smoked black archways of the kitchen were high enough for Emery to walk below them with ease, and the space well-stocked. Three more of those delicious hams hung from the beams, along with bundles of dried herbs and chains of plaited onions.

A cake sat cooling on the table, a poppyseed cake, and all together the room smelled so delicious that Emery's stomach should have rumbled again.

But perhaps the turmoil in her brain had squashed its function.

"Are you sure you want me to tell her ladyship that you're here?" The cook had clearly seen Emery's shabby dress and taken her as more beggar than visitor. "I can give you a couple of onions and a bit of bread, if you need."

Emery felt the laughter bubbling up inside her was in danger of breaking her. "No, thank you. I don't need bread."

She couldn't stand still, digging a toe into the groove between the flagstones of the floor as the woman disappeared up the stairs.

A little kitchen maid, no bigger than Sal, went on scouring pots in a corner, watching Emery with one eye. But Emery didn't care.

Part of her couldn't believe she had marched straight to this grand house, with its windows placidly disdaining the view over the square, and asked to come in. But another part of her couldn't think to do anything else.

She didn't really grasp anything about her sisters' view of men, or the marriages they were contemplating. It all seemed unnecessarily complicated, and except as a threat to her home, none of it applied to her.

But she had a few ideas strung together on a fragile little string, and they all led her here.

That one gave gifts to make an impression upon someone one found interesting.

That the money value of gifts mattered less than the intention.

That even Mr. Morley saw marriage as a source of comfort, and of company.

And that Lady Arnold insisted on coming to the bakery

herself at least once a week to buy cake. Always when Emery was at the counter.

When Lady Arnold came sweeping down the stairs, her deep blue skirts trailing behind her, hair falling over her shoulder and shining like sunbeams, Emery looked hard at her, trying to see whatever it was the lady wanted to say.

And when their eyes met, Emery saw there was a great deal.

"It's all right, Beatrice, you can go up," Lady Arnold said absently, waving the little girl away from the pots with one hand.

Gladly the kitchen maid disappeared up the stairs, leaving Lady Arnold to address her guest in the middle of her kitchen.

She drew closer, those yards and yards of skirts rustling all around and making Emery feel awkward just to be near them. The skin on Emery's hands was so rough with work that it actually caught on the soft cotton of her own gown.

But this woman—*this* woman—had sent her a ham.

"I received your ham, Lady Arnold; thank you." Perhaps Emery should have curtseyed. But she wasn't sure how.

"Oh!" The lady's breath went out, as if she had been holding it. She waved a dismissive hand. "Think nothing of it, please! I only wanted to help you celebrate."

Lady Arnold wasn't tiny, Emery realized; only smaller than Emery. She had a heart-shaped face and the kind of eyes that didn't hit you till you looked at them twice.

Emery looked.

Emery was a blunt sort of person, and still had a great deal of bread to bake that day.

So she went to the heart of it. "Did you mean to send it only to me?"

Something seemed to affect Lady Arnold's breathing. It was fast, and shallow. "I knew you would share with your sisters, of course. But I felt like you and I had become friends, a little. Haven't we?" She looked up into Emery's eyes. "A little?"

"I wouldn't have dared call you a friend, madam." Emery wasn't imagining it. The look in Lady Arnold's eyes—eagerness, a little trepidation, some boldness, the anxiousness that came from anticipation. Emery only knew that look from wearing it.

When Lady Arnold's expression fell, Emery added quickly, "There is so much difference between us. But admiration, certainly. Perhaps we've talked enough to admire each other a little."

Was that safe to say?

The next moment Emery knew it was, because Lady Arnold smiled the most brilliant smile. She seemed suddenly to become herself, a soft woman instead of a bag of awkward elbows.

"Thank you for saying so," Lady Arnold almost whispered. "I would never have found the courage."

This exquisite lady needed courage to talk to Emery?

No, Emery didn't feel right as the *target* of such emotion, not at all.

But it was very nice, to be looked at that way. For now, having found her courage, Lady Arnold was looking at Emery with the kind of admiration that was unmistakable.

Or perhaps Emery had just learned to see it.

"So... thank you for the ham," Emery said again. Those were all the words she had.

"Oh!" Unwilling to let their interview be over so quickly, Lady Arnold clearly cast about for something else. "You must... you must come to dinner some night and see how my cook prepares it! I would be so interested to hear how it differs from the way you do it."

"Would you?" Emery had never felt so tall or so awkward,

or so beautiful or so interesting, ever before in her life. She didn't know where to put her hands. Leaving them hanging at her side seemed stupid.

This would take a great deal of getting used to.

"I would, yes! I'll see you when I come get my cake, and we will decide on a suitable evening. I would so like that." The accomplished lady, widow and mother of lords, suddenly looked shy. "Would you?"

"Yes," said Emery, her thoughts blank, her *feelings* saying that she wanted that, she wanted that very much. "I would."

"Mrs. Parker. I wonder if I might have a word with Captain Brice."

Jane was twisting her bonnet in her hands and edging toward the stairs.

The hotel clerk hadn't let Jane go up to the rooms, and she didn't know how else to find Captain Brice unless she stood in the street and shouted. Jane didn't feel quite that desperate.

But she was getting close.

The clerk had finally relented enough to at least send a footman, which had resulted in Mrs. Parker seeing her like this, the darkness tugging at her skirts betrayed by the way her hands viciously twisted that bonnet.

Jane didn't want to fall on her knees and claw at the woman's skirts, but she would if she had to.

"Please."

The Captain's housekeeper looked startled at such an impassioned plea from one of the Bickering sisters who, at best, seemed to tolerate the Captain's interest.

"I don't think he'd mind, Miss Bickering, if you want to come up."

The day before, the idea of going to a man's rooms in a hotel would have been too shocking even for Jane, for whom *brazen* was simply an impractical word.

Had she told herself the truth, she'd have realized that Captain Brice's presence in those rooms was a draw more enticing than any danger, real or perceived by society.

But Jane did not tell herself the truth, and even as she walked through his door she thought, *This is for Anna.*

"Captain Brice." She tossed aside her sadly used bonnet and shawl the moment she saw him.

"Miss Bickering! Is all well?"

He rose from his chair like the surge of a wave. A pen lay by some cut paper on his desk, a civilized picture at odds with his hair. As always, he looked blown about by sea winds, and the ends of his neckcloth flapped in the nonexistent sea breeze, too.

He looked like an unyielding cliff battered by nature's passion. Jane knew that inside, he was that steady rock. They all knew that. And it was the only thing that might dissuade her sister from taking a terrible course.

"No, Captain, things aren't at all well. I'm sorry to disturb you. You have been so kind. But if I do not impose upon you one more time, I'm afraid the damage will be done."

"What sort of damage?" His dark eyes swept her over, looked behind her as if demons might follow her. "A person? A fire?"

"A bad decision. Captain..." How was she to put this?

If Jane knew anything, she knew Anna was full of heart. That she wanted love, desperately. And that she wouldn't find it with Lord Boislegrand.

Oh, she might be comfortable, and companionable. She might even have children. She would smile kindly at him, and he at her, and they would gladly help each other to the butter over the dinner table.

But it wouldn't be right.

Jane had felt hard and angry for so long that she'd forgotten she'd once been more like Anna. She wanted that back. Wanted herself back. If she couldn't save Anna from a cold marriage based on hard truths, how could she save herself?

And Captain Brice was part of it. He was passion personified, and looking at him made Jane *feel* all the winds that swirled around him. She could feel them now, tearing up her insides. He was the medicine Anna needed, and saving Anna would let Jane cling to some ragged hopes that she still needed.

It also meant realizing, with the cold clarity that only Jane had, that the Captain had never looked at Jane the way he'd once looked at Anna. If tying him to Anna was the price of Anna's future and Jane's ability to hope, so be it.

How to explain that to the kind sea captain who seemed to view them as he had the children, like lost cats in need of help?

The same way he ought to have explained from the beginning why he wanted to buy bread, she supposed. Bluntly.

"Anna is going to marry Lord Boislegrand, I'm afraid."

"*Marry?*" Bracing his legs wide as if on a ship's deck, the captain folded his arms over his chest and whistled a long, low whistle. "I didn't think the old goat would go that far."

"You see? You think he's an old goat! And he wants to marry her!"

"Pardon me, Miss Bickering, I just meant..."

"I know what you meant!" Jane's eyes flashed as she thrust out an arm towards what she thought might be the bakery. She was really quite lost. "You think he's a goat. He wants to *goat my sister!*"

"All right, all right." His voice lowered, grew more soothing, and he put his hands out with the palms facing down as if calming a crowd. "He wants to *marry* your sister."

"It's not right!"

The Captain's eyes looked into hers, and they were dark and deep and sad. Eyes that saw pain everywhere and couldn't heal it all. "It's as right as it can be," he said.

Jane had not crushed half her dreams, and humiliated herself to the leering little man downstairs besides, to hear that.

"Don't you shrug your shoulders and say that. You get down there and do something about it."

"Uh... like what?"

"*You* marry her."

"Miss Bickering, your sister does not even *like* me."

"She'll get over it."

"She'll get over not liking me if we're married? But she won't do the same with Lord Boislegrand? May I remind you he has actually *asked* to marry her?" His big shoulders shrugged under his thick brocade coat. "It sounds like he likes her."

"Oh God. This cannot be happening."

Her knees suddenly felt weak. She sank into a chair.

Just looking at the Captain made Jane feel foolish. Surely Anna would feel the same way? Once she really looked? Everything about him said that he was a man, the kind of man who would sweep away a woman's fears and carry her off to bed with conviction it would be impossible to escape. Indeed, that it would be a pleasure to give in to.

That kind of passion would keep Anna from dying an old maid. The married kind of old maid, married but still robbed.

Jane's face fell into her hands. "I thought you had some tenderness for my sister."

"I wish her well. Truth be told she's more alarming than anything else."

"You mentioned offering for her once."

"I thought the alternative would be that she might end up in the streets. You all would. Pardon my bluntness, Miss Bickering, but if she married Lord Boislegrand, she wouldn't be in the streets."

"She would be dead."

"On the contrary, she would be very well fed. I believe Lord Boislegrand really loves your cake."

He didn't see. He didn't get it. He was a sudden kind of man; why didn't he march out there, get sweet, perfectly feminine little Anna, carry her off over his shoulder and... and have lots of babies on board his ship through mechanisms Jane only faintly guessed?

The very image of it made Jane feel ill. But she had to stop Anna from running back to the life she knew. The Captain wouldn't be her past; he would be her future.

If he would go. Somehow Jane had thought if she just pushed him, he would go. But he wasn't.

"What am I going to do?" Anna was exhausted, that was plain enough, and her sisters were not the comfort she needed. Jane couldn't explain to the Captain if he didn't already understand. "I don't know what to do if you don't go," she whispered.

As always, the appearance of plight seemed to motivate the man. "Here now. It's not that dire. I will speak to her, Miss Bickering, all right?"

"Will you?" She looked up, all the way up, to his sunbrowned face.

It was to her a vision of hope.

"Yes. I will. Mrs. Parker, do see Miss Bickering home, won't you? I'm sorry I can't come now, but I will. Miss Bickering. Don't despair."

She picked up her things languidly, thinking of those

moments at Aunt Eden's home when remembering the past had really felt like hope.

Hadn't that been her only bright moment since they'd come here?

No. The ducal visit had changed things. They could scrape by, if they could keep together.

Though that wasn't to be either, since Rose was getting married.

"Oh, and Rose, ah—" She stopped. Why did she have this urge to *tell* him things?

"Yes? Is Miss Rose well?"

Jane likely ought not get the Captain involved in *that*. "Ah, yes, she's fine. Fine, really. Fine."

"Good." His dark eyes narrowed, missing nothing, but if Jane wasn't about to give more information, then that was the end of it. "I'm glad you brought it up if there's nothing to worry about."

Those watchful eyes. His *presence*. His powerful body was always poised for action. The very way he balanced on the balls of his feet made Jane feel... impossible things.

Maybe Anna would see it if he talked to her. Maybe it would make things better.

Maybe.

WHEN EMERY CAME BACK TO THE BAKERY PROPER, BY THE door from the mews as she most often did, Sal was already there, washing the endless stack of bowls their new prescription required.

And Jordan was there too, stirring a vat of dough but with a frown instead of his usual faraway look.

"You don't have to do that." Emery moved to his side and took the spoon, a long club half as tall as Jordan himself.

"I *want* it." He snatched it back; Emery let it go in time to keep him from pulling so hard he whacked himself with it.

"Very well."

She stood next to him for a while, watching him stir, just being with him. At the big sink, Sal went on washing. Emery felt like they had made the space for him to speak, if and when he wished.

Finally she saw his shoulders sag a little. Had he grown wider? Taller? In the time she knew him?

"I'm not stupid," Jordan said, hands grown strong from work moving the heavy dough in a circle.

"No, you're not."

The splashing in the sink got louder for a moment, but then subsided.

Jordan just shot a glare toward his sister. "Sal said that too."

"Not surprising," Emery said, just as Sal shouted, "Because you're not!"

"All right, that's two."

"Two what?" What happened when Emery left them alone in the bakery?

"Two people who think I'm not stupid. There's a lot more who think I am."

"*They're* stupid," said Sal, sloshing water down her front.

Well, it was a warm day, she would dry.

"Jordan." Emery took the spoon and leaned it upright in the dough. This felt like a trap, the kind children sprang on adults. She didn't want to agree with Sal that someone else was stupid, but... "You're not stupid, and anyone who thinks you are is just wrong."

"I like bread!"

That made Emery drop down to one knee. He'd grown taller, but from here she was closer to looking him in the eye. "I like bread too!"

He knew it was true, and Emery's grin made it that much more obvious.

"I know. You do." He did know. They had that in common, both treating the dough almost like a pet, one that bred more and more loaves to feed them and lots of other people.

"I don't care about much else," he went on. "So... am I like my dad?"

Stomach dropping, Emery wondered if this were a hugging occasion. She wasn't good at it.

Well, she did it anyway.

Wrapping his sturdy body in her arms, Emery squeezed him tight. "You have hair as dark as his, like sons sometimes do. And you're both related to your sister. You're *family*, Jordan. That doesn't make you terribly alike." A thought struck her. "Am I very much like Anna?"

"Uh..." Surprisingly, he paused before he answered. "A little. Not much."

She wondered what Jordan thought she and Anna had in common.

But instead of asking, she said, "Your father's not well, Jordan. But you're fine. Does that answer your question?"

"It's all right to *me*."

The way he said it made Emery want to find whoever had been taunting her Jordan—for he was her Jordan, after all this time, her apprentice and friend and responsibility—and give that person a few whacks with a bread paddle.

Fortunately or unfortunately, she didn't have time.

But he went on. "They say if I don't sneak out to chase girls instead of making bread all day, that I'm slow like my dad."

The confusing feelings brought on by ham fell away and Emery felt only the clean fury of anyone who would make her Jordan feel bad because he didn't act like every other boy.

How much could she say to him with Sal listening? Not that Sal wasn't fiercely loyal to her brother; she always was. But she might say the wrong thing at the wrong time to the wrong people.

Emery just took both of Jordan's shoulders in her hands and squeezed again.

"Jordan, you are made up of a hundred hundred things, from your toenails right up to the last dream in your head, and no one, *no one*, knows everything you are but you. No one can tell you those things, either. You get to say what makes up *you*. And you don't have to tell anyone, either."

It was a day for looking deep into others' eyes, and finding it rattling. Jordan's dark eyes, too, seemed full of things he was surely too young to feel. Who had made him so worried about his own feelings, so frightened?

"However you feel about anything is just fine, Jordan." Emery whispered it to him and smiled. "Whoever you want to chase or not chase. It's all right."

She tried to put into her words, her eyes, whatever he needed from her right now.

And it seemed to be enough.

That broad brow smoothed and took on its more habitual placid look. "Want to shape loaves?" he said, just like any other day.

Emery wanted to hug him again, but instead she stood and just nodded. "Yes I do."

THE WAY THE CAPTAIN SWEPT IN WHEN MRS. BUNIONS left, Anna suspected he had been waiting for the shop to empty.

It was too hot for him to wear a cloak, but at least he had shoved on a hat.

"Miss Bickering."

"Yes?"

Anna was in no mood for this today. Surely if he had some bad news, he could take it to someone else? And if he had good news... Well, he never had good news.

The next moment, she felt herself ungracious. He had helped them with the water bill, so much. And treated them to a sumptuous dinner the likes of which she might never see again. Even if the men from Jacquier's Hotel all now treated her and her sisters like ladies of the evening, it had been a wonderful dinner and he had only been kind.

So she tried to look more gracious and waited for whatever he had to say.

It certainly wasn't making him calm. He was sweating. Though that might be the summer warmth.

"Miss Bickering..."

Anna just waited.

"I wondered," he finally said, and something seemed to thicken his voice, but he managed to force out the words. "I wondered if you wanted to marry me."

Anna's jaw dropped open.

"I am not asking you *to* marry me," the Captain rushed to add. "I should make that clear."

"Yes, you should."

"I'm only here to ask. Because—" He seemed to think twice about revealing his reasons. "I wished to know."

"If I wanted to marry you."

"Yes."

"And you thought you would just march in here and ask. Like that."

He looked behind him, as if back along his steps. Turned back to her. "How else?"

She'd forgotten how bizarre he was. Utterly twisted. She

didn't have words to express what she thought of *that* question.

"Captain Brice..." Now it was she who was having trouble finding words. She didn't wish to be rude. But the question, so bluntly put, seemed to require a very blunt response. "I do not want to marry you. At all."

He breathed out a sigh of relief.

Anna's nerves were a bit raw for that. "Thank you very much!"

"My apologies. I didn't mean... See here, Miss Bickering." More relaxed, he leaned closer; Anna leaned away. He said, "I'm a man of the sea. I have things I must do, and I am often away for long stretches of time. I wouldn't be able to offer anyone much of a marriage. And some things I do... if I didn't come home, it would be a poor way to serve a wife."

That sounded ominous. "Then you should always come home, Captain Brice."

The deep groove on one side of his mouth deepened with a rueful half-smile. "We are not always the masters of our fates."

They shared a moment of charity while both of them contemplated that truth.

"But if you *needed* to marry for some reason—"

Anna threw her hand up to stop him, almost into his face. She pushed it forward, and he stepped back, and again, her hand and the air between them pressing him back and back.

"Don't finish that sentence, Captain. Neither of us deserve it. I do not *have* to marry; I will never *have* to marry. But if I did—and I mean this in a way I hope you will find comforting, given the obvious reluctance of your insulting question—if I did have to marry, I would marry any other man I have *ever* met before I would marry you."

His back was against the shop door.

There was a twinkle in his dark eyes as he looked down at

her. "I believe you, madam. Then you are not marrying Lord Boislegrand out of some dire need?"

That reminded her of the blackberry.

The blackberry that meant no way out.

Anna moved away. "There are different types of needs, sir."

"And are any of them dire?"

When she looked up again, she found the look in his eyes entirely uncomfortable. It was a look that said he saw everything, accepted everything.

Well, the devil did.

"It is no business of yours if I accept Lord Boislegrand's proposal of marriage for any reason I like."

That pulled his brows into a frown. "I've often been told what I care most about is not my business. It hasn't stopped me yet."

SHE LOOKED PUZZLED. WELL, WHY HAD HE SAID IT THAT way? Brice cared about a lot of things, but it wasn't as though Miss Bickering was one of them.

Rather, he did; but in no deeply personal way.

Though perhaps that wasn't the right way to say it either. His interest in the Bickering sisters was personal. He would take it amiss if something happened to them on his watch.

But not Miss Anna more than any of them.

She had a pretty little frown, as little-ladyish as the rest of her. She looked like she didn't know to what cares he referred. She was so little interested in *his* affairs, she likely did not listen to gossip about them.

Which was all to the good. He respected women; he had sisters. He really could not bring himself to marry a wife—

God forbid he bed her—and sail off into the ocean to face death.

Unless the rich Portuguese man made good on his promise of a ship to accompany the *Halia*, the death was near-certain.

No, he'd come only to satisfy Miss Jane's pleading, and to see for himself that Anna wasn't being coerced.

She seemed clear-eyed to Brice. She knew what she was doing, and she was going to do it.

"I wish you all the best, Miss Bickering," he said, and tipped his hat.

He left before she could say anything else.

He wasn't going to marry her *or* bed her.

But it wasn't easy, preparing to face what he prepared to face.

And he'd just discovered even the palest wisp of concern from a pretty lady didn't make it easier.

"Mrs. Scrope, I don't have any more excuses not to fix that bakery counter."

Mrs. Scrope looked the carpenter up and down the way one would a six-foot-tall ant. "I said leave it alone."

"Even if those girls fail," the carpenter said, blowing hair out of his eyes—he had not had time to get his hair cut in the last four weeks—"you'll have another tenant in there. Likely a bakery. You'll need the counters refinished. Let me get to them while I have a minute."

"I don't want to be seen supporting them in any way! It can only cause trouble for Mr. Scrope if it is noised about that he gave aid and support to those girls."

He scratched his nose. It wasn't like giving aid to the enemy in one of their wars, after all. "They're your tenants."

"Ssshhh!" Mrs. Scrope flapped the ends of her lace shawl to shush him.

Darenot Harding knew little about women. His mother had died when he was young, and his father and brother knew little more than he did. He understood oak and ash; lace, not so much.

But this was admonishing lace, and for the life of him, he couldn't think of a reason for it.

Fortunately, Darenot Harding's father had raised him to be a simple man. Cut trees, hew them, make useful things from the timber. Life didn't have to be complicated, and he tried not to let it.

He wasn't gallant; but he did have two Puritan grandfathers and an inability to ignore work.

"You don't have to pay me till the job is done," he told her, lifting the straw hat in which he had just shored up a roof beam.

Since Mrs. Scrope wouldn't have expected to, she watched him leave with some suspicion.

But Mr. Scrope's rents didn't gather themselves, and she had work to do. And she wasn't likely to chase a carpenter into the street.

Captain Brice's abrupt departure bothered Anna. Of course, the Captain was given to abrupt arrivals and departures. But the look in his eyes when he tipped his hat...

Jane slipped in the front door looking pale, and Anna forgot the Captain in worrying about whether Jane had eaten enough that morning. Had she left before eating her toast? "Jane, should you eat?"

Jane just shook her head, and before Anna could go to her, Sal opened the door to the bakery proper and Rose brought in a basket of bread. "The second bake is ready," said Rose.

The customers were well aware of the schedule, and as if chased by a bear, three women pushed through the door together, all of them in desperate need of a quartern loaf.

The rush of custom distracted Anna until it ebbed, another shower of everlasting crumbs leading the way to the door that still squealed every time someone pushed it open.

Perhaps in winter it would just fit. But by then…

The door screeched again, and when Anna looked up, the carpenter stood there.

He was frowning at the thing, running his fingers along its top and letting in all the sounds of the street.

Anna had an urge to throw a rope around him and tie him to the counter.

"*Mr. Harding!*"

He jumped at Anna's shout—had she shouted? Oh dear, she had—and looked behind him, as if there might be a row of Mr. Hardings and she was shouting at some other one.

Anna rushed to grab his sleeve and drag him unceremoniously into the shop.

"Mr. Harding! You're going to fix the counters! *Are* you going to fix the counters? Please don't toy with me; it's been a very difficult day."

The bemusement on his face made Anna pause; but she didn't let go of his sleeve.

"You must realize," she said, "that I am startled to see you, and unwilling to let you go."

"Of course, ma'am. I'm used to ladies being so happy to see me."

If he was, he didn't look it.

"You can start with the counter." Anna used her apron to wave Jane, still silent, away from the counter, and then to fan away the last remaining crumbs.

"No, I'll do the door first."

Anna dropped her apron. "Last time you said it would be fivepence extra, and that we didn't even need it."

The carpenter had a sun-reddened face, the bones of it as planed and sharp as the edge of one of his wood planks, but the mention of those five pence seemed to bring a blush to his face that showed. With that mop of wavy golden hair on his head, he must have been a fair-faced child.

"Do you still want it?" His rough question was half-hidden by his turned-away face.

"Yes!"

"All right then, I'll do it first. No extra price."

Clearly used to working with whatever was at hand, he spotted the stools he'd left on his last visit by the Bear Street window, and snagged one.

Even as he climbed atop it, Anna wanted to tell him she didn't want his feet on the stools where they all sat; but she was afraid any interruption would send him disappearing into the street.

If that happened, he might never be seen again.

He had just applied his plane to the top of the half-open door when Lord Boislegrand walked in.

His lordship shoved the door a bit more open to make way for himself, knocking the carpenter backwards.

Only Mr. Harding's quick grab at the top of the door saved him from a fall; as it was, he was left hanging from the top of the door like a bell rope.

"Oh!" Anna ran and righted the stool, placing it under his feet.

"Sorry," Lord Boislegrand said, looking up at last and seeing a carpenter dangling above him. "Didn't see you there. Miss Anna. Are you quite well today?"

While in other circumstances his focus on her would be flattering, at the moment it seemed excessive.

"Quite well. Have you your footing back, Mr. Harding?"

"Yah," said the carpenter with a laconic drawl, but he gave Lord Boislegrand a sharp look around the side of the door.

"Sorry," his lordship said again. "I apologize for sounding eager," he said to Anna, much more sincerely, "but I could no longer wait. Have you given any thought to my proposal?"

"Oh yes."

"Anna, don't."

Anna and his lordship both turned to see Jane, hands clenched to the edge of the bread counter, eyes large and dark and staring at her sister.

"Jane, are you sure you're well?"

"I'm fine. Don't do it."

"It will be all right, Jane."

A long, slow scraping noise issued from the top of the door, and a curl of wood floated down to land atop Lord Boislegrand's stovepipe hat.

He did not notice.

"Anna." Jane hissed at her sister over the counter. "You said we ought not to have to marry to live."

Anna looked away from Jane and back to Lord Boislegrand, his hands gripping each other out of anticipation, maybe worry, and brushing the gold chain of his pocket watch. The thought hit her that it was beyond foolish for his lordship to wear a pocket watch, as he never had to be anywhere on time.

The slight sway of the chain stopped against the gentle slope of his belly, just a little curve, and Anna thought again how gentle he was.

He really was so kind.

She looked back at Jane. "No one is forcing me to do this."

"Quite right!" Lord Boislegrand looked nearly beside himself with worry. "I would never dream of forcing your hand, dear lady! I only await your permission to make you the happiest woman in the world."

He did. He wanted to do that. He would endow her with all his worldly goods.

Anna felt a little shudder. She didn't just want his worldly goods; that felt wrong. She wanted *peace.*

"*Anna.*" It looked like Jane's fingernails were cutting into the wood of the counter. "*Is this what Mother would have wanted?*"

That made an avalanche of memories crowd into Anna's mind all at the same time. Her mother making bread with her; her mother sewing lace onto a handkerchief for Anna's first ball. Her mother's gentle eyes.

Her mother crying over the empty butter dish. Because they were poor.

Her mother as Anna reported the words of the unkind man at the ball, and Aunt Eden's pronouncement that she was too poor to look for love.

Her mother had nursed Anna's hopes, Anna saw now, to protect them. She'd wanted hope for Anna, hope and antic-ipation.

Anna smiled at her sister. "You still can," she said, and she knew Jane understood what she meant.

She turned back to Lord Boislegrand just as another long slow curl of wood dropped onto his hat.

"Really, Mr. Harding." Anna reached up and brushed them off; Lord Boislegrand bent a little to let her.

It brought them close enough that she could see into his eyes.

"Yes, I will marry you," she told him.

He smiled so hard that his eyes nearly disappeared. Both her hands were caught up in his; he kissed them, both of them, his lips pressed against one set of knuckles and then the other, very sweetly.

"Thank you, Miss Bickering. Truly, thank you."

It felt like giving him an enormous present.

A third curl of wood was scraped away above their heads and dribbled down to cling again to the top of Lord Boislegrand's hat.

"Mr. Harding!"

"I think I'm done," that fellow said in a careless tone from above them, and Anna heard him stepping down heavily from the stool.

The door still stood open, and two more women came in, sidling around Lord Boislegrand and giving him curious looks.

They were followed by Mrs. Baby with her two youngest. She'd never come in without the oldest before; perhaps he had been judged old enough now to run about as he pleased.

The two women together approached Jane at the counter. "Half a pound of the maslin, please," said one.

Jane was still looking at Anna with lost eyes.

"Excuse me," she said, and fled.

Astonished, Anna watched the door to the bakery proper close after her.

She'd abandoned the till.

"I'll help you, ladies," she said, moving behind the counter.

"I need to work on that," the carpenter said, pointing at the counter.

"You needn't," said Lord Boislegrand, as if he expected her to drop everything in the shop and simply come away with him.

Perhaps he did, but Anna wouldn't do that. "We can discuss the details later, sir," she said, giving him a warm smile.

"Yes. Quite. All right." So dazzled was he by the smile that he tipped his hat to her, turned and left without taking his usual cake.

Or perhaps he felt he no longer needed cake.

When the two bread customers had gone, Anna crossed the shop to stand near Mrs. Baby while the carpenter attacked the main counter they used all day with his plane.

"You look happy," said Mrs. Baby, clamping the toddler between her knees to shift the baby from one side to the other. The toddler only squeaked; the baby cried.

"I agreed to marry his lordship," Anna said before she thought. Then, "Not that it's to tell."

Why didn't she want that gossip spreading?

Mrs. Baby didn't look inclined to tell anyone anything. "It's just as you choose," she said, obviously more occupied with bouncing the baby on her knee to get it to stop its crying.

It felt odd, Anna thought, that the woman hadn't congratulated her. They had known each other for months now; Anna had thought the woman was interested in the bakery, having fed the bread starter while they visited Aunt Eden. "Won't you wish me well?"

Mrs. Baby's thin face looked drawn. "I've stopped congratulating that," she said bluntly.

"Oh." From appearances, Anna could well imagine Mrs. Baby had become disillusioned with marriage. "Marriage wasn't what you expected?" she asked gently.

"It never is." It was the closest the patient young woman ever sounded to snapping.

Rose had come out just in time to hear the last exchange. "Mine will be," she said, moving toward the counter, only to have Anna come take her hand and lead her away.

"The carpenter is finally smoothing the counters."

"Never say so!"

"And you aren't getting married."

Rose didn't argue, just smiled as she patted Anna's hand. "Yes, I am."

She sounded so certain. Far more certain than Anna, and Anna had only agreed to be married in the last few minutes.

A long abrasive *skraackk* and a shaving flew away from the counter. At least there would be something to sweep away tonight besides crumbs, Anna thought a little wildly. The calm of the last few minutes was seeping out through the soles of her shoes.

"You sure you want to marry him?" Mr. Harding asked as he positioned his plane again.

Such a blunt question from a mere bystander stiffened Anna's spine. "I beg your pardon?" The man had just heard her accept him!

"I'm just sayin'. You could've picked any one of a lot of fellows. Not sure why you picked that bacon-faced calf."

"Mr. Harding! I'm not going to allow you to speak of him that way."

"Just sayin'." The carpenter swung around the counter to plane the other way, and his eyes met hers over the hard swell of muscle in his sleeves. "You're a hard worker, pretty to look at, calm enough. Well, pretty, anyway. Likely anyone would have married you. I would have."

His sturdy calm and shocking words sent Anna's thoughts tumbling after one another. If marriage were simply joining forces toward staying alive, she likely *could* have married the carpenter. Or anyone.

"You didn't offer."

He shrugged, scraped the blade of his tool across the counter's surface again. "Barely know ya."

No, that was it. Lord Boislegrand had *wanted* to know her. He had pursued her.

It wasn't only that he was rich. It wasn't that.

Rose seemed at least willing to rebuff Mr. Harding's odd observation on her behalf. "Don't tease a lady, sir, especially in a vulnerable moment." She elbowed Anna. "You're vulnerable right now, right?"

"Rose, *please!*"

Rose just laughed.

Rose, who faced goodness-knew-what, marrying a politician likely to lose and trying to whip up the neighborhood into all sorts of moral ideas. Rose was happy.

Happy.

Anna wasn't.

The door to the shop opened—

It just opened. It didn't scrape along the top at all.

The shock of it jerked Anna from her thoughts.

"We want some bread."

This was pronounced by a woman wearing a long twill skirt liberally sprinkled with wax.

Behind her, an astonishing collection of women laughed and jostled their way into the shop. Two women in spotless white with forearms almost as corded with muscle as Mr. Harding's; a woman with fuzz stuck in her hair and on her sleeves; one with nameless dark stains around the hem of her skirt and a fat healthy face, and one who smelled, even at a distance, of gin.

It was the smell of gin that startled Anna into speaking. Better her to help than Rose, since a man with a sharp instrument stood between her and the bread.

"Of course, ladies; how may I serve you?"

There were half a dozen of them—no, nearly a dozen!

"Bread," said the one with fuzzy sleeves simply. "We heard this was the best place to get it."

"We heard it was a ladies' bakery," said one behind her in white.

"That's for us," said the gin-smelling one, clearly completely sober.

Something clicked in Anna's mind and she saw who they

were. Women she'd probably walked past a hundred times in the street. A candlemaker; a liquor seller; a butcher, two milkmaids, and someone who worked with felt. A hatmaker perhaps. And more besides.

And their words...

"We've been here for a while, ladies," said Anna, moving to grab the basket of bread behind Mr. Harding and take it to the second counter they never used.

"Aye, but Tilly told us we'd rather come here. And we would!" The hat-maker was staring in open awe at Lady Arnold's bowl-like vase. "If it's for ladies, it's for us."

"No men to bother *us*," said one of the milkmaids, and the rest of the women laughed.

They were working women, with trades. Like the Bickering sisters. Like Anna.

And they were happy.

One word stood out in Anna's swirling thoughts. "Tilly?"

"Sure. She's told all of us at her rooming house and the one nearby. Told us if we want bread as good as our own without having to make it, t' come here."

The hatmaker sniffed the air appreciably. "She was right!"

It was a whole new wave of customers, and in moments they'd bought out the rest of the afternoon bread.

"We must bake some more," Anna whispered to Rose, who nodded. "Not just for today." If these became regular customers...

"But how?" Rose wasn't disagreeing; just wondering. "If you and I go back to bake, who will help customers?"

This was the same old question they'd asked before, but then it had been only an exercise. Now they had customers. If these customers came back...

"Tilly." Rose was shaking her head in disbelief as she split a loaf between two of the women. "Tilly," she whispered.

Anna, carrying the till that Jane had abandoned behind

her, was giving the women their due returns as fast as she could.

Surely Tilly was not the answer.

Before she left, the butcher woman cocked her head at Anna to pull her into a little side conversation. "Ah've got a table n'chairs Ah'm sellin'. Ah've bought meself nicer ones. Tilly said you mi' want."

Her accent was a bit thick, but Anna gathered that this was an offer of a table. And chairs. Cheaply, no doubt. Via Tilly.

"We may well want, thank you."

The butcher woman just nodded stoutly and marched out. Anna worried a little what she'd just agreed to, but obviously, details would be forthcoming.

Tilly.

Rose moved closer. "Tilly can wait on the customers, can't you see?"

"Tilly is a disaster."

"She never comes on time, but she dotes on customers when they're here."

"She'll get lost talking and half the customers will leave!"

"She brought half the customers *in*. We must give it a try."

Anna moaned. "Tilly?"

Tilly.

Anna was going to have to apologize to Tilly.

JANE HAD LEFT THE MEWS WITHOUT SHAWL OR BONNET, walking bare-faced through the streets.

She couldn't cry, but she wanted to.

Stupid Anna couldn't see. Jane *used* to think of being wed the way Anna was thinking of it now. Couldn't Anna see when she was just plain wrong? Or remember when she'd been right?

The paving-men had moved around to the far side of the square, still on the southern half. Jane marched straight there, and whatever was on her face, no one hooted or called at her.

When she saw him, she jerked her head back. "A word?"

His mates all certainly hooted at *him* as he scowled and picked his way over the gravel and rock, following her around the corner to a spot behind a gate that was largely out of sight.

"What d'you want?"

"You know what I want." Jane felt like fire was eating her heart up from the inside. She'd sent the Captain, she'd sent the very Captain, and Anna hadn't even paused to consider what life with him would be like before she'd accepted that wet piece of toast.

Her sister wasn't even her sister anymore.

He leaned a hand white with gravel dust against the wall over her head. "Y'know, I'm startin' to feel like what those lightskirt women must feel like when a man leaves the money and goes." He rubbed his other thumb, also dusty and calloused, across his lower lip. "I don't like it."

"I'm sorry," said Jane, not meaning it at all, and pulled his head down to kiss him.

He jerked for a second like a balky colt, but at her second tug he gave in.

She didn't even mind the taste of gravel dust on his lips. She wanted salty and earthy. She wanted rough.

Marriage was a trap that was swallowing two of her sisters. Jane would never fall for it again.

But a hard, hot kiss? When she wanted one, she'd get one.

ROSE WAS STILL MULLING OVER THE IDEA OF EMPLOYING Tilly when she heard the door open again. It was so quiet now, hey'd need to have a bell for it.

Ah, the problems of a properly working door.

The footsteps that approached were slower and heavier than most of their customers, and the man's deep voice confirmed it. "You do not have any cakes today?"

It was him. The man who'd come to sniff at them before. The hotel man.

"I believe we do have cakes," Rose said as politely as she could, sidling toward the bakery door to rap on it three quick times.

Emery and Anna appeared quickly, both of them rustling towels in their hands.

"It's the man from before," Rose whispered to Emery, and heard Emery whisper it along before Anna said, "How may we serve you, sir?"

"He wishes to buy cakes," Rose said aloud, quickly.

"I did not say I wished to buy cakes."

They all paused, silently.

"Well," Anna finally said, "if you don't wish to buy cakes, why did you ask about them?"

His voice, nasal, cold, didn't seem like the voice of a man who doubted himself. But Rose heard his shoes shuffling a little.

Finally he said, "I may wish to buy cakes, but not today, and not for myself."

Perhaps Anna was still muddled from deciding to get married, because she didn't answer for long enough that Emery chimed in, who usually stayed out of business discussions. "Is it a riddle? Did you come in to ask us a riddle?"

The man let out a huff of exasperation. "It would be for *l'Hôtel*." He pronounced it the French way.

"Not Jacquier's." Anna seemed a bit breathless.

"Yes." He sounded as though something or someone had forced him to be standing here offering to buy cakes for his hotel. "I would buy three cakes a day to begin and see if our *clientèle* enjoy them."

Rose wanted to hold on to something.

She wanted to hold Anna's hand.

Anna, on the other side of Emery, might still be shaky but her voice was firm as she said, "We would be happy to sell you cakes at our regular price of two shillings for each."

"I would expect a lower price for *l'Hotèl*," he said quickly.

"If you agree to a long arrangement, I am sure we could do that for you," Anna said back just as quick.

"Hmm." He was prowling around the bakery again, just as he had the first time. But this time all Rose's sisters were there—well, not Jane.

But Jane wouldn't object to making money.

"Done," he said as he concluded his circuit of the store. "We will try it for a month. In exchange, you will not sell the cakes elsewhere."

"We will certainly sell them here." Anna *was* quick.

"But not to other establishments."

"If you like." Anna made it sound careless.

There were no other establishments. Not yet. But Jacquier's was not the only restaurant in or near the square. If he were nervous about that...

"And you'll make your men stop shouting at us." The words were out of Rose's mouth before she knew she was going to say them.

Instantly, Rose wondered if she had just spoiled their business deal.

But Anna added her voice to Rose's. "Yes, you must stop their harassment."

"Harassment?" He sounded puzzled, and his French accent thickened.

"Yes," Emery added, just as firm as her sisters. "Harassment."

"It isn't seemly for a hotel of your quality," Anna put in smoothly.

"No, of course not." He seemed to mull the idea over.

Whether or not he took the injunction to stop his employees from shouting at women seriously, he seemed very serious about the cake. "We will begin tomorrow."

"Very good." Anna said nothing else, so he said nothing else. Neither did Emery, so neither did Rose.

After some long, tense moments of silence, he simply left.

The odd sound of the door actually closing and latching was engulfed by the sensation of selling so many cakes.

"Anna!"

Her sister gripped Rose around the waist and hugged her hard. "Twenty-one shillings in profit a week!"

Emery just sounded stunned. "He meant it."

Anna grabbed Emery and pulled her into the hug. "Twenty-one shillings a week! A *week!*"

Laughing, Emery's long arms went around them both, and her hug pulled them into a tight knot of Bickering sisters with, for once, no space between them.

"Where's Jane?" Rose hadn't heard her leave, but she hadn't come at Rose's knock.

"Somewhere nearby. Can you imagine when we tell her? Twenty-one shillings a week!"

"It's your Duchess," Emery said suddenly, giving Rose a squeeze. "Your Duchess friend."

"Mine and Jane's if anyone's," Anna said tartly, "as we hatched that plan. Oh I think it is, I think it is!"

"I think he was considering making the offer before," Rose said.

"If so, the Duke and Duchess' visit seems to have pushed

him over the edge," Anna replied, and Rose couldn't help but agree.

"With that much money we could..." Anna's voice trailed away. "All those women. Working so hard, and happy... because they can live. Oh, no."

Rose couldn't quite follow what Anna was thinking. "What?"

"Where is Jane?" was all Anna replied. "We should all be here for this."

"Why?" Emery backed away, and even in the warm summer afternoon, it made Rose feel a little cold. "Won't you and Rose soon be gone, anyway? In fact, we shouldn't have promised him cake if you won't be here to—"

"I promised *you* that I would be the last one to ever close the door on this bakery, and I meant it." Anna's tone was more harsh and fierce than Rose ever heard her.

"If you say so," but it was clear Emery didn't believe.

Rose wasn't sure what to say. She didn't intend to leave either, but she and Mr. Russell hadn't discussed how she would stay. The all-consuming topic of *getting married* had eclipsed any other real discussion of what the marriage would *be* like day to day.

But surely he understood she had no intention of leaving her sisters.

The door slid open again, nearly silently. Only a whisper of friction marked its opening and closing again.

"That's new," Jane's voice said by the door.

"Jane! We must tell you! The most exciting news!"

"No one say *marriage* to me or I will do myself an injury."

"No no! Cakes!"

In a rush of words from all three sisters, they made it plain that a gentleman from Jacquier's Hotel had engaged them for a regular supply of cakes.

"Your cakes?" Jane sounded a little more like herself, and her arm went around Rose's waist. "Your cakes, muffin?"

"My cakes, certainly," said Anna a little tartly, "but... yes, Rose's cakes. Sugarless cakes."

The feeling swelling in Rose would do something awful if she let it out. She tried to keep it inside, but it did feel as if she were bursting.

"And a flood of new customers for bread!" she added, reaching out to find Emery again and squeeze her hand.

Emery squeezed back.

"New customers? What's all this? I leave for five minutes and the door closes and we have all these new customers?" Jane did sound much more like herself. Her old self, before the bakery and the money and even before their mother had died.

"Because of Tilly!" Anna's astonishment blanketed them all.

"*Tilly?!*"

"Yes, and she might have gotten us a table and chairs too!"

"We must be nicer to her," Rose said soberly, "if she's to wait on our customers while we bake more bread."

"I must apologize to her. We will be fine, isn't it wonderful, Jane? We will be fine!" Anna's question had an odd tang to it, and Jane didn't answer.

But Jane did lean down and press her cheek to Rose's temple. "Look what you did," she said softly.

"We all did it," but Rose was overcome with that feeling again that she might burst.

For the first time, she felt grateful to her sisters for listening. It had been her dream, her need, to follow in her mother's footsteps and just to do what was right. But they had listened.

"And we would never have had a bakery in which to bake cakes *or* bread if Anna hadn't seen the advertisement."

"It's my job." Anna sounded muffled now. Was she crying? Into her hands, or someone's shoulder? "I'm the oldest."

"I'm the youngest, but I think I did my job well too."

"Which job?" Emery sounded as though she really wanted to know.

"Dream," said Rose, and hugged her sisters tight.

Don't miss Rose's wedding! *Get your Season One bonus episode, Rose's Wedding, available exclusively here.*
And never fear, this is far from the end; it's only the beginning!

Stay tuned for Season Two of Ladies' Own Bakery
From Judith Lynne

Historical Notes

My readers know I always have historical notes for them, little tastes of the research that go into my books. Rather than releasing them episode by episode, for Ladies' Own Bakery I keep them on my website, judithlynne.com, on their own page here, so that no one will see spoilers they don't want to see.

I love hearing from readers, and if you are curious about something in one of my books (or just want to connect), feel free to send me a note through my website too. I'm always wishing you good books, time to read, and joy.

Enjoyed the Ladies' Own Bakery?
Invite your friends!

The story doesn't end here—I hope we'll see each other again!

Sign up here to be among the first to know when more LOB drops, and (*psst*) you can even elect to get new episodes right in your inbox. **Four seasons are planned!**

Missed an episode? Right now, you can get Seasons One and Two at your favorite bookstore. And if you download the bonus chapter, you'll be signed up to receive future episodes *free* as they come out!

(If you want to chat about Ladies' Own Bakery there's a Facebook group just for that, or feel free to send me a message via my website. I love to hear from readers even more than I love baking.)

Questions? They're probably answered on the Ladies' Own Bakery page of my website.

Looking forward to the future of the Ladies' Own Bakery!

About the Author

Judith Lynne writes rule-breaking romances with love around every corner. Her characters tend to have deep convictions, electric pleasures, and, sometimes, weaponry.

She loves to write stories where characters are shaken by life, shaken down to their core, put out their hand...and love is there.

A history nerd with too many degrees, Judith Lynne lives in that other paradise, Ohio, with a truly adorable spouse, a small domestic jungle, and a misgendered turtle. Her screenwriting and science fiction efforts ranged from aspiring to award-winning and back again. Now she writes passionate Regency romances with a rich sense of place and time.

If you enjoyed Ladies' Own Bakery, *keep these books coming - share a review at your favorite bookstore, Bookbub, or Goodreads!*

Sign up for the author's newsletter, including exclusive book news and sneak peeks,
at judithlynne.com.

Also by Judith Lynne

Lords and Undefeated Ladies

Not Like a Lady

The Countess Invention

What a Duchess Does

Crown of Hearts

He Stole the Lady

No Titled Lady *Series prequel*

Maids Done Waiting

The Lord Trap

The Lady Escape *Forthcoming*

Cloaks and Countesses

The Caped Countess

The Clandestine Countess

The Castaway Countess *Forthcoming*

Ladies' Own Bakery

Ladies' Own Bakery Season One: The Collected Episodes

Ladies' Own Bakery Season Two: The Collected Episodes

www.ingramcontent.com/pod-product-compliance
Lightning Source LLC
Chambersburg PA
CBHW061531190726
48289CB00004B/1001